We'll Meet Again

By Mary Nichols

The Summer House

The Fountain

The Kirilov Star

The Girl on the Beach

Escape by Moonlight

A Different World

We'll Meet Again

a&b

We'll Meet Again

MARY NICHOLS

Allison & Busby Limited
12 Fitzroy Mews
London W1T 6DW
allisonandbusby.com

First published in Great Britain by Allison & Busby in 2015.

A CIP catalogue record for this book is available from the British Library.

First Edition

ISBN 978-0-7490-1798-9

Typeset in 11/16 pt Adobe Garamond Pro by
Allison & Busby Ltd.

The paper used for this Allison & Busby publication has been produced from trees that have been legally sourced from well-managed and credibly certified forests.

Printed and bound by
CPI Group (UK) Ltd, Croydon, CR0 4YY

The first casualty when war comes is truth

Chapter One

Saturday 7th September 1940

Sheila stood and looked at the pile of rubble, her mind and body so numb she could not think, could not cry, could not even move. Her home, which had stood near the corner of Mile End Road and White Horse Lane, was gone. She couldn't take it in.

The day had started out so well too. Although it was the beginning of September, it had been more like midsummer with the blue, cloudless skies and the sun beating down on a population making plans for the evening. Her friend Janet, who worked alongside her at Morton's general store in Hackney, had suggested going to a dance – they both loved dancing – and they had, between customers, been deciding what to wear. Being wartime, there wasn't much choice, but whether the evening would be as warm as the day and they could wear summer frocks or if the going down of the sun might bring a chill to the air and they would be better in a skirt, blouse and cardigan was the gist of their conversation, not Hitler and his bombs.

'Bert will call for me and we'll meet you outside,' Janet had said. 'Chris will come too, won't he?'

'I expect so. He'll be at the football match this afternoon, but he'll be back by the time we leave off. I'll call on my way home and ask him.'

Sheila had known Christopher Jarrett since schooldays, as she had Janet and Bert Harris, and they often went about as a foursome. Whether Chris would end up being her permanent boyfriend, she didn't know. He was good-looking with his fair hair and blue eyes, and she liked him a lot but was that enough? Ma said they were both young and there was plenty of time to find Mr Right, which had made her laugh because Ma had married Pa when she was only seventeen and theirs had been a true love match.

She had just finished serving a customer when the air raid siren went, but apart from looking up from adding up the lady's bill, she took little notice. At the beginning of the war, that banshee up-and-down wail had driven them all to the shelters as soon as they heard it, but they had become blasé about it now and only went down to the basement when they heard aeroplanes overhead and the uneven drone of their engines told them they were German. Sheila and Janet saw no reason to panic. There had been raids before, a few bombs dropped here and there, but nothing to what the airfields around the capital and the south coast had endured, and in due course the All Clear had sounded and they went on working with hardly a pause. At going home time, they might see a bomb crater where once a house or shop had stood, and houses with windows and doors blown out, and they might wonder about casualties but, so far, that had been all.

This Saturday was different. Almost before the siren had stopped its wailing, they heard the drone of aeroplanes and had gone to the shop door to see the sky filled with a mass of bombers, too many to count. An ARP warden had cycled up the road blowing a whistle and shouting, 'Take cover! Take cover! It's going to be a bad one.'

'Down to the cellar, you two,' Mr Morton had said, coming up behind them. 'And don't forget your gas masks.'

Even as they turned to obey, they could see the bombs leaving the aircraft and spiralling earthwards. Grabbing their gas masks and handbags they had clattered down the stone steps into the basement, normally used to store stock. There among the shelves and boxes a space had been cleared for a few chairs and a table on which stood an oil lamp and some matches.

Mr and Mrs Morton had followed them down a minute or two later. He was carrying a canvas bag of money taken from the till, and she had a flask and some mugs. They sat drinking tea and listening to the thuds and bangs, feeling the earth shake and speculating on what was happening above them. 'I'm worried about Mum and the kids,' Sheila had said, trying not to sound scared when an extra large bang made the table rock and they saw the walls bulging. Miraculously they settled back without crashing down. 'I hope they're all right.'

'They'll be in a shelter, won't they?' Janet said.

'I hope so. The kids might have been out playing, but they'd have run home when the siren went, I expect.' Sheila's family was a large one, each sibling a little less than two years younger than the one above. At seventeen Sheila was the oldest, then Charlie, not quite sixteen, who worked at the docks with their father. The rest, five of them, were still at school. Mum had refused to let them be evacuated with the rest of the school, saying if they were going to be killed, they might as well all die together. 'Pa and Charlie will be at work.'

'Where does your father work?' Mrs Morton asked.

'At the Commercial Docks, in the office. But he's a part-time fireman, so he might have to go on duty. Charlie works down there too, as a messenger.'

'My pa's in the Merchant navy,' Janet told them. 'He's at sea.'

'I don't envy him that,' Mrs Morton said.

'He said he'd rather drown than be shot or wounded in the trenches, and besides, the sea is the only life he knows. It's great when his ship comes in, we have a grand time, going out and about.'

'There's the All Clear,' Mr Morton said as the steady wail penetrated the walls of the cellar. It was six o'clock. They made their way up the steps behind him. Something had fallen against the cellar door and he could not open it. It looked as though they were trapped but by dint of much shoving and pushing, he opened it far enough for them to squeeze through. Treading on broken glass, they stood and surveyed the scene. The shop window had blown in and glass, vegetables and daily papers were scattered everywhere. It was one of the display shelves that had fallen and blocked the cellar door; tins of foodstuffs, flour and bags of precious sugar which had been stacked on it were strewn over the broken glass. The shop door was lying out on the pavement.

Over to the south-east, flames reached above the roof tops, casting the sky in a pinkish orange glow, suffused by smoke and grey-brown dust which hung in the air and blotted out the sun. Everyone was coming out of their houses and shops and standing about mesmerised, many were coughing on the dust.

The warden they had seen before came cycling back. His clothes were so covered in dust they were a dirty brown colour, as was everything about him including his face. 'Any casualties down here?' he asked.

'No. Where did they hit?' Sheila called out to him.

'The docks,' he said, dismounting to answer her. 'Everything down there is a shambles. The West India docks are alight from one end to the other and the timber stacks are burning on the Commercial docks. There's rum, oil and molten pitch from the tar factory running all over the road. Ships and barges are on fire on the river. There are bits of blazing wood flying all over the place and starting new fires. You can't get near it. God knows how the firemen will deal with it.'

'I must get home,' Sheila said, turning to Mr Morton. 'Mum will be out of her mind.'

'Go on then. You too, Janet. Me and the missus will clear up here. Thank God tomorrow's Sunday.'

Sheila thought she knew every inch of every road in the district. It was her home, had been her playground, was where she worked, but it was a nightmare trying to find her way round blocked-off roads, rubble spilling into streets, and a cityscape changed almost beyond recognition. The nearer she came to home, the worse it was. And then she had stopped, transfixed.

This street of rubble had once been a row of terrace houses. Now you couldn't tell one from the other. Stones, bricks, bits of wood, broken roof tiles, twisted water pipes, smashed furniture, scraps of cloth and shattered glass were piled up like some giant bonfire. 'Mum,' she murmured, unable to take it in.

'Sheila. Sheila Phipps.' The voice was almost against her ear, but it hardly penetrated her confused brain. 'Sheila.'

She turned to face Bob Bennett. He was in his thirties, wearing an armband that told everyone he was ARP and a tin hat on which was stencilled 'Air Raid Warden'.

'Mr Bennett. Where's Mum? And the kids? And Pa? Where are they?'

He put his hand on her shoulder. 'Your mum and the children were at home when it happened.'

'Under that?' She nodded towards the rubble that had once been their house.

'I'm afraid so. It got a direct hit. They wouldn't have known anything about it. The rescue squad got them out. They were taken to the school to be made ready for identification and burial.'

'All of them? Every single one?'

He nodded. 'Annie was still alive when we dug them out, but she died on the way to hospital.'

'Oh.' She was too numb to shed tears. She felt as dry as the dust that lay thick over everything. It was still very warm but she felt cold as ice and could not stop shivering. She found her voice with a monumental effort. 'And Pa? And Charlie?'

'We haven't seen either of them. They'd be at work, wouldn't they?' Since the beginning of the war, they had been working longer shifts and free Saturday afternoons had become a thing of the past. Bob, who worked in a munitions factory when he wasn't being an Air Raid Warden, was working every other Sunday.

'Yes. They'd be due home at half past six, except Pa is in the AFS.'

'He'd be putting out fires then?'

'I suppose so. P'rhaps Charlie stayed with him.'

'Very likely. You can't stand here, you know. You need to report to the Rest Centre to register as homeless. The WVS will give you a cup of tea and a bite to eat and find you some clothes and a bed for the night.'

'I don't want to rest. I want to see Mum and my brothers and sisters.'

'Are you sure?'

'Yes.'

'Very well. I'll take you.'

He took her to the local school where the bodies were laid on the hall floor in rows, covered with sheets. If the rescuers knew who they were, they were carefully labelled, though in some cases, they could not be identified. Sheila, following Mr Bennett up and down the rows, thought she must be in the middle of a terrible nightmare. He stopped and bent to read a label. Then slowly drew the sheet back from the face.

Mum looked so peaceful, serene almost. Usually she was dashing about cooking, washing, sweeping up and shouting at one or the other of them for not tidying away their things or getting under her feet, flapping at them with a damp tea towel while wisps of auburn hair escaped its pins. Now she slept a final sleep and the lines of worry had gone from her face and she looked like the beautiful woman she had been on her wedding photograph. No wonder Pa had fallen in love with her.

'That is your Mum, isn't it?' Mr Bennett queried, though he knew the answer very well.

She nodded without speaking. He covered the face again and went on to the next and the next. They were all there, except Charlie: Dickie, Dorrie, Maggie, Bobby and little Annie, who had only this term joined her brothers and sisters at school. Tonight the school was a morgue.

'We found them all huddled together,' he said. 'Your mother was lying on top of them, trying to shield them. Of course she couldn't, but it was brave of her to try.'

'I should have been there,' she said dully. 'I should have been with them. Ma said we'd all die together.'

'She couldn't have known that, could she? What with your father and Charlie and you all at work.'

'I expect she thought if there were raids, they'd be at night when we were all at home. I don't know what Pa is going to say. He doesn't know, does he?'

'We've sent someone to find him. Now, are you ready for the rest centre?'

'I ought to go and look for Pa.'

'Leave it to us, my dear. You can't go into that inferno and he wouldn't want to lose you too, would he?'

'No, I s'pose not.'

He took her to the South Hallsville school which had been utilised for bombed-out families. They were lying on mattresses all over the floor. Some were asleep, some crying, some staring in bewilderment, unable to take in what had happened to them. Some women were breast-feeding babies, others nursing minor wounds; those with more severe injuries had been taken to hospital. The children's reactions were as diverse as the adults about them. They cried, they laughed, they dashed about shouting and pretending to be aeroplanes with arms outstretched. Some, who had lost parents, sat huddled in corners looking petrified or weeping heartbrokenly. At the end of the assembly hall, a couple of tables had been set up and here Civil Defence and the Women's Voluntary Service worked side by side, taking names, suggesting places to go for the night, handing out tea and sandwiches.

Mr Bennett took her to one of the tables and introduced her, then left. He looked exhausted but Sheila knew he wasn't going home, not yet, not until he had accounted for everyone on his patch. He had a list of the occupants of every house and business for which he and his men were responsible and he was duty-bound to match bodies and survivors against his list.

'Sheila Phipps, that's your name, is it?' the lady in the WVS uniform queried.

'Yes.'

'Your address?'

She told her, told her the names of her mother and siblings, of her father who worked at the docks and her brother who worked in the same office as a messenger. She heard her voice but it didn't seem to be her voice; it seemed far away, like an echo. This nightmare must surely end soon and she would wake up in her bed and the sun would be shining again and her mother would be bustling about getting breakfast, singing as she did so. Ma had a lovely voice. Thinking of that was her undoing. The ice melted and swamped the dryness in her mouth. Tears welled in her eyes and rained down her cheeks.

'Oh, you poor dear,' the woman came round the table and took the girl into her arms. 'There, you have a good cry. Don't mind me.'

After a couple of minutes, the weeping stopped as suddenly at it had begun and Sheila's back stiffened. For the first time in her life she felt hate, hate for Hitler and everyone who fought for him, hate so intense her fists were balled. If she met a German now she would kill him with her bare hands. 'I'm worried about Pa,' she said, stuffing her handkerchief back into the pocket of her dress. 'This will break his heart.'

'Have you got any relatives or neighbours you can go to until your father comes?'

'No.'

'Then you'd best stay here. He'll find you here. There are buses coming to take everyone to a place of safety. He'll be notified where you are. There's tea and sandwiches, nothing hot, I'm afraid, and a blanket and pillow. Find a spot and try to rest.'

She sat wrapped in a blanket, with her back to a wall, seeing, in her mind's eye, what it must have been like for Mum and the little ones with bombs falling all around them. They would have been terrified, huddling together for comfort. They had been poor, but Mum kept a spotless home and she and Pa made sure they were clothed and well fed. Not until now, when it had all gone, did she appreciate that. The tears started again but this time they were a silent stream making a furrow down her grubby face.

'I feel so sorry for that poor kid,' Bob Bennett told his wife, referring to Sheila. He was dog tired but satisfied that he had accounted for every one on his patch, dead or alive, all except Charlie Phipps. 'It's bad enough losing her mother and her brothers and sisters, but now I've got more bad news for her. She's stuck in that school all alone.'

'Poor thing,' June said.

'I was thinking, do you think we could have her here for a bit? Would you mind?'

'No, go and fetch her. I'll make up a bed in the spare room. I don't suppose she's got any night things.'

'No, only what she's wearing.'

He finished the bowl of soup he had been drinking, found his tin hat and his gas mask. 'If the siren goes again while I'm gone, make sure you go into the shelter.'

'Surely it won't go again tonight.'

'You never know.' He kissed her cheek and went out again.

He was only at the end of the road when the siren sounded again. He hesitated, wondering whether to go back to June, but then carried on, driven by the need to speak to Sheila and, somehow or other, try to comfort her. There were so many tragedies being enacted this night, the wonder of it was how stoical everyone seemed to be. It was shock he supposed, it had numbed their senses, but what of the morrow when reality dawned? All these people bereaved and homeless. And children like Sheila Phipps, who was still a child for all her seventeen years, left orphans. What was to become of them all? The authorities seemed to have concentrated on the need to deal with the dead, not the survivors.

There was pandemonium in the school as some of the survivors of the first bombing tried to find shelter from the second and others elected to remain where they were. Bob helped to settle everyone down in the corridors away from flying glass and then went in search of Sheila. She was sitting huddled against a wall, a cold cup of tea and a curled-up sandwich on a plate beside her. She didn't seem to be aware of her surroundings.

He bent to touch her arm. 'Sheila, I've come to fetch you. We'll give you a bed for the night. Up with you.' He helped her to her feet.

'Will Pa find me?'

'I should think so.' He said no more as he led her out of the school and into the road, just as the bombers arrived again. They could not see them for the haze of smoke and dust but they could hear them. 'Let's hurry,' he said. 'We've got an Anderson shelter in our garden. June will be in there.'

'We didn't have a garden so we couldn't have one.'

'I know.'

They could hear bombs whistling down and ducked every time, but they were not close and all they knew of them was the explosion as they hit the ground a little way off and then a wall of dust, smoke and flame added to what was already there. Searchlights were sweeping the sky and ack-ack guns were firing, at what they could not see. They were running now, in too much of a hurry to talk, for which he was glad. The middle of a street in an air raid was not the place to impart bad news. He kept that until they were safely in the Anderson shelter in his garden and his wife was pouring tea from a Thermos for them. Anderson shelters, though only made of curved corrugated iron, were supposed to withstand all but a direct hit. They were damp and airless, and flying debris – stones, bits of masonry and broken glass – rattling on the roof didn't help already shattered nerves.

He watched her as she sipped her tea. She was a pretty girl, with thick auburn hair inherited from her mother, hazel eyes and a softly burgeoning figure, although swollen red eyes and the tears drying on her pale cheeks did not enhance her appearance.

'Sheila,' he said gently, putting his cup down and leaning forward. 'I am afraid I have more bad news for you . . .'

'Pa?'

'Yes, I'm afraid so. He was with a bunch of fire-fighters, pumping water onto a burning warehouse, when the wall collapsed on them. There were no survivors. I'm sorry.'

She was silent for a minute digesting this, then she said flatly, 'He's gone too. I hope there's a heaven, I hope somewhere, up there, he and Mum and all the others are together.'

'I'm sure they are.'

'And Charlie?'

'I don't know what happened to him. According to the people I spoke to from his office, Mr Phipps sent the boy home when the siren went, telling him to look after his mother and brothers and sisters. The last they saw of him he was cycling up the road hell for leather.'

'He wasn't in our house?'

'No. He may have gone into a shelter somewhere and will turn up later. Of course, he could have been injured and sent to hospital. We'll find out in the morning.' He knew that there were bodies and bits of bodies that would never be identified, but he kept silent on that score.

It was dawn before the bombing stopped, the sound of aircraft faded, the guns went silent and the All Clear sounded. They straightened stiffened limbs and left their shelter. Apart from the crackle of fires, the heat of which they could feel half a mile away, everywhere was eerily silent. Bob's house was undamaged, apart from one broken window, and they lost no time going indoors.

'I'll make some breakfast,' June said. 'Then we can go to bed and try and get some sleep.'

'I'll have to go out again,' Bob said. 'I might be needed.'

'Needed or not you'll stay and have something to eat before you go,' June said. 'I've got a bit of bacon and I can fry some bread.'

'I must go and look for Charlie,' Sheila said.

'Not until you've had some rest,' June told her. 'You're all in. Then you can decide what you're going to do.' She put the frying pan on the gas stove and turned the tap. 'Drat it, there's no gas.'

'I'll get the primus stove.' Bob fetched it from the Anderson shelter and set about pumping and lighting it. He put the kettle on it, glad that they had taken the precaution of filling it before the raid; there was no water coming out of the tap. 'Tea first,' he said. 'Then food.'

Half an hour later, having consumed a slice of fried bread, a rasher of bacon and some reconstituted egg, washed down with the inevitable cup of tea, he reached for his tin hat again. 'I'll make enquiries about your brother, if I get the chance,' he told Sheila as he left.

June piled the dirty plates and cups into the sink to wait for the water to be reconnected and conducted Sheila upstairs where she showed her into a small bedroom. On the bed was a nightdress, a toothbrush, a flannel and towel. 'Make yourself at home,' she said. 'The bathroom is the door opposite. There might just be enough water in the tank for a quick wash. I'll wait until you're done.'

Afraid to use the water, Sheila put a dribble into the basin to get the worst of the dirt off her hands and face, then returned to the bedroom, stripped off her clothes and put on the nightdress.

As she did so and climbed into bed, it came to her that those few items of clothing were all she possessed. Her week's pay packet lay unopened in her handbag. She usually gave it to her mother every Saturday evening and was given half a crown back to spend on herself. It made her feel guilty that now she had it all to herself and could perhaps buy a few necessities. That was not the only guilt she felt. Why had she survived when everyone else was gone? She was no better person than the others, no more deserving to live than they did. What sense did it make?

She did not think she would sleep, but she did, only to be woken by nightmares which frightened her so much she dare not go to sleep again. At noon she rose, put on her dirty clothes and went downstairs to the kitchen. June was listening to the wireless while she washed up. The water and gas were back on. Sheila picked up a tea towel to help.

'Some damage has been caused to docks, residential areas and industrial premises,' they heard the newsreader saying. 'So far as is known at present, three churches and two hospitals, including a children's nursing home, have been damaged. Some people were made homeless but they have been removed from the danger area and steps taken to provide them with food and shelter.'

'Good God! Where did they get that from?' June said. 'You've only got to use your eyes and ears and nose to know there was a lot more to it than that.'

'They wouldn't want the Germans to know that, would they?' Sheila said. 'They'd have to tone it down a bit.'

'No s'pose not. We'll get a Sunday paper later, if there are such things, that is.'

'Has Mr Bennett been back?'

'No.'

'I think I'll go to the rest centre and see if Charlie's turned up there.' It was something positive to do, something to concentrate on, to stop herself thinking too much about Ma and Pa and the others and a bleak future without them. If she let her thoughts wander in that direction she would collapse in a heap. Surely someone had survived?

'You do that, dear. If you don't find him, come back here. Bob might know something.'

The refugees in the school were still stoically waiting for the buses to take them away from the horror. Charlie was not there and her enquiries drew a blank. There were other rest centres in the area and she went round them all. There was no sign of her brother. She decided to trace the route he would have taken to come home from the Commercial docks where he worked, but the nearer she got to the river the worse was the devastation. Some of the fires had been put out, but some still raged. She could feel the heat and smell the sickening mixture of burning tar, rum, oil, sugar and death. It made her gulp for air. How could anything be alive in that? But there were people, wandering aimlessly about like lost souls, picking up bits of debris and dropping them again. But there was no sign of Charlie.

She was stopped by a warden. 'You can't go any further, miss. It's not safe.'

'I'm looking for my brother. He didn't come home last night.'

'He most likely went into a shelter.'

'But he'd have come home when the All Clear sounded, wouldn't he?'

'Tell me his name. I'll keep an eye out for him.'

'Charlie Phipps. He worked with my father at the Commercial dock.'

'I know Mr Phipps.'

'He died.'

'Yes, I know. Brave man he was, didn't think of his own safety at all.'

'But you didn't see Charlie?'

'No. Go on home, I'll let you know if I learn anything. Where d'you live?'

'We were bombed out. Everyone's gone except me. I stayed with Mr and Mrs Bennett last night. They told me to go back if I didn't find Charlie, but I don't like imposing on them. I ought to go back to the rest centre but they are sending everyone away and I don't want to leave without finding my brother.' It was the longest speech she had managed since it happened.

'Go back to your friends. You need friends at a time like this. They'll look after you.'

Her feet dragged as she went back to the Bennett's home. Guilt overwhelmed her. She had no right to be alive. The feeling stayed with her all day, a day of anxiety and misery, of no appetite and endless cups of tea. She hardly paid attention to Bob and June when they asked her, over the evening meal, if she had any other relatives, grandparents, uncles, aunts, people who ought to be informed of the tragedy, who would want to attend the joint funeral, people who might give her a home. Their questions finally penetrated her numbed brain. 'I think my mother had a sister. I believe there was some trouble, I don't know what. They didn't keep in touch.'

'What's her name?'

'Name? Who?'

'Your aunt. We ought to let her know.'

'Oh, Connie, I think. Mum's maiden name was Robins. Don't know if her sister married.'

'Do you know where she lives?'

'Can't say I do.'

'Look, dear, do make an effort,' June said. 'We are trying to help you. I know it's hard, but try and think.'

'I'm sorry. She didn't live in London, I'm sure. I think it was somewhere beginning with a B. Bl . . . something.'

'Blackpool?'

'No. Bletchley, that's it. Bletchley. Just before the war began, I remember Mum saying something about Connie and Bletchley being safer than London, being in the country.'

'Perhaps she was thinking of evacuating the children there,' Bob said. 'She couldn't have fallen out with her sister so badly if she was considering that.'

'No, but she said Connie wouldn't want to know and we should all stay together and Pa agreed. She was nearly right, wasn't she, about everyone dying together? Except me. Why not me too? I should be dead.'

'We'll get the Red Cross onto it,' he went on as if she had not spoken. 'They'll find her.'

'I don't want to be a nuisance to you. I think I should go back to South Hallsville school and be sent away with all the others.'

'You'll do no such thing,' June said. 'You'll stay with us until we can find your aunt.'

'And Charlie.'

'And Charlie,' June repeated, looking at Bob, but he simply shook his head without speaking. 'I've been through my wardrobe and found a few clothes that might fit you,' she went on. 'I think when you're bombed out, the WVS provide you with some clothes. You'll need to go to the school for those. And you'll need a new ration book. The council offices will provide that. You can do that tomorrow. Have you got any money?'

'I've got this week's pay packet in my bag.'

'Good, but that won't go far. You might get a handout too.'

'I don't want handouts. Mum never did that, however hard up we were.' She was indignant. 'I'm not going to start now. I've got a job. I can work.'

'Of course you can, dear,' June said placatingly. 'But this is an emergency, you know. And the funeral will have to be paid for. Did your parents have any insurance?'

'I think they paid into the Prudential.'

'That's something else for you to find out tomorrow. It will keep you busy.'

'But I have to go to work.'

'No, you don't. Bob will go and tell Mr Morton why you can't go in, won't you, Bob?'

'Of course. It's on my way to the factory.' He had no sooner spoken than they heard the wail of the siren.

'Oh, not again,' June said. 'Haven't we had enough?'

'Apparently not,' he said. 'Come on, into the shelter with you.' He reached for his tin hat. 'I'll have to go on duty.'

He saw them into the shelter with a Thermos flask of tea, some sandwiches and an attaché case of essential documents and treasured photos, some knitting and a couple of newspapers. He lit an oil lamp for them and then left, securing the door behind him. They settled in deckchairs with cushions and blankets for another night of terror. June picked up her knitting and Sheila glanced at the newspaper, but she wasn't concentrating and the words didn't make sense.

'What does it say about last night's raid?' June asked above the drone of aeroplanes and the noise of guns and the intermittent crump of bombs exploding.

Sheila obediently turned to the reports; it helped her ignore the noise outside. 'Biggest daylight raid of the war beaten off,' she read aloud. 'Thousands enjoyed the glorious weather and watched their favourite football teams. Crowds at the greyhound stadium stayed to watch the dog fights overhead. There is no reason whatever for dejection or depression. The RAF is more than holding its own.' She looked up. 'Do you believe that?'

'Well, they can't tell the truth, can they? That would really give Herr Hitler something to crow about. If he thinks he can bomb us into submission, he's got another think coming.'

'You don't think we're beaten?'

'No, certainly not. Did you know Mr Churchill came down to the East End today to look at the damage and speak to some of the bombed-out people? They say he was moved to tears but very upbeat. He'll see us through.'

'I wish I could understand . . .'

'Understand what?'

'The reason for it all. The world's gone mad and I've lost my whole family because of it.' She tried hard not to weep again, but the tears defeated her. She scrubbed at her eyes and pretended to go on reading the paper, but the words were blurred and made even less sense.

'I can't tell you,' June said. 'But no doubt there is a divine purpose for it all and we must trust in God.'

'Trust in God!' Sheila's voice rose. 'Trust in a God that allows such things to happen?'

'Hush, dear, we are all given free will. It is mankind that has allowed it to happen, not God, and with God's help it will be mankind who puts it right.'

'I wish I had your faith.'

June did not answer that, instead she said, 'Shall we turn down the lamp and try to sleep? You must be very tired.'

Although June turned down the wick to a glimmer, Sheila knew she would not sleep. The cacophony overhead would be enough to keep her awake, even without the thoughts going round and round in her head and leading nowhere. It ended at last and the All Clear sounded. They emerged and went indoors, not stopping to look at the fresh fires that raged all round them, thankful that they still had a house to go to. They went to bed and this time Sheila did sleep.

Bob returned for breakfast. He was so exhausted, so dirty and smoke-begrimed, he had nothing to say and after swallowing a cup of tea, went upstairs to have a bath and go to bed. He obviously had no news of Charlie or he would have told them. As soon as she had helped June wash up and sweep up the thick layer of dust that had gathered overnight, Shelia set off for South Hallsville school to find out what she was supposed to do to try and put her life together again.

She couldn't believe the devastation, worse than the night before and that had been bad enough. Hardly anything was recognisable: craters where buildings had been, heaps of rubble where streets should have been, flames still flickering among scorched wood, firemen with hoses snaking all over the place, rescue squads digging in the rubble, signs saying 'No entry. Unexploded Bomb', and others on windowless shops saying 'Business as usual'. There were houses with the fronts blown off but still standing, reminding her of the doll's house she had once had where you could open the front to reveal the contents. It had been handed down to each sister in turn and Annie had it now. She stopped suddenly. Annie was no more and neither was the doll's house. She felt the tears returning and blinked hard. She must not cry again, she must not. She must find Charlie.

She was in for another shock when she reached the school. It was in ruins. She was stopped from going closer by a warden. 'That's as far as you can go, miss. Did you know someone there?' He nodded towards the remains of the school.

'I was here the night before last,' she said dully. 'I left.'

'Good job you did or you wouldn't be here to tell the tale. There were hundreds in there. Whole families. The buses didn't come, some mix up about where they were supposed to go.'

'Oh my God.'

She turned away. She had been spared by Providence a second time. But why? Why, of all the people in her neighbourhood, had she been singled out to survive when so many more deserving people, like her parents and siblings, had perished? Divine intervention or something altogether more cruel?

She went to the council offices and was given a new ration card – her identity card was safely in her handbag – and was directed to a building where the WVS were handing out clothes. Taking the bundle she had been fitted out with, one item of which was a black skirt to wear at the funeral, she made her way back to the Bennett's. They had been good to her, but she would have to find somewhere to live soon. The trouble was her brain was moving so slowly, she didn't seem able to rouse herself enough to think properly.

'Sheila!' The voice was a shout that made her look up.

'Chris.' She had forgotten all about him.

'I thought you were a goner. I went to your house yesterday. I couldn't believe my eyes. The neighbours told me you'd all died.'

'Everyone else but me. Dad was killed down by the docks and Charlie is missing.'

'Oh, you poor thing.' He attempted to hug her but she pushed him away.

'Don't make a fuss of me, Chris, you'll only make me cry again.'

'But I want to comfort you.'

'I know. I'm sorry. It's just . . . Oh, I can't explain.'

'OK, but you aren't going to send me away, are you?'

'No. Course not.'

He turned to walk beside her. 'D'you want to come and stay with us? Mum won't mind.'

She thought of Chris's untidy house, all his rowdy brothers and sisters and his scruffy mother who smoked while she cooked, dropping ash everywhere. 'Thanks, but it's all right, Chris. I'm staying with Mr and Mrs Bennett. They've got more room than you have.'

'D'you want to come out with me tonight, flicks or something?'

'No thanks, I don't feel like it. Sorry.'

'Righto.' They had reached the Bennetts' door. 'I'll see you around then, shall I?'

'I expect so.'

She watched him walk away, rueful that she had been so brusque with him, but she couldn't deal with sympathy, she really couldn't. He meant well but that only made it worse.

Chapter Two

Prue brought her chestnut mare to a halt at the level crossing and waited a few yards from the gate as a train thundered through. It was a freight train and very long. Although the wagons were covered with tarpaulin, it was not difficult to see they carried guns. Making for London, she supposed, to help bring down the bombers that were devastating the city. The BBC and the newspapers played it down, of course, but it was easy to read between the lines. It was like the bombing in Spain, indiscriminate and merciless. The Nazis didn't care where the bombs fell, so long as they terrified the inhabitants into demanding peace. From what she had read, far from doing that, they had produced anger and defiance.

The gatekeeper came out of his house beside the line and opened the gates when the last wagon had passed through. 'Good afternoon, my lady,' he said. 'Nice day, isn't it? Not so good as last week, but warm for the time of year.'

'Yes, Mr Potts, though I imagine the poor East Enders must be praying for bad weather.'

'True. I'm right glad I don't live there. There's some evacuees at the school come from there, I did hear, bombed out, many of 'em. They'll be wanting homes. I reckon me and the missus will take one.'

Walking her horse, she crossed the line, and rode along the lane to the lodge gates of Longfordham Hall. There were trees either side of the drive, many of them sweet chestnut, almost ripe, she noticed. Nearer the house were flower gardens and a terrace. She rode round the house to the stables and dismounted. Bill Stevens, the groom who had served with her father in the First World War but was too old and bent to fight in the latest conflict, took the bridle. 'Master Gilbert is home, Miss Prudence,' he said. 'He arrived an hour ago.'

'Oh, good.' She smiled to herself. Stevens, who had known them both from birth, had never managed to make the transition from addressing Gilbert as 'my lord' after a lifetime of 'Master Gilbert', or her as 'my lady', when her father had inherited the Earldom of Winterton three years before. Indeed, she could not get used to it herself. It sounded so pretentious and she much preferred her proper name of Prudence Le Strange.

She hurried indoors and ran to the drawing room, where she could hear voices, and flung open the door. Her mother and brother were having afternoon tea. The Countess, who was seated on a sofa with the tea tray on a table at her side, wore a green silk afternoon gown, her dark hair elegantly coiffured. Her brother, sitting opposite his mother, was in his army officer's uniform. 'Gillie, Stevens said you were home.'

'Prue, I wish you would not come in here in your riding clothes,' her mother said. 'You smell of horses.'

'I'll go and change. I just wanted to say hallo to Gillie.'

'He will still be here when you come down, decently clad.'

Gilbert winked at her and she smiled at him, before taking

herself off to change. She and Gillie were especially close, being only eighteen months apart in age. He was twenty-two and she was a month short of her twenty-first birthday. In peacetime she would have had a come-out at a débutante's ball and been presented at court, but she doubted that would happen now. She might be lucky and have a party. The trouble was that all her friends were scattered, some in the forces, others doing war work of one kind or another, and she doubted they would be able to rustle up a decent number.

'Hitler has a lot to answer for,' she murmured, as she stripped off her riding clothes. The shirt and underwear she put in the laundry basket and hung the jodhpurs and jacket in one of the spacious cupboards in her room and went to have a shower.

Half an hour later, she returned to the drawing room, demure in a printed cotton frock and cardigan, and took her place beside the Countess.

'Timothy rang while you were out,' her mother said. 'He has some leave and asked if he might drop in on his way home. I told him to come for dinner and stay overnight. He'll be on the five o'clock train.'

'Oh good. It seems ages since I saw him.'

She had met Timothy Mortimer at a friend's come-out ball in 1938. It had been a glittering affair, but overshadowed by the news from Czechoslovakia and Chamberlain's appeasement of Hitler. Everyone drank too much, and sounded just a little too animated, conscious perhaps that it was the last event of its kind they might have for a very long time. Tim had seen her standing just inside the door and moved over, two full glasses of champagne in hand, to speak to her.

'Someone as pretty as you should not be alone,' he had said, giving her one of the glasses.

'I shan't be alone for long.'

He had laughed, making a lock of his fair hair fall over his forehead. He pushed it back, a gesture with which she would become familiar. 'No, I should think not, but I want to get my bid in first. What's your name?'

'Prue Le Strange. What's yours?'

'Tim Mortimer. Do you know everyone here?'

'Most of them. Do you?'

'Most of them. How come we've never met before?'

He was far too forward and she ought to have rebuffed him, but he was fun to talk to and during the course of the evening, they had danced and joked and eventually exchanged telephone numbers.

It was not until their third or fourth meeting he discovered she was the daughter of an earl. 'You might have told me,' he said. 'I've made a complete fool of myself.'

'Why? It doesn't make any difference to me. I'm still the same person, a title doesn't change anything. If it does, then you are not the man I thought you were.'

'It's not that, it's the fact that you kept it secret.'

'I didn't keep it secret, it's simply that I do not consider it important and I certainly wouldn't boast about it. Come and stay the weekend with my family. You'll find we're very ordinary.'

After a little persuasion, he had come and Mama had been kind to him and Papa jovial and he had relaxed and told them about his parents, that he had a brother and sister, both younger than he was, that his home was in a village near Stowmarket and he was in his last year at Cambridge and hoped to follow his father into law. 'That's if there is no war,' he had said. 'If there is, I shall join the air force.'

He had been as good as his word and was now a flight

lieutenant, stationed at Scampton in Lincolnshire. He had learnt to fly while at Cambridge which gave him an advantage over some other recruits, but even so he had not become a pilot, but a navigator. 'Everyone wants to be a fighter pilot,' he had told her at the beginning of his training the year before. 'There's no shortage of recruits for fighters, so I've landed up in Bomber Command. It's like being back at school with text books, instruments and charts.' Since then they had seen each other only occasionally but made up for it by corresponding regularly.

'I'll meet him off the train,' she said, then turned to her brother. 'Now, Gillie, tell me all your news.'

'Nothing to tell. We train, we eat and sleep and we train some more. We go on night exercises, do rifle drill, then eat and sleep some more. We lost so many men at Dunkirk, we are nowhere near up to strength again yet and the new recruits have to be trained. There's talk of North Africa, India or the Far East, but that's all it is, talk. No one knows anything for sure. We will almost certainly be sent abroad. I can't see us staying in England for the rest of the war.'

He was a different man from the haggard, exhausted one who had come back from Dunkirk in stinking clothes that he'd been wearing nearly a week, his handsome face lined with fatigue and his dark hair unkempt and full of grit. All he'd wanted to do was have a bath and a long sleep, but by the end of his leave he appeared to have recovered his usual spirits, at least on the surface, and went back to his unit, only to find they were not destined to return to active service immediately. Their mother might be glad of that, but he was itching to get his revenge for the suffering of his comrades. Although he had tried to tell Prue what it had been like, he had said nothing to his mother and had asked his sister not to mention it either. The harsh reality of war had seemed not to have hit the Countess and she carried on in her serene way, doing what good she could in the village and keeping up a correspondence with friends and family, retaining the ritual of afternoon tea and changing for dinner.

'We will have to have troops in England if there's an invasion,' Prue said. 'Papa and his Home Guard won't be able to hold them off alone, even if he thinks he can.'

The Earl's enthusiasm for the Home Guard made them smile, but he treated it very seriously. Teaching warfare to the local volunteers was the next best thing to being back in the army himself, he had said, and made him feel he was doing his bit.

'There won't be an invasion,' Gilbert said firmly. 'Not while we've got an air force.'

'I certainly hope not,' Prue said. 'But I want to do something useful. I think I'll join up.'

'You certainly will not,' her mother said. 'I never heard such a thing. Your father will never allow it.'

'I might have to, if not in the forces, then for war work of some kind and I'd rather choose what I do than be directed. I can't sit about idle, Mama, when so many of my friends are doing interesting things. Besides, it's not patriotic. Papa understands that. Where is he, by the way?'

'Where do you think? With his precious Home Guard. I don't know what he finds to occupy them for so long. He was very secretive about it when I asked him. He trotted out the usual excuse, "Careless talk costs lives". As if telling me is careless talk! It makes me think he doesn't trust me.'

Gilbert laughed. 'Let him have his secrets, Mama, it makes him feel important.'

'He is important. At least he is to me.'

'Of course he is and not just to you. All the Home Guard are, so are the fire-fighters, the ARP and the police. Civilian or not, everyone has a part to play . . .'

'Except me,' Prue put in.

'You will find your niche, Sis.'

'If you are going to the station, you had better go,' her mother told her.

'You can take my car,' Gillie said, throwing her the keys.

Marcus Le Strange, fifth Earl of Winterton, Lieutenant-Colonel in the Great War, now Captain of the Longfordham Home Guard, faced his company of part-time soldiers in a barn on the estate. They were a mixed bunch of old and young and a few in between who were in reserved occupations. Many of them were his own employees, farmers or employees of the farms on the estate and he had known every one of them all their lives. One or two, like Bill Stevens, had served with him in the Great War. Being country folk, used to farming, they did not need to be taught how to use a rifle, but they had only recently been issued with those and had happily started popping off blank ammunition at anything that moved. They needed discipline.

He conceded that discipline of the square-bashing type that took place in the regular army would not do for these rugged countrymen. They needed to understand what they were being asked to do and why. 'In the event of an invasion,' he told them. 'We will undoubtedly be outnumbered, but that does not mean we can expect to be defeated. Defeat is not a word we recognise. We know our terrain, we know our neighbours, we know where to hide ourselves and pick off a target and not let loose with everything we've got.'

'I thought we were meant to defend our homes and families,' one of them said.

'And that we must undoubtedly do,' he told them. 'But standing at your garden gate shooting at the advancing horde will do no good at all. We must be cleverer than that.' He paused. 'There will be an exercise next weekend to test the security of the airfield. We will meet here at nineteen hundred hours on Saturday. Do not be late.'

They nodded agreement and he dismissed them. All but six drifted away, talking among themselves. The six, including Bill Stevens, had been asked privately to stay behind. 'I have been asked to form a special unit to be deployed in the event of an invasion,' he told them. 'And you six have been selected as being suitable to join it. It is entirely voluntary, of course, but if you agree, we will be trained in guerrilla warfare. In the unlikely event the country is occupied, we will be there to carry on the fight. We will do our work swiftly and silently and melt away again into secret hideaways.'

'Do you think we will be, my lord?' Bill Stevens asked. 'Occupied, I mean.'

'Highly unlikely, but the enemy might try. We must be prepared. It is absolutely imperative we do not talk about what we are doing, not to anyone, not to wives, sweethearts or the people we work with every day, is that understood?'

'Yes, my lord,' they said in unison.

'If anyone wants to back out, now is the time to do it.'

'Not on your life,' Bill said, and everyone echoed that with a 'Hear. Hear.'

'Good. These units will be called Auxiliary Units and will be part of a special Battalion, but to all intents and purposes, an adjunct of the Home Guard. We must pretend what we are doing is normal Home Guard exercise, nothing more. Do you understand?'

'Yes, my lord.'

'Our next meeting will be after the weekend exercise when I will probably have more details for you.'

He dismissed them, beckoning his gamekeeper to join him. 'George, we have to have a secret underground bunker and we need to construct it ourselves with the help of some Royal Engineers. It must be invisible on the surface. I'm thinking of putting it in the wood. You know every inch of the woods and I need your advice on the best place to site it. We've got to be able to dig down about twelve feet.'

'Twelve feet, my lord, that's a fair ol' distance.'

'Yes, but it has to house us all and store weapons and ammunition and have an escape tunnel.'

'And that's all to be done in secret, my lord?'

'Yes. The woods are part of the estate and the villagers won't be able to see what is going on from the road. And I can trust you to see off any trespassers.'

'Yes, but what about the Countess and Lady Prudence, what will you tell them?'

'I'll think of something,' he said. 'The same goes for your wife. Something to do with a Home Guard exercise perhaps.'

They parted company and Marcus walked home alone, musing on the problem. Having told the men they must not say anything to their wives, he could not break his own rules and tell Chloe. But how often could he say 'Careless talk costs lives' before she exploded in anger?

His family was everything to him and their safety was of paramount importance. Gilbert was in the army and would have to take his chances with that, but what of Chloe and Prudence? How could he make sure they were safe? He had considered sending them to Canada – he had cousins there – but Chloe would not hear of going without him. 'If the Queen can stay with the King, then I can surely stay with you,' she had said. As for Prue, being young and beautiful, she would be especially vulnerable. Thinking about it made his blood run cold. It was why he had agreed to set up this local resistance unit. If there were enough of them scattered about the country they might do some good.

He found Gilbert in the gun room. There were several pairs of Wellington boots and walking shoes arranged in rows beneath pegs on which hung coats and mackintoshes. On a shelf above them were a couple of deer stalker caps, some riding hats and a tin hat. A cupboard housed their sporting guns and a few boxes of cartridges for the pheasant season, but these had been augmented with a couple of army-issue rifles, boxes of ammunition and grenades stacked in a corner.

'Hallo,' he said. 'Spot of leave?'

'Long weekend. You've got a fair arsenal here.'

'A lot of it is Home Guard stuff. The men have taken their rifles home, but I've got the ammunition here, couldn't risk children getting hold of it.'

'No, but it could make quite a bang here.'

'It's safe enough. We are going to build somewhere to store it.'

'Secure, I hope.'

Marcus laughed and tapped the side of his nose. 'So secret no one will have an inkling it's there.'

Gilbert laughed too. 'In a village like this, you must be joking.'

'Then I'll just have to trust everyone to keep their mouths shut, won't I?'

'Did you know Prue is anxious to do something for the war effort?'

'Yes, she's been nagging me about it.'

'Are you going to let her go?'

'I can't really stop her, can I? She'll be twenty-one next month. I can only try to influence her decision.' He paused. 'Come on, let's go and change for dinner.'

'Tim Mortimer is coming. Prue has gone to meet his train.'

'Oh. Don't know what to make of that. Is it serious, do you think?'

Gilbert shrugged. 'Only they know that. Seems a nice enough chap.'

Prue parked the little red MG on the road near the station and ran up the slope onto the platform just as the train drew in. There were several workers from the airfield waiting to board it, but Tim was the only one to alight. 'Hallo, gorgeous,' he said, bending to kiss her cheek.

She smiled at the flattery. 'Hello yourself. Did you have a good journey?'

'Not bad, at least the train was on time.'

'You are looking tired.' They began to walk down the platform towards the level crossing gates as the train continued on its way to London.

'I'm OK. All the better for seeing you. I hope your parents didn't mind me asking to come, but I couldn't go on leave without seeing you.'

'No, of course they didn't mind.'

'And you?'

'Need you ask? It seems ages since I saw you last.'

'All of three months,' he said.

'Well, it seems longer than that. I've been bored. Everyone seems to be getting into uniform.' She turned to look at him as they reached the car. 'You look very dashing in yours. I bet you are driving all the WAAFs wild.'

Laughing, he settled himself in the passenger seat. 'If you are fishing for reassurance that I wouldn't give any of them a second glance, then you have it.'

'I believe you, thousands wouldn't.' She started the car up, did a competent three-point turn and set off for the hall.

'Gillie is home on leave,' she said. 'Please don't ask him about Dunkirk, not in front of Mama, anyway.'

'I won't. I know how awful it was. From the air we could see all those troops on the beach, completely exposed and long lines of them stretching into the sea. We were trying to harass the enemy, to help our chaps get away, but we couldn't do much except go after the airfields and shipping. It was a miracle they got so many off.'

'So Gillie said. He was in a dreadful state when he came home and worried Mama to death. He seems all right again now, though maybe that's put on for our benefit.'

She turned in at the gates of the hall and drove slowly up the drive to the front door and stopped. 'Here we are.'

Dinner was served in the dining room on a table properly laid with a pristine napery and the second-best cutlery and dinner service. Marcus and Gilbert were in dinner jackets but Tim was in uniform, for which he apologised. 'I didn't have a dinner jacket on the base,' he said. 'There doesn't seem much call for it.'

'It doesn't matter in the least,' Prue said, sitting beside him. 'Does it, Mama?'

'No, of course not,' her mother said. 'We are glad you were able to join us. It is wartime after all and the fare is very simple.'

'It looks delicious,' he said, as a maid served onion soup.

'Cook grumbles that it is no better than the farm hands have to eat,' the Countess went on. 'But there is was a war on and rationing affects everyone. We are lucky that we have home-grown produce, vegetables from the kitchen garden and plums from the orchard. Even the chicken is one from the home farm which had ceased to lay.'

The soup was followed by roast chicken and then plum crumble. While they ate, they spoke of generalities, but the conduct of the war inevitably came to the fore. The newspaper report of the latest air raids, while admitting there had been much damage to property, played down the loss of life. According to them, the attacks were failing because of the numbers of enemy aeroplanes shot down and because they had not succeeded in bringing the docks and factories to a standstill. Schools, churches and hospitals had been hit, but the general mood of the people was defiance.

'I wonder how true that is,' Prue said.

'I imagine it has been somewhat edited,' Tim said. 'The authorities would not want to spread fear and panic. The real facts will be kept from the general public.'

'I don't see how you can keep people in the dark,' Gillie said. 'I came through London on my way home and it was pretty grim. There's bomb damage everywhere, great craters and ruined buildings, but everyone is trying to carry on as normal. I think that's what the newspapers mean.'

'It seems to me that this war is making liars of us all,' Chloe said. 'We must not say this, we must not say that, we must not be told the truth. We are not children who have to be protected from unpleasantness.'

'I don't think it's that,' her husband said. 'We don't want Hitler to know what we're up to.'

'No, nor even your wives,' she said with some asperity.

'What have you been up to, Tim?' Gilbert asked in the embarrassed silence that followed. 'Operational yet?'

'Yes, have been since the spring. Our main task at the moment is trying to prevent an invasion. We've been targeting German shipping and the Channel ports, anything to stop them moving troops by sea.'

'There, I told you,' Gilbert said to his mother. 'There won't be an invasion while we've got chaps like Tim to prevent it.'

'That doesn't mean the threat isn't very real,' the Earl said. 'We still need the Home Guard.'

'Oh, you and your Home Guard,' the Countess said.

He was saved having to reply by the sound of the telephone in the hall. They heard the butler answer it. After a moment Hedges came into the room. 'My lord, there is a telephone call for you. It is Mr Welchman. I told him you were at dinner and he asked if you would ring him back when you have a moment. I have written his number on the pad.'

'What the devil does he want?' Marcus said.

'We have finished our meal, so go and find out,' Chloe said. 'I'll have coffee sent to the drawing room.'

'Coffee?' queried Gilbert, as his father disappeared. 'Have you still got coffee, Mama?'

'I stocked up last year, but unless I can find a new supply we shall soon run out. We'll have to drink that dreadful Camp. God knows what that's made of, but it's not coffee beans. Let's go into the drawing room so that Margaret can clear away.'

On the way, they passed the Earl, apparently listening intently to his caller. 'Can't you tell me anything about it?' they heard him say before going out of earshot.

He followed them a few minutes later and accepted a cup of black coffee from his wife. 'What was that all about?' she asked him.

'I don't know. It's all very hush-hush. He wants me to take Prue to see him.'

'Me?' she queried in astonishment. 'Whatever for?'

'He might have a job for you. He wouldn't tell me what it was except that it is important for the war effort. If you are interested we have to go up to London tomorrow.'

'What sort of job?'

'I haven't the faintest idea.'

'All these secrets,' Chloe said. 'I hate secrets and I hate it when you won't tell me.'

'I can't tell you because I don't know myself.'

'Well, I hope it's not dangerous.'

They smiled at this. Everyone was in some measure of danger, whatever they did. You didn't have to be in the forces or even in London; in Longfordham with an airfield being built on their doorstep they were also vulnerable. 'I was assured it was not,' he said.

'Why me?' Prue asked.

'I don't know that either, but he mentioned being given your name by Edward Travis.'

'Who is Edward Travis?'

'Commander Edward Travis. I knew him years ago. He went into the navy. I haven't seen him in years.'

'The answer to your prayers, Sis,' Gilbert said.

'I don't know what it is yet.'

'What time will you have to leave?' Tim asked.

'We'll go up on the nine o'clock train,' the Earl told him. 'But you don't have to hurry away. Stay as long as you like.'

'Thank you, but my parents are expecting me, so I'll catch the eight o'clock to Cambridge. I can get a connection there.' He reached for Prue's hand and squeezed it. 'But it was very good of you to have me.'

'You are very welcome,' the Countess said.

'Let's go and have a wander in the grounds,' Prue said, standing up.

The clocks had gone forward two hours in March – they called it double summer time – because the extra daylight helped the farmers who were expected to grow most of the nation's food. In September it was light until late in the evening and still warm, so they fetched jackets and left the house by a side door and wandered down the drive. She hung onto his arm and put her head on his shoulder. 'I love this place,' she said. 'It's so peaceful. You'd never know there's a war on, except all the young, fit men are disappearing one by one.'

'Let's pray it always stays peaceful,' he said. 'Haven't you any idea what you are wanted for?'

'Not a clue.'

'I hope it won't mean living in London. I couldn't bear to think of you being bombed. I need to feel you are safe.'

'You are being very serious all of a sudden.'

'War is a serious business. And my feelings for you are serious. You do know that, don't you?'

'I was beginning to wonder.'

'What about you? May I hope?'

'Of course you may hope.'

'Oh, Prue.' He looked back. They were out of sight of the house. He pulled her into his arms and kissed her soundly. 'I don't think it's right to get married at the moment,' he went on. 'You never know . . .'

'So this isn't a proposal?' She looked up at his face. He was watching her intently, scanning her face with his grey-green eyes and she knew she ought not to tease him.

'Not exactly.'

'How so, not exactly?'

'I'm simply giving you due notice that if I survive this war, I shall ask you properly.'

'Then I hope it doesn't last too long.' She reached up and pulled his head down to hers and kissed him hard on the mouth. 'Let's go back through the woods.' She linked her arm in his and they left the path to plunge into the wood. The setting sun, shining through the trees onto leaves already turning colour, gave them a golden luminosity that was magical. She stooped to pick up a few chestnuts that had fallen and put them in her pocket. 'It's a pity we have no time to build a fire and roast them,' she said. 'But when you come again, that's what we'll do.'

'I shall look forward to that.' He grinned and stopped to kiss her. 'And lots of other things besides. This is something on account.' And he kissed her again. 'We won't have the chance to say goodbye properly tomorrow, so I'll say cheerio now.' This involved more kissing until she broke away. 'Tim, you are making me all breathless.'

'Don't you like it?'

'Need you ask.' She reached up and pecked his cheek. 'There, that will have to do until we meet again.'

'Until we meet again,' he repeated. 'I'll hold you to that.'

Arm-in-arm, they turned to go back to the house. She had been brought up to be poised and self-contained, to have a sort of feminine equivalent of the stiff upper lip, and she found it difficult to give her emotions free rein. But they were there, all the same, just below the surface. Perhaps one day she would learn to let go, but now was neither the time nor the place.

She saw Tim at breakfast, but there was no opportunity to do more than say goodbye and good luck, before he was taken off to the station by Stevens to catch his train. Gilbert took her and her father an hour later.

Arriving in London, they took a taxi to the address he had been given in St James's Park. On the way they passed evidence of the bombing, gaps in the rows of buildings, big craters filled with water, boarded-up windows. 'It's horrible, isn't it?' she said. 'All this destruction.'

'Yes.'

'What do you think Mr Welchman wants me for? Didn't he give you any clues?'

'None, but we'll soon know.'

He paid off the taxi and they went into the building and were shown up to the fourth floor where they met the gentleman in question. He was not a tall man but he was, in Prue's eyes, a handsome one with dark wavy hair and a neat moustache.

After the preliminary greeting, Mr Welchman turned to Prue. 'Tell me about yourself,' he said. 'Education, interests, that sort of thing.'

'Why?' she demanded.

'You are curious, I understand that, but I need to get to know you so, I'm afraid, you are going to have to indulge me and answer my questions. It is important, not idle curiosity.'

'I was taught at home until I went to Rodean and then to Switzerland . . .'

'Finishing school?'

'No, university. I studied languages.'

'Ah. What languages?'

'German and French.'

'What do you make of this?' He pushed a piece of paper across his desk to her.

At first what was written on it seemed a jumble of meaningless letters arranged in groups of five, but on closer inspection she realised they were German words with the spaces in the wrong place. Once she had separated them, the translation was easy. '"I have nothing to offer but blood, toil, tears and sweat.",' she read aloud. 'Mr Churchill's words.'

'Good.' He took the paper away and replaced it with another. 'Try this.'

She puzzled over it for some time. 'It doesn't make sense as it stands,' she said. 'But if you replace all the "o"s with "e"s and the "g" with a "c", it reads: "*Denn eben wo Begriffe fehlen, da stellt ein Wort zur rechten Zeit sich ein.*"'

'And the translation?'

'"For just when ideas fail, a word comes in to save the situation." It's Goethe.'

'Well done,' he said. 'We can use you.'

'For my German?'

'Among other things. Do you want to do something for the war effort, something important, so important that I cannot tell you anything about it until you get there?'

'Sounds intriguing. Yes, of course.'

'Go home now. Report to Commander Travis at Bletchley Park at noon on Monday morning. Be prepared to stay.'

'Where's Bletchley Park?' she asked.

'It's a country house in Buckinghamshire, about fifty miles north-west of London. You can get there easily by train from Cambridge.'

They shook hands and Prue and her father left. They found a restaurant where they had a frugal lunch.

'It's all very mysterious,' Prue said, looking with distaste at the meat pie on her plate. 'I'm intrigued.'

'I expect it's translation work of some kind.'

'That doesn't sound very exciting.'

'Depends what it is you are translating. It could be secret stuff.'

'Secret! Whatever will we say to Mama?'

'Oh, we'll think of something. She will be glad you are not going to be in the services, I expect.'

'Papa, have you engineered this?'

'No, not at all. Alice Harridan is going to do similar work, according to her father. He told Edward Travis about you and Travis told Gordon Welchman, who is responsible for recruiting suitable people.'

'I haven't seen Alice since school. She was a bit of a swot, I remember. The rest of us used to tease her about it.'

'That was unkind.'

'She didn't seem to mind.'

They finished their meal and took a taxi to Liverpool Street station to catch a train, and arrived home in time for dinner.

Being told by her husband that Prue was going to do office work in a country house and would be in no danger at all, the Countess accepted that her daughter was going to be leaving home. 'It'll be like going back to school,' Prue told her. 'I'll be home for the hols.'

Gilbert left on Sunday evening and on Monday morning Prue caught a train to Cambridge. It wasn't until she left the train at Bletchley and was standing on the platform looking about for a porter that she realised Alice had been on the same train. They greeted each other warily. Alice was little different from the schoolgirl Prue had known. She still wore her hair cut short and spectacles on a rather aquiline nose. She was wearing a tweed suit and flat-heeled shoes, in contrast to Prue's wool dress, warm cape and high heels.

They soon discovered there was no porter and they would have to hump their cases to the park. 'That's it,' the ticket collector told them, shrugging towards a high, chain-link fence. 'If you follow the path round that, you'll come to the gate.'

'My God, it looks like a prison,' Prue said, as they struggled along the path. They could not see what was on the other side for trees. Her case was heavy and she was beginning to wish she had packed fewer clothes and had the rest sent on. 'Do you think they'll dress us in overalls with arrows on them?'

'I was told security would be tight,' Alice said. 'I'm sure you were too.'

'Do you know what we're going to do?'

'No idea.' They had reached a guarded gate and, on giving their names to the sentry, were allowed in and made their way up to the house, passing a lake and several newly constructed wooden huts on the way. There were people, quite a lot of them, going in and out of these huts, some in naval uniform, some in khaki, most in civvies. They paid no attention to the newcomers, who made their way to the front entrance of the sprawling inelegant mansion and announced their presence to a receptionist who sent them upstairs to Commander Travis's office. He was a plump, balding man with an engaging smile, who told them he was the deputy head of Station X.

'I knew your father well, many years ago,' he told Prue as they shook hands. 'How is he?'

'He is well, thank you.'

He moved on to Alice, shook her hand and mentioned her father too. It seemed this was a job for the boys or, in this case, girls.

'The work we do here is highly sensitive,' he said, after telling them to be seated. 'I cannot stress that too strongly and so before we go any further, you are required to sign the Official Secrets Act. It means you cannot under any circumstances tell anyone what you are doing here, and I mean no one, not even your nearest and dearest.' He handed them each a sheet of paper and a pen and watched them read and sign it. 'You will be assigned to different sections of our work and you do not speak of it, even to each other. Is that clear?'

'As crystal,' Prue said, handing back her signed paper. Alice did likewise.

'Good,' he said. 'Welcome to the Government Code and Cypher School, GC & CS for short, also known as Station X, but we always refer to it as Bletchley Park or BP. I'll have someone show you where you'll be working and order a car to take you to your digs.'

'We're not living in, then?' Prue said. 'I thought all the huts . . .'

'They are where we work, not where we sleep. I am afraid there is no accommodation on the premises, but because we work a twenty-four-hour shift system and people are coming and going all the time, we have buses and cars to bring you in and take you home. The billets have been chosen with care, but you do not say a word to your hosts about your work. I doubt they will ask.' He rang a bell and a girl in a W.R.N.S uniform appeared and was told to take Prue to Hut Six and Alice to Hut Eight.

Hut Six was a long building with a central corridor and rooms to the left and right in which people of both sexes worked at plain desks. Prue found Mr Welchman in the first of them. Having ascertained that she had signed the secrecy document, he explained what was happening. 'In a nutshell we are in the business of intercepting and decoding enemy radio traffic, most of which is brought to us by motorcycle from listening stations,' he said. 'The enemy uses a very clever machine called an enigma, to encipher their messages. Our job is to find the key to unscrambling it all and thus reading what they have to say. We pass the decoded information on to whoever needs it.

'We have a modified Type X machine made to work like an enigma, and other more complicated electro-mechanical machines called bombes, which do the job of checking what we think might be the key, but they won't work unless we have a crib to start them off, things like call signs, transmission times, the length of the message and, more often than Herr Hitler would like if he knew about it, the silly mistakes of the German operators. Without those there are 58 million million million possibilities.

'Our work is further complicated because there is no universal setting; every section of the army, navy, air force and intelligence services all use different machines and different settings and they are changed every twenty-four hours on the stroke of midnight. Then we have to begin all over again.'

'Gosh! What a task. Can it be done?'

'Oh yes, we are doing it. In this hut we are dealing with German army and air force signals. Other huts are doing other things and working on different aspects of decrypting, but you do not need to know about those. I have only told you this much so that you can understand how vital the work is and how important it is to be accurate and never to breathe a word to anyone of what you do.'

'I understand.'

'The decoded messages are in German, naturally, and that is where you come in. You will be working next door in Hut Three. I'll take you there now to meet Commander Saunders.'

It was in Hut Three that the five letter groups were separated into German words, a process called 'emending' and then passed to the translators who sat round a table with the leader of the Watch facing them. 'Sometimes there are gaps in the message because of poor reception or the mistakes of the sender and these can sometimes be guessed at,' she was told. 'Or we could ask for it to be run again or sometimes the same message would have been sent to someone else and that might reveal the answer. It is painstaking work and needs accuracy, dedication and the utmost secrecy. The enemy must never know how we have obtained our information. In fact, most of our own side don't know either. When we send on the information, we have to say it comes from a most reliable source. Sometimes we make it look as though it is a report from a spy.'

'I understand.' Now she understood that strange translation she had made for Mr Welchman. Only later would she realise that had been child's play to what she would be asked to do.

'I'll take you back to the office to find out what shifts you are on for the next three weeks,' Mr Welchman said, leading the way back to the main house. 'There's a canteen and some facilities for recreation. Is there anything else you want to know? About your job here, I mean. There is no need for you to know what everyone else is doing. It is actively discouraged. Oh, and you will need to know the password to get around in the grounds.'

'Am I allowed to write letters?'

'Of course you are, but they will be censored, naturally. And letters addressed to you must come via a box number at the Foreign Office. No post leaves here with a Bletchley post mark either. Letters are taken away from the site to be sent from a number of different locations. Now I suggest you go and have some lunch and then find your billet. Admin will tell you where that is. Report to Hut Three . . .' He consulted a chart on the wall of his office. 'Sixteen hundred hours.'

So she was going to be on Watch B, the evening shift, which didn't give her much time to settle into her billet before starting work. She felt excited and a little apprehensive and would have loved to tell her mother or Tim what she was going to do, but she could not say a word. She would write to Tim tonight and give him the Foreign Office box number, though what she would tell him, she was not at all sure. As to what to tell her mother, that posed an even bigger problem.

A wren in uniform came to drive her to her lodgings in the town, and she picked up her bag and followed her guide out to a large Humber car.

Chapter Three

'We've found your aunt,' the Red Cross lady told Sheila. 'You were right, she does live in Bletchley. Her name is Mrs Constance Tranter and she is a widow. She has agreed to take you in.'

'What about Charlie?' They were talking in the Bennett's front room. June was busy pouring out tea for them.

'We have no information about him, I'm afraid, but if we hear anything we'll let you know straight away.' She paused. 'I think that after all this time we will have to assume he perished.'

She didn't want to hear that, however true it might be. 'When am I to go?'

'As soon as you are ready.'

'I'm ready now. It isn't as if I've got much to pack.' She had never been used to much in the way of possessions but even so her wardrobe was meagre by any standards. Besides the clothes she was wearing she had a wool skirt, two blouses, a cardigan, two pairs of pyjamas, some underwear, socks and stockings, a pair of slippers and toiletries, all donated, none of it new. There was also a rucksack to put them all in. With the money she earned she had bought a second-hand dress, an overcoat, a scarf and a pair of gloves. The Indian summer had gone and there was a distinct nip in the air as September came to an end. She had also treated herself to a little make-up for her pride's sake.

'You don't need to rush off today,' June said. 'Tomorrow will do.'

Sheila didn't want to go at all. It meant leaving her family behind. The fact that all but one of them had been buried and all that was left of them were seven new graves, side by side in the churchyard, made no difference. She felt as if she were deserting them, turning her back on everything she had known and loved. More importantly it meant abandoning her search for her brother. When not at work, she and Chris had combed the streets between her old home and the docks, looking for him. They had found no sign of him, no evidence at all that he had ever existed. She had steeled herself to go to the morgue and the places where they laid out the dead, but Charlie was not among them. 'If he's not there, he must still be alive somewhere,' she had said to Chris, ignoring the fact that many bodies were so mutilated they could not be identified, a fact she was well aware of but refused to acknowledge.

Chris had been a stalwart, putting up with her moods which swung from despair to hope, from snapping at him to leaning on him to cry out her misery, anger and frustration. She would have to say goodbye to him too. And what would she find at the end of her journey? The Red Cross lady's words, 'agreed to take you in', sounded as if her aunt had needed some persuasion.

'You needn't stay there if you don't like it,' Chris said, when she told him later that day as they walked the streets. 'You can always come back to live with us. The evacuation's on again and Ma's going to send the kids to the country. There'll be room.' Chris's younger brothers and sisters had been evacuated the year before, but when the prophesied bombing had not happened their mother had brought them home again, as many others had done, which made the present bombing all the more dreadful. There had been raids every night since that fateful one that had killed her family, adding more damage, more casualties.

'Thank you,' she said, dully. 'I'll bear that in mind.'

'You'll write to me, won't you? Tell me how things are.'

'Course I will. I'm not going far away.' Her grief had made her numb to all other feelings: hope, joy, love, even to misery. To give Chris his due, he had tried to understand and had stuck by her even when she was ratty or silent, walking the streets with his arm about her shoulder or sitting silently beside her in the Bennett's front room, while she stared at the wallpaper with unseeing eyes. He was her prop and she was going to miss him more than she liked to say. 'I'll be back.'

He came to see her off, carrying her rucksack on the bus to Euston station. On the platform he gave it to her and made a clumsy attempt to kiss her. She turned her head away and his lips contacted her ear lobe. Afterwards, sitting in the train with the rucksack on the luggage rack above her head, she regretted that. Poor Chris! He had been so good to her and she had not even let him kiss her goodbye. As soon as she was settled she would write him an affectionate letter to make up for it.

Settled was hardly the word she would use by the time she went to her room that night and took out her pencil and notepaper. She had started off on the wrong foot simply by addressing her aunt as Auntie Connie.

'I am your Aunt Constance,' the lady had said repressively. 'I wish you to address me properly.' She was tall and thin, with iron-grey hair pulled back tightly into a bun. She wore a black skirt and a grey twinset. There were pearls at her throat.

'Sorry. It's what Mum said and I thought . . .'

'Your mother never did have any sense of what was right and proper. She would never have married Walter Phipps if she had, but then what choice did she have?'

'Pa was a fine man and a good father. He always thought of others before himself and he died doing his duty. I won't have you insulting him, nor Ma neither. She was a smashing mum and we all loved her.' Anger prevented her from weeping, which she might easily have done under the circumstances.

'Your loyalty does you credit, I give you that. Now, let's take your things up to your room and settle you in.'

Victoria Villa was a detached four-bedroom house whose name was etched in the lintel above the front door. It was double-fronted with bay windows either side. Inside it was well furnished and spotless and smelt of disinfectant and Mansion polish. The hall and stairs were covered in fawn carpet. Sheila followed her hostess up the stairs and was shown into a small bedroom at the back of the house. There was a single bed beside which was a little table, a built-in wardrobe, a dressing table and an upright chair. The floor was laid with linoleum and there was a single rug alongside the bed. 'This is your room,' her aunt told her. 'You will keep it clean and tidy at all times and you will avoid making a noise. I have another guest who is working on shifts and she sometimes needs to sleep during the day. She is, for your information, a real lady. Her father is the Earl of Winterton and her brother is a viscount. But you don't need to worry about that. You are never likely to meet them.'

'I shan't be here much during the day, shall I? I have to find a job to pay my way.'

'Of course but, until then, you can help me in the house. My daily help has left to do war work.' While she spoke she opened

Sheila's rucksack and began taking garments from it and holding them up for inspection. 'Is this all you have?' It was said with an expression of distaste.

'Yes. Most of it was given to me by the Red Cross. I only had what I was wearing on the day the house was bombed.'

'It's adequate for you, I suppose.' She tidied the clothes away in the wardrobe and drawers and put the empty rucksack on top of the wardrobe. 'The bathroom is at the end of the landing and the water can be heated by turning up the pilot light on the geyser. I do not expect you to spend long in there and you will leave it as you find it. Lady Prudence Le Strange will take precedence, of course.'

'Of course,' Sheila said with bitter irony while she wondered what the lady would be like. A carbon copy of her aunt perhaps?

'Good. I am glad you understand. Now let's go down to the kitchen. Ah, that sounds like the bus. Lady Prudence will be in time for tea.'

They had reached the hall when the front door opened and a young woman breezed in. She could not have been more unlike a Puritan aunt. She was tall, fair-haired and well-proportioned, but it was not that which attracted Sheila, it was her cheerful smile and expressive blue eyes. 'You must be Sheila,' she said, holding out her right hand. 'Mrs Tranter told me she was expecting you today. Welcome to Bletchley.'

Sheila shook the hand. 'Thank you, miss.'

'My lady,' her aunt corrected her.

'Nonsense,' Prue said. 'I'm Prue. I can't be bothered with all that "my lady" stuff.'

'You will be ready for a cup of tea,' Constance said, ignoring that. 'I was just going to put the kettle on.'

'Oh, good. I'll dump my bag in my room and be down in a jiffy.' She raced up the stairs two at a time.

'I don't know what the world is coming to,' Constance said, watching her go. 'Come, Sheila, into the kitchen with you.'

The kitchen was large, with a red-tiled floor, a kitchen range as well as a gas cooker. There was a gas water heater over the deep white sink and a long dresser on whose shelves crockery was displayed. It had drawers and cupboards beneath the shelves. A small table stood in the middle of the room. A tabby cat snoozed in a basket by the hearth. Sheila bent to stroke it. 'What's it called?'

'It is a she and her name is Tiddles. She keeps the mice down. You can set out the tea tray while I make the tea.'

Sheila had no idea what was meant by 'set out the tea tray', but was soon being instructed by her aunt. 'Tray cloth first,' she said, pointing to a drawer in the dresser. 'Cups and saucers, milk in a jug, sugar in a bowl, the stand for the teapot.' Each item was accompanied by a pointing finger. 'You will find tea plates in that cupboard and a cake tin. The cake goes on a stand. That's it, there. You will need a knife from the drawer.'

By this time the kettle was beginning to sing on the gas stove, a much more elegant version of the stove that had been in their own kitchen. Her aunt warmed the pot, added three spoonfuls of tea leaves and then the boiling water. 'Have you brought your ration book?' she asked. 'I will need that.'

'It's in my bag. I'll fetch it.'

'Not now. It will do after we have had tea.' She removed the third cup and saucer, picked up the tray and carried it into the sitting room whose bay window looked out onto a small front garden and beyond that the street. It was furnished with a three piece suite, a display cabinet containing ornaments, a book shelf, a bureau and a small coffee table on which Constance put the tray. They were joined almost immediately by Prue. She sat on the settee and patted the seat beside her. 'Come and sit by me, Sheila, and tell me all about yourself. I gather you've been bombed out.'

'Lady Prudence,' Constance said. 'Sheila will have her tea in the kitchen when she has finished serving you.'

'But I understood she was your niece, not a servant,' Prue said.

'Yes, but she is not used to titled company . . .'

'Goodness, I won't have anyone standing on ceremony on my account. I've no doubt Sheila is dying for a cup of tea. I know I am.'

Her aunt sighed. 'Go and fetch yourself a cup and saucer, Sheila.'

'It's all right, I don't mind,' Sheila murmured.

'But I do.' Prue was adamant. 'Go on, Sheila, fetch another cup and saucer. I want to hear all about you. The blitz must have been horrendous.'

Sheila escaped to the kitchen, in two minds whether to return or not. Her aunt was impossibly snobbish and she would just as soon keep herself to herself. She smiled. Lady Prudence Le Strange had the measure of the lady and was used to having her own way. She carried a cup and saucer back to the sitting room and took her place beside Prue. Prompted, she was soon telling her new friend what had happened and about her search for her brother and how kind the Bennetts had been. 'It's like that in our part of London,' she said. 'We all look out for each other.'

'How dreadful for you. I cannot imagine what it must have been like. I've only got one brother and he's in the army. I don't know what I'd do if I lost him.'

'I imagine you would be sort of numb, like me. I didn't seem able to think straight and every thought led back to Ma and Pa and the kids. I tried not to think about them and at the same time I wanted to remember them, remember everything about them, the things we did, what we said to each other, the laughs we had.'

'It sounds like a happy childhood.'

'It was.'

'Nine crammed into a two-up two-down,' Constance said.

'It wasn't two up, two down. We had three bedrooms, a sitting room, a dining room and a kitchen. We used the dining room as a fourth bedroom and managed just fine.'

'No bathroom. How on earth did you keep clean?' her aunt went on. 'But then I suppose you didn't.'

'We were all clean,' she said indignantly. 'The kids got dirty playing out, but Ma soon cleaned them up again. There was a bath hanging on the back wall. We used to bring it in when we needed a bath. The house was spotless too, Ma saw to that.' She felt the tears gathering in her eyes as the memories rushed back, and tried unsuccessfully to blink them back.

'You poor thing,' Prue said, taking her hand. 'I won't ask you any more questions. You tell me when you want to, when you're ready.'

Sheila found her handkerchief from her sleeve and blew her nose. 'I'm sorry. I can't seem to help it.'

'You'll have to pull yourself together if you want to find a job,' her aunt said. 'No one wants to employ a cry baby.'

Prue ignored her and turned to Sheila. 'Will you be looking for a job?'

'Yes. I'll have to earn my keep.'

'What can you do?'

'I served in a general store. I was at work when the bomb fell on our house. I should have been with them all. I feel bad about that.'

'Don't, for goodness' sake. It wasn't your fault. I'm sure you will have no difficulty finding work. I might be able to help.'

'You don't mean up at Bletchley Park, surely?' Constance queried.

'Yes, why not? I can't promise anything, of course, but I'll do my best.' She turned to Sheila. 'Would you like to go for a walk before dinner? I'll show you round.'

'Yes, that would be nice.' Sheila had had her dinner at the Bennetts' before she left, but afraid to show her ignorance, she did not mention it. She fetched her new coat and joined Prue in the hall.

'Don't you have to go back to work?' she asked as they set off.

'No. We do shift work. I'm on eight to four this week.'

'What do you do?'

'Can't tell you, I'm afraid. Hush-hush, you understand.'

'Sorry I asked.'

'She's an old battle-axe, isn't she? Your aunt, I mean.'

'Yes. I never met her before today. She and Ma didn't get on.'

'I'm not surprised, but I've found that if I stand up to her, she backs down.'

'That's because you are a lady and she is a snob.'

Prue laughed. 'Oh, we are going to get on like a house of fire, you and I. Together against the dragon.'

'I dare not cross her. I've nowhere else to go.' She paused. 'No, that's not quite true, I could go back to Chris's place . . .'

'Chris?'

'My boyfriend. At least, that's what he calls himself, but I've known him since we were at infant school and I'm not sure that's what he is. A friend who just happens to be a boy, I suppose. Trouble is, his house is overcrowded as it is and his mother is not the cleanest person in the world.'

'Then stick it out here. It will get better when the dragon realises she can't browbeat you.'

'Have you got a boyfriend?'

'Yes, you could say that. He's in the air force.'

'You must worry about him.'

'Yes, I do, but it's all-out war and we all have to do our bit. He's in Bomber Command.'

'Good for him. Is he a lord?'

'No. A flight lieutenant. He's . . .' She laughed. 'How can I describe him? A year older than me, very tall and handsome with fair hair and gorgeous greeny-grey eyes. Sometimes he's funny, sometimes he's serious . . .'

'Are you engaged?'

'Not exactly but we have an understanding.' She stopped and waved her arms to encompass the street. 'This is Bletchley, known only for its railway junction and its brickworks, and not much else. There are the usual shops, butcher, baker, candlestick-maker.' She laughed. 'There's a Co-op, W H Smith, fishmonger and hairdresser. You can get a meal at the British restaurant. There's a department store, but if you want to buy clothes I suggest a trip to Bedford or London. Not much in the way of entertainment, except a handful of pubs and a couple of cinemas: the Studio and the Palace. We've got leisure pursuits laid on at the Park but that's only for the people who work there.'

'Where is this park you keep talking about?'

'Near the station. You must have seen the fence when you got off the train. It goes all round it. You can't get in unless you work there.'

Sheila was bewildered; why would anyone work in a park, except gardeners? She wanted to go home, where she was secure and loved, but home had gone, swept away in a single night, along with her family and everything she had known, and with it went her childhood. 'Why am I here?' she asked suddenly.

'Here? Because you need a home, I expect.'

'I didn't mean that. I meant, why am I alive? Why have I been left behind when everyone I love has gone?'

'I can't answer that, Sheila. Maybe there is a reason behind it all, maybe you are destined for great things.'

She forced a laugh. 'Me? I'm a nobody. What great things can I do? I'm not even educated.'

'That can easily be remedied. And you are not a nobody, you are Sheila Phipps, very much a somebody.'

'I never hated anyone before, but I hate all Germans now.'

'I can understand you saying that, but you can't hate a whole race of people. I've known some very nice Germans who would deplore this killing as much as we do. The men in those aeroplanes are obeying orders, just as our men must. They are killing too. War is like that. It is horrible.'

'Are you a conchie?'

'No, I am not, though I think some of those are brave men to stand up for what they believe in, braver than I would be.'

'You aren't in the forces though.'

'No, I'm a civilian, but even civilians have a job to do to help the war effort. The sooner it's over, the better.'

'Do you think it will soon be over?'

'I have no idea but I doubt it.'

'But what you are doing is important?'

Prue smiled. 'So I am told. Come, let us go back. Mrs Tranter cooks dinner for me when I am on early turn, but when I am working evenings and nights I eat at BP.'

'BP?'

'Bletchley Park.'

'Oh, I see.'

They returned to eat an evening meal with their hostess, who spent much of the time apologising to Prue for the poor fare. 'I know it's not what you are used to, my lady,' she said. 'But it is impossible to buy the ingredients for anything but the simplest meal.'

'It is delicious,' Prue said. 'Don't you think so, Sheila?'

'Yes.' There was nothing wrong with the meal but Sheila had no appetite. Her stomach was churning and she wanted to cry again. She put a forkful of mashed potato in her mouth and forced it down.

'I don't know how you can be so fussy,' her aunt said. 'It's better food than you'd get at home, I know.'

'Ma was a good cook and you've no call to say nasty things like that. We were all well fed.'

'Then eat what's on your plate. We can't afford to waste good food.'

Sheila made another attempt to eat and then rushed from the room.

'Well!' Constance said. 'She really will have to be taught some manners.'

'Sheila can't help it, Mrs Tranter. She's all stirred up inside. I would be if I had lost my entire family to Hitler's bombs. Just imagine what that must be like. Give her time.'

Constance lapsed into silence. Prue glanced across and noticed the woman's cheeks were crimson. Embarrassment, she supposed, guilt perhaps. Whatever it was, it had shut her up. Prue went on eating, although her hostess had put down her knife and fork, her own meal half-eaten. The silence was almost tangible.

The first course was cleared away and stewed apples and custard produced for dessert, all in silence. It was obvious to Prue the lady did not like being criticised. As soon as she decently could, she excused herself on the grounds she had to be up early next morning and needed her sleep.

She stood outside Sheila's room for a moment, wondering whether to go in to say goodnight, when she heard the sound of sobbing. She opened the door. Sheila was sitting on the bed in her oversized pyjamas, crying as if her heart would break. Beside her on the counterpane was a notepad and pencil. Prue rushed across to sit beside her and take her in her arms. 'Have a good cry,' she said. 'I would if I were you.' She glanced down at the notepad. On the top of the page was written 'Dear Ma and Pa'.

'I wanted to tell them,' Sheila sniffed. 'I wanted to tell them what it was like here.'

'Of course you did.'

'I wrote their names and then I realised . . . What am I to do? How can I go on living without them?'

'You will find the strength, Sheila. It will come from somewhere. Why don't you write the letter anyway? It might make you feel better. A sort of journal, if you like.'

Sheila gave her a watery smile. 'Yes, I think I will. I must write to Mr and Mrs Bennett too, to let them know I've arrived safely. And Chris. I promised him I would.'

'Will you be OK now?'

Sheila nodded. 'Yes, thank you.'

'Goodnight. I'll probably be gone when you get up in the morning. I'll try not to wake you.'

'Don't worry, I'm used to getting up early. I had to help with the younger ones before I went to work. We couldn't all get washed at once.'

Prue left her and went to her own room. Poor, poor girl. Whatever must she be going through? If someone came to her and said Mama and Papa and Gillie had all been killed and her home was a pile of rubble, how would she feel? Mrs Tranter had hardly been sympathetic. She would look out for the poor kid. Could she persuade Mr Welchman to give her a job? There were new people arriving at BP all the time and they needed back-up services, cleaners, waitresses, cooks, clerks, messengers. She would have to hold her tongue about it, of course, but as the only relative she had in the world appeared to be Mrs Tranter, she didn't think that would be a problem. There was the boyfriend, of course. How close was that relationship?

She finished undressing and jumped into bed. That would be Mr Welchman's problem, not hers.

As she had predicted, Prue had left when Sheila went down next morning. She spent the morning doing housework. After lunch her aunt brought down a pile of garments and heaped them on the dining-room table. They smelt strongly of mothballs. 'See if there is anything there you can use. I've finished with them. Can you sew?'

'A bit. Ma took in sewing and I sometimes helped her.'

'Good. I'll show you how to use my sewing machine and you can alter what you can use.'

'I ought to go and sign on at the labour exchange.'

'You can do that tomorrow.'

'Perhaps Prue will get me a job with her.'

'She is Lady Prudence to you, miss. And she was only saying that to be kind. The people who work up at the Park are all upper-class, educated people, you've only got to look at them to know that. What would they want with a little gutter urchin like you?'

'I am not a gutter urchin. That's an insult. Ma would be disgusted if she could hear you.'

'But she can't, can she?'

'I'm going to my room.' She gathered up the clothes and ran upstairs and into her bedroom, where she dropped the garments on the floor and flung herself face down on the bed. She must stop this bursting into tears all the time, but she couldn't help it; she missed everyone so much. Aunt Constance didn't help with her constant innuendo about Ma. What had made her like that? As sisters, they couldn't have been more unalike. She didn't want to stay here. Mrs Jarrett's overcrowded and untidy house would be preferable. The trouble was that she was not at all sure Chris had asked his mother before issuing the invitation. Besides, until she had earned it, she didn't have the train fare, let alone money for her keep. And she had a distinct feeling that her aunt wanted her for a general dogsbody to replace her daily help and there would be no wages for that.

She scrubbed at her eyes and sat up when she heard a footstep on the stairs, but it was not her aunt but Prue who knocked gently on her door and put her head round it. 'There you are,' she said cheerfully, then looking down at the bundle on the floor, 'What's all this?'

'Some clothes my aunt has finished with. I'm supposed to alter them to fit me.'

Prue picked up a shapeless woollen dress in a drab brown. 'Good God! This must have come out of the ark.' She dropped it and picked up another. 'This too. If you need clothes, I can do better than that.'

'It's all right.'

'No, it isn't. Come into my room and let's see what I've got.'

'I can't take your clothes.' Nevertheless, she followed Prue to a spacious bedroom with a bay window that looked out of the front of the house. It was carpeted and the furniture was solid, if old-fashioned. It also had a small fireplace shining with black lead.

'I think that was the marital bed,' Prue said, nodding towards the double bed with its brass knobs. 'I can't imagine what went on there, can you?'

Sheila giggled. 'I feel sorry for her husband.'

'He didn't last long. He was gassed in the last war. Horrible way to go.'

'Did she tell you that?'

'Yes, when I first came.' She opened her wardrobe door and began pulling out clothes. 'This might fit you,' she said, holding up a blue dress in a fine wool. It had a flared skirt, nipped-in waist and long sleeves. Its bodice was embroidered in matching wool. 'You will need something for the cooler weather. And here's a grey skirt and a Fair Isle jumper. They will do you for work.'

'But, I can't take those. They're too good for me.'

'Don't be silly. Nothing is too good for you, after what you've been through. I've got plenty of clothes, more than I'll ever wear. If I need more I can always send home for them. Try them on.'

'What do I tell my aunt? She's already against me, I don't want to make it worse.'

'Leave her to me.'

'I don't think she wants me to get a job,' Sheila said as she tried on the skirt and jumper. 'She kept me so busy today I didn't have time to go to the labour exchange.'

'You don't need to. I've got an interview for you at BP.'

'My aunt said that you were all toffs up there and you wouldn't want me.'

'Well, she's wrong on both counts. I've been instructed to take you in with me tomorrow, so you wear that. It might have been made for you.'

Sheila sank onto a stool by the dressing table and looked at herself in the mirror. The skirt and jumper certainly suited her. 'What am I supposed to do there?'

'We'll wait and see what my boss says, shall we?' Prue picked up a hair brush and began drawing it through Sheila's auburn locks. 'You've got lovely hair, Sheila, so thick and vibrant. I do like the colour.'

'They used to call me Carrots at school.'

'It's nothing like the colour of a carrot, it's a rich, dark auburn and I envy you. Hold your head up, Sheila, you are as good as anyone. Don't forget that.'

'But you don't really know me, do you? I might be really wicked. Is that why I survived? The devil looks after his own.'

'Tommy rot! You survived because that is your destiny.'

She sniffed and rooted in her pocket for a handkerchief. 'I wish I knew what happened to Charlie. I know I have to accept he's probably dead like all the others, but I'd just like to know how it happened and where. According to what I was told he was on his way home on his bike when he disappeared. He loved that old bike. Pa bought it for him second-hand. Funny, the bike never turned up either.'

Prue had no answer to that. She put down the brush, picked up the blue dress and Sheila's discarded clothes and thrust them into her arms. 'Take these back to your room and come down for dinner. Show that aunt of yours what you're made of.'

At a quarter to eight the following morning, Sheila, dressed in the skirt and jumper, topped by her new overcoat, was allowed through the gates of Bletchley Park and had her first view of the sprawling mansion, its lake and garden and the dozens of wooden huts that filled the grounds. Everywhere seemed to be a hive of activity as people came and went. Some were in uniform of one kind or another but most were in civvies. She stared round her, while sticking close to Prue.

They entered the front door of the house, where a receptionist checked that she was expected and Prue left her. 'I'll see you later,' she said, leaving Sheila to follow a guide to the first floor.

Sheila liked the gentleman who greeted her and asked her about herself, though it appeared he had been briefed by Prue.

'Can you keep a secret?' he asked suddenly when she paused from answering him.

'Yes, I think so. Why?'

'Only think so?'

'I am sure.'

'Good, because what we do there is hush-hush and you'll be sworn to secrecy. But it's very important for the war effort.'

'I understand.'

He pushed a document across the desk to her and handed her a fountain pen. 'I'm afraid you will have to sign that. It's the Official Secrets Act.'

'Does that mean you are going to give me a job?'

'Sign that first and I'll tell you.'

She put her name to the paper which was headed Government Code and Cypher School, which meant nothing to her. 'What sort of job?' she asked, pushing the paper back to him.

'How do you like the idea of being a messenger? You will be required to deliver letters, packages, parcels to all the huts and carry messages between them. You do not need to know what goes on inside the huts, nor what is in the envelopes you are carrying. It may not seem important to you, but it is vital you do the job well, I cannot stress that too strongly.' He gave her a reassuring smile. 'Do you want to do it?'

'Yes, please.'

'You will be on a shift system like everyone else here. We never stop, twenty-four hours a day, seven days a week. We'll let you know when you can start, probably in a day or two. Can you find your way home again?'

'Yes. Thank you, sir.'

He asked a uniformed wren to escort her to the gate and see her safely through it. She walked down the road feeling elated. Not only did she have a job, but it was one that was going to help defeat Hitler. Ma and Pa and the kids were going to be avenged.

For the first time since she lost them all, she felt herself coming alive again, ready to face the future, even putting up with Aunt Constance.

Constance did not approve of young girls being given ideas above their station. Her niece came from the slums and to the slums she would return, but she couldn't make Lady Prudence see that. Of course, her ladyship was only amusing herself befriending the girl and Sheila would discover that for herself in the end. She had no idea what went on up at the Park. It was fenced off and heavily guarded and the people who worked up there were mostly from the upper classes, very clever most of them, that much she knew from acquaintances who also billeted them. Where, in heaven's name, did Sheila Phipps fit into all that? She had refused to say.

The girl had no right to be so secretive. Anyone would think she had something to hide and Constance knew all about keeping secrets. Sheila could not possibly know the truth . . . Unless Ellen had told her. But Ellen was dead and if Sheila said anything it could be dismissed as lies.

She and Ellen had never got on, not even in childhood. Her sister had been six years younger and her father's pet. Even their mother made light of her naughtiness, while condemning her other daughter for the slightest thing she did wrong, on the grounds she was older and ought to know better. Her solidly middle-class parents had even condoned Ellen's marriage to Percy Phipps at the age of seventeen and given her the wedding of her dreams. She had married that hulk of a docker with his winning smile and not a penny to his name, and gone to live in the East End of London, had seven children and been happy. How could anyone be happy under those circumstances? It just wasn't fair. She should have been the happy one, not Ellen. The duster in her hand polished the same few inches of table over and over as she meditated on this.

She had married Clifford Tranter, a well-to-do businessman, in 1917 in London. He was not in the forces, but in the upper echelons of the railway business which brought them to Bletchley. He had bought this house with all its modern conveniences and she had been so proud of it, proud of their status in the town. And look what happened. No, she would not think of it. It had lain hidden for over twenty years and it had best stay hidden.

'We're not often on the same shift,' Prue said one afternoon after Sheila had been at Bletchley a month. 'Let's make the most of it.' They were in Prue's bedroom, where they spent much of their time when they were in the house. It was the only place to talk without Constance joining in with her hurtful comments. 'There's a dance in the Assembly Rooms this evening. I've no idea what the band is like, but there's a crowd of us going. It's my treat . . .'

'Oh but you can't . . .'

'Yes, I can. It's my twenty-first birthday and I mean to celebrate. It will be fun.'

'Your birthday? You never said. I haven't got you anything . . .'

'That's precisely why I didn't tell you. I don't want you spending your money on me. I'll have loads of presents when I go home on leave next week. So what do you say? You can dance, can't you?'

'Oh, yes, I used to go with Chris and my friend Janet and her boyfriend.'

'Then you'll come?'

'But I haven't got a partner.'

'Oh, you'll soon find someone and if you don't, we can always dance together.' She smiled. 'If you don't go, you'll end up mending your aunt's underwear all evening while you listen to more nagging. And I shall feel guilty for leaving you behind.'

Sheila laughed. 'I'm so glad I've got you for a friend.'

'And I you.' Prue stood up and held out her arms. 'May I have the pleasure of this dance, Miss Phipps?'

Sheila stood up and they began to dance while Prue hummed a tune. It was a song Sheila knew, 'We'll meet again', and she began to sing the words.

'You've got a lovely voice, Sheila. Good enough to sing in public.'

'Don't be silly. Ma had a smashing voice, better than mine. She knew all the popular songs and she used to sing while she worked about the house. Sometimes Pa joined in.' She felt her eyes filling again and blinked hard. 'I don't think I'll ever get over it, Prue.'

'No, of course you won't. But you will learn to live with it. Remember the good times and think they are all together now in a happier place than we have down here.'

'Do you believe that? Really?'

'Yes, and you must too. It will help you to bear it.'

Downstairs a bitter woman heard the clear voice; it was as if the past were coming back to haunt her, the voice was so like Ellen's. How was she going to stand having that child round her all the time, reminding her?

Chapter Four

It was the second time that morning the gardener had passed the breakfast room window with a wheelbarrow loaded with soil. 'Just what is Tom Green doing?' Chloe asked her husband.

'It's good soil, full of leaf mould, just right for the vegetables, fertiliser being difficult to get hold of.'

'Marcus, since when have you interested yourself in the vegetable garden? That's what we've got gardeners for.'

'Had gardeners, you mean. There's only Tom Green and young Billy Smith left, one too old and one too young to be in the forces. I need to put in some time myself. We've all been exhorted to grow as much of our own food as possible. "Dig for Victory" and all that.'

'Am I supposed to believe that nonsense? It's more likely it's got something to do with the Home Guard.'

'Why do you say that?'

'Oh, Marcus, do you take me for a fool? You go out at all hours in uniform and when you come back your boots are caked in mud. The same mud that Mr Green is carting. And what are those soldiers doing in the wood? Are you going to tell me they are they digging for victory?'

'You could say that.' He smiled as he scraped a tiny pat of butter onto his toast. 'It's only an exercise in digging trenches.'

'In case of invasion?'

'Yes.'

'Marcus, tell me honestly, is an invasion imminent? Is that what it's all about?'

'I don't know, any more than you do. But if it is, the Home Guard must be prepared.'

'The women in the knitting circle are all talking about it. Edith Stevens told everyone that it was such a deep secret the men have been sworn not to tell a soul, not even their wives. Naturally the wives are agog with curiosity and asked me.'

'I hope you haven't undertaken to find out for them.'

'Of course not. I pretended ignorance. But you might at least tell me if there's something going on. I won't pass it on.'

He reached out and put a hand over hers. 'Darling, if the men have been told not to tell their wives, then I must set a good example and keep mum myself. It's nothing really, just preparations in case of invasion. That's what the Home Guard is for: making it as difficult as possible for the invaders and keeping our loved ones safe. If anyone asks you, that is what you tell them.' He put down his napkin and stood up. 'I must go. I've got a meeting in Cambridge this morning, I should be back for luncheon, but don't wait if I'm not.' He dropped a kiss on the top of her head.

She watched him as he left the room and a few moments later saw him waylay Thomas on his way back with the empty barrow, no doubt to tell him to find a different route from the wood to the vegetable garden. She sighed. How she hated secrets.

She finished her tea, which at least still tasted like it was supposed to, which was more than the coffee did, and went up to her room for her coat and hat. Then she went out, taking the path towards the railway crossing which would take her past the woods. It was the shortest way to the village where she intended to visit Nanny Bright. Miss Bright had been her own nanny as well as nanny to Gilbert and Prudence and had stayed with the household until old age and failing health meant she had to be pensioned off. She lived in a little cottage near the station and loved watching people getting on and off the trains. Chloe loved her and visited frequently.

She could see from the single wheel tracks in the mud where the wheelbarrow had come from and smiled to herself. There were also tyre tracks from a vehicle. Anyone bent on mischief would have no difficulty in finding out what was going on. She stepped off the path into the wood and was met by the gamekeeper. 'Were you looking for his lordship, my lady?' he queried, standing in front of her, so that she would have to ask him to step aside if she wanted to go on.

'No, Mr Burrows. I wondered if there was a chance of having a couple of pheasants for tomorrow's dinner. My daughter is coming home on leave.'

'I'll see what I can do, my lady. I'll bring them up to the house, shall I?'

'Yes, please. How is Mrs Burrows?'

'A martyr to her rheumatism, my lady, but she don't complain.'

'If there is anything I can do, please let me know, won't you?'

'Yes, my lady. Thank you.'

Curious as she was, she could not insist on walking further into the wood and turned to continue on her way to the village. She had not gone far when she saw a figure flitting between the trees and strode after him. 'Hey, young man, where do you think you are off to?'

Surprised, he turned and faced her. He was about ten or eleven and not one of the village children; she knew all those. He was dressed in short trousers and a ragged jacket. His shoes were down at heel and his socks were wrinkled about his ankles. 'Nowhere,' he said, not in the least shame-faced. 'Just exploring.'

'This is private property and you should not be here.'

He shrugged. 'Didn't know that, did I?'

'Shouldn't you be in school?'

'School's boring.'

'What is your name?'

'Ronnie Barlow.'

'Where are you from?'

'Over by the railway crossing. I'm with Mrs Potts.'

'You are an evacuee?'

'Yes. I didn't ask to be one. I weren't given no choice.'

'I expect it was for your own safety. Where is your home? London, is it?'

'West Ham. I 'ad to leave me ma on 'er own. That ain't right. She ain't got anyone to look after 'er, 'cep' me.'

'Where's your father?'

'In the army, missus.'

'Oh, I see. I am going towards the crossing, we'll walk together, shall we?'

He turned reluctantly to walk beside her. 'What are they doin' all that diggin' in the wood for?' he asked.

'I really don't know that they are digging.'

'It must be a secret. I can keep a secret, you know.'

'I am glad to hear it.'

'So you ain't going to tell me?'

'No, I am not.' They had reached the lodge gate which, before the Home Guard began whatever it was doing in the wood, always stood open but which was now closed. She opened it and ushered him through, shutting it behind them. 'Did you come in this way?'

'No, I found a gap in the fence along the railway line.'

'You surely haven't been on the line? It is dreadfully dangerous. You could be killed.'

'Not me, missus. Me ma says I'm inde . . . indestructible.'

She laughed. 'I don't think it is very wise to put your faith in that, young man. Now, are you going back to Mrs Potts or shall you go to school? I'll go to the school with you, if you like.'

'If you go with me, will it stop me getting the cane?'

'I can't promise that, but I'll try.'

'Good-o. It's school then.'

They walked up the lane to the village. 'Why don't you like school?'

'Like I said, it's boring. Times tables and spellings and dates of kings and queens. Who wants to know about boring kings and queens?'

'Surely you learn more than that?'

'Not much.'

'How old are you?'

'Eleven and three-quarters.'

He was small for his age, she thought. 'You are not the only evacuee at the school, are you?'

'No, there's all my class.'

'And are they all like you?'

He shrugged. 'Shouldn't think so.' He paused. 'Do you live in a palace?'

'Good gracious, no. What gave you that idea?'

'It looks like a palace. I saw Buckingham Palace once. It's gigantic.'

'Buckingham Palace is very big, that's true, much, much bigger and grander than the house I live in. Where I live is called Longfordham Hall. I take it you have been up there and looked?'

'Yes, I was exploring.'

'It is also trespassing.'

'What's that?'

'Going where you shouldn't go. You can be prosecuted for it.'

'Prosecuted? You mean arrested and sent to prison?'

'No, I don't think you would be sent to prison. You might be fined.'

'Tha's all right then,' he said complacently. 'I haven't got any money, so fining me wouldn't do no good, would it?'

She laughed. 'No, I suppose not, but confine your exploring to the village and the heath in future, will you?'

They arrived at the school which stood on the corner of the crossroads. It was a very small building, having only two classrooms and a small playground. She ushered him in front of her to the room where the head was teaching the older pupils. She saw Chloe through the glass in the door and hurried out to her.

'My lady, this is an unexpected pleasure.'

'Miss Green, I've found one of your flock and have brought him back to you.'

'Oh, it's that naughty Ronald Barlow. He's more often absent than present, I'm afraid.' She gave him a little push. 'Go into class, young man, and stay there until you are sent home.'

He grinned at Chloe and sauntered into the classroom. Chloe watched him go. 'He's quite a cheeky little fellow,' she said.

'I hope he hasn't been rude to you, my lady.'

'Not at all. I found his conversation quite refreshing. Please don't punish him too severely.'

'I expect he'll be given some lines and kept in at playtime. Would you like to see what the children are doing? I was about to give them dictation. And the younger ones could sing a song for you.'

Chloe went into the classroom and wandered from desk to desk as the children were writing, some of them were sitting three to a desk meant for two. Then she stood at the back while they sang 'Golden Slumbers', a little too robustly for a lullaby.

'We are awfully crowded what with twenty evacuees besides our own children,' Miss Green explained as she conducted Chloe to the door afterwards. 'If you could use your influence to have the evacuees accommodated elsewhere, my lady, it would be most appreciated. I know we should be compassionate after what the children have been through in London, but most of them have no idea how to behave and they are teaching our own pupils bad habits. And some of the language is appalling.'

'I am sorry to hear that, Miss Green. I'll speak to the Chairman of the Governors, but I don't know what else we can do. I'm afraid we all have to make sacrifices in this war.'

'I know that, my lady, but the children should not have to suffer because of it. The children are our future.'

'You are right, of course. I'll see what I can do.'

She left and continued on her way. Why everyone in the village thought she could wave a magic wand and solve all their problems, she did not know. Marcus said it was her own fault for being so approachable and bending over backwards to help them. As far as she was concerned, it was a pleasure as well as a duty. Being a member of the aristocracy gave her responsibilities as well as privileges, and even those were being slowly eroded.

She smiled and knocked on the back door of Miss Bright's little cottage and then opened the door to call, 'It's me, Nanny.'

She was soon ensconced beside the fire in a sitting room that was tiny but cheerful. On every surface were snapshots of children; she and her brother looking self-conscious and old-fashioned, Gilbert and Prudence, playing and laughing, another of them riding their ponies. Nanny Bright hobbled about making tea and producing biscuits but she wouldn't accept help as Chloe well knew. 'They are very plain, my lady, not like the biscuits we had at the big house before the war. How are you managing up there with half the staff in the forces?'

'Oh, we manage well enough. Prue is coming home on leave tomorrow. I expect she will find time to come and see you. She will want to thank you for the birthday present you sent her.' Miss Bright had knitted a scarf and beret in warm white wool.

'Did she have a good birthday?' She put a cup of tea and a small plate on a little table beside Chloe's chair.

'She and a few of her colleagues had a celebratory glass of champagne at work and in the evening they went to a dance at the assembly hall near her billet.'

Nanny smiled. 'A bit different from your twenty-first then. I recall a glittering ball, oceans of champagne and punch and heaps of food, not to mention dozens of young men eager to pay court to you. But you did well, catching an earl.'

'It wasn't the earl I married, Nanny, but the man. And I have never regretted it.'

'And now my poor Prudence celebrates with nothing more to mark that important milestone than a glass of champagne.'

'Well, times have changed, haven't they? She was lucky to have that. We will try and make it up to her when she comes home.'

'What is she doing exactly?'

'I don't know. It's all very hush-hush. She says she's only a clerk, but I think there's more to it than that.'

'Of course there is. She is a very bright girl and I should know. What about Master Gilbert? He's in his father's old regiment, isn't he?'

'Yes, but tells me he's volunteered for the Parachute Regiment.'

'Oh dear, that sounds dangerous.'

'He says it isn't. "Easy as falling off a log", he told me.'

'Believe that, if you like.'

'I have to, otherwise I should be worried to death.'

'And his lordship? Is he well?'

'Very well. Involved with the Home Guard.'

'So I heard. I saw Mrs Stevens in the shop and she told me Bill was doing hours and hours of overtime up at the hall and she hardly ever sees him. What's more, he's being very secretive. There's a rumour that they're digging an underground tunnel from the hall to the station. Goodness knows what for. He wouldn't say. She said Mrs Potts had seen dozens of soldiers coming and going in trucks bringing equipment.'

'I really don't know what it's about, Nanny. No one tells me anything, but I can't believe that's true. I'm sure his lordship would have told me.'

'That's what I told her. If people don't know what's going on, they make something up and she would do better to keep her mouth shut on the subject.'

'Oh, Nanny, you didn't.'

'Yes, I did. And I'll say the same to anyone, no matter who they are.' She offered the plate. 'Would you like another biscuit?'

'No, thank you. I must be off. Lots to do. I'll come again when I can. Is there anything you need?'

'No, thank you, my lady. I'm very comfortable here, thanks to you and his lordship.'

Chloe went home and later that afternoon she tackled Marcus about the rumours and all he did was laugh without explaining anything. Later that night, he was obliged to tell her.

Prue was glad to be home, but it was a home bowed down with misery. It appeared her parents were hardly speaking to each other. This was so unusual, she was immediately concerned and waylaid her mother when she went up to change for dinner. 'Mama, what's wrong? I never saw such long faces.'

Her mother followed her into her bedroom and shut the door. 'Bill Stevens is dead. And Edith is blaming your father.'

Prue sat down heavily on the bed and stared at her mother. 'Dead? How? Why is Edith blaming Papa?'

'The Home Guard were building an underground bunker in the woods. It was all so secret and so silly. The roof caved in on Bill and he was buried. If it hadn't been for the blacksmith, they'd never have got him out. He was alive then but died on the way to hospital.'

Prue didn't know what to say. She was as shocked as everyone in the village must be. Bill Stevens was well known and well liked. He had taught her and Gillie to ride as soon as they were big enough to sit on a small pony and he had often told them stories of her father's heroism in the Great War, which they only half believed. He had been a stalwart friend as well as a servant and she could not imagine Longfordham Hall without him. 'Oh, how awful. And you say Mrs Stevens is blaming Papa.'

'Yes. There was a team of regular sappers helping them during the day and they made sure it was safe, but your father decided to carry on digging after they'd gone. He was anxious to get it finished, heaven knows why, unless he thought the invasion was imminent. We aren't told these things, are we? I was asleep in bed when I heard him come in and pick up the telephone in the hall. I went out on the landing and heard him telling Doctor Hewitt there had been an accident in the wood and Bill Stevens had been hurt. I went down to ask him about it, but he just told me to go back to bed.'

'But you didn't.'

'Of course not. I dressed and followed him back to his men. It was a dreadful scene, ghostly almost. They were in a clearing lit by a hurricane lamp hanging on a tree. There was earth piled up everywhere. Bill Stevens was lying on the ground with half a dozen men standing over him. Someone had covered him with an army greatcoat and folded another under his head. He was deeply unconscious and very dirty, but I couldn't see any injury. Your father squatted down beside him. I was concerned that Edith would have to be told, so I went and roused her. We got back just as the ambulance arrived and she went in it with him, but he died before they got him to hospital. He was too crushed, you see, and he wasn't a young man.'

'Oh dear, poor Mrs Stevens. Poor Papa. He must be feeling awful.'

'I am extremely angry with him. The whole scheme was mad from beginning to end. And a good man has died needlessly.'

'Mama,' she said, taking both her mother's hands in her own. 'This is not the time to be angry. Papa needs you.'

'If he had told me what he was doing, I might have been able to dissuade him, but no, it had to be a secret, as if everyone in the village didn't know something odd was going on. There were rumours that he was digging a tunnel from the hall to the station so that we could escape if no one else could.'

'Surely no one believes that of him?'

'Edith does.'

'She is upset. She will calm down. Have you talked to her?'

'She won't listen.' She pulled her hands away from Prue's and walked to the window, staring out across the garden. The flowers had long gone and it was looking bleak and damp. 'This war is spoiling everyone's lives, making liars out of truthful men and making them do things they would never have dreamt of doing in peacetime. Your father was always open and above board and now he can't tell his wife what he is doing, nor look me in the face.'

'Oh, Mama, I am so sorry. Is there anything I can do?'

'No, just be your usual sunny self.' She turned back into the room. 'Let's get changed. Cook won't be pleased if we keep dinner waiting, though how I shall manage to swallow it, I don't know. And I so wanted this to be a happy occasion to make up for the birthday party you didn't have.'

'This is not the time to be worrying about birthdays, Mama. I have Papa's cheque and very generous it is too, and I did have a little shindig with the people at work. Tim sent me a lovely brooch, the wings of his squadron in silver.'

'Not a ring? I wondered . . .'

'Not the right time for that either.'

Dinner was a sombre affair: the gamekeeper had evidently forgotten about the pheasants and they had some kind of hotpot, eaten mostly in silence, and as soon as it was over, her father disappeared into his study. Prue excused herself and went after him.

She found him slumped onto a leather covered sofa, his head in his hands. 'Papa, Mama told me about Mr Stevens.'

'I expected she would. She is angry.'

She sat beside him. 'I know, but it won't last. She loves you too much to be out of sorts with you for long.'

'I hope you are right, but I'm angry with myself.'

'Can you tell me about it?'

'I oughtn't to. We were sworn to secrecy.' He gave her a wan smile. 'But I know you've signed the Official Secrets Act and won't pass it on. I was approached by the Ministry of Defence to form a special squad to harass the enemy if the country was ever occupied. I was asked to recruit six or seven men who would go into hiding the minute the Germans arrived. Our task was information-gathering, observing and reporting, harassing the enemy, disrupting their communications, sabotage and anything else we could think of to hinder them. And we were to do it from hidden underground bunkers. We were excavating a bunker with the help of sappers. It had to be big enough to accommodate all of us and our weapons and ammunition. And it had to have an escape tunnel in case the entrance was discovered. The main room was almost finished and we were working on the tunnel. That's where Bill was when the roof fell in. We'd shored it up as we went. I checked the supports myself before Bill started and I swear they were all sound. But I was wrong, so wrong. Bill came across a tree root and was hacking away at it when the roof gave way. It buried him.'

'Oh, Papa.'

'Everyone in the village knows about the bunker now but they think I was doing it off my own bat, not because of instructions from the MOD with a time set for it to be completed. I can't tell them there are dozens of these secret bunkers all over East Anglia.'

'And so they believe the worst?'

'Yes. What is it they say? The first casualty of war is truth. How right they are.'

'What does Mama know?'

'After what happened, I had to tell her something but not

everything. She came to the site when Bill was lying unconscious after the blacksmith pulled him out, and she could see some of it. We can't use it now, too many people know about it, so I've told the men to close it up and make it safe. It was all for nothing. Bill died for nothing.' His voice cracked. 'Mrs Stevens blames me and I don't blame her. I have lost a faithful servant and a good friend and I can't forgive myself so how can I expect anyone else to forgive me?'

'Oh, Papa, you must not feel like that. It was an accident. Mr Stevens was a casualty of war, just the same as if he were in the front line trenches, flying an aeroplane or sailing the seas. You were both doing your duty.'

He turned to smile at her. 'Bless you, child, do you think I have not tried to comfort myself with that? The trouble is that I can't see past the funeral and the knowledge I shall have to say something to the congregation. I don't know how I'm going to get through it.'

'You will, Papa, because you are strong and honourable, and Mama will come round, you'll see.'

He sighed and patted her hand. 'I hope you are right. You had better go back to her, she needs you.'

The funeral was held the day before Prue was due to go back to Bletchley. The whole village turned up, even the schoolchildren, who were shepherded into the back pews by Miss Green. The Earl and the Countess, with Prue between them, sat in the Le Strange pew. She was holding their hands, hoping her love and strength might flow from one to the other through her. Never in her whole life had she known her parents to be so at odds with each other and it was hurting badly. She wished Gillie were there. He was so strong he would be able to knock their heads together, which is what she felt like doing.

She listened to the Reverend Mr Bradshaw intone, 'I said I

will take heed to my ways; that I offend not in my tongue. I will keep my mouth as it were a bridle while the ungodly is in my sight. I held my tongue and spake nothing. I kept silence, yes, even from good words, but it was pain and grief to me . . .' Who, she wondered, had chosen that psalm? She squeezed her father's hand and he turned to look at her and then at his wife. She was staring straight ahead.

The Rector finished. 'As it was in the beginning, is now and ever shall be: world without end.'

The congregation murmured 'Amen' and the Earl rose and went to stand beside the coffin. Everyone watched him expectantly. He cleared his throat several times, then put his hand on the coffin, as if drawing strength from it. 'Bill Stevens was more than a servant to me,' he said. 'He was my companion and friend through thick and thin. We served together in France in the Great War when we were young. We grew old together. But this war is different. It involves the whole population, men and women, old and young, servicemen and civilians. It is total. Bill understood that. He wanted to do his duty to protect those he loved and he died doing it. I . . .' He paused to collect himself. 'I regret the manner of his death more than I can say and my thoughts are with his wife and family at this sad time . . .' His voice trailed away. He looked down at the coffin. 'Goodbye, Bill, my friend, may you rest in peace.' And with that he stumbled back to his seat. Except for Edith Stevens who was sobbing quietly, the congregation was utterly silent, there was not even a cough, a murmur or the rustle of hymn book pages. Prue could almost feel their stares on the back of her neck.

The Rector read the twenty-third psalm and the service ended with the singing of 'Abide with Me', after which they followed the coffin to the newly dug grave for the interment.

It was over and yet it was far from over. No one would ever forget what had happened; tongues would continue to wag. Edith would go on grieving for a long time and she would continue to vilify the Earl. Prue prayed that her mother would come to understand why her husband had behaved in the way he had and be reconciled with him. All three walked back to the Hall in silence.

After luncheon Prue decided to go for a ride. It was often the first thing she did on arriving home, but this time she had not felt like leaving her mother. But Copper needed some exercise and so did she before returning to Bletchley and the sedentary job of translating German communications in smoky Hut Three.

It was when she went to the stables that it hit her. Stevens was not there to saddle her mare. The stables were deserted and the three horses whose home it was were looking over their stalls as if questioning why no one was busy around them. Even the stable boy was nowhere to be seen. She stroked the three noses, one by one. 'I know you are sad, we all are.' Hearing a sound, she climbed the stairs above the stable which had, many years before, been the living quarters of the head groom, and there she found sixteen-year-old Terry, sitting on a rickety chair crying heartbrokenly. He scrambled to his feet when he saw her. 'My lady.'

'Terry, I know it is a very miserable day, but the horses don't know that, do they? They still need looking after and it's up to you to see to them now.'

He wiped his face on his sleeve. 'Yes, my lady.'

'Off you go then.'

He preceded her downstairs. 'Shall I saddle Copper for you, my lady?' His voice was watery but he was no longer crying.

'No, I'll do it myself. You look after the others.'

She saddled up, mounted and set off for the heath, but today there was no joy in her ride. The war had come to Longfordham with a vengeance and her cosy life was changing irrevocably.

Sheila missed Prue. Without her friend's leavening influence, life at Victoria Villa was miserable. Aunt Constance never left off grumbling and scoffing at her. What had she to be so superior about? She had a nice house and didn't seem short of money, but money and a house did not bring happiness, not as there had been with Pa and Ma in West Ham. Sometimes the sadness rose to the surface and on those days she wanted to hide herself away and be miserable in private. But Victoria Villa wasn't an easy place to be private in. Her aunt had no patience with displays of emotion, maintaining they were a sign of weakness. Prue said she understood how she felt, but how could she? No one who had not been through the same tragedy could understand. She spent her off-duty time in her unheated bedroom, sitting on the bed with the eiderdown round her to keep warm and wrote her journal and letters to the Bennetts, to Janet and to Chris.

'Dear Chris,' she wrote. 'I went to the pictures with my friend Prue last week. We saw *The Wizard of Oz*. It is really for children but I enjoyed the singing and it took my mind off the war for a little while. We went to a dance too, to celebrate Prue's twenty-first birthday. She has lots of friends and some of them danced with me, but I would rather be dancing with you.' Unable to talk about her work, she went on to write about the town and the countryside in autumn. Running out of things to say, she concluded, 'I hope you are well and able to keep warm. Write to me soon, Love from Sheila.'

After that she turned to the notebook she used to write her journal letters to her parents. She imagined them at home, eagerly waiting to hear from her and so she let her mind and pencil run away with her. It was all there: her homesickness, her first impressions of her aunt, her job as a post girl, her friendship with Prue which made it all bearable, although she was careful not to say anything about her work in case the book was found by someone who had no business knowing about it.

An early entry read:

Prue is a real lady, her father is an earl. She is really great fun and not at all snobbish. Aunt Constance is though. I wonder why she is like that? Why didn't you ever tell me about her? She seems to have a grudge against you. I don't listen to nonsense like that, I promise you. Anyway, Prue has the measure of her and Aunt is not as bad when she's around. I've had no news of Charlie. When I get some leave, I'll go to London and see if I can find anything out.

On another page she had written:

I've been exploring Bletchley and borrowed a bike to go for a ride with Prue. The countryside is lovely in autumn with all the trees turning colour. I hope this winter is not as cold as the last one. Do you remember how we had to dig our way out of the house because the snow was halfway up the door? And how icy the pavements were? The kids made a slide in the road and Pa told them off because it was dangerous for people walking. He spread a bucket of sand on it, didn't he?

The last entry continued:

I'm getting used to the work now, it isn't difficult. I just have to remember where all the huts and offices are. The trouble is it's mostly out of doors and I have to go from place to place, and no excuses if it's cold and wet. It is practically impossible to get my things dry in this house. There's no heating in my room and Aunt Constance doesn't like me putting my wet things round the kitchen fire.

She turned to the next blank page and wrote:

Prue has gone on a week's leave so I'm here alone with Aunt Constance. And the cat, of course. She's a big tabby called Tiddles and if she can get away with it, she comes up and curls on my bed to sleep, which is strictly against the rules. Aunt Constance has her to keep the mice down. Not that there's anything much for mice to eat; the house is spotless and any food we leave on our plates, which isn't much, is given to the cat.

Prue is my best friend, but I have made one or two other friends at work. Some of the people there are really brainy. You see them wandering about deep in thought, puffing on pipes or cigarettes. There's one we call the Prof. who goes running a lot and sometimes rides a funny bicycle wearing his gas mask. I thought he was dotty but Prue assures me he is a genius. I don't think he is the only one, there are more like him and some of them have real tantrums. Of course, I am the lowest of the low and don't have much to do with any of them, though Prue chats to them.

I still miss you dreadfully, but I am trying to be brave. Until we meet again, always your loving Sheila.

She closed the book and hid it in her rucksack on top of the wardrobe. Tonight she was beginning a week of night shifts, walking about in the park with her letters and packages by the light of a feeble torch. She wasn't looking forward to it.

Prue arrived back just as she was leaving and they only had time to exchange a few words before they parted again. To Sheila's question, 'Did you enjoy your leave?' Prue said, 'Not exactly. Something happened. I'll tell you about it tomorrow.'

As she left the house, wrapped in a warm coat, a beret, scarf and gloves, she heard her aunt come out from the kitchen and ask Prue if she wanted dinner. 'We had ours earlier,' she said. 'But I can rustle up something . . .' She didn't hear Prue's reply as she shut the front door behind her and set off for Bletchley Park, lighting her way with the torch, the only way to get about in the blackout.

Chapter Five

The grounds of the park took on an eerie atmosphere at night. There were still people moving about from hut to hut or coming and going from the house to the cottage, a converted stable block to the side of the house, or arriving and leaving at the gate, each with a shaded torch, like so many glow worms. The lake was a lighter patch and the walls of the house, with its blacked-out windows, were dark and rather menacing. The huts were dark, shuttered blocks, but the smoke coming from their stovepipe chimneys could be seen against the lighter sky.

She made her way to the post room, which was to the side of the main house, to be given her first delivery and then with a canvas bag over her shoulder, went out again. She knew where all the huts were now and there were more being added all the time. She went from one to another, briefly into warmth and light and then out into the dark again and on to the next. Sometimes she was given notes or packages to take to other huts or back to the post room to be put in the mail, which was given to a motorcyclist. There were several of those who came and went all the time. She had no idea what she was carrying. She had been told curiosity would be her undoing and she believed it.

Halfway through her shift she went to a hut that had been set aside for making tea and coffee. Sometimes there were biscuits, but they soon disappeared. Other people came and went and chatted to her about the weather, or the news published in the newspapers or broadcast by the BBC, films they had seen or jokes that were doing the rounds, but never about their work. She knew some of their first names but no more. They all knew what she did. This evening there was only one other person in the room. She set about making a pot of tea.

'You are Sheila Phipps, aren't you?' he said, watching her from a chair at the table.

'Yes. Who are you?'

'I'm James Barry,' he said. 'I work in one of the huts, but I'm also on the entertainments committee. A little bird told me you have a fine singing voice.'

'Would that little bird be called Prue, by any chance?' She poured two cups of tea and pushed one towards him.

'Yes. I'm looking for people to take part in a pantomime we are putting on at the Assembly Rooms on Boxing Day. Would you care to audition? It's *Cinderella*.'

She laughed. 'One of the ugly sisters, I suppose.'

'Most definitely not. Depending on the voice, of course, it could be Cinderella or the handsome prince or one of the chorus. What do you say?'

'When do you want me to do the audition?'

'How about when you finish work? There's a piano in the ballroom.'

'OK.'

'Right, I'll see you there.' He drained his cup and left.

She washed up the teapot and mugs and went to the post room to fetch more envelopes and packages to finish her shift. She couldn't help smiling in the dark as she went from hut to hut. Someone had deigned to notice her and apparently wanted her to sing for him. She would tell Ma and Pa about him and the audition in her next letter and Chris too, of course. As soon as her last delivery had been made, she went to the ballroom.

The main house was a hive of activity. There were desks and files in every room and trestle tables in the corridors, all piled with papers. Sheila didn't often go there, but she knew where the ballroom was. It was a large wood-panelled room, with a high ornate ceiling and a polished wood floor. It had housed the telephone exchange and teleprinter earlier but that had been moved to its own hut and the room was now used for recreational purposes. James was waiting for her by the piano. 'Hallo again,' he said. 'What do you like to sing?'

'All sorts,' she said. 'Popular ballads mostly.'

He sorted through some sheet music. 'How about "Apple Blossom Time"? Know that?'

'Yes.'

He sat down and began to play. She started diffidently. 'Don't be shy,' he said. 'Fill the room with sound.'

So she did. When she finished, he swivelled round on the stool. 'Who taught you to sing like that?'

'No one, but my mother had a lovely voice.'

'Had?'

'She was killed in an air raid, so was everyone else. I had three brothers and three sisters, all gone except perhaps Charlie. He disappeared on the night of the raid that killed the others and

I don't know what happened to him. I was at work and didn't know anything about it until I went home. The house was a wreck. Pa died fighting fires down by the docks . . .' she stopped, gulping back tears. She really hadn't meant to talk about it; as long as she could push it to the back of her mind, she could cope, just about.

'Please don't cry.' He stood up and put his arm round her shoulders and drew her to him. 'I wish I hadn't asked.'

She pulled a handkerchief from her pocket and blew her nose. 'I'm all right now. It's just that sometimes it hits me all over again.'

'You poor girl. This war is evil, don't you think?'

'Yes I do. The sooner we send Hitler packing, the better.'

'And I must do my small bit towards it. First rehearsal on Saturday afternoon. Can you make it? There's no time to waste, Christmas is a-coming.'

'You mean you want me?'

'Oh, yes, definitely.'

'Then I'll be there.'

'Good.' He dropped a kiss on her forehead and left her standing there, bewildered by the speed of it all and his familiarity.

To save her aunt cooking, she had breakfast in the canteen which was just outside the main gate of the Park – only the most senior staff used the dining room in the main house – before catching the bus back to Victoria Villa and going to bed for a few hours. She was getting used to the irregular hours, but it was always difficult the first day or so after a changeover. Today it took her some time to get to sleep; her head was whirring with the idea of singing in public. Could she really do it?

Prue woke her when she came off the early shift. 'Come on, lazy-bones. Up you get.'

'It's warm in here. I don't want to stir.'

'I can understand that, this room is icy. Get dressed and come into my room. We can talk there.'

'Where's my aunt?'

'Downstairs, entertaining the vicar with tea and biscuits. No doubt they are putting the world to rights.'

Prue left and Sheila hastily washed and dressed and joined her. They sat side by side on the bed with the eiderdown draped round their shoulders. Aunt Constance did not believe in fires in bedrooms.

'You said something happened while you were on leave,' Sheila said.

'Yes, it was awful.' She went on to recount what had happened, ending, 'It's the first casualty of the war I've had contact with and what made it worse is that my mother and all the village are blaming Papa. Oh, I know it's not like losing your whole family, but it really brought home to me what war is all about. Good men dying.'

'Women and children too.'

'Yes. Now I have made you miserable. I'm sorry, I didn't mean to.'

'It's all right. I'm trying not to be sad. And I have a bit of news.'

'Go on.'

'You should know, since you've been telling tales behind my back.'

'Me? What have I done?'

'You told James Barry about me singing. He's putting on a panto and he asked me to sing for him. He's offered me the part of Cinderella.'

'Oh, Sheila, that's wonderful news. You said yes, of course.'

'It helps, you see.'

Prue did see. 'Let's go for a walk before dinner. I need some fresh air, even if you don't. The people in my hut smoke like chimneys and so does the stove and with the windows boarded up because of the blackout, it creates a real fug.'

'OK. I'll go and get my coat.'

Constance was seething. That little gutter rat was off her head, writing letters to her dead parents. It was ghoulish and the things she put in the letters about her were beyond belief. Snobbish, she had called her. Well, if it was snobbish to expect good manners and deference to one's betters and to want things done tastefully, then she was guilty. And to say Lady Prudence had the measure of her was ridiculous. No one had the measure of her, no one knew what went on inside her head, what secrets were kept hidden, nor would they ever, because it was evident Sheila did not know. That was a relief at least. The girl was going to end up like her mother, if she wasn't watched: pregnant and unmarried. It didn't make any difference that Ellen was married before she began to show, Sheila was still a bastard.

'What are you doing?'

Startled, she turned to face her niece, the notebook still in her hand. 'Tidying up,' she said quickly. 'Your mother seems not to have taught you about housework.'

'This room is perfectly tidy and you have no right to go poking into my private affairs. Not even Ma would do such a thing. Give me that book.' She held out her hand for it.

Constance ignored it. 'I was dusting the top of the wardrobe, thick with dust it was, and when I picked up the bag, the book fell out.'

'Then you should have put it back where you found it, not read it. It's private.'

'So it needs to be. If a doctor read it, I've no doubt he would certify you insane. Can't you accept that your parents are dead? Dead! Dead!' Her voice rose almost to a shriek.

'Of course I know. Give it back to me.'

'You are an ungrateful wretch. After all I've done for you, taking you in, feeding and clothing you . . .'

'Clothing me! With your fuddy-duddy cast-offs you haven't worn in years. Give me back my book.' She reached out to grab it and then began a fierce struggle, with neither of them prepared to give way.

'Give it back,' Sheila shouted, as the cover was torn off it. 'Now look what you've done.'

'What on earth is going on here?' Prue's voice stopped them in their tracks. She was standing in the doorway in her dressing gown with a towel round her head, having just come from the bathroom. They had been caught in a rainstorm while out walking and been drenched, which was why they had returned earlier than expected.

Constance, flustered, threw the book on the bed. 'The girl is off her head, writing rubbish like that.' Then she stalked out past Prue who stood aside to let her go.

Sheila sank onto the bed and picked up her book. 'She was snooping. She read my letters. I'm not really off my head, am I?'

Prue came into the room and sat beside her. 'Of course you're not, silly. Anyway, I was the one suggested it, so if that's the case, I must be off my head too.'

'I feel awful. I can't have any private life at all. Perhaps I shouldn't have said those things about her.'

'What you write in private is no one's affair but your own.' She paused. 'You didn't write anything about your work or what goes on at BP, did you? It would be a breach of security, if you did.'

'Only about finding my way round the huts. Now, I suppose

I'll have to stop writing it. She'll snoop again when I'm out. It was only luck I caught her at it this time.'

'Does it help doing it?'

'It makes me feel closer to Ma and Pa, like you said, and I can let off steam if I want to.'

'Then you keep writing. I'll look after the book for you. She won't dare poke about among my things.'

'I ought to find different digs.'

'No, don't do that. I should miss you. We'll get the better of her.' She laughed suddenly. 'I was wondering what to give you for Christmas and now I know. You shall have a lockable box to keep your private things in.' She stood up. 'You had better get those wet clothes off or you'll catch your death. You can't sing if you're ill and that would be a shame.'

'Oh, Prue, what would I do without you? It is only because you're here that I put up with it.'

The war did not stop for Christmas. Neither she nor Sheila had any extra time off for the festivity. Fortunately they were both on the first watch from eight until four and had their Christmas dinner in the canteen before joining the party in the main building. There would be dancing to records, paper hats and silly games and a great deal to drink. Constance had gone to spend the day with the vicar and his wife, so they had no need to feel guilty about leaving her on her own.

Prue had loaned Sheila a party frock. It was a pale-green silk, with a nipped-in waist, a full skirt and a little matching shoulder cape. 'You look gorgeous,' she said as they changed from jumpers and skirts into the frocks in the ladies' cloakroom after coming off their shift. 'You'll knock them out.'

'You don't look so bad yourself.'

Prue's own dress was a blue and white stripe with a boat-shaped neckline and huge puff sleeves. She linked her arm in Sheila's. 'Come on, the party's already noisy, we've some catching up to do.'

They drifted into the crowded ballroom. James Barry, as Master of Ceremonies, was operating the gramophone in an alcove, originally intended for an orchestra. He winked at Sheila and beckoned her over. 'Are you going to sing for your supper, Sheila?'

'What, now?'

'Yes, give them a taste of what's to come tomorrow night. We've still got empty seats to fill.' He didn't wait for her to agree, but handed her the microphone.

'Go on, Sheila,' Prue urged her. 'Give it to them.'

There was so much noise going on, they hardly heard her begin to sing 'A Nightingale Sang in Berkeley Square'. She stopped and turned to James. 'Let's have something to wake them up instead.'

He sorted through his music and found 'Bless 'em all, the long and the short and the tall . . .' Sheila belted it out and before long she had her audience. She followed it with 'Boogie, Woogie, Bugle Boy' and 'Chattanooga Choo Choo'. They clapped and whistled when she finished and shouted, 'Encore! Encore!' Now she had their attention, she went back to Berkeley Square and its nightingale.

'That's it,' James told them when that came to an end. 'If you want more, come to the show tomorrow night.' He kissed Sheila's cheek and let her go.

'You've made a conquest there,' Prue said, as she rejoined her.

'Don't be daft.'

They drank, they danced, they played musical chairs and blind man's buff and the ballroom became even more crammed as people drifted in from work or from festivities elsewhere. Apart from sitting down to dinner, Sheila had been on her feet since before eight o'clock that morning and she knew she could not keep going much longer. She found Prue talking to her friend Alice. 'Prue, I'm going home. I'm whacked.'

'OK, I'll come with you.'

'No need, you stay and enjoy yourself.'

'I'm not letting you go home alone. Besides, I've had enough myself.' She said goodnight to Alice, seized Sheila's arm and marched her out of the room to change back into their daytime clothes and find a taxi.

Constance was in the drawing room knitting and listening to a carol concert on the wireless when they arrived. 'We're back, Mrs Tranter,' Prue said, 'Did you have a nice day?'

'Very nice, thank you, my lady. Can I get you anything?'

'No, thank you, we've had plenty to eat and drink. We'll go up to bed now. Sheila needs her sleep. She has the panto tomorrow.'

'Yes, of course, the pantomime.'

'You could come if you want,' Sheila said. 'I could get you a ticket.'

'No, thank you. I have never liked pantomime, it all seems very silly to me.'

'You'd think she'd make the effort for your sake, wouldn't you?' Prue said in an undertone as they made their way upstairs.

'Well, I don't care. She would probably find fault anyway.'

'True.' They stopped outside Sheila's bedroom door. 'Bed now or you'll never get through tomorrow's performance.'

'I feel all woozy.'

'Drink plenty of water.'

'You aren't tipsy.'

'Perhaps I'm more used to wine than you are.' She took Sheila's hand. 'Come on, I'll see you safely in bed. Lucky you, having tomorrow off, you can have a lie in. I have to go to work.'

Left alone with the room revolving around her and her

stomach definitely uneasy, Sheila reflected on the evening's events. It had been good to feel part of the fun and jollity, but she also felt guilty that she had enjoyed herself when her family were lying in the cold, dark earth and Charlie was goodness knows where. She wondered how Chris had spent his day and whether he liked the tie she had sent him. Tomorrow she would have thank-you letters to write to Chris for the 'Evening in Paris' scent, Janet for handkerchiefs, Bob and June for slippers.

She heard her aunt come up to bed just as she drifted off to sleep. Tomorrow she would pull herself together and sing her heart out for them all. If she couldn't do anything else, she could sing.

The pantomime was a great success. Sheila did sing her heart out and was rewarded with enthusiastic applause. Prue was one of the first to congratulate her. 'You were stupendous,' she said, watching Sheila change and clean off her make-up.

'Thank you. James managed to get the best out of everyone.'

'Especially you.'

'You are just saying that.'

'No, I mean it. Are you ready to go home?'

'Yes, let's walk. I need to clear my head.'

It was bitterly cold but there was no snow. The sky was like a blue-black pincushion studded with shiny pinhead stars. A moon hung low just above the tree tops. They didn't need their torches.

'A bomber's moon,' Sheila said. 'No doubt they'll be over London again tonight, Christmas or no Christmas.'

'I suppose our boys will be over Germany too.'

'Are you worried about Tim?'

'Yes, wouldn't you be? I listen to the news about where we've bombed and how many aeroplanes were lost and I can't help wondering whether he was among them.'

'You would hear if he was.'

'Not directly. I'm not next of kin, but I expect his mother would let me know.'

'When are you going to see him again?'

Prue shrugged. 'I don't know. He's been transferred to Wyton in Huntingdonshire and that's not so far to go as Scampton. I'll go when we both have a weekend free.'

'I've got leave. I'm off to London tomorrow.'

'How long will you be gone?'

'A week. I'll go to the Bennetts' first and then to my friend, Janet. If they can't put me up, I'll find a boarding house. And I'll see Chris, of course.'

'He's important to you, isn't he?'

'I suppose he is. He writes me lovely letters. It's almost as if I can hear him talking to me. He reminds me of home.'

'What do you want to go back there for?' Constance demanded when she was told about the trip to London. 'There's no one there you know.'

'There's Mr and Mrs Bennett and my friend, Janet, and seven graves I want to visit . . .'

'Oh, so you've finally come to your senses and admitted they're all dead.'

'I never denied it. And they might not all be dead. Charlie might be alive somewhere.'

'If he were, you'd have heard long before now. And the name is Charles not Charlie. I do so hate it when people mangle names.'

'I'm still going to try and find out what happened to him. I'll catch the first train in the morning.'

'Sheila! My goodness, where have you sprung from?' June Bennett held the door open to admit her. 'Come on in, I'll make some tea and you can tell me what you've been up to.'

'I've got a week's holiday, so I thought I'd look up my old friends.' She followed June into the kitchen where there was a fire in the range and sat at the table watching her as she busied herself with kettle and teapot.

'Where are you staying?'

'I thought I'd find a boarding house, if there's one still operating. The bomb damage is scary, isn't it?'

'Yes, we've only had one night without a raid since September. Poor Bob is feeling the strain.' She poured two cups of tea and fetched out a tin of biscuits. 'Only plain I'm afraid.'

'Thank you.' She took the tea but not a biscuit. 'Mr Bennett is still a warden, then?'

'Yes, he didn't pass the medical for the forces. He's mad about it, but I'm glad, though I sometimes wonder if he's any safer here than in the front line. What about you? Are you happy with your aunt?'

'She's OK, I suppose. An awful snob, not a bit like Mum. I've got a job as a post girl with a company in Bletchley.' That was the nearest she dare go to the truth.

'Will you see Chris while you're here?'

'I expect so. I want to see Janet too. She's a very poor letter writer. And I might call on the Mortons.'

'The shop got hit a few weeks ago, Mrs Morton lost a leg and poor old Mr Morton is finding it hard to cope with looking after her and the shop. They repaired the damage and he's still trading, but how long for I don't know.'

'Oh, how dreadful. I want to see if I can find out what happened to Charlie, too. I don't suppose Mr Bennett has discovered anything?'

'No, we would have written and told you if he had. Sheila, I think you must accept that your brother is dead. If he were alive, he'd have come home.'

'But there's no home to come home to, that's the trouble. He'd have seen that hole in the ground and gone away again.'

'But where? Sheila, this is his home ground. He wouldn't have strayed far, especially if he learnt you had survived. People would have seen him.'

'Yes, I know you are right, but it's so difficult to let go.'

'Oh, my dear, I am so sorry. You know if Bob or I could help, we would.'

'Yes, I know.'

'You can stay here, if you like, use it as a base.' She laughed. 'You might find yourself in the Anderson shelter again if there's a raid.'

'Thank you. I'd like to stay if I may. I've brought my ration book.'

Bob was equally pleased to see her when he came home from work, but reiterated what his wife had said, that he didn't think they would ever know what had happened to Charlie. 'It's not just the damage caused on that first night,' he said, 'It's all the destruction later. He could have been buried many times over.' He saw her shiver. 'I'm sorry, Sheila, but it's best you face the truth.'

What was the truth? It was not knowing that which gave her sleepless nights. She smiled. 'You are probably right.'

They had hardly finished their evening meal when the siren sounded. Bob left the table and reached for his coat, tin hat and gas mask. 'No rest for the wicked,' he said. 'See you later.'

'I don't know how much longer he can keep going,' June said after he had gone. 'Working all day in the factory, up half the night, and the sights he sees are enough to give anyone nightmares. He's tired out. But then, aren't we all?'

'Perhaps the raid won't last long.'

They sat in the kitchen because that was the only place where June kept a fire in. It also had a sturdy table they could dive under if they had to. It was not long before they heard the bombers overhead, wave after wave of them. And then explosions which shook the house. 'I don't like the sound of it,' June said, pouring the remainder of the tea from the pot into a Thermos flask. 'I think we'd better go into the shelter.'

She banked down the fire and they gathered up gas masks, cushions, bags, knitting, a newspaper and the flask and, making sure the gas and electricity were turned off, let themselves out of the back door. In whatever direction they looked, the whole sky was orange with flames and smoke and it wasn't just the east end and the docks; to the west and north, London was on fire. 'God! It's the worst yet,' June said as they stood and watched in awe. Incendiaries were being rained down from hundreds of bombers, causing fires which gave the bombers something to aim at with their high explosives. They saw one or two aircraft caught in searchlights and heard the guns firing at them. They even saw one brought down. But still they came.

'Come on,' June said, as Sheila hesitated. 'We'd better get under cover.'

'What a way to start a holiday,' Sheila said, as they sat on deck chairs in the Anderson shelter, drinking the rather stewed tea and straining their ears to catch the all-too-familiar noises.

'Haven't you had any raids?'

'We had one that did a bit of damage, not like this though. We were told it was a single bomber who'd lost his way and saw the railway lines. I was off duty at the time, so was Prue.'

'Prue's your new friend, is she?'

'Yes. We work for the same company and she lodges with my

aunt.' She laughed. 'You'll never believe it, but she is the daughter of an earl and her real title is Lady Prudence Le Strange. There's no side to her at all and she's been a good friend to me.'

'Going up in the world, are you?'

'I don't know about that, but I would like to better myself. I want to make Ma and Pa proud of me. I'd like to sing on the stage. I was Cinderella in the firm's pantomime. It was hard work, but I really enjoyed it.'

'Your mother sang in the church choir for years. She had a lovely voice.'

'I know.'

'I wonder where Bob is. I can't rest easy when I know he's out on the streets in the thick of it.'

They fell silent. June knitted furiously and Sheila tried to read by the light of an oil lamp, the sort every household had before the advent of electricity, now hard to come by. The allies were defeating the Italians in North Africa and the Dutch fleet had made a daring escape and arrived in Hull loaded with volunteers, but that was all the good news. The rest was about air raids, rationing, new regulations and the black market, which was seen as criminal if not downright treason. She let the paper drop and shut her eyes.

Now she was back in London it was mostly of Charlie she was thinking, wondering where he was and if he had suffered. If he was still alive, why hadn't she been able to find him? In spite of the noise outside, she dozed a little and dreamt of home, a home with everyone there sitting round the dining table, smiling and happy, everyone except Charlie. The extraordinary thing was that no one seemed troubled by his absence. 'He's all right,' her mother said. 'Don't worry about him.'

'There's the All Clear.' June's voice roused her, as the steady sound told them the raid was over. 'And we're still alive to tell the tale.'

They gathered up their belongings and returned to the house. It was still intact, as were the other houses at their end of the street. They had been spared, but the rest of the great city seemed to be on fire. 'It reminds me of stories of the Great Fire of London I heard about at school,' Sheila said. 'But most of the buildings in those days were wooden.'

It was only half past nine, earlier than most raids ended, and they wondered if there might be more to come later. In the meantime they would go to bed.

Sheila had hardly drifted off to sleep when she was woken by sounds coming from downstairs. Grabbing her dressing gown, she wrapped it round her and left her room to investigate. There was a light on in the kitchen and she could hear voices, June's and a lower voice she took to be Bob's. She knocked gently and entered. Bob was sitting at the table with his back to her, one arm stretched out in front of him covered in blood. The sleeve of his shirt was in shreds. June had a bowl of water on the table which was red with blood. 'Don't make such a fuss,' he was saying as she tried to clean the wound. 'It's only a scratch . . .'

'Can I help?'

They both turned towards her. June was looking worried but it was Bob's face that caught her attention. It had no colour at all, unless chalky, begrimed dust was a colour. And even that was marked by deep scratches that oozed blood. His hair, his eyebrows and his clothes were all scorched. There was a smell about him of acrid smoke. His hands had been burnt too.

'He was trying to get a baby out of a burning building,' June said.

'I was cut by glass when the windows blew out,' he said. 'It's nothing much.'

'Well, there's glass in this cut,' June said. 'I'm not competent enough to deal with it. I think you need a doctor.'

'I'll get one,' Sheila said. 'Just give me a minute to throw on some clothes.' She ran upstairs to dress, then flung herself out of the front door. She didn't need a torch, the fires were enough to light her way, though in the shadow of tall buildings it was dark. The contrast was eerie and might have unnerved her if she hadn't been in such a hurry. The doctor was out, looking after casualties at the first aid centre, but a nurse agreed to go back with her. She set to work on Bob at once, stitching the wound and bandaging him up. She treated the cuts on his face too, but he still looked dreadful.

'Go to bed and stay at home for a day or two,' she said, giving June some ointment for his burns. 'They can manage without you for once. I'll come back tomorrow.' She snapped her bag shut. 'I expect to find you here.'

'Do you know what happened to the baby?' he asked her.

'No, but I'll try and find out for you.' And she was gone.

June, who was drooping with tiredness, threw out the blood-stained water and rinsed the bowl. 'Let's get you up to bed.' She put her arm about her husband's waist and helped him to stand. Together they negotiated the stairs with Sheila behind them. 'Thanks, Sheila,' she said, at their bedroom door. 'I am jolly glad you were here. Go back to bed. I can manage now.'

The fires had indeed been greater than the Great Fire of 1666, and had done extensive damage to some of the most beautiful and historic buildings in the city. Worse still, there were thousands of casualties. But there were tales of great heroism too, which resulted in St Paul's Cathedral being saved, and on a smaller scale, one tiny month-old baby had been given a second chance of life. The infant Bob had rescued was alive and apparently none the worse, they learnt when the nurse arrived the following morning to dress his cuts. 'The poor thing lost his parents, but the Red Cross are trying to find relatives who might take him.'

'We'll look after him,' June said. 'Until they find his relations.'

'Don't you think you've got enough on your plate looking after your husband?'

'I'll heal,' he said. 'I'm better already and I feel sort of responsible for the little one.'

He was more shaken up than he cared to admit, but he did agree to stay in bed with June fussing round him. Sheila took the opportunity to visit the cemetery with flowers and then went to the Mortons' shop.

Everywhere were signs of devastation and fires still burning. Firemen with blackened faces went off duty and fresh-faced ones took their place. She had to make a detour, stepping over snaking hoses, to pass a building that was declared unsafe and again when a road was closed because of an unexploded bomb which the army were dealing with. It was not only sights and sounds that filled her vision, but strange smells too, of scorched cloth and burning wood, hot tar and death.

The Morton shop had been badly damaged; for the second time had lost its windows and door and for the second time the stock had been ruined. 'If that wasn't bad enough, the shop was looted while I was at the hospital with my wife,' Mr Morton told her. His once-grey hair was now snow-white and his pale eyes reflected the strain he was under. He had a hopelessness about him as if nothing mattered any more. 'How can people do such a thing?'

'I am so sorry.'

'Janet has been a brick. I don't know what we would have done without her.' He jerked his head towards the door behind him. 'She's in the stockroom. Go and say hallo.'

Janet was weighing sugar from a sack into stiff, blue paper bags, eight ounces into each. 'Hallo, Jan.'

'Sheila! Well I never. What brings you here?'

'I'm on holiday and catching up on old friends. How are you?'

'I'm OK.' She looked behind her towards the door into the shop and then whispered. 'Mrs Morton lost a leg in an air raid. She was caught out when the raid happened and went into a public shelter that got a direct hit. Poor Mr Morton is really cut up about it, he seems to blame himself for letting her go out. They can't live upstairs any more, so rent a ground-floor flat somewhere. He doesn't come in every day. Leaves most of the work to me. He's talking of making me manager and letting me have the upstairs flat.'

'That will be handy for you. What about Bert?'

'In the army. He comes home on leave sometimes, but it's not the same, is it?'

'No. Nothing is.'

'Have you seen Chris?'

'He'll be at work. I'll go round after tea.'

The baby Bob had rescued had been brought to the house and June was busy mixing up baby food for him when a newspaper reporter and cameraman arrived. They had heard of Bob's bravery and wanted to make a feature of it. Sheila, watching them fuss about asking questions, felt sure that the authorities at Bletchley Park would frown on any of their employees attracting publicity, and slipped away to see Chris.

His face lit up when he saw her on the doorstep. 'Sheila!' He dragged her inside, hugged and kissed her. 'Why didn't you say you were coming?'

‘I wanted to surprise you.’

‘Well, you have that.’ He looked behind him. His mother had just come from the kitchen to see who was at the door.

‘It’s Sheila,’ he said. ‘She’s back. We’re going out.’

‘But you haven’t finished your tea.’

‘Yes, I have.’ He seized his coat from a hook on the wall and ushered Sheila into the street. ‘We can’t talk with Ma ear-wigging,’ he said, taking her arm. ‘Tell me all your news. Are you back for good?’

‘No, I’m on holiday. I’m staying with Bob and June.’

‘So how’s life in Bletchley?’

‘It’s OK. My aunt is a bit of a tartar, but she doesn’t worry me, not any more. What about you?’

‘Same as ever. Work, eat and sleep. I think about you a lot, wondering what you are up to.’

‘I think about you too. Sometimes I get dreadfully homesick and then I realise there’s no home to come back to and I’ve got to put up with it.’

‘What shall we do tonight? Fancy the flicks?’

They queued up at the cinema to see Laurence Olivier and Joan Fontaine in *Rebecca*. They sat in the back row and he put his arm about her.

Halfway through the film, a message flashed on the screen. ‘Air Raid Warning.’ Half a dozen people left but the rest stayed where they were and the film continued. The noises outside were muffled by the soundtrack. After the main film, they watched the Pathé News. Pictures of London burning were shown with the St Paul’s Cathedral standing proud amid the smoking ruins, which were accompanied by stories of stoicism and bravery, of firemen directing hoses on burning buildings, just as her father had done – had died doing. There were pictures of the King and

Queen touring the damaged areas. Since Buckingham Palace had itself been bombed the previous September, the East Enders had changed towards the Royal couple and they were welcomed everywhere.

'Charlie!' Sheila cried suddenly, grabbing Chris's arm. 'He was there in the crowd just behind the King and Queen.'

People sitting near them were turning towards them, telling them to 'Shush.'

Sheila got up, banging back her seat, and edged her way out, followed by Chris. 'How can you be so sure?' he said when they reached the foyer. 'There were crowds of people and the camera was focusing on the King and Queen. I didn't see him.'

'I'm sure it was him.'

'What do you want to do about it?'

'I don't know. I don't know.' She paced up and down.

'We could come back tomorrow and look at it again.'

'You want to see that film all over again?'

'If I've got you beside me, I'd see it a dozen times.'

'Oh, Chris! I am a great trial to you, aren't I?'

'No, of course you're not. You are my sweetheart. The girl I love most in all the world. I would do anything for you.' The sound of the All Clear penetrated the foyer. 'Come on, I'll walk you home.'

She was silent as they walked. The night was clear and moonlit. The Londoners all wished for cloud to give them some respite, but there hadn't been enough to deter the bombers. It was the first time he had said he loved her and it gave her a warm glow to think she mattered to someone, but was that enough for her to think of him as her sweetheart? She really didn't know.

'When do you think you will be coming back to West Ham again?' he asked.

'I don't know. It depends. We don't get leave all that often. My work may be boring but it is war work. I'll come when I can.'

'Trouble is, I might not be here. I've had my call-up papers. I have to report for a medical next week.'

'You're going in the army?'

'No, the navy.'

'The navy?' she queried in surprise. 'Why? Your father died at sea.'

'I know, but he loved the life and I don't fancy being stuck in a trench, nor shot at it in the sky.'

'Your mother will miss you.'

'She's as ratty as hell about it, but it can't be helped. More to the point, will you miss me?'

'Of course I will, but we can still write to each other and see each other when we're both on leave.'

'Can't see that happening very often, can you?'

'No, I suppose not. Blame the war and Adolf Hitler.'

They reached the Bennetts' door. He kissed her. 'I'll call for you tomorrow at a quarter to seven if you want to see that film again.'

It was a different newsreel the following evening. She cried bitter tears of disappointment, especially as her certainty had begun to waver. One boy in a crowd, not even wearing anything outstanding, had flashed by in a second. She really couldn't be sure, especially as she had to admit to June that she had often imagined she had seen him in the street, but on a closer look it had turned out not to be her brother.

She divided the rest of her leave between June and Chris. They wanted to make the most of their time together, going for walks, well wrapped up against the cold, visiting the cemetery with flowers, going to a dance on New Year's Eve to see the New Year in, or simply sitting in June's front room, holding hands and talking quietly. The night before she was due to go back to Bletchley, he came to say goodbye to her. 'I'll write,' he said. 'You'll write too?'

'Of course I will.'

The next day she went back to her aunt, happy to think her old friends remembered her and Chris had not changed, probably never would change. But she was still in the dark about what had happened to her brother.

Chapter Six

Prue was more sympathetic than June but she was still dubious. 'It is so easy to imagine you have seen someone simply because that's the person you most want to see,' she said, when Sheila arrived back at Victoria Villa at the end of her leave and told her about the newsreel. As usual, they were talking in Prue's bedroom. 'The mind plays funny tricks sometimes.'

'I know. I keep telling myself that.'

'Have you said anything to your aunt?'

'Lord, no! She'd laugh at me. I think you must be laughing at me too.'

'No, I'm not. But supposing, just for a minute, that it was your brother you saw, what can you do about it? Just because he was on the film, doesn't mean the news people know who he is. He was just one in a crowd, there and gone in a moment.'

'I know.' She sighed. 'I'm trying not to think about it. But if he's alive, that's good, isn't it? And there was that strange dream. Was Ma trying to tell me something?'

'No, it was your inner self telling you not to worry.'

'If it was, my inner self hasn't made a very good job of it.'

Prue got up off the bed, and pulled Sheila up beside her. 'Go to bed. We're on early shift tomorrow.'

Sheila went to her own room leaving Prue musing on what she had told her. Had Sheila really seen her brother? But if he were alive, what possible reason could he have for not contacting her? Unless he thought she was dead along with the rest of her family. Being reunited with her brother might make up in some measure for the loss of the rest of her family but how could it be done? Not without Sheila seeing that piece of film again and pointing out the figure she thought was her brother. Newsreels, as Sheila had already discovered, were changed almost every day. Events moved on, yesterday's news was yesterday's news. And, really, should she be thinking about it? If they failed, which was almost certain, would the disappointment be too much for Sheila to bear? Best leave well alone, unless Sheila herself brought up the subject again.

'Let's go for a bike ride this afternoon,' Sheila suggested, as they cycled home after coming off night shift at eight o'clock one morning. They had both bought second-hand bicycles which saved them having to walk to work.

'OK, after I've had a bit of shut-eye.' They were changing shifts and were not expected back on duty until the following morning which meant they had nearly twenty-four hours in which to please themselves, and being young and healthy, sleep was not a major concern. Although they had become used to changing shifts and sleep patterns, it was never easy to sleep during daylight hours. There were noises in the street, milkmen clattering milk bottles, the postman rattling the letterbox, dogs barking and errand boys whistling. After a couple of hours, Prue gave up and went to rouse Sheila.

Wearing slacks and wrapped up in coats, scarves and gloves, they set off away from the town to the open countryside. Prue was glad to be out in the fresh air, even on a freezing February day. Her work required unremitting concentration. Some phrases she was translating didn't make sense at all and they often had to ask if the same message had been picked up elsewhere which might be clearer. A mistake could have been made by the original sender, or during the decode, or it might have been that the signal was just too faint. Sometimes the slip of paper was passed from hand to hand to see if anyone else could decipher it. If the translation was an educated guess, that had to be noted. Then there was all the technical jargon and abbreviations to interpret. By the end of her shift she was frequently exhausted and suffering from a headache. But she was no worse off than anyone else at BP. The war was testing the stamina of everyone.

Cycling along the lanes bordered by leafless trees, she reflected on the part of it that affected her, not only her job but that of others around her. Papa liked to pretend he was young again but he had been looking very tired the last time she had been home and Stevens' death hadn't helped. It was so unlike Mama to snap at Papa and no doubt they were worried about Gillie and what he was up to. At least her brother was still in England and not off to the Far East with his old regiment, though why that was she did not know; he was up to something.

Sheila was whizzing down the hill ahead of her with her feet off the pedals and stuck out in front of her, singing.

Daisy, daisy, give me your answer do,
I'm half crazy, all for the love of you.
It won't be a stylish marriage,

I can't afford a carriage,
But you'd look sweet upon the seat
Of a bicycle made for two.

Prue smiled. The poor girl had had more than most to contend with but she had shown extraordinary resilience. Writing up that journal seemed to help and her singing bolstered her confidence, but she must have bad days when she felt overwhelmed by tragedy. She was clinging on to the hope that her brother had survived, but it was such a forlorn hope she was sure Sheila must realise it. 'Oh, let there be some good news soon,' she prayed, pedalling after her friend.

One of the recent messages translated in Hut Three was an admission by Hitler that the bombing campaign against Britain had not achieved the result he had hoped for and had had no measurable impact on morale or the will to resist; instead the bombing of shipping and ports would be increased. If he couldn't terrorise the British people into giving up, perhaps starvation would. Whether this message would be made public she did not know, but what she did know was that its source would never be revealed. Knowledge like that lay heavy on her shoulders.

'The Drama Society is going to put on a revue for Easter,' Sheila said. They were toiling uphill now, side by side. 'They want me to sing in it.'

'Good for you. It's a pity you are under age, or we could go to a pub for a drink.'

'I'm not under age, not any more.'

Prue braked hard and stood down, making Sheila stop too. 'You mean you've had a birthday?'

'Yes.'

'When? Why didn't you say?'

'Yesterday. I didn't want a fuss.'

'Oh, Sheila, I wish I'd known. But it's not too late. Come on, we're going to celebrate with a pub lunch and a bottle of wine.' She got back on her bicycle and cycled back the way they had come.

Sheila followed her. 'Is it all right for us to go in a pub without a man? My mother never would.'

Prue laughed. 'Nor mine, but this is an enlightened age. If women can go into the forces and do war work, then they can please themselves what they do in their spare time.' She stopped outside the Duncombe Arms. 'This'll do.'

Inside there was a good fire and they settled at a table in a corner. While Prue went off to order, Sheila looked about her. She had never been in a public house in her life before. Her father had not been a great drinker, unlike most of his mates, and she had never been required to go and fetch him from the pub to come home for his dinner, as so many of her young friends did. Even so, she did not think the pubs that stood on almost every corner of the East End were anything like this. It was warm and cosy and crowded with young people, some of whom she recognised as working at BP. Away from their working environment they lost the air of distraction they seemed to have when grappling with a problem and were cheerful and noisy. Prue knew some of them and went over to speak to them with the result they all turned towards her and raised their glasses in salute.

Prue returned followed by a waiter with two glasses and a green bottle, which he proceeded to open with a great deal of ceremony. The cork flew up and hit the ceiling, making Sheila jump.

'Food will be coming in a few minutes,' Prue said, handing Sheila a glass of sparkling liquid.

'What is it?'

'Champagne.' She raised her glass. 'Happy birthday, Sheila. May you have many, many more and live to be a ripe old age.'

'Oh, Prue . . .'

'You're not going to go all tearful on me, are you?'

Sheila blinked hard. 'No. I've never drunk champagne before. I've never even been in a pub.'

'There's a first time for everything and today is your initiation into the world of grown-ups.'

Sheila sipped her wine and twitched her nose when the bubbles went up it. 'It's nice.'

'Well, don't drink it too quickly, it's got quite a kick if you're not used to it.'

The young men and women at the bar broke into a chorus of 'Happy Birthday' and then came over to shake her hand. 'You are our lovely nightingale,' one of the young men said. 'I thought I was too old for panto, but you converted me. When are we going to hear you again?'

'We're doing a revue for Easter.'

'Do we have to wait that long? Can't you give us a taste?'

'Yes, sing for us,' one of the others said.

'What, now?' She gave Prue a questioning look and her friend nodded. She began to sing 'Ave Maria'. Her clear voice silenced everyone as they listened. At the end, they all applauded, even the publican, who didn't have a licence for music and would be obliged to stop any idea of an encore.

Riding home was a problem. Sheila was giggling so much she could hardly steer straight and her feet kept slipping off the pedals. 'Whatever will Aunt Constance shay when she shees me?' she said.

'Who cares.' Prue was riding beside her, watching she came to no harm. 'It's not every day you have a birthday and it was mean of her to forget it.'

'I don' sh'pose she ever knew it.'

Thankfully, Constance was out and by the time she returned Sheila was asleep on her bed, cuddling Tiddles who had once again evaded Constance to reach the bedroom.

Prue went out again to buy her friend a birthday present and was browsing among the limited selection of perfumes at the chemist's when one of the young men she had spoken to in the Duncombe Arms came in to buy shaving soap.

'Your friend got home safely?' he asked. He had brown hair, carefully parted, and thick, black-rimmed glasses.

'Yes. I left her asleep and came out to buy her a birthday present. Poor thing, she had no one to remember it and she never told anyone, not even me until today.'

'You work in Hut Three, don't you?'

'Yes.'

'I'm in Hut Eight.'

Hut Eight worked on the German naval cyphers and they were the most difficult of all to crack, the coding being more complex than the army and air force messages Prue dealt with. She did not ask him any questions about it, and instead chose and paid for some perfume and they left the shop together. 'I'm Hugh Wentworth, by the way,' he said, holding out his right hand.

She took it. 'Prue Le Strange.'

'Lady Prudence Le Strange, I believe.'

'How did you know that?'

'Your friend, Alice, told me. I asked her when I saw you at the Christmas party. Mind if I walk with you?'

'Not at all.'

They chatted inconsequentially as they walked, about the weather, the blitz, the rationing and their favourite likes and dislikes. She learnt that he was the only son of a doctor. 'My father wanted me to follow in his footsteps, but I think you have to have a calling for that sort of thing and I didn't feel called. I did an engineering degree and that got me interested in the technical side of radio. I hadn't quite made up my mind about a career when the war started and I landed up here, fiddling with wires.'

She gathered from that he was working on the bombes. 'Would you rather be here or in the forces?'

'I don't know, but I think I'm doing more good here. I'd make a lousy soldier. Besides, I've been told they won't let any of us chaps into the forces in case we're captured and spill the beans about BP. That pleases my mother.'

'Mine too. She thinks I'm doing a boring office job. It's dreadful how we have to lie, isn't it?'

'Well, not lie exactly, stretch the truth a bit. How did your little friend come to be working at BP? She doesn't seem the type.'

'Type? What type?'

'Educated, classy, self-assured.' He laughed. 'Like you.'

'The only difference between us is that my family had money and hers didn't. She's intelligent in her way, certainly very talented, and she's had a rough time. She lost her entire family in the Blitz and the only relation she has is an embittered aunt. I've taken her under my wing.'

'I didn't mean it as a criticism.'

'I certainly hope not.' She stopped outside Victoria Villa. 'This is where I'm billeted.'

'I'll say cheerio then.' He paused. 'Look here, I don't want us to get off on the wrong foot. Will you come out with me some time? A drink perhaps, or we could go to the pictures.'

'We haven't got off on any foot at all, Mr Wentworth, wrong or otherwise.'

'Message received and understood. I'll be on my way then.'

She watched him go off down the road and went indoors. She had been rather brusque with him, but she hated snobbery of any kind, especially when it concerned Sheila. Pity, because he was rather good-looking and reminded her of Gillie, with his dark hair cut short, amber eyes and boyish charm. She hadn't seen her brother for months, but they corresponded regularly. It was funny how it was possible to write long letters without saying anything of importance at all. She had not divulged what she did at Bletchley Park and he had not said exactly what he was doing. All he had said was that he was doing parachute training.

Constance, alone in the house, was doing some washing when she heard the front door knocker. It was too early for the postman and it wasn't the butcher's day, not that he brought her anything worth having these days. She dried her hands and went to answer it.

A young man in a scruffy suit stood on the doorstep. He took off his cap to her. 'Is Sheila at home?'

'Who are you? You're not Charles, are you?'

'Charles?' he queried, then smiled. 'No, I'm not Charlie. I'm Chris. Are you Sheila's Auntie Connie?'

'I am Mrs Tranter to you. And who is Chris, when he's at home?'

'Christopher Jarrett. I'm Sheila's boyfriend. I came to see her.'

'Boyfriend, ridiculous! She's only seventeen, not old enough for boyfriends.'

'She's eighteen now. Is she here?'

'No, she isn't, and I suggest you go back where you came from.'

'I'm not going back until I've seen her.'

'Then you have a long wait. She's at work. She won't be home before nine o'clock, not then if she goes gallivanting with her new friends.'

'Where does she work? She never said.'

'No, she wouldn't. She's trying to put the past behind her and that means anything to do with her old life. You are wasting your time.'

'I don't believe it.'

'I am not accustomed to being called a liar, young man. Now I suggest you go before I call the police.'

'OK, I'm going. Tell me where she works.'

Constance laughed. 'Bletchley Park. Go there if you must but don't blame me if you find yourself locked up.' She slammed the door in his face.

Chris always gave most of his wages to his mother and it had taken a few weeks to save enough for the train fare and the ring he had in his pocket. Three pounds it had cost him, over a week's wages, and he did not intend to go home until he had put it on Sheila's finger.

Everyone in the town knew where Bletchley Park was and it wasn't long before he found himself at the gate and confronting a sentry in naval uniform. 'You can't come in here.'

'I want to see my girl. She works here.'

'Makes no odds, you can't come in.'

'Then fetch her out to me. I must see her. Her name is Sheila Phipps.'

'I don't know the names of all people who work here, lad. There are hundreds of us and security is tighter than your arse.'

'Can't you turn your back for a moment?'

'Certainly not.'

'Then I'll just have to hang around 'til she comes out.'

'D'you want to get yourself arrested?'

'No, course not. But I have to see her. I'm off to Chatham on Monday and I want to say goodbye to her.'

'Go to her billet.'

'The old battleaxe wouldn't let me in either.'

The sentry laughed. 'Wait here.' He turned and picked up a telephone in the sentry box and spoke to someone. 'There's a young lad at the gate wants to come in and speak to his girl.' Pause. 'No, he won't go away.' Another pause. 'Yes, sir.' He put the phone down and turned back to Chris. 'Someone's coming.'

Chris peered through the gate. There was a path and some gardens but he couldn't see much else. People came and went through the gate after having their passes scrutinised by the sentry. He tried to slip in behind one of them, but was grabbed by his jacket collar and hauled back. 'No, you don't young feller, m'lad. You wait here.'

A couple of military policemen arrived and, before he knew it, he was being blindfolded and frog-marched he knew not where. They took him into a building and up some stairs where they removed the blindfold. He was in an office and there was a naval commander facing him. 'Sit down,' he said, indicating a chair.

Chris sat and then began a thorough interrogation which scared him half to death. It wasn't that the man laid hands on him, because he was politeness itself, but the fact that he was suspected of breaking some law he knew nothing about and according to his interrogator the punishment was dire. He would probably spend the rest of the war in clink. 'I don't know anything about what goes on here, Sheila never said,' he insisted. 'I didn't even know she worked here, until today.'

'How did you find out? Did she tell you?'

'No, her landlady did. She said I'd be arrested if I came and she weren't far wrong.'

'You haven't been arrested – yet.'

'If you arrest me, you'll have to answer to the Admiralty. I'm due to report at Chatham for war service on Monday.'

'I can soon check that.'

'You do that, sir, then perhaps you'll believe me. I've done no wrong and if I've messed up your security, then I'm sorry. It weren't intended.'

The man laughed. 'I believe you. What did you see as you came in?'

'Nothing, those MPs blindfolded me.'

'You will have to go out the same way, I'm afraid.'

'But I want to see Sheila. I've got a ring in my pocket for her.'

'Do you know what she does here?'

'I haven't the faintest idea, but I can't think what she does that has to be so secret; she's only an ordinary working girl, a shop assistant until a couple of months ago.'

'We all have our part to play, Mr Jarrett. But sit still, I'll see what I can do.'

He went into an adjoining room. Chris heard the murmur of voices and then the officer came back. 'They'll have to find her, it might take a few minutes. You can wait here.'

'Thank you, sir.'

The officer went back to the work on his desk and Chris simply sat and waited. Neither spoke. Ten minutes later, a breathless Sheila arrived. Chris stood up, a broad grin on his face.

'Chris, what on earth are you doing here?'

'I came to see you.'

'And they let you in?'

'Yes.' He glanced towards the officer, who showed no sign of leaving them alone. 'I'm off into the navy next week and I wanted to say goodbye and . . .' He fumbled in his jacket pocket and took out the box containing the ring and flipped it open. 'I wanted to give you this.'

If he had expected delight and an eagerness to pick up the ring and slip it on, he was disappointed. She simply stared at it. 'Chris, you shouldn't have.'

'Why not? You know how I feel about you. I wanted to make it official.'

'Oh, Chris, why didn't you ask me before you spent the money?'

'Are you turning me down?' He was miserable and bitterly disappointed and she had changed. Not so much in looks but the way she held herself and the way she spoke, especially in the way she spoke. Posh-like.

'But it's the wrong time. We are both young, there is a war on . . . Who knows what will happen.'

'It won't change the way I feel.'

'I'm sorry, Chris, truly I am, but I just don't think it's the right time.'

'Your aunt said you'd found new friends.'

'Of course I have. You can't get along without friends, Chris, and you are one of the best.'

'Then I'll wait for you to change your mind. If I get killed you might be sorry.'

'Of course I would be sorry. I'm not hard-hearted, Chris, but . . .'

'Oh, I understand. You've got above yourself, that's what. P'raps I never was good enough for you.'

'That's not true. I haven't changed. I'm still me.' After a pause she added, 'Are you staying in Bletchley tonight?'

He had planned to do so, to take her out somewhere and

celebrate, but in the face of her rejection, he changed his mind. 'No, I promised Ma I'd be back. Tomorrow's my last day at home.'

She held out her hand. 'Then good luck.'

He ignored it and made to leave but the officer stopped him. 'Sorry, old chap, you have to be escorted off the premises. Miss Phipps, you may return to duty.'

She smiled at Chris as she left. 'Sorry, Chris, so very sorry. Perhaps I'll see you when we both get leave.' Then she was gone.

He put the ring back in his pocket and waited for his escort, mentally cursing the officer whose presence had inhibited him. He could have said so much more, would have persuaded her, he was sure. He had never felt so miserable in his life.

'I felt an absolute heel,' Sheila told Prue later that day, as they sat together on the bed in Prue's room. 'But I couldn't pretend, could I?'

'No definitely not. He'll get over it and you are still very young. There's plenty of time.'

'I hope so. Miss Reed gave me a lecture about security which went on and on. It wasn't my fault, I didn't ask Chris to come and make a fuss. I didn't even tell him where I worked, Aunt Constance did. He knew her address because I told him when I knew I was coming here and we've been writing to each other. In any case I don't know what goes on at BP. I just do my job, carrying envelopes and packages from place to place. I don't even know what you do.'

'Boring office work. Miss Reed must have believed you or you would have been out on your ear.'

'Aunt Constance has been nagging me about Chris. She says it's disgusting to have boyfriends at my age and no doubt I'll go the way of my mother. I've no idea what she meant by that. I wouldn't mind being like my mother. She was the best. She and Pa loved each other. And they loved all us kids.'

'Take no notice, the old dragon is repressed.'

'I just need someone to love.'

'Oh, Sheila.' Prue put her arm round the girl's shoulder and hugged her. 'I know it's not the same, but you can love me.'

'Oh, I do.'

'Just hold onto this thought: if it is meant to be, he'll be back.'

Dear Ma and Pa,

Chris came to BP today and made a fuss. He brought a ring and wanted us to get engaged before he left for the navy. It was awful because Mr Welchman was there the whole time and we couldn't talk properly. I felt he was secretly laughing at us. I know Chris loves me, he puts it in every letter, but it was such a surprise, I'm afraid I turned him down and he didn't understand why. I couldn't explain, not with Mr Welchman there. It's just that I don't think it's right with the war and everything. Who knows how we'll feel in a year or two. I wish you were here to advise me. Prue tries, but it's not the same. She has gone to meet Tim this weekend. She was very excited about it and spent ages deciding what to wear. I think she really is in love.

Until we meet again,
your loving daughter,
Sheila.

Tim and Prue came out of the smoky warmth of the cinema into the cold crisp air of a late January night and, arms linked, made for the Black Bull in Huntingdon where Prue had taken a room. The film they had just seen was *The Lion Has Wings*, about an RAF attack on a German battleship and how the Luftwaffe bombers were turned back from London by barrage balloons.

Part newsreel, part acting, it starred Ralph Richardson and Merle Oberon and had been doing the rounds of the country's cinemas for nearly a year.

Tim was incensed. 'Blatant propaganda,' he said. 'Lies from beginning to end. They couldn't even get their facts right. All those pre-war biplanes whizzing about and everyone fearless and patriotic. And that German bomber was actually an airliner. My God, do they think people are going to be taken in by it? And the speech by Merle Oberon at the end was so cloying, it was unbelievable. I don't wonder Ralph Richardson fell asleep while she was giving it. Why couldn't they tell it like it really is?'

Prue hugged his arm with both hands. 'I suppose it was made before the Blitz started. It was meant to make people feel cheerful and optimistic.'

'Well, it hasn't made me feel cheerful. I felt like throwing something at the screen.'

She laughed. 'I'm glad you didn't.'

The river was wide and deep before swirling under the ancient bridge. They stood in one of the embrasures and looked down at the fast-flowing water. The moonlight shining on it made it gleam like a silver ribbon. 'Rivers make good landmarks,' he said. 'We always try to identify rivers when we're over there.'

'Is it very bad? Silly question, of course it is. Do you want to talk about it?'

'Not really. Let's get in the warm.' He took her arm to walk the short distance to the inn. 'Do you think they'll have anything to eat at that hotel of yours?'

'I expect they'll rustle up a sandwich if we ask nicely.'

'Good. The food we get is pretty basic, except before an op, when we are served bacon and eggs.' He gave a hollow chuckle. 'The condemned man ate a hearty breakfast.'

'Do you have to go back to Wyton tonight?'

He turned and grinned at her. 'Is that an invitation?'

'Could be. So when are you due back?'

'I have to report by eight in the morning.'

'How will you get back?'

'There's buses or a taxi or I could walk.'

The lounge was deserted but they were able to obtain sandwiches and a bottle of wine and two glasses by ringing the bell in reception, and sat in a corner to eat and drink.

'Do you think we could sneak this up to your room?' he asked.

There was no one about; the staff had evidently gone home or gone to bed. The porter who had taken their order had disappeared in the direction of the kitchen. They successfully negotiated the stairs to Prue's room, carrying the bottle, glasses and sandwiches. 'I feel very wicked,' she said, laughing and taking off her coat and hat and throwing them on a chair.

'Good,' he said, pouring wine. 'I shan't have a fight on my hands.'

'What would you do if I did resist?' she asked, sitting on the side of the bed.

He handed her a full glass. 'I suppose I should have to behave like a gentleman. But you aren't going to resist, are you?' He took off his jacket and sat down beside her.

'I don't know. I've often wondered what I would do.'

'You mean you're an innocent?' He affected surprise.

'Not so much innocent as inexperienced. I've led a sheltered life, home and girls' school. Not that I haven't had my chances,' she added, laughing. 'I never felt the inclination.'

'War changes things,' he said thoughtfully. 'It changes people. Things we would never dream of doing in peacetime become commonplace. Men who have seen the murky side of war try and relieve it by picking up the first willing girl and making love to her.'

'That's not love, that's lust.'

'True. War makes us lusty, not that we weren't lusty before, simply schooled to be patient and restrain ourselves.' He took a gulp of wine. 'Now there isn't time. We might be dead tomorrow.'

'Oh, Tim, don't talk like that.' The film had evidently touched a raw nerve and the wine was making his mood worse.

'Why not? It's true. Have you any idea of the casualties we've suffered?'

'I think so,' she said quietly.

'I don't mean what they put out on the news. That's lies, like everything else. Bomber Command has lost hundreds of men and aeroplanes, a lot more than Fighter Command, who get all the praise. And for what? So that we can fly in the cold and the dark for hours on end to pulverise a German city. There are men, women and children in those cities, people who didn't want this war any more than we did. And I'm expected to murder them.'

'Oh, Tim.' She put her glass on the bedside table, took his from him and put that down too, so that she could take both his hands in her own. 'It's no more than they are doing to us. You should hear my friend, Sheila, on the subject. She lost her whole family, mother, father and six siblings.'

'Two wrongs don't make a right.'

'No, of course they don't, but what else can we do? If we stood back and did nothing, what do you think would happen? We would lose the war and be occupied like France and the Netherlands, Norway and poor Poland. We simply cannot let that happen. Since Dunkirk, bombing is about the only weapon we have.'

'I know. I tell myself that all the time, but it isn't as if we're doing a lot of good. At Brest we were trying to hit the *Scharnhorst* and *Gneisenau* but we couldn't see them for cloud and I don't think we did a bit of damage. I didn't mind doing that. After all, the men on the ships are all combatants, but then we switched to bombing industrial targets. Precision bombing they call it.' He gave a cracked laugh. 'We're not getting within fifteen miles of the target and what are we hitting instead? People's homes.' He took his hand away and raked it through his hair. 'I didn't mean to go on like this. I'm sorry.'

'I wish we hadn't gone to see that damned film.'

'It wasn't that. Or only partly. I've lost a lot of good pals and films like that, glorifying war, make me sick.'

'Can't you ask to be taken off operations for a while?'

'Can't do that. It would mean abandoning my crew and they'd be a man short and have to put up with a new navigator or be scattered to other crews. They wouldn't thank me for it. We're like another family: live together, work together, let off steam together and look out for each other. I couldn't break that up. Besides, what reason could I give, except blue funk? The RAF has a way of punishing that. LMF, lack of moral fibre, they call it and you get stripped of your rank and sent to do all the dirty work on the base, like washing up and cleaning the lavatories. I can't think of anything more humiliating.'

'Oh, Tim.' She took his face in both her hands and kissed his lips and then she saw the tears gathering in his eyes and knew he was exhausted. 'Tim, darling, you're too tired for all this soul-searching. Shall we try and forget it, just for a little while?'

He nodded, unable to speak. Gently she pushed him back onto the bed, lifted his feet onto it and took off his shoes. By the time she had done that, he was snoring gently.

Sipping the last of her wine, she sat and watched him. In sleep he looked little more than a boy with his fair hair flopping over his face. She, who was a year younger, felt quite motherly. That she had had every intention of losing her virginity that night lost its appeal. She put down her glass and curled up beside him with her arm across his chest.

He was gone when she woke. She went to the window and drew back the blackout curtain. It was just beginning to get light. She stripped off to wash, put her clothes back on and took the glasses, plates and empty bottle down to the lounge and left them on the table where they had been sitting. She did not believe, for a minute, that it would fool the inn's staff but she didn't really care. She had paid her bill in advance, so there was no need to stay. She set off to walk to the station to catch a train to Cambridge and thence to Bletchley.

It was a cold, overcast morning, but still fine. People were moving about the streets in the half light of dawn, going about their daily business in factories, offices, inns, driving vans, buses and trains. Life had to go on, some sense of normality maintained, but she was still filled with the image of Tim fighting back tears. There had been no evidence of the light-hearted young man who had joined the Royal Air Force the day after war was declared, keen to do his bit. She knew as well as anyone that whatever was said publicly about industrial targets, the bombing was far from accurate. And he knew it too. Poor man! His gentle soul had imagined what was going on beneath his wings and made him sick. In that condition, how long would it be before he snapped? She prayed someone in authority would recognise the signs and do something about it.

* * *

'Lady Prudence,' Constance said, when Prue arrived back at Victoria Villa. 'I wasn't expecting you back just yet. I haven't prepared a meal, I'm afraid.'

'That's all right, Mrs Tranter. I can always eat out. Where is Sheila?'

'In her room, I think. She came in and walked straight by me and up to her room without a word. I despair of ever teaching that girl manners.'

'I'll go up to her.' She picked up her overnight bag which she had dropped in the hall and climbed the stairs. Leaving the bag on her bed, she went and knocked on Sheila's door. 'Sheila, it's me. I'm back.'

'Come in.' The voice did not sound in the least sulky.

She went in to find Sheila putting away her journal. 'Your aunt said you had walked straight past her without speaking.'

'I did say hallo, but she was listening to the news and didn't hear me, so I came up here.'

'She hasn't cooked dinner.'

'I know. She doesn't when you're not here.'

'Come on, we're going out to eat. You can tell me all about it on the way.'

'Now, tell me what's happened,' Prue said, as they walked quietly through the town in the dark, in search of somewhere to eat. 'I know by the look of you, something has.'

'James came on a bit strong and I had to fend him off. It was in the corridor of the main house, I'd gone there to pick up some post. He tried to pull me into one of the empty offices . . .'

'I thought you were growing rather fond of him.'

'No. It was the music, nothing more. What made him think I'd . . .' She shuddered. 'I didn't give him any encouragement even though he said I did. I was only trying to please him over the panto, that didn't mean I wanted him all over me. Just shows how stupid I am, doesn't it?'

'You are not stupid. Far from it. How did you get away in the end?'

'I kneed him in the groin.'

Prue laughed. 'Oh, dear, I bet that made his eyes water.'

'It made him let go of me and I ran. I'm always making a mess of things. First Chris then James. Will it always be like that?'

'No, of course not. You are still very young. There's plenty of time to meet Mr Right.'

'Perhaps I have and I turned him down.'

'Oh. And you regret that?'

'I don't know. I couldn't begin to think of anything like that when I was still grieving for Ma and Pa and the kids, but I want to stay friends with him. I've written to him, but he hasn't replied.'

'There could be any number of reasons for that. Do you know where he is?'

'No, in training somewhere, I think. I sent a letter to his mother to forward. I think he's done with me.'

'If he has, he's a fool. There's plenty more fish in the sea.'

They turned into the British Restaurant which served cheap but nourishing food and were soon eating chicken and chips.

'I was thinking I might like to go on the stage after the war,' Sheila said. 'I loved doing the panto.'

'Going on the stage is a precarious sort of life as a profession.'

'So what if it is? I've no one to please but myself.'

No one, Prue mused. What must it be like to have no one? She didn't count Mrs Tranter, who was a cold fish if ever there was one, and would deride whatever Sheila tried to do. It would be interesting to know what had made her like that. Was it simply jealousy? 'Then good luck to you,' she said. 'I'll come to all your first nights.'

The rest of the evening was spent imagining Sheila as a star with her name in lights and stage door johnnies queuing up to take her out to supper. Prue said nothing of her own weekend; it was not something she wanted to share with anyone, not even Sheila. It was late when they returned to Victoria Villa and Constance had already gone to bed. They crept up the stairs giggling.

Chapter Seven

Work went on apace at Bletchley Park. More huts were built, more bombe machines were installed, more people arrived and some left, including James Barry who was being transferred. He stayed to stage the revue and afterwards there was a party to send him on his way. Sheila had considered withdrawing from the cast but Prue persuaded her to keep going. 'If you want to be a professional you are going to have to deal with men like him,' she said. 'Just pretend it never happened.'

He must have wanted to do that himself, or perhaps he realised that without Sheila the revue wouldn't be half the success it was because they managed to work together and the performance was received warmly. She even went to his party and shook his hand afterwards as he went round everyone, kissing some of them. He didn't kiss her.

Although the news was heavily vetted, it was impossible to keep the bad news from the public. Ships were still being sunk, Greece and Yugoslavia had been lost, Crete invaded, Malta under siege and nothing going the Allied way in North Africa where

German troops, under General Rommel, had come to the aid of the Italians and were pounding Tobruk, which had only a couple of months before been taken by British and Australian troops. Prue was kept busy translating the German army and air force traffic, which didn't make light reading. She knew that the Russians and Germans had signed a pact of mutual help. In return for industrial raw materials to make weapons, and grain from the Ukraine, the Russians would receive machinery for their factories. But she also knew that Hitler was planning to invade Russia. Stalin would surely not have signed that agreement if he had known of that. Had no one told him? Naturally she said nothing to anyone; her job was not to reason why.

It was June before she had leave and was able to go home. To her surprise and delight, she found her brother, also on leave. He looked extremely fit, heavier than he used to be and more mature, but it suited him.

But she didn't think her mother looked well at all. She was thinner, her complexion pale and everything seemed an effort, although she tried not to let it show. 'Go and unpack and change,' she told her. 'Dinner won't be long.'

Prue made her way up to the room which had been hers since childhood. Nothing had changed; the furniture was exactly as it had always been, her dolls and teddy bear still sat in a row along a shelf. Her books still filled other shelves and a tennis racket and hockey stick were still propped in a corner. She smiled to herself as she opened her wardrobe door to select something to wear for dinner. Clothing had been rationed and what there was was subject to so much restriction; it was good to wear something which didn't have the utility mark sewn into it. She chose a blue silk dress, the colour of a summer sky, with a very full skirt and a nipped-in waist. The gong sounded for dinner as she was going downstairs.

'It's good to have everyone together again,' Marcus said, as all four sat down to eat. 'How have things been with you both?'

He knew a little about Prue's job and the need for secrecy, so he didn't ask her about that. But she told him about the Easter revue in which her friend, Sheila, starred. 'It was a roaring success,' she said. 'Sheila is hoping to go on the stage after the war. She's saving up all her money to have proper singing lessons. She's got a voice like an angel. I think singing helps her to get over what happened to her family, but she won't give up the idea that her brother is still alive. She thinks she saw him on a newsreel at the beginning of the year. If he is alive, it would be wonderful if they could be reunited. I wish I could help, but I don't know how to. You haven't got any ideas, have you, Papa?'

'Short of putting an ad in the newspapers, I haven't. She could try the film people, I suppose. I expect they keep copies of newsreels in archives.'

'This little waif seems to have tickled your fancy,' Gilbert said.

'She's not a little waif, Gillie. She is quite tall and has a gorgeous figure. And she's strong, mentally as well as physically. I don't know that I would have coped half as well as she has. You'd know that if you met her.'

'I can't wait,' he said, laughing.

'Next time we all have leave together I'll arrange it.'

'Don't know when that will be. I might have to go abroad.'

'Abroad? Where? When?' his mother demanded.

'I don't know yet. I'll tell you when I do.' Unwilling to elaborate, he turned to his father. 'Enough of me. What's been happening here in Longfordham?'

'Not a great deal. The Home Guard and the estate keep me busy and the airfield is nearly finished. I hope when the war is over, they put it back to what it was. All that concrete is an eyesore. Your mother is kept busy with the Women's Institute and the WVS.'

'I am the evacuee co-ordinator,' Chloe said. 'I'm always having to settle disputes or chase parents who haven't sent the money for the children's keep. Ronald's mother is particularly bad at that, though Mrs Potts doesn't seem to mind. I think she is growing rather fond of the boy and perhaps that's not a good thing. She will have to part with him eventually.'

'I hope it is not all too much for you,' Prue said, turning to her mother. 'You look tired.'

'We are all tired,' she said. 'Tired of this dreadful war. There seems no end to it and all we hear is bad news. How is anyone ever going to stop it?'

'We will, Mama,' Gilbert said. 'We will.'

'The servants are all gone except Cook, a couple of maids and Hedges, who is too old to be called up,' she went on as if he had not spoken. 'And what with rationing and one thing and another, it's a daily struggle to maintain standards. The house is beginning to look quite shabby. And people aren't honest any more.'

'What do you mean, not honest?' Prue asked, wondering if her mother was complaining she hadn't been told what she did at Bletchley. She felt constrained from joining in any discussion or speculation about the conduct of the war because she was afraid she might inadvertently let slip something of the knowledge she had acquired in her job. She wondered if her mother had noticed it.

'We've had things stolen,' her father put in. 'Oh, not valuables from the house, but eggs, vegetables, flowers, bags of chicken feed and garden implements. Someone's going round at night taking them. It's worrying your mother because she thinks whoever it is will come into the house next.'

'Do you think it's just someone who's hungry?' Prue asked.

'They are taking an awful lot if it is. It's not only us but others have had things go missing. We are going to set up a watch tonight and catch whoever it is red-handed. It will give the Home Guard something useful to do.'

'I'll stand watch with you,' Gilbert said.

It was about ten that evening when someone was spotted darting about in the woods. Gilbert and a handful of Home Guard gave chase, but in the dark they lost whoever it was.

'He must have realised he was walking into a trap and turned tail,' Gilbert said to Prue after they had given up and returned to the house. 'He led us a merry dance. I think he got out onto the railway line. There's a hole in the fence.'

'I'll get it mended tomorrow and we'll watch there tomorrow night,' their father said. 'Might as well turn in now.'

Gilbert went to bed and slept like a log. He did not hear the bombers going over on their way to Germany, though Prue did and she prayed for their crews, especially Tim. Was he still on ops, still dropping bombs on German cities? She felt sure he would never ask to be relieved of his duties. He would view that as failing everyone, his crew, his country, himself most of all.

After breakfast next morning, Prue and Gilbert went riding on the heath. It had always been their favourite place to ride, but now half of it was covered with concrete and ugly buildings although there were still places where the old heath survived, where the grass was rough and gorse bushes bloomed all year round. As she clicked her tongue and urged the horse forward over the railway crossing, she wondered about the wild creatures that had called the heath home, the hares and rabbits and skylarks. The war was affecting animals too.

'I'm worried about Mama,' she said, after they had had a gallop and were walking their horses. 'She doesn't look well.'

'The war is having that effect on all of us, don't you think?'

'Not you. You look fit as a fiddle.'

'That's because I am. You don't look so bad yourself, blooming in fact. New boyfriend is it? Or are you being faithful to old Tim?'

'He's not old, only a year older than me.' She paused. 'I'm worried he's cracking up. When I last saw him, he was really down because of bombing German cities. He was concerned that there were innocent people being killed . . .'

'Innocent people are being killed in this country too.'

'So I pointed out to him, but it didn't seem to help.'

'The bomber boys are having a rough time of it. Terrible casualties.'

'So he said. What about you?'

'I'm not cracking up if that's what you mean.'

'No, I meant your love life.'

'That would be telling.'

'Then tell.'

'Her name is Esme and she's very pretty and very tiny. Comes up to here.' He put his hand just below his chin. 'She's in the ATS.'

'When am I going to meet her?'

He shrugged. 'Who knows?'

'You said you might be going abroad.'

'Yes.'

'Where?'

'Can't tell you.'

'Yes you can. I won't tell a soul. Knowing you, I bet it's somewhere where there's some action.'

'If you must know, it might be France.'

'Gillie!' she exclaimed. 'That's what the parachuting is all about. Does Papa know?'

'Yes, but don't you dare tell Mama.'

'I won't.'

'I've told you my secret, what about yours?'

'Secret, what secret? All open and above board, that's me.' She paused. 'Come on, let's go back. It's nearly lunchtime and I'm starving.'

Mr Potts was standing by the railway gates when they approached. He tipped his cap to them. 'Good afternoon, my lord, my lady. You haven't seen that pesky evacuee of mine, have you?'

'No, sorry,' Prue said. 'What's he been up to now?'

The man sighed. 'I wish I knew. He's never around when he's wanted. Miss Green says he's been playing truant again and when he is in school he seems half asleep.'

'Oh, dear, I wish I could help you, but we didn't see anyone except the men working on the airfield, did we, Gillie?'

'No, 'fraid not. I expect he'll turn up.'

'He'll get my hand on his britches when he does.' He opened the gates for them and they rode across the lines and made their way home.

'Do you think the evacuee could be our secret thief?' Gilbert queried.

'A boy of twelve?'

'Why not? Children grow up fast nowadays.'

'Mama told me she caught the young scamp wandering in the grounds,' Prue said. 'She said he's a cheeky beggar, but I think she rather likes him. He's not used to the freedom of the countryside and I think he's making the most of it. You can't really blame him. It doesn't make him a thief.'

'Perhaps not, but he'll bear watching.'

'Is this all you've got?' Aggie Barlow surveyed the contents of the sack that Ronnie had dumped on the kitchen table. There were six eggs, some carrots and parsnips, a couple of small onions, a pound or two of potatoes, some stored apples with wrinkled skins, a dead chicken and a bottle of wine.

'That's all there was. It's too early in the year for peas and beans and things like that. I had to dig the spuds out of a clamp.' He looked round at the kitchen of the tiny ground floor which had been his home before going to Longfordham. He had never realised how filthy it was. The oilcloth on the table was so badly stained it was difficult to make out the pattern on it. There were unwashed plates and glasses in the sink, the cooker was caked with grease and he didn't think the floor had seen a mop for a year. Until he had learnt about cleanliness from Auntie Jean, he hadn't noticed how bad it was. Now it disgusted him.

'A clamp?' She was dressed in a black skirt whose hem had come undone, an off-white blouse and a black cardigan with holes in the elbows. Her hair was in steel curlers and covered with a scarf. It was what she wore in the house. When she went out, she changed into a smart frock, silk stockings which had been nicked from a bombed-out house in the west end, her best shoes, a tweed jacket and a felt hat with a long feather. Her face would be made up with red lipstick and dark eye make-up and her hair would be waved. Ronnie knew perfectly well what she was up to, but he dreaded the day his dad came home and caught her at it.

'It's a big heap of spuds covered in straw and earth,' he explained. 'It's supposed to stop them freezin' and rottin'. The onions are hung up in a shed on a string. The carrots and the parsnips I had to dig out o' the ground. It's bloody risky. I nearly got caught the other night. A whole platoon of Home Guard was chasing me.'

'Your pa would clip your ear if he was 'ere.'

'Well, 'e ain't, is 'e?' Ronnie knew very well his father would not punish him for thieving, but for failing to deliver. But at least he hadn't been caught, which was more than his dad could say. It looked as though his errant father would spend the war in Pentonville.

'No, more's the pity. 'E'd 'ave us in clover if 'e was, what with all the bombing makin' it easy. You could come back, you know. You don't have to stay in the country.'

'I like it there.' The prospect of coming home did not appeal to him at all. 'I could bring you flowers, there's lots growing in the gardens at the hall. They wouldn't be missed.'

'OK.'

Ronnie left her sorting through what he had brought. She'd have it all down at Queen's Market in the shake of a lamb's tail. He wanted to help her, but she was never satisfied. It was a good thing he already had some stuff stashed away in his special hiding place. He had caught a glimpse of the men digging in the wood before that man died and his curiosity had led him to discover the entrance, even though the Home Guard had concreted the trapdoor in, rolled a heavy boulder over it and stuck dead leaves and bracken all round it. They thought they had sealed it and no one would find it. More fool them! The boulder had been too heavy to lift but he had managed to hitch it away, inch by inch, and dug out the cement round the trapdoor. Once he had broken it open it made a super hiding place. The ladder had been removed when the bunker was sealed off, but he had made a new one with some rough pieces of wood and could go in and out at will. He didn't put the boulder back, it was too heavy to keep moving, but if he covered the trapdoor with leaves and bracken, anyone who knew about it would imagine the boulder was still over the entrance. So long as the gamekeeper didn't catch sight of him coming and going, it couldn't be safer. He had dived into it the other night and pulled the trapdoor back in place, laughing softly to himself when he heard his pursuers pass over the top of him.

Liverpool Street Station was crowded with people getting on and off trains. It was easy to slip past and get on a train. If someone saw him they'd think he was with a grown-up. If he was questioned, all he had to do was pipe his eye and say his Ma had got on the train while he was going for a pee and he had to join her. Usually, they took him along the platform and asked him to point his mother out to them. He'd point and say, 'There she is!' and rush to get on the train to join the unsuspecting woman just as it drew out. Getting off at Longfordham could be tricky, but he knew if he walked down the line a little way he would come to the crossing by the heath. He didn't have to go through the booking hall.

The trouble was, he was getting fed up with it all. He didn't get enough sleep and the village was so small everyone knew what everyone else was doing and he couldn't keep ducking school. Besides, it would be easier to sell the stuff to the men building the airfield. He could send the money to his mother. The difficulty with that was that he didn't write very well and addressing an envelope might be a problem. And supposing someone nicked the money before it got to his mother? He sighed as he locked himself in the toilet on the train. The ticket collector was coming along the corridor. Life was full of problems.

Mr Potts was waiting for him when he arrived. He grabbed him by his collar. 'Where the devil have you been? We've got the whole village out searching for you. His lordship wants a word with you.'

'What for? I ain't done nothin'.'

'We'll see about that. Come along with me.'

He was taken to a side door of the hall and they were conducted by a servant into a carpeted corridor with doors all along it. There were huge pictures on the walls in gilt frames and vases of flowers on little tables. They stopped in front of one door, the servant knocked and opened it. 'Mr Potts and the evacuee, my lord.'

Ronnie found himself in a large sitting room containing two sofas, half a dozen armchairs, little tables on which stood china ornaments and photographs in silver frames. There were display cabinets full of interesting things and more pictures on the walls. Ronnie stared about him in awe, weighing up how much he could get for some of the ornaments if he could lay his hands on them. Standing by the fireplace, surveying him beneath beetling brows, was the Earl.

'Ah, Potts,' he said. 'You found him then?'

Potts had pulled off his uniform cap and was holding it in front of him with both hands 'Yes, my lord.'

His lordship turned to Ronnie. 'Where have you been hiding today, young man?'

'I ain't bin 'idin'. I went home to see me mum.'

'To London?' he queried. 'How did you get there?'

'On a train.'

'How did you pay for your ticket?'

'Ma sent me the money.'

'I see. And how is your mother?'

'OK.'

'You were seen getting on the train with a sack.'

'So what if I was?'

'What was in it?'

'What you want to know that for?'

'I think it contained vegetables and eggs. I am right, aren't I?'

'I bought them fair and square.'

'Who sold them to you?'

'A man. 'E said 'e'd got more'n he needed. Don' know 'is name so it ain't no good to ask me.'

The Earl smiled. 'Do you know the story of Pinocchio?'

'It were on at the flicks a few weeks back. I saw it at the fleapit in Royston.'

'Then you will know that every time he told a lie, his nose grew longer, until it was so long it was an embarrassment. Do you want that to happen to you?'

'Don't be daft, tha's a fairy story.' Ronnie put a hand to his nose just to make sure it was its usual size.

Mr Potts clipped him round the ear with his cap. 'Don't you be disrespectful to his lordship.'

'You know, if you had asked if you could have something to take home to your mother, I would have given them to you,' his lordship said. 'As it is, I shall have to devise a punishment.'

'You ain't never goin' to 'and me over to the constable, are yer?'

'I ought to, but it would be a shame to have a criminal record, don't you think? That lasts you all your life.'

Ronnie knew that perfectly well; his father had one as long as his arm. 'You can't prove nothin'.'

'Oh, I think we can. The night before last, you were in my woods and being chased by several of my men . . .'

'Not me. I was in me bed.'

'That you weren't,' Mr Potts said. 'Your bed weren't slept in. You were out all night. I heard you come in just as I was getting up.'

'I stayed with a pal.' He was beginning to panic, but one thing he was determined on and that was keeping his hide-out secret. If they found what he had been hiding there, then he really would be in the soup.

'Ronald,' his lordship said patiently. 'We have spent the day searching for you and in the course of that, spoken to every one of your school friends and some who denied they were your friends. None had seen you since yesterday afternoon, when you went off by yourself. This morning you were seen carrying a sack on the train.' He paused while Ronnie squirmed. 'Lying only makes things worse, you know. Come clean and I'll be lenient.'

Ronnie didn't know what lenient meant but it was obviously better than being handed over to the constable. 'So I took a few spuds and eggs to take home to me ma, so what?'

'Do you know what a magistrate is?'

'He's a kind o' judge, only there ain't no jury.'

'Right. I am a magistrate and I can dole out punishments. My punishment for you is that you attend school every day without fail, and you help my gardener on Saturdays. And I want you to promise never to steal again. Will you do that?'

'OK.'

'Off you go then. Mrs Potts will have your supper ready.'

Ronnie left with Mr Potts, apparently contrite. He'd got off lightly and he knew it. He'd had nothing to eat all day and his belly was rumbling.

It was just as well he did not hear Marcus laughing. How did the boy come to know what a magistrate was?

It was Nanny Bright who had told Gillie and Prue she had seen Mr Potts' evacuee boarding the train carrying what looked like a heavy sack. They had gone to visit her as they always did when they were home and had mentioned the search that was going on for the boy. 'I'm fairly sure he didn't buy a ticket,' she had said. 'He came onto the platform from the line. One of these days he'll be hit by a train if he keeps doing that.'

'I talked to my father about Charlie,' Prue told Sheila the day after she returned from leave. She and Sheila had come off the afternoon shift together and were cycling home. 'He suggested writing to Pathé News to see if they can tell you anything. What do you think?'

'I've often wondered about that, but I didn't think it would do any good.'

'You'll never know if you don't try. You would need to describe the scene as carefully as you can, so they can identify it.'

'Then what?'

'It depends what they say. They might have a still photo they can send, then you would be able to look at it more closely and make up your mind if it really is your brother.'

'Do you think they'd do that?'

'Don't see why not. I don't suppose it's the first time they've been asked something like that. I'll help you write the letter if you like, two heads are better than one.'

'OK, but not a word to Aunt Constance.'

'As if I would.'

The letter was written after dinner that evening, on notepaper headed with the Earl of Winterton's crest. 'It might carry a bit of weight,' Prue said, putting a pad of it onto the table in her bedroom and unscrewing the top of her fountain pen. 'Here, use this.'

'No, you do it. Your handwriting is so lovely and neat and I don't want to spoil your pen.'

'If that's what you want.'

'Yes. Your signature and the headed paper is sure to make someone sit up and take notice.'

'OK.' She took a seat at the table. 'I want the date you saw the film and an exact description of the scene so it can be identified.'

'It was the 28th of December, the day after the big blitz. The King and Queen were talking to a woman who had been bombed out. There was the rubble of a bombed house behind them, and there were people standing round, being kept in order by a policeman; they were all smiling. Can't think of anything else.'

'Where was your brother?'

'He must have been standing on some of the ruins, that's why I noticed him; he stood out from the others.'

'What was he wearing?'

'I only saw the top half of him. Nothing out of the ordinary. A jacket and a cap I think.'

Prue began to write, a whole page of it, while Sheila went to stand looking out of the window. There were people walking about, a few bicycles and a van on the tree-lined road. She wondered what she and Charlie would do if they were reunited. It would depend on what he had been doing since they parted. She found it difficult to envisage him ever coming to live at Victoria Villa.

'There, how's that?' Prue's voice interrupted her thoughts.

She turned to take the sheet of paper. 'Heavens, you've got the story of my life here.'

'I needed to gain sympathy for you. Will it do?'

'Yes, thank you.'

Prue signed it, found an envelope, which she addressed to British Pathé at Elstree Studios, and stuck a stamp on it. 'Let's go and post it, then we can have a drink on the way back.'

'I wonder if we'll get a reply,' Sheila said later when they were sitting in the lounge bar of the Shoulder of Mutton, sipping gin and tonic. Sheila preferred orange with her gin but they didn't have any. 'They might just throw it in the wastepaper basket.'

'True, but it was worth a try, don't you think?'

'Yes, but it's got me all fidgety. I keep wondering and thinking . . .'

'Best thing to do is forget it, then if you do hear from them it will be a pleasant surprise.'

* * *

Sheila went on her next leave as much in the dark about Charlie as ever. As usual she made for the Bennetts'. The baby was still there. Efforts to find his family had failed and Bob and June were hoping to adopt him. He was plump and happy and thoroughly spoilt. Sheila sat cuddling him while bringing June up to date on what had been happening in her life and telling them about the letter to Pathé. 'They haven't replied,' she said.

'Perhaps they couldn't find the bit of film you were talking about.'

'Perhaps. Anyway, I'm going to spend my leave wandering about here. I can't believe he would stray far from home, even though there's no home there any more.'

'The site has been cleared, but there won't be any rebuilding until after the war. It's dreadful seeing these great gaps in rows of houses and wondering what happened to the people who used to live there. We have been so lucky, only a few broken windows.'

Since the Germans had invaded Russia, they had been kept busy on their eastern front and the bombing of Britain had virtually stopped and, apart from an occasional sharp reminder from Hitler that he had not forgotten them, Londoners were breathing easily and sleeping in their beds again. The aeroplanes that flew overhead now were British bombers and their fighter escorts.

'I'll go and see Janet too. She's living above the shop now. We'll probably have a night out somewhere.' She handed Noel back to June who put him in his high chair in order to give him his dinner. When Bob came in, the three adults had theirs and afterwards Sheila went to visit Janet.

Her friend had moved into the flat above the shop and made it very comfortable. 'It's where Bert comes when he's on leave,' she said. 'But there won't be any of that for a bit. He's in North

Africa and complaining about the heat and the sand getting into everything.'

'It's warm enough here at the moment.'

'Yes. This flat is lovely in the winter, the heat comes up from the shop, but in summer it's like an oven even with all the windows open.'

'D'you want to go to the pictures tonight?'

'OK. I'll meet you outside. It won't be the same without the boys though, will it?'

'No.'

'Have you heard from Chris?'

'We've drifted apart somehow.'

'Pity that. I thought he was really gone on you.'

'No, well, people change.'

On the way back to the Bennetts', she called on Mrs Jarrett. Her welcome was hardly cordial and she wasn't invited over the threshold. 'What are you doing here, Sheila Phipps?' the lady demanded. There was a cigarette dangling from the corner of her mouth and steel curlers in her dark hair. She was wearing a stained apron and felt slippers.

'I'm on holiday and came to see how you are and if you've heard from Chris.'

'Of course I hear from Chris.' She took the cigarette from her mouth and tapped the ash off it. Her fingers were stained brown. 'Did you think he wouldn't write to his own mother?'

'Is he all right?'

'He's at sea, as you very well know. Last time I heard he was OK but none the better for the way you treated him. Wicked that was. He came home in a foul temper and it took ages before he'd tell me what was wrong. Money wasted it was. Rings don't come cheap.'

'I'm sorry, Mrs Jarrett, but I couldn't pretend to feelings I didn't have. I thought it better to be honest with him. I'm still trying to get over my family going like that.' She gulped. 'That doesn't mean I didn't want to stay friends with him, and I'm sorry if he took it the wrong way.'

'Wrong way! What other way was there to take it? You trampled on his feelings without a care in the world and him on those Atlantic convoys and likely to be blown to bits at any minute.'

'I did care and I didn't know where he was.'

'No? Well it's no business of yours now, is it?'

'No, I suppose not. I'm sorry I troubled you.' She turned to leave, then hesitated. 'You did pass my letters on to him, didn't you?'

'Course I did. If he chooses not to answer, that's his affair.'

Dejectedly, she left. It wasn't that she had changed her mind about Chris; her reasons for turning him down were as valid as ever, it was because it had left such rancour behind.

Chapter Eight

'Tim, are we anywhere near the target?' Graham's voice came to him over the intercom. 'I can't see a thing through this cloud.'

'Two minutes to go, Skip.'

'Good. Let's get down to it. I want to be getting home and warm.'

'Hear. Hear,' came from Ken in the tail. 'I can't feel my feet.' Intense cold was one of the worst parts of flying. No matter how many layers of clothes you wore, how many pairs of gloves and socks, your hands and feet froze.

The weatherman had told them there would be cloud over England but the skies over the target would be clear, but in fact the opposite had been true. The only advantage was that no enemy fighters had come up to harass them. That hadn't stopped the anti-aircraft guns which were taking pot shots at them as they descended towards the target. There were flashes of bright light and puffs of smoke all about them and once a rattle against the fuselage which told them at least one of the shells had struck home.

'Anyone hurt?' Graham asked.

'No, Skip,' came from four voices, one after the other.

One of the Wellingtons on their port side suddenly exploded, lighting up the sky in a blinding flash and littering the air with burning debris which spiralled slowly downwards. No one made any comment, they were too busy praying they wouldn't be next. With a full load of bombs on board, they had no chance of survival, any more than their colleagues had. They would mourn the men who had been lost when they were safely back themselves.

'I saw the glow of fires a minute ago,' Gerry, the nose gunner-cum-observer, put in, when the last flickering flame of the dying bomber had faded and they were in the dark again, except for the searchlights.

'That doesn't mean it's the target,' Tim said. 'If some silly fool has dropped his bombs on the wrong place, we don't have to follow suit.'

Below them Hamburg, a city with genuine industrial targets, also housed women and children and old men. He could not hit one without the other. On the other hand, he reminded himself, only the month before London had suffered its worst Blitz since the war started, worse even than the one in September the previous year, worse than the one just after Christmas which had set the city alight. And there was Coventry, Portsmouth and Norwich and all the other places that had suffered from German bombs. Why did he feel no urge for vengeance? Instead he felt sick and decidedly dizzy, almost as if he were drunk, but all he had had to drink on the long, cold flight was a flask of coffee.

'Tim.' Graham's voice came over the intercom again, a little impatient this time.

'Right,' he said, leaving his seat to take up his position on the floor with his eye to the bomb sight. 'Start the run in.'

Tim usually guided this with directions such as, 'Left a little, right a little, hold it there', but tonight all he said was 'Steady as she goes', and then, 'Bombs gone'. The aircraft bucked upwards as the weight of bombs left it.

'Thank God for that,' Graham said, peeling away and gaining height rapidly. 'Set course for home.'

Tim returned to his seat and his charts.

The flak over the coast had been bad on the outward journey. Now the enemy knew where they were, it was worse. Tim, sitting with his maps, sextant and compass on the board in front of him, found himself shaking. He wanted to be back at base, to be safely on the ground again, but at the same time he dreaded the debriefing. How far off the target had they been? If only there was some way to improve accuracy, he wouldn't feel so bad about what he was doing.

Graham was busy flying the Wellington and trying to avoid being shot down, but the other four, David, the radio operator, Gerry, who had pointed out the previous fires, and the two other gunners, Sid and Ken, while remaining alert for enemy fighters, relieved of immediate pressure were chatting and joking and talking about having a pint in the Jolly Brewers that evening. Tim didn't join in; it was just too much of an effort. He managed to give Graham navigational directions in a croak, but that was all.

'North Sea,' Gerry said. The danger was still not over; the flak might be behind them, but there was always the chance of being spotted by enemy fighters. The nearer they came to safety, the more their tension mounted. Once safely back it would be another operation to notch up towards the thirty they needed before being taken off for a rest.

They landed back at Wyton an hour later and tumbled

thankfully out onto the runway. 'What's up, Tim?' Graham asked him as they walked towards the airfield buildings, leaving the ground crew to take care of the Wellington. 'You've been like a bear with a sore head all night.'

'Nothing's up. I'm tired, that's all. Feel a bit giddy, as matter of fact.'

'Too tired to do your job properly,' Gerry put in. 'You overshot the target by miles. Waste of bombs, that was.'

'No, I didn't.'

'I think you did, Tim,' Graham said quietly. 'I'm afraid I'm going to have to say so at debriefing.'

'That's up to you.' He really didn't care any more. He could hardly walk straight and it seemed as if the ground was heaving in front of him. He stumbled and would have fallen if Graham hadn't grabbed his arm. 'You need to see the M.O., old chap.'

Prue learnt Tim was in hospital after Tim's mother had telephoned the Countess, who had passed on the news to Prue in a letter. Worried as Prue was, she could not get away immediately and it was a week before she had a whole day off and could visit him. And then she was told by the ward sister she could not see him. He had expressly said he did not want visitors.

'What exactly is the matter with him?' Prue demanded.

'I'm afraid I can't say. I am sorry you have had a wasted journey, Miss . . .'

'Le Strange.' Prue supplied her name. 'Can I write to him?'

'Of course.'

'Tell him I was here, will you, please? Give him my love.'

The nurse watched her turn and leave. It was a pity she had to send the girl away, she might have been able to cheer the young man up. She walked along the ward to Tim's bed. He was lying flat on his back, staring at the ceiling. 'You had a visitor, Flight Lieutenant, a Miss Le Strange. I sent her away. That was what you wanted, wasn't it?'

'Yes,' he said, without turning his head. 'And she's not Miss, she's Lady Prudence Le Strange, daughter of the Earl of Winterton.'

'She's very pretty.'

'I know that.'

'Why wouldn't you see her?'

'That's my business.'

'Sorry I spoke.'

'Sorry, Sister. Leave me, will you?'

He dare not turn his head because it brought on the awful nausea, but he knew she had gone from the crackle of her starched apron. He was being looked after and treated like a hero when he was nothing of the sort. Why that raid over Hamburg should be any worse than those that had gone before he did not know, but it had not been the intense cold that had made him freeze, it was the conviction that what he was doing was wrong. His conscience was doing battle with his patriotism and his loyalty to the rest of the crew and he was in a mess.

His salvation had come in the form of a genuinely acceptable complaint. Labyrinthitis, a problem with the inner ear which affected his sense of balance, was common among air crews. It may have been caused by the rarefied atmosphere of the altitude in spite of oxygen masks, or it might have been the swaying and bucking of the aeroplane, which was disorientating, but it was certainly exacerbated by stress. Those suffering from it were immediately taken off active service. What would happen when he was cured, he did not know. More of the same? His crew had been given a temporary navigator and he knew any disruption of an established crew that worked well together was a bad omen. Nearly all aircrew were superstitious and something like that made them vulnerable. He felt he had let them down badly. And Prue.

The last time he had seen her he had behaved stupidly, telling her what he should have kept to himself, and he felt embarrassed and ashamed. And then to fall asleep on her bed! What she must have thought of him, he hated to think. His plans for a romantic night had ended in farce. He couldn't face her the following morning and had crept away long before dawn and walked back to Wyton. The letters she had written to him since were full of things she and her friends had done, the concert parties, the films they had seen, the story of the thieving evacuee, anything and everything except any reference to their last meeting. Was she as embarrassed about it as he was? If she saw him now, she would pity him and pity he could not abide. Better to end their romance here and now.

Prue could not understand the letter from Tim. The words were plain enough, but the reason behind them was unfathomable. His conscience had been troubling him, he had written, and it was unfair to her to go on seeing her when nothing could come of it. It would be kinder all round if they had no more contact and this would be his last letter to her. He wished her the very best of luck for her future and sincerely hoped she would find happiness with someone else.

She read it over and over again, then wrote and said she didn't understand. What had she done wrong? He did not reply. After three weeks of watching for a letter, she realised he had been as good as his word.

'Men!' she said to Sheila one afternoon as they were cycling home from work after coming off the early shift. 'You can't trust them an inch.'

'Have you quarrelled with Tim?'

'No, we haven't quarrelled. He simply said he didn't want to see me or write to me again. I can't believe that's all there is to it.'

'How much does it matter to you?'

'Not at all,' she said airily. 'He's not the only fish in the sea. I've had offers.'

'Oh, and who might that be?'

'If you must know Hugh Wentworth has been asking me to go out with him for ages. He works in Hut Eight.'

'I know, I take post to him. He's a nice man, but it seems to me that going out with someone on the rebound is hardly fair.'

'All right, clever clogs, what would you do if you were me?'

'I can't tell you what to do. Look into your heart, it's what's there that counts.'

'Oh, Sheila, you're a tonic, you really are. So naïve one minute, so worldly-wise the next.'

'Stuff!'

They were laughing when they dismounted and wheeled their bicycles round the side of the house to the back shed. 'What are we going to do this evening?' Prue queried, as they made their way into the house by the kitchen door.

'Whatever you like.'

They passed through the kitchen and spoke to Constance who was cooking the evening meal, before going upstairs to their rooms.

'Let's go to the pictures. Leslie Howard's in *Pimpernel Smith*. I've heard it's good.'

In the film Leslie Howard updated his role in the Scarlet Pimpernel to outwit the Nazis and rescue the inmates from concentration camps. It took Prue's mind off Tim for a little while, but concentrated it on her brother. Had he gone to France? It would be a highly secret operation if he had and she was unlikely to hear anything of it before the war finished.

The ground came up more quickly than expected and Gilbert landed heavily which for a moment winded him, but he was safely down and no bones broken. He knew his first priority was to leave the field and bury his parachute before Jerry turned up. He sat up, thumped the disc on his chest to unclip the parachute and began rolling it up, hoping as he did so that the men running across the field towards him were friendly. Not far away Esme was busy with her 'chute and, tangled in a bush a little further off, was the canister containing supplies, including Esme's wireless set, which had been dropped separately.

Two men, dressed in dark clothes, were busy putting out the flares which had guided the Whitley into the dropping zone, two more were untangling the canister from the parachute. He stood up as another approached him. 'Boris?'

'*Oui*.' Gilbert had lived with that code name for weeks until it had become second nature to answer to it. He looked round to find Esme beside him. 'This is Arlene.'

'*Bon*,' the man said. 'I am Jean. Leave the parachutes to the others and come with me. We must be quick.'

They followed their guide across the field, through a patch of woodland and out onto a country road where a small van waited for them. Jean hefted the canister in the back, motioned to Gilbert and Esme to climb in and then joined the driver in the front.

'That jump in the dark was scary,' Esme said as they moved off. 'I couldn't see the ground at all.'

Esmeralda Favelle, code name Arlene, was five foot nothing, but her slight frame hid a great deal of courage and determination and a quick wit. She was going to need all those in the weeks to come. As he was. If the powers-that-be had known how he felt about her, they would certainly not have allowed them to work together on the grounds that emotions might interfere with efficiency and, in a tight corner, he might put them both and the whole operation at risk. But he wanted to protect her and he couldn't do that if they were in different sectors which were forbidden to communicate with each other. He had never told Esme how he felt: it was safer for her not to know. She laughingly called him her partner in crime.

They had met during their early training when they were often paired and he found himself admiring her grit and determination. In one so small, it amazed him. What he had no idea of was what her life had been before she came to SOE. Her cover story was all he was required to know, just as it was all she knew of him. Each knew the other's real name but that was all. Could love blossom under such circumstances?

Their parachute training had consisted of practice in the hangar from a fan, a descent from a tethered balloon, one daylight drop from an aircraft and one in the dark. That had been after they had gone through rigorous physical training, learning how to kill silently, escape and evade and how to stand up to interrogation if caught, all conducted in French and German, all designed to test their physical and mental fitness to the limit.

The Special Operations Executive had been formed in July the previous year. Their brief was to work behind enemy lines, recruiting resistance workers and organising them to be ready to assist the Allies when they invaded, which they surely would. There was already a network of *resistants* in the country who had begun simply as publishers of newspapers and pamphlets to keep the spirit of unconquered France alive, but that had escalated into acts of sabotage, though not everyone approved. Some actively co-operated with the invaders on the grounds that the Allies could not possibly win the war and they would rather be on the winning side. Others were simply compliant; it was easier that way.

There had recently been a concerted round-up by the Gestapo and the *Brigade Speciales* of the Vichy police, which had left the *resistant* ranks decimated. London had no idea how this had worked on their morale. Those who were left did not have enough explosives and money to carry on the fight to any great degree. His task was to find out what they could do and what they needed. Esme's was to operate a wireless set to send and receive messages from London. Once the circuit was in place, they would be sent arms and ammunition, explosives and anything else they might need. What happened after that was in the lap of the gods.

He had told his mother he was going into the parachute regiment and that had been his original intention, but when the call came for French-speaking volunteers, he had put his name forward. Goodness knew what she would make of what he was doing now, but as he was not allowed to tell her, she was still in ignorance. HQ had a series of postcards and letters from him which they would post to her at intervals while they knew he was still alive. Whether she would be deceived by that, he did not know. His whole life from now into the foreseeable future would be one of deception. He was reminded of his mother saying the war was making liars of everyone. She was probably thanking God that he had not gone out to Singapore with the rest of his battalion. He would either be dead or a Japanese prisoner of war by now.

The van turned off the road onto what must have been a rutted cart track, judging by the jolting. Five minutes later it stopped. They heard Jean get out and come round to let them out. The van door was flung open and Jean held out his hand to help Esme down. 'Welcome to Chez Duport, *mes amis*.'

They found themselves in a farmyard facing a building which they took to be a farmhouse. Its blackout was complete and they could only see its dark shape and chimneys silhouetted against the night sky. As they picked their way carefully towards it, the door was opened and a large woman in a black dress was outlined in the light which flooded out into the yard. 'So you are here. I heard the aeroplane. Come in, come in.' She stood aside to let them enter. 'You are welcome.'

'My mother,' Jean said.

They shook hands with her and in no time at all they were seated at a table in the kitchen along with Jean and three other men. Jean introduced them as Anton, Philippe and Gustave. Anton was Jean's younger brother, the other two were neighbours. They were all dressed in rough working clothes, stalwart men with unshaven chins. 'We have already sabotaged some trains,' Jean said, as his mother bustled about filling soup bowls with thick vegetable soup. 'But we did not have enough explosive to do any lasting damage to the lines. London will send us explosives, no?'

'And money,' Gustave chimed in. 'We need money for bribes.'

'Whom do you bribe?' Gilbert asked.

'Railway officials, people in the mayor's office for identity papers and ration cards,' Jean said. 'Sometimes Vichy police and German soldiers. They tell us what is worth attacking and what is unimportant, and warn us when there is a search on for us, but they ask a great many francs for their information.'

'How many of you are there?'

'The four of us and the men who were on the field when you arrived, but we need more. We need to persuade those who sit on their backsides and let the Boche rule us that France is not beaten, can never be beaten.'

Gilbert smiled. There was no doubt the men were keen and

patriotic, but he guessed they might also be foolhardy and take unacceptable risks. It was up to him to instil discipline.

'I must send in my report,' Esme said, going to the canister which was lying on the floor beneath the window. 'I need somewhere to hang the aerial.'

'There's a tree directly outside one of the bedroom windows,' Jean said. 'We could string it to that.'

'Will it be seen from the road?'

'No, it's at the back and we are fairly isolated here. The Boche don't bother with us so long as they get their milk and eggs.'

'There's always a first time,' Gilbert murmured.

Anton, carrying the wireless, led Esme from the room.

'What have you done with the parachutes?' Gilbert asked Jean.

'They have been hidden for now. Tomorrow we will bury them.'

'Bury that canister too, good and deep. If it's found here, we will all be in trouble.'

'We will do that, monsieur.'

'You know why I am here?'

'To find out what we need and London will send it,' Jean said.

'More than that. I am instructed to organise a resistance group with a proper chain of command, not only to sabotage, but to gather information and send it back to London. There are other groups in other parts of France and the occupied countries being told the same thing. It must all be co-ordinated, a secret army, ready to rise up when the time is ripe.'

'A secret army, I like the sound of that,' Jean said, laughing. 'I'll drink to that.' He held up his wine glass and clinked it against Gilbert's. '*L'armee secrete.*'

'*L'armee secrete.*' Gilbert watched him drink and took a mouthful from his own glass. 'You will be expected to take your orders from me.'

'Never! *Sacre Dieu!* What do you take me for? A lap dog?'

'No.' Gilbert smiled to soften what he had to say. 'Not a lapdog, but perhaps a fearsome wolf. Wolves fight best in packs and there has to be a leader. I'm afraid it has to be me.'

'I am the leader. I have been from the first. Everyone acknowledges it. I say what we do.'

Gilbert shrugged. 'No compliance, no money, no explosives.'

Gilbert's assessment that Jean might be hot-headed was borne out when he rose to his feet, fists clenched. The last thing Gilbert wanted was a fight; he refused to rise. 'Sit down, *mon ami*, we can work together. We have to, to defeat the common enemy. I am the head, but you are the arms and legs and the beating heart. You will give your men their orders, even though ultimately they have come from me, or rather from my bosses who will have the last word. This is not a local issue, what we do affects the whole war effort. Little groups working independently might prick the Germans, but they won't defeat Hitler.'

Deflated, Jean sat down again. 'You are right, *mon ami*. I will agree.'

'Good.' Gilbert held out his hand and the other shook it. 'Now, let us get down to business. First things first, accommodation for myself and Arlene.'

'You will stay here for the rest of tonight,' Jean said. 'Tomorrow you will go into Ville Sainte Jeanne and find the bicycle business of my cousin, Paul. I have an *ausweiss*, a pass to go from the free zone to the occupied zone because some of my fields are on the other side. Paul will take you to lodgings where you may stay while you do your work. Arlene can stay here. Safer for her. We will think of a cover story for her presence if anyone should come asking.'

The area close to the River Cher had been chosen for the drop because Jean was known to the people in SOE and also because there were railway marshalling yards a few kilometres away and an airfield used by the Germans for its fighters, which harried the British bombers as they crossed the channel. They had been earmarked for sabotage. Its situation on the demarcation line was another plus because if saboteurs were being hunted they might be able to disappear into the free zone. It wasn't free in the accepted sense of the word, because it was ruled by the Vichy government who collaborated with the Germans, but without occupying troops. He hoped to find a way of moving between one zone and the other, as Jean seemed able to do, but he would need a pass to do it openly. How that was to be obtained he did not yet know.

Esme came back into the room followed by Anton. 'Message gone and London says well done and take care. The next transmission is scheduled for tomorrow evening at seven o'clock.'

'Good.' He turned to Jean. 'I shall need a courier to contact people and take messages to Arlene for transmission and to pass on instructions from London.'

'I can do that,' Madame Duport said. 'I often go into Ville Sainte Jeanne to shop and take produce to the market. No one takes any notice of me. I am a nobody.'

'Are you sure you want to do it?' Gilbert asked. 'It could be dangerous.'

'Pah! If my sons can work to free our beloved France from the Boche, then so can I.'

'If anyone wants to know, I am Gerard Lebonier, an insurance salesman,' Gilbert went on. 'It will explain why I move around a lot visiting people.' He went over to the canister and took out a briefcase. 'My stock in trade, forms for people to fill in to obtain insurance.' The forms were headed with the name of a well-known French insurance firm, which he had been assured were authentic.

'And Arlene?' Madame queried. 'She looks too young to be doing this work.'

Gilbert smiled. 'We know Arlene looks nearer sixteen than twenty-two,' he said. 'And so that is what her identity documents say. Born Madeleine Tillon in Algiers in 1925. Her parents were killed in a motoring accident in 1936 and she came to live with her Aunt Matilde in France.'

'I will say Matilde was my cousin but she has recently died,' Madame Duport said. 'So she has come to stay with me.'

'Do you have a cousin who has recently died, madame?' Gilbert asked.

'No, but I can invent one. It would be better for her to be attached to a family.'

'If you are sure,' Esme said. 'That would work very well. I will call you Tante Gabriellle.'

'Tante Gabby will do. Now, I think we should all go to bed. It will soon be dawn. Jean, Anton, you have work to do tomorrow.'

'As have I,' Gustave said, rising. 'Come, Philippe.'

The two men left and Madame showed Gilbert and Esme up to their bedrooms, each carrying the small pack that contained a change of clothes and toiletries, all French of course. Esme was given the room from which she had radioed London. Gilbert said goodnight to her before going into his room. It was very small with a sloping ceiling, so that it was only possible to stand upright in one half of the room. Stripping off his clothes, he climbed into bed.

It seemed a lifetime ago since he had stood on the Tarmac of Tangmere airfield, waiting to board the Whitley, but it was only five or six hours. In that time he had entered a different world, a clandestine world where one wrong move, one unconsidered word, could result in death, not only his but of everyone around him. It was a fearful responsibility.

All that training, running with a heavy pack for miles, vaulting over obstacles, diving into muddy streams, target practice with a pistol, learning to kill silently with a knife, unarmed combat, learning about explosives, being interrogated by men in Nazi uniforms with loud, harsh voices, at all hours of the night and day, sticking to his story, had been leading to this. And there was no going back before the job was done, not then if London couldn't get him away. He was well aware of the risks and the odds of living through it. If he didn't, would his family, father, mother and Prue, ever learn what he had been doing?

He had a feeling that Prue might. She knew more about what was going on than she was saying. Why, for instance, had she been called to the Foreign Office and then been given a job which involved 'boring office work', in a place like Bletchley Park which was full of boffins and where security was so tight it was like a prison? He had tried to visit her soon after she went there and been turned away, and then had gone to her billet, a typical suburban house, kept by a thin, austere woman who practically curtsied to him when she realised he was Prue's brother and a viscount. He smiled at the memory.

Unable to talk privately at the house, he and Prue had gone to the hotel where he had taken a room. They had talked about home, their parents and friends, who was in which service, and who had been turned down on medical grounds, who was marrying whom. She had not divulged anything about her work. He guessed it was quite taxing mentally because she was looking tired and sometimes did not seem to take in what he was saying, as if she was thinking of something else.

Her last letter, received only a week before, talked about the changes at Longfordham where American engineers had arrived to help complete the extension of the aerodrome ready for their bombers. 'They need long, hard runways,' she had written, 'so every bush and tree, every tussock of grass is being uprooted, every hollow filled in, and covered with concrete. Goodness knows what the rabbits and partridges and skylarks and all the little animals will do about that.' She went on to write about her friend, Sheila, and their failed attempt to find the girl's brother, about the weather and the films she had seen. It was as if his sister had to fill her letters with inconsequential chatter to avoid writing what was really on her mind. But he had been guilty of the same thing. And now she would not hear from him for weeks, months, maybe years, and would have to rely on those cards he had already written to his parents, which would tell them nothing.

He woke when he heard people moving about on the landing outside his room, and reached for his pistol, but it was only Jean coming to tell him it was time to get up. 'I will take you into Ville St Jeanne to the bicycle shop,' he said. He was newly shaved and his dark hair had been combed and oiled. 'Breakfast is ready in the kitchen.'

Esme was already seated at the kitchen table, eating a boiled egg with some bread and butter. She greeted him cheerfully. 'Did you sleep well?'

'Like a log. And you?'

'OK, but it's funny to think we are in France at last. It's almost like an anticlimax after all that training. I can't believe it's real.'

'You will know it's real enough when you come across the Boche,' Jean said, offering Gilbert an egg. 'And the *Brigade Speciales*. They may be French but they are every bit as bad as the Gestapo. There was a big round-up of *resistants* last year, all taken to prison, many of them were tortured and shot, others simply disappeared. You will need to keep your wits about you.'

They had been briefed about the situation before leaving England. Almost as soon as the Armistice had been signed and the

Germans arrived in the occupied zone, people began trying to cross to the *Zone Libre*, survivors of Dunkirk, refugees, Jews, foreigners, escaped prisoners of war, downed airmen, and they were helped on their way by *passeurs* who risked their lives doing it, hiding them, feeding them, supplying them with forged documents, guiding them from safe house to safe house, through the Free Zone which was anything but free, until they reached Spain and safety.

There was no doubt that the Gestapo and the Vichy police knew about them and the round-up of suspects had led to others and, one by one, men, women and young girls alike were mopped up. Some confessed under torture or threats to harm their families, others were defiant to the end. 'Be extra vigilant,' he had been told. 'Vary your route and your clothes when moving about and make absolutely certain of someone before confiding anything. You cannot be sure passwords are not known. And if someone fails to turn up for a *rendez vous*, do not go looking for them. Change your address frequently. If you stay in one place for any length of time, make sure you receive mail. A man who has no correspondence must be in hiding. Write to yourself if you have to.'

'And you too,' Gilbert told Jean.

Jean laughed. 'Me, I am a simple farmer, minding my own business, trying to earn a living and keep out of trouble. Today, I go into Ville Sainte Jeanne to sell my milk, most of which the Boche will take for themselves, and *Maman* comes too, to go to market, so when you are ready, we will go.'

Gilbert said goodbye to Esme, telling her to write to him, so that he could be seen to receive post, then he followed Jean and Madame Duport out to the van. He climbed into the back beside two churns of milk, the door was shut and they were on their way. He hadn't liked leaving Esme, but she seemed happy about it. She was a very confident person. When the war was over and they were back at home, he would enjoy getting to know more about her.

They were stopped by a German guard and a French policeman on the bridge across the river where Jean and Madame's passes were examined. Gilbert, trying to make himself as small as possible behind the milk churns, held his breath. He could hear Jean laughing and joking with the policeman and was relieved when they were on their way again.

A few minutes later the van drew up in a side street just short of a large dairy. Jean came round to let Gilbert out. 'The bicycle shop is just round the corner,' he said, handing Gilbert a torn train ticket. 'Paul has the other half of this, so show it to him when you tell him you have come from his cousin in Lyon. Maman will come to the shop this afternoon to ask Paul if you have any messages for Arlene before she returns to the farm.'

Gilbert nodded and walked off without looking back.

The bicycle repair business was situated in a converted stable beside an old inn called Le Coq Rouge. Gilbert made his way past bicycles in every state of repair to where a man was busy working on one propped upside down. It was old and rusty and had only one wheel which he was replacing with one cannibalised from another, less-roadworthy, machine. 'Monsieur Paul Duport?' he asked.

'Who wants to know?' The man straightened up. He was taller than his cousins, broader too, and he had a weather-beaten countenance.

'I am Gerard Lebonier from Lyon. I sell insurance. I have been told by your cousin you need insurance, Monsieur. For your business.'

'Perhaps,' the man said guardedly. 'From my cousin in Lyon, you say?'

'Yes, from Lyon. Perhaps this will convince you.' He proffered the half ticket.

Paul took it and matched it with a half he took from his own waistcoat pocket and then returned it. 'Keep it, Monsieur, you might have need of it. At the moment I am busy with this bicycle. The German who requisitioned it is coming back soon to collect it, so I cannot leave. Go into the inn, order an aperitif and wait for me.'

Gilbert did as he was told. He sat in a corner, sipping his wine and watching the people come and go. Most of them were German who spoke in loud voices, laughing among themselves and issuing orders for drinks without the courtesy of a please or thank you. It seemed strange to be sitting so close to the enemy and really brought home to him how precarious his safety was. He felt more like bolting than sitting patiently waiting for a stranger, but he knew that would be fatal. Instead he opened his briefcase and took out a sheaf of papers and pretended to study them, his eyes and ears alert. He knew the first few hours, the first couple of days, on the ground could be the most risky. He needed to look confident, but not too confident, to blend in with whatever was happening around him and on no account to stand out. After a few minutes, without any sense of urgency, he stacked the papers and put them back in his briefcase.

The man sitting at the next table had finished reading his newspaper and folded it on the table. Gilbert asked him if he might he borrow it. The man pushed it towards him. He thanked him and began to read.

'Ah, *mon ami*, you are here before me. I am sorry I was delayed.' Paul sat down beside him and called to the waiter to bring him a glass of wine.

He sipped it, apparently in no hurry to leave. Gilbert was fidgeting to be off but had to take his cue from his companion. 'We will leave in a few minutes,' Paul said in an undertone. 'There is a patrol car in the street checking everyone's papers. It happens nearly every day. We will wait until they have gone.'

They heard screaming and protests and a car door slamming, and then there was silence. A few minutes later, the car drove past the window. 'Someone is off to prison,' Paul said. 'Poor devil. Finish your drink. Now we can go.'

They went out into the street. Everything seemed normal, in so far as it was normal for French people to scurry past anyone in a German uniform. No one was standing about gossiping. All Gilbert's senses were racing, heightened by an awareness of danger on every corner. He was going to have to get used to it, if he was to do the job he had come to do.

He was taken to Paul's home in a leafy avenue in the outskirts of the town where Sylvie, Paul's wife, made him welcome and showed him to a room in the cellar. It was sparsely furnished but there was a bed with sheets and blankets, a chair and a cupboard. Facing onto the street was a grille at head height. He could see little from it except the feet of passers-by. That might be enough to identify people by their footwear: the highly polished boots of the Germans or the down-a-heel shoes of the French. More importantly, there was a door at the back that led into a walled courtyard. He scrambled up to look over this and discovered it backed onto the garden of the house in the next street. This would be his escape route if he needed one.

Chapter Nine

In August, a letter from Pathé News arrived for Prue, forwarded from Longfordham Hall. It contained three photographs and a hope that one of them might be the one she wanted.

Sitting on Prue's bed, Sheila studied them eagerly and one of them did show the boy she had thought was Charlie, but the picture was grainy and the focus was on the people in the forefront of the picture, so that those in the background were blurred. 'It looks like Charlie,' she said. 'But I couldn't swear to it.'

'You don't want to give up, do you?' Prue asked. 'At least someone might recognise the boy even if it isn't Charlie. Better to know one way or another, don't you think?'

'Yes, I suppose so.' She really wasn't sure. Knowing it wasn't her brother meant she would be back to believing he was dead. 'What are you planning to do?'

'We'll send the picture to the newspapers with a ring round the boy, asking them to publish it to see if anyone can identify him.'

'You wrote the letter in the first place, so you do it, Prue. Please.'

Prue agreed because it helped her to get over Tim's rejection of her and, besides, she loved a mystery. The solving of this one would give her immense satisfaction.

The result was that Longfordham Hall became the destination of reporters hoping to interview Lady Prudence Le Strange; the aristocracy were always newsworthy and especially tied in with a girl from the East End and her sad story. They were not pleased to discover she was not there and her whereabouts could not be divulged. 'You had better get in touch with them,' the Countess wrote to her daughter. 'Your papa and I dislike being the object of newspaper attention. If you can't give them your real address, use the flat, but make sure you are not a nuisance to Mrs Gault.'

The flat was in Mayfair and Mrs Gault was the housekeeper. The Earl used it on his now-infrequent trips to London, mainly when he wanted to attend a debate in the House of Lords which necessitated an overnight stay. Before the war, the Countess had used it when she went to London on shopping expeditions, but she had stopped going when the Blitz started. Prue had sometimes slept there when she had a day off, but it wasn't enough time to go home to Longfordham.

Arranging to meet the press there took some organising. She and Sheila had to have leave together, and a time and date booked, and it was October before anything could be arranged. Prue had decided to give the *Daily Express* an exclusive interview, on the grounds they would be more likely to act diligently, and it was also a popular paper, read by the masses. Prue was enjoying what she called their adventure, but Sheila was full of trepidation. Ma wouldn't like her making a spectacle of herself for all the world to see and perhaps Charlie had his reasons for not wanting to be found. What those could be she could not even guess. And the apartment overawed her. It was on the top floor of the building with large, high-ceilinged rooms and long windows from which they could glimpse Hyde Park. Its heavy curtains and thick carpets, into which her feet sank, highly polished furniture and sumptuous sofas made her realise that her preconceived ideas of what constituted 'posh' were way off the mark. This was the stuff of film sets.

She sat on one of the sofas, with her hands in her lap, and allowed Prue to do all the talking, only speaking when she was addressed directly. But she flared up when she perceived a criticism of her family and the way they lived. 'We never went short of food or clothes and we were all clean,' she insisted when it was suggested her brother might have wanted to disappear to get away from the slum they lived in. 'We were a happy family. Charlie would have no reason to hide from me.'

'He may have believed his sister had died with the rest of the family,' Prue put in. 'He might not know she is alive and looking for him.'

'And what is your interest in the affair, Lady Prudence?' she was asked.

'Miss Phipps is now my maid and I want to help her if I can.' She dug Sheila with her elbow when she appeared to be going to contradict her.

After a few more questions about Charlie, where he had worked, what he liked doing in his spare time, they agreed it would make an uplifting story in the middle of all the bad news if brother and sister could be reunited. But they wouldn't do it without a picture of Prue and Sheila together.

'Prue, we can't do that,' Sheila whispered. 'We'll get the sack.'

'Sheila is camera-shy,' Prue told the photographer who had accompanied the reporter.

'No picture, no story,' the reporter said.

Sheila was beginning to wish she had never agreed to come,

though Prue seemed to be enjoying herself. And the man with the camera was already clicking away.

The two men left at last and Sheila relaxed a little. 'Why did you say I was your maid?' she demanded.

'Because we couldn't have them delving into our work at BP, could we? They would never have had the temerity to ask what I did for a living and would assume I was one of the idle rich. And it was best they didn't know what you do either. Telling them it's a secret would only have whetted their appetites.'

'I see. What do we do now?'

'We wait to see if anything turns up. But since we are in town, let's go to a show and have supper somewhere. We've got the whole weekend, so we could stay here tonight and go back to Bletchley tomorrow.'

'I'd like go and see June and Janet before I go back, if that's all right with you.'

'Of course it is. You go and see them in the morning. Hugh is in town and I'll catch up with him.' She wasn't sure how she felt about Hugh. Anyone as unlike Tim would be hard to find. He was rather a serious man, but then it was serious and intricate work he did which needed maximum concentration and perhaps under different circumstances he might unbend. Meeting him in town might uncover a different Hugh. 'We'll meet at Euston station in the afternoon. There's a train at five-thirty.'

'If you are sure Mrs Gault won't mind.'

'She won't mind. That's what she's paid for.'

Sheila was in a cheerful mood as she walked from the underground station to the Bennetts' home. Something was being done about Charlie and she was feeling hopeful. The show they had seen at The Windmill had been very good and she had sat entranced by the singing and dancing. It had given her ambition a boost to watch them, even if the girls were more scantily clad than she would want to be.

June was busy in her kitchen when she knocked on the back door and poked her head round it. 'Sheila, what a lovely surprise!'

'I've been in town being interviewed by the newspaper about Charlie being missing. They might be able to find him for us and as I had a day to spare I decided to come and see you.'

'Come on in. I was just going to give Noel his dinner. We can have ours afterwards. Bob has gone on some training course for his work. It might mean promotion.'

'Thank you. I'm meeting Prue at half past five and I want to see Janet as well.'

Noel was using a chair to try and pull himself up on his feet. Sheila picked him up and sat down to cuddle him. 'There's one who couldn't care less about the war.'

'But it's the children we are fighting for, isn't it? So they can have a future in peace.'

'Any news about the little one's family?'

'No, and the adoption is taking simply ages. There's so much red tape and so many forms to fill in. The adoption society we approached want to know every little thing about us and I suppose it's right they should. The fact they are not sure he has no relatives makes it more complicated.'

'He's a little bit like me then. In a kind of limbo. Am I alone in the world, or aren't I? I wish I knew.'

'You've got your aunt.'

'So I have.' She laughed suddenly. 'She's not the cuddling sort!'

'Then you'll have to make do with us and your friend Prue. Look at that child, he's worth a cuddle now, isn't he?'

'Of course he is.' She kissed the top of his curly head.

'I was just about to write to you, but now you're here I can tell you. I don't suppose anyone else has let you know.'

'Let me know what?'

'Chris's ship was sunk in the Arctic on one of those Russian convoys about three weeks ago. He's been reported killed in action. Apparently they can't survive more than a few minutes in the water before the cold gets to them.'

Chris dead? She sat nuzzling her face in Noel's curly head, so shocked she couldn't take it in. Chris gone, gone like everyone else. He had been so full of life and he had loved her. She supposed it was her own fault Mrs Jarrett hadn't let her know. She hadn't been very kind to him. Guilt overwhelmed her.

'Chris was Mrs Jarrett's eldest and her favourite, especially since his dad died,' June went on. 'She can't seem to get over it. The house is more of a shambles than ever. She blames the government, and Mr Churchill in particular, for not protecting the convoys better, and doesn't keep her opinion to herself. Bob had to speak to her for spreading alarm and despondency.'

Sheila had known Chris's job was dangerous, more so than most, but she had never dwelt on the possibility that he might die. Now he was gone, she felt a kind of longing for him, a wish that he might still be with her, walking down the road beside her, talking a load of nonsense, making her laugh. He had spent hours with her searching for Charlie and he had come all the way to Bletchley to propose to her before going to war. Ought she have pretended to love him, to have said yes, simply to make him happy? Would it have been pretence? Was the truth that she did love him, had loved him all along and it was only the rawness of her grief over her family that made her turn him down? Given time, would they have made a proper loving couple? She would never know now.

'I must go and see Mrs Jarrett.'

'She might not welcome you.'

'There's nothing new in that, but I still have to go, it's only right. I'll go this afternoon.'

June was right, Mrs Jarrett's welcome was less than cordial. She looked grubby and unwashed and her hair was a tangle. 'What do you want? Come to gloat, have you?'

'No, Mrs Jarrett, nothing of the sort. I have come to offer my condolences and tell you how very sorry I am. I've only just heard or I would have written to you.' She felt more like weeping but would not give the woman the satisfaction of seeing it.

'What's the point of being sorry? It's too late for that. My boy is at the bottom of the ocean. I don't even have a body to bury. At least you've got graves, you know where your folks are.'

'All except Charlie.'

Mrs Jarrett ignored that. 'I knew he weren't comin' back, the last time he were 'ome. I felt it in me bones and I reckon he knew it too.'

Sheila didn't know what to say. She didn't have the right words. There had been so many instances of young men, in the prime of life, having premonitions of their own deaths which had turned out to be right, she felt she could not contradict the woman.

'Anyways,' Mrs Jarrett went on, while Sheila debated whether to go or stay. 'He left something for you, made me promise to give it to you, or I wouldn't bother. Wait here.' She left Sheila standing on the step while she went indoors. She came back a few moments later and thrust a small package into Sheila's hand. 'There! I done what he asked, so now you can clear off. I don' want none o' yer condolences. They won't bring 'im back.' She went inside and slammed the door.

Sheila turned and left. She had no idea what was in her hand, but whatever it was made her feel worse than ever. She went to the park and found a convenient bench to sit and undo the packet. It contained a letter and, in a little box, the engagement ring she had spurned. It was small and probably not expensive as rings went, a slim gold band with a single small stone, but it must have cost him several weeks' wages and it had been chosen with love. Tears filled her eyes as she unfolded the letter and began to read:

My dearest darling Sheila,

You will always be that to me whatever you say. I had hoped to come home and court you properly, to make you change your mind and realise that I was the one for you because I love you so much. I know I could have made you happy, if only I had been given the chance. If you are reading this, then you must know that I won't be coming back after all, that I died thinking of you. I would like to think you are grieving just a little bit, but not too much. I go to a better place than this war-torn world and life for you has to go on.

Be happy.

Please keep the ring in memory of me.

Your ever-loving Chris.

The tears were pouring down her face by the time she finished reading and she could hardly make out the words. She took the ring from its box and sat with it in the palm of her hand for a long time as thoughts and memories crowded in, some happy, some sad. Chris, with holes in his shorts, chasing her in the playground of their infant school in a game of tag, Chris defending her from the class bully in secondary school. His first hesitant kiss, his laughter, his serious side when he talked of joining the navy to help win the war, 'Because it has to be won,' he had said, and his insistence on seeing her at Bletchley and that awkward proposal in front of Mr

Welchman. He had been part of her life and now he was gone, gone knowing she had rejected him. Not since her family perished had she felt so miserable.

Around her people were going on their way, some purposefully, some loitering; mothers playing with toddlers, throwing balls or pushing them back and forth on the swings. Those with young babies wheeled their prams. They were largely safe from bombs now, but the war still went on, soldiers, sailors and airmen were still dying in order that others might live. That was the propaganda of the day, fed to them by the BBC and the cinema newsreels. It didn't make her feel any better. She scrubbed at her eyes with a handkerchief, slipped the ring on the third finger of her right hand, put the letter and empty box in her handbag and left the park.

She bought a bunch of flowers from a barrow boy and took them to the cemetery where she knelt on the grass beside her mother's grave and poured out her heart to her. It was peaceful there among the gravestones, with the sun warm on her back, and gradually she felt calmer. She could almost hear her mother saying, 'You can't do anything about it now, love. You have to get on with your life. Sing your heart out for me and your dad, and for Chris too. You have to live.'

She laid the flowers on the grave, then rose and went to pay Janet a flying visit. Her friend was wearing an engagement ring and was full of wedding plans. Sheila hadn't the heart to mention Chris. She congratulated her and left to meet Prue.

The war ground on. Everyone was exhausted and fed up with it, but the end was nowhere in sight. Prue and Sheila would read the newspapers but because of the shortage of paper they only consisted of four cramped pages. It was better to listen to the wireless. They heard how the poor people of Malta were struggling to survive as ships sent to supply them were sunk. And in the East the relentless German advance into Russia continued; the important city of Leningrad was under siege and it looked as if Moscow would be next. Prue wondered whether Tim had changed his mind about what he was doing, since only the bombers were having any sort of success. But even here, doubts were being raised about the accuracy of the bombing, something Tim had told her on that night in Huntingdon. But most people didn't care what was hit so long as something was.

The stark situation was played down by the propagandists, but Prue was only too well aware of how bad things were. The signals came in thick and fast and the analysis, decoding and translating went on day and night. With the help of the bombes, the German army and air force traffic was being decoded and translated. The German naval code was more difficult. The people in Hut Eight, which included Hugh and Alice, had only been able to crack some of it with the help of an enigma machine and codebooks found on a captured enemy U-boat. The result was that losses at sea were not quite as bad as they had been and the navy had scored a great victory against the Italian fleet at Cape Matapan off the island of Crete. Information supplied by Hut Eight also helped locate and sink the German battleship, *Bismark*, in May, although BP's part in that was not made public, though the rumours were flying around BP and Hugh confirmed it. Successes like that were few and far between and hadn't stopped other British ships being sunk.

Everyone at Bletchley Park was working flat out and looking exhausted. After a visit by Mr Churchill in September, more resources were put at the disposal of the Bletchley Park chiefs and a new tennis court built for everyone to enjoy. The dilapidated huts were slowly being replaced with brick buildings, though they were still referred to by their hut numbers; it was, according to Prue, a sure sign they were in for a long haul.

By November it was being reported that German guns could be heard in Moscow, the fighting in the North African desert was as fierce as ever and the news from the Far East was worrying. At the beginning of December the Japanese attacked the American fleet at Pearl Harbour and brought the United States into the war. 'Thank goodness for that,' Hugh told Prue on one of their evenings out. How long it would be before they made a significant impact on the war situation in Europe was anybody's guess.

Sheila was busy rehearsing hard for a wartime take on *Aladdin*. The traditional story was being embellished with contemporary jokes about the war and the characters at BP. 'It isn't malicious,' she told Prue. 'We just want to cheer everyone up.'

She needed cheering up herself. A young man had contacted the *Daily Express* and identified himself as the boy in the picture and it was not Charlie. The newspaper bosses had been less than sympathetic when they realised their uplifting story was nothing of the sort. They more or less accused Prue of attention-seeking. The Earl and Countess were annoyed with her too, especially since she had claimed Sheila was one of their employees and she could not explain why she had done it.

For Sheila, the disappointment, coming on top of the news about Chris, was a real blow. She had been so optimistic and now she felt deflated and forced to listen to all those people who said Charlie could not have survived, including her aunt who had seen the article in the newspaper and been incensed that Sheila had resorted to such a cheap trick to gain publicity. 'I am surprised her ladyship demeaned herself by agreeing to it,' she said.

'It was my idea, Mrs Tranter,' Prue said. 'Sheila was sure the boy was her brother.'

'How could he have been? If Charles were alive, we would have known about it long before now.'

It was an argument that seemed unanswerable.

Christmas passed with no pause in the work, though there was the usual party and that was followed on Boxing Day by the first of two performances of *Aladdin*. Sheila put her misery behind her and sang her heart out. She sang for Ma and Pa and her siblings, for Chris whom she had hurt and for Charlie who was lost. She sang for all the people in the audience taking time off from their gruelling work to listen to her. She sang 'A Nightingale Sang in Berkeley Square' and 'You Made Me Love You' and a rousing rendition of 'Bless 'em all' in which the audience joined. It was exhausting and exhilarating at the same time. She fell into bed as soon as she arrived home and was soon asleep.

Prue, who had been one of those lucky enough to go home for Christmas, returned on New Year's Day. It was bitterly cold and snowing and her train had been held up several times because snow was building up on the line and they had to fasten a snow plough to the front of it. In spite of that she was in a cheerful mood and brought a big bag of sweet chestnuts stored since the autumn, some chocolates and two bottles of wine. 'We'll scoff them later,' she told Sheila, who was sitting on her bed watching her unpack. She still seemed to have a mountain of good clothes and hardly needed her clothing coupons.

'Were your parents still cross with you?'

'No, of course not. They were fine when I explained everything to them, though Mama is still a bit peeved that I won't tell her what I'm doing here. Anyway, I've been told to take you home with me when we manage to have leave at the same time. I told them all about you and they are keen to meet you.'

Sheila wasn't so sure. She thought the Earl and his wife might be fearsome and she would let herself down by not knowing how to behave. That's what Aunt Constance said anyway. She smiled. 'So Christmas was all right, was it?'

'Yes, except Gillie wasn't there.'

'What about Tim? Did you hear from him?'

'No, I assume he's flying again.'

'Why don't you try contacting him?'

'And risk a put-down? I think not. If he wants me, he knows where to find me.'

'I wish I'd made it up with Chris before it was too late,' Sheila said wistfully.

'Don't dwell on it, Sheila, you can't change anything.'

'No, but you can.'

'Leave off lecturing me. You're as bad as Mama.'

'OK, not another word.'

Tim was flying again, but his old crew had settled down with a different navigator and he was assigned to a new crew. He was glad in a way because the new men would not know how he had so nearly failed. They were young and inexperienced and he was looked up to as a kind of patriarch, though he was only three or four years older than they were, a lifetime in a bomber crew's life. They were given one of the new Lancasters, which had a seven-man crew, and with new navigational equipment on board and with the role of navigator separated from bomb-aimer, he felt a little happier about it.

In March, when the long, cold winter was coming to an end, they were off to Hamburg again and he could not help thinking of the last time he had gone there. He had not realised at the time what was wrong with him, nor that it would take several months to put right. He could have been taken off flying altogether, since added stress could bring on a recurrence, but he had insisted on coming back. He had to prove to Prue and, more importantly, to himself that it was not cowardice that had caused his breakdown, but a physical ailment. It didn't alter what he thought about the accuracy of their bombing. He hoped the new radio device, code-named Gee, would help him find the target more accurately.

He wished whole-heartedly that he had not written that stupid letter to Prue. 'You can't do this to me,' she had replied. 'I am not some pick-up to be discarded when you tire of me. I deserve an explanation. If it is something I have done to make you turn against me, then I want the right of reply.' Oh, she had been angry and he didn't blame her. He had replied, trying to tell her that the fault lay not with her but with him. He had been unhappy, confused, unsure of himself, sick and very, very tired. He had asked her forgiveness. He loved her and always would. He had asked for her continuing support and patience.

She had not replied and had evidently taken him at his word and considered their relationship severed for good. Perhaps she had found someone else. She was beautiful and popular, so had he been kidding himself to think she would wait for him? His mother had sent him a newspaper cutting of the search for Charlie Phipps which had made him smile. It was typical of Prue to take up arms for the underdog and he wondered what the outcome had been. He also wondered why she had said Sheila was her maid and nothing about her own war work. It confirmed his belief that what she was doing was considered top-secret. How had she come to be doing it? There were some aspects of Prue's life and character that were a complete mystery to him.

The Lancasters were able to cruise at a height that the coastal guns found difficult to reach accurately but they still had to keep a sharp lookout for enemy fighters. It was while losing height towards the target they became really vulnerable. He had to get them to it with as little delay as possible and then out again and on their way home. He had the assistance of the gunner-cum-observer in the nose turret. And it would be the bomb aimer, on the floor peering through the bomb sight, who would guide the bomber in and call out, 'Bombs gone!' He was glad he had been relieved of that task.

They were accompanied by Wellingtons, Stirlings and Halifaxes, together with a fighter escort some of the way. His pre-op nerves left him as they left the ground behind them and made off over the Wash to the point where they would meet up with other squadrons to form one huge formation. Sitting behind the pilot and flight engineer with his lamps shielded from the outside world by a curtain, he set about plotting the course given to them at the briefing. Opposite him sat the wireless operator, listening in for signals. The night was clear and there was a good moon.

Searchlights swept the skies in a wide arc and it was then the guns opened up from the ground. He felt the familiar thumping in his chest and his mouth drying up as the bursts of light and puffs of smoke told them the aircraft had been seen, despite Colin, his pilot, throwing the heavy bomber about in an effort to stay out of the glare. Tim calculated they would be able to see the target visually before too long and they began the descent.

'Hold her steady on course,' he told Colin, as they approached the run in, then handed over to the bomb aimer to do his work. After a few minutes which seemed like hours, during which flak was exploding all around them and their hearts were in their mouths, the bomb aimer called, 'Bombs gone.' The sudden lift of the aircraft as the load left it also served to save their lives as a shell caught the bomb doors before they could be closed, ripping them off. If they had been a few feet lower, it would have hit the fuselage or perhaps a wing and its fuel tanks.

Colin climbed as fast as he dare, leaving the burning city behind them, but Tim didn't have time to set course for home before the night fighters were onto them. Colin corkscrewed the aircraft down and then up again in an effort to throw them off. At first they thought they had escaped, but just as they were breathing again, another Messerschmitt came at them from nowhere and raked them with cannon fire.

'Port wing on fire!' the gunner in the mid-upper turret called out. Tim knew they had been hit because the force of it, just behind him, had slammed his back into his instrument panel and sent a sharp pain through his shoulder blade.

Colin tried diving to put it out, but that failed and he reluctantly gave the order for everyone to bail out. The bomb aimer went out through a hatch in the floor of the nose cone and the tail gunner rotated his turret and dropped out through the rear turret doors. Everyone else made for the side crew door, scrambling over the wing spars as they did so. The heat in the aircraft was intense, the noise of its faltering engines loud in their ears. Tim helped the younger ones out before following. He felt a jerk that momentarily knocked the breath from his body as his parachute opened.

He was floating down apparently unharmed except for the pain in his shoulder, while the Lancaster, with Colin still on board, flew on in a steeper and steeper dive. Tim watched it, hoping and praying to see Colin come out and parachute to safety, but he did not appear before the aeroplane hit the ground and exploded. He had no time to dwell on the loss of his pilot because he had to prepare himself for the landing. There were trees below him and a river and he could, in the dawn light, just make out a building, probably a farmhouse. It was Germany below him, not an occupied country, and he wondered what his fate would be. He did not expect mercy.

* * *

Prue heard Tim was missing on a raid through her mother, who had been told by Tim's mother. 'Mrs Mortimer is hopeful he is alive, and either a prisoner of war or being looked after by the people in the underground,' the Countess had written. 'A lot depends on whether he managed to bail out and where he came down. It will be a few days before they hear for sure. I know you quarrelled with Tim, but I think it would be a courtesy to write to Mrs Mortimer.'

'I don't need Mama to tell me how to be polite,' Prue murmured to herself when she read it. 'Anyway we didn't quarrel, he ditched me. I don't suppose he told his mother that, nor the reason, which I never understood anyway.' Nevertheless she did write and asked to be told when there was any news.

After several days of uncertainty, Prue heard that Tim had been taken prisoner and, apart from a cracked shoulder blade, was safe and well. She couldn't help feeling that Tim might even be relieved that he would take no further part in the bombing. The new Commander-in-Chief of Bomber Command, Sir Arthur Harris, was convinced the war could be won by air power alone. He maintained that if sufficient bombs were dropped on German cities to devastate them and demoralise the inhabitants, they would turn against their rulers and insist they make peace. It was a controversial strategy but, over-ruling the doubters, he had put his theory into practice and a thousand bombers at a time were setting fire to German cities. Tim would hate that. For the moment he was relatively safe. She sent a parcel to the address the Red Cross had given Mrs Mortimer.

To Ronnie, the arrival of the Americans on the airfield was manna from heaven. They gave him so much he no longer needed to nick things. His hiding place in the woods was full of chewing gum, chocolate bars, sweets they called candy, cigarettes, tins of peaches and spam. All of it could be sold or taken to his mother, not that he went to see her any more often than he had to. Getting on and off trains without paying was becoming increasingly difficult. The old lady in the cottage by the line was always peering out of her window, watching everyone coming and going. He had a good idea it was she who had shopped him before. He could, with his new wealth, buy a ticket, but that went against the grain. You never paid for anything you could get for nothing.

He liked the Americans. They had an easy-going way with them; they accepted him on face value and didn't ask too many questions. He wasn't supposed to go onto the airfield, but it wasn't fenced and though the perimeter was patrolled, the guards simply grinned at him and let him go, just telling him to keep off the runways. He was, in their eyes, just a kid. He was thankful that he was small for his age.

He rode a bicycle he had found abandoned in a ditch, probably by one of the airmen who had 'borrowed' it to get back to base. Old Tom Green, the gardener up at the hall, had given him some black paint for it and helped him fit a new tyre and he was very proud of it. He cycled for miles, usually alone. He didn't have pals, mainly because they couldn't be trusted to keep his secret and they would definitely inhibit him when he saw an opportunity for a little enterprise. Not only that, they were jealous of his rapport with the GIs.

Their bombers were huge and called Flying Fortresses. There was one often parked on the corner of the field close to the railway crossing where it seemed to dwarf the Potts' cottage. Mrs Potts was nervous when it was there. 'Asking to be bombed, it is,' she would say to whoever would listen. Indeed, on one occasion a German aeroplane flew so low along the railway line Ronnie could plainly see the pilot looking over at him and dived into a hedge. But the fortress had not been there that day and the German had machine-gunned the line and then veered off when one of the anti-aircraft guns on the base had started firing at it. Ronnie could hardly contain his excitement as he retrieved his cycle and went on his way along the old lane to the airfield. It was, according to Johnnie, off-limits to civilians, but Ronnie took no notice of that.

He had been going onto the heath ever since he came to Longfordham. In the beginning he watched the workman pouring tons and tons of concrete for the runways and perimeter track and had made a footprint in one corner which was still there. He went to sell the workmen whatever he had to offer, but now he came because those huge bombers fascinated him, and so did the fliers. He soon learnt he could not sell them anything because they had everything: stuff he hadn't seen in England since the outbreak of war, oranges and lemons and tinned fruit, spam and bully beef, chewing gum and a dark sweet drink called Coca-Cola. The sad tale he had told them of a father fighting in the desert and a mother bombed out and unable to cope may have increased their natural generosity.

'Did you see it?' he demanded of Johnnie when he reached the Nissan hut where his particular friends had their quarters. Captain Johnnie Howard was a pilot. He was sitting beside his bed writing a letter. The rest of the ten-man crew were either doing the same, sprawled out on their beds or playing poker round a small table. 'Johnnie, did you see that Jerry? I saw his face as plain as day. It was a Messerschmitt, weren't it?'

'Sure was.'

'Did they shoot it down?'

'No, don't think so. What are you doing here?'

'Just mooching. It's Saturday. No school. Ain't you flyin' today?'

'No, it's a rest day. D'you want a Coke?' He threw the boy a can, who caught it deftly.

'Ta.'

Johnnie put his letter in the locker by his bed and looked at his watch. 'Opening time. I'm going to the King's Head before it shuts again. Any of you guys coming?'

Martin and Oscar said they would, but the poker players, unwilling to abandon a good pot, elected to stay where they were. Ronnie followed them out and put the can of Coke into the saddlebag of his bicycle which he had propped against the wall, then wheeled it beside the men as they set off for the railway crossing. The only pub in the village was on the other side of the line.

'That's a mighty fine machine,' Johnnie said. 'Can I take a ride?'

'Sure.' Ronnie was even beginning to talk like them.

Johnnie took the bike and wobbled up the road. 'You ride on the left, remember?' the boy shouted after him. The American veered over to the left, just missing a jeep coming in the opposite direction. He turned and rode back. The other two took their turn at trying the bicycle, wobbling about and laughing joyously.

'I could do with something like that to get around,' Johnnie said to Ronnie as they used the pedestrian gate to cross the line. 'Do you know where I could get one?'

'I could find one for you. It'll cost you.'

'How much?'

'Don't know. I'll have to find out.'

'You do that.'

Ronnie could not enter the public house, so they parted at its doors. He rode on to Royston where he knew of a man who sold and repaired bicycles. His was a good trade to be in, when petrol was so severely rationed you could only get if for essential work so it was a bicycle for short journeys, a bus or the train for longer ones.

He hid his bicycle in a hedge before entering the shop. It was only a converted blacksmith's forge and the front was open to the elements. There was an elderly man working on an upturned bicycle.

'I want to buy a bike,' Ronnie told him. 'But I ain't got much money, only my pocket money and what I saved from doing odd jobs. It don't matter if it's clapped-out, I can do it up.'

The man looked at the boy, sizing him up. Ronnie put on his best butter-wouldn't-melt-in-his-mouth expression and produced a half a crown from his pocket. 'Will this do?'

The man laughed. 'No, bor, I can get more than that for a boneshaker outa the ark.' When Ronnie screwed up his face ready to weep with disappointment, he added, 'Tell you what. You work here on Saturdays and I'll let you have one for that half a crown.'

'How many Saturdays? Two do?'

'You drive a hard bargain for a little 'un, bor. Make it three.'

Ronnie worked on Saturdays for the gardener at the Hall, but he'd have to skip that for three weeks. It was a pity because he liked old Tom and even enjoyed working in the garden. At this time of the year it was mostly raking up leaves and cutting down what Tom referred to as herbaceous plants ready for the winter. Sometimes the Earl came out to speak to him and ask how he was getting along. The old boy had been good to him, so he made it a rule not to pinch anything from him. Besides, nowadays he didn't need to.

'OK,' he said. 'Can I start now?'

Mr Tweed agreed and he worked hard all afternoon. He also watched and learnt. One day he would start his own workshop, buying and selling bicycles. There were thousands of Yanks up on the 'drome and they were all potential customers.

It was dark as pitch when he left to go home and he didn't have the glimmer of a light, not even the blackout ones which had the glass covered with blue tissue paper. He knew the road so it didn't matter, except he needed to watch out for potholes and keep alert for other traffic. He was late for his tea.

'Where d'you think you've been?' Auntie Jean demanded. 'You can't have been working in the Earl's garden in the dark.'

'There isn't much to do at this time of year, so I've been working at Mr Tweed's bike shop. I need some money for a birthday present for me mum.'

'That's all right then. But tell us next time, I don't like not knowing where you are. You'd better get your tea. We had ours half an hour ago.'

Ronnie smiled to himself as he sat at the kitchen table to wolf down paste sandwiches and cheese scones spread with real butter. Country living was a lot better than town living, especially when there were farmers with cows in the meadows. He had long since got over his fear of the animals, just as he had learnt to groom the horses in the Earl's stables, instructed by Terry.

Johnnie's bicycle was delivered two weeks later, for which he received five pounds. Ronnie was gleeful, especially as Johnnie seemed to think he had a bargain and others asked him to find them bicycles. He most definitely didn't want to go home to London and he was equally sure his mother didn't want him to.

Chapter Ten

Johnnie Howard loved the English countryside, even in winter when the trees were bare and the air was damp and misty, and in summer it couldn't be bettered, it was so lush and green. It was the country of his forbears, it was where he had been born, not to the couple he called Mom and Pops, but to an unknown English mother and father. He knew very little about them. As far as Mom and Pops were concerned, it was a closed subject. When, as a child, he had asked them how he came to be adopted, they told him he wasn't wanted by his natural parents, but he was wanted by them. They adored him and spoilt him and so he had refrained from asking again. That didn't mean he was no longer curious.

When he told his mom he was being sent to England, she had said. 'Look up my folks, Johnnie, if you get the chance. They will be thrilled to see you. They haven't seen you since you were a tiny baby.' She had given him an address in Derbyshire. He had written to his grandparents as soon as he arrived in England and his grandmother had replied, welcoming him, but so far he had not managed to get to see them. He was aware they were not his real grandparents, but they might be able to tell him something. He didn't like going behind Mom's back, but this wanting to know was eating at him, especially since he came to England. He looked at every woman of the right age and wondered if she could be his mother. He knew it was stupid; after all, he had no idea where she came from, nor even if she were alive. He was due eight days' furlough in the New Year, he'd make the trip then. In the meantime, there was a war to wage and the Hun to beat.

Their missions were conducted in daylight, but it was still dark when they were roused for breakfast and went through the routine of every crew flying that day. Wash, dress, shave and have breakfast of eggs, bacon and toast, real eggs when they were flying. From there they made their way to the briefing hut where they sat and smoked, waiting for the sheet to be pulled off the big map hanging on the wall to reveal their target for that day. Sometimes it was in the occupied countries, not too far to go, and referred to as a 'milk run', which gave them reasonable odds for returning in one piece. But just recently it had been deep inside Germany itself, places like Essen, Kiel, Duisberg, Schweinfurt and Hamburg, which was altogether different.

It meant spending long, cold hours being battered by flak and trying to avoid enemy fighters even before the target was reached. Over the target it was murderous because only the bombardier had anything to do and they felt like sitting ducks. After they had dropped their bombs, it was the same all the way back again. The fighter escort could only go so far to protect them. The longer the trip, the shorter the odds for survival. It churned everyone's stomach and many a breakfast was lost even before they left the ground.

When the chatter had died down, they were given the details by other officers, shown maps, pictures and diagrams, told about the route and where the heaviest concentration of flak was and the anticipated strength of the fighters. There wasn't much talking as cigarettes were extinguished and they went to get into flying gear and were driven out to the aircraft on which the ground crew had been working all night.

The bombers were not called Flying Fortresses for nothing. They were big, well armed and could take a lot of punishment, often coming back to base riddled with holes and one or sometimes two engines not functioning. Even so, losses of aeroplanes and, more importantly, crews had been horrendously high. New crews came and went before they even had a chance to get to know them. It was up to him to maintain good morale among his own crew. At twenty-five, he was considered old compared to the others who were all two or three years his junior; they looked up to him and called him Pappy. He was aware that they relied on him to get them home safely after every mission; it was a huge responsibility which weighed heavily on him. So far they had been lucky.

They were all aware of the importance of luck and everyone had a talisman, taken with them on every mission. Others had a ritual they observed when preparing to go. He had a very small teddy bear, only six inches long, which he had had all his life. It had survived being sat on, kicked about, even drenched in the shower. It had sat on the dressing table in his bedroom all the years of his growing up; it waited for him when he went off to college; it came with him when he went to war. No one laughed. They all had similar lucky charms.

Towards Christmas someone suggested they give a Christmas party for the local kids and the idea was enthusiastically taken up. Johnnie was delegated to visit the school and put the suggestion to the headmistress.

The arrival of the tall American in the middle of a history

lesson set the children giggling. Miss Green frowned at them. 'Get on with your reading, all of you, while I speak to our visitor. There will be questions afterwards.'

They bent to their books but they weren't reading. Their ears were alert for what was being said, especially Ronnie who struggled with his reading anyway.

'Ma'am,' the American began. 'We up at the base would like to share some of our Christmas with the children. We thought we'd give them a party.'

'That's very kind of you, Captain. How many of the children, where and when?'

'All of them, ma'am. We'll send a truck to pick them up and take them home again. We thought we would have it on the afternoon of Saturday the nineteenth. Would that suit?'

She turned to the children, who were grinning and laughing and talking excitedly. 'Be quiet! Anyone behaving badly between now and then won't go.'

They subsided immediately. 'We break up on the eighteenth,' she told Johnnie, 'so that would be an ideal time from my point of view.'

'OK, the nineteenth it is.' He smiled at her. 'You are included, ma'am, and the other teachers too. We are going to hold a dance too, for the New Year, and we need partners. It will be properly organised, I promise you, no funny stuff allowed. So will you come? And any other ladies you know. The more the merrier, isn't that what you say?'

'Why thank you. That will be lovely.'

'Then will you spread the word? I will let you know the arrangements in good time.' He touched his forehead, replaced his cap and left. He smiled at the noise behind him which all her shouting could not subdue.

Now all he had to do was survive the next few missions, each bringing him nearer to the twenty-five he needed to complete his tour and maybe, just maybe, Hitler and his commanders willing, he would be able to enjoy Christmas. It would be their first Christmas away from home and loved ones, but it would be the Limeys' fourth. No wonder they were all looking washed-out. Folks at home had no idea what it was like. Nor could they understand what their menfolk were having to endure; the sheer terror, the long, cold flights deep into enemy territory, the fighters, the blinding searchlights and the flak, seeing your buddies killed and injured, the smell of hot oil, cordite, blood and guts spilling out onto the floor, aeroplanes flying beside you suddenly disappearing in flames. You couldn't write home about that.

'You're coming home with me for the New Year,' Prue told Sheila one Sunday in November. They both had the day off and were sitting over a late breakfast listening to the church bells. General Montgomery had won the Battle of El Alamein and was forcing General Rommel into retreat. For the first time since the war began, church bells were ringing out all over the country to mark the victory. Even Constance was seen to smile when she set off for morning service.

'How do you know we'll have leave?'

'I saw the list in the office. We're on duty over Christmas but we've both got seven days starting the Tuesday afterwards. So it's off to Longfordham.'

'I don't want to put you to any trouble. I'll be all right here.'

'No, you will not. And you won't be any trouble. Whatever gave you that idea? Anyway, I won't go without you. You don't want to condemn us both to a week with your aunt, do you?'

'If you're sure.'

'Of course I'm sure, I wouldn't have said it otherwise. There's an American air base only a stone's throw from our house and there's to be a New Year dance up there and we're invited. My parents often have some of the American officers to the house for tea or drinks or to have a bath, and they've got to know them, so they approve. It'll be fun.'

'What'll I wear?'

'Oh, we'll soon find something to wear. I've loads of clothes.'

It was evident Prue was not going to take no for an answer, indeed had not even posed the invitation as a question. She smiled. 'All right, if you insist.'

'Good. I'm told the Yanks really know how to lay on a party, so we'll say goodbye to the old year and all its troubles and hallo to the new in style.'

'I shan't be sorry to see the end of the old year, what with Chris dying and that boy not being Charlie after all.'

'Yes, I'm sorry about that. Perhaps I shouldn't have encouraged you.'

'It's just as well to know. Do you know where your brother is?'

'No, not really. I'm just glad he wasn't with his regiment in Singapore when it fell. He would be dead or a prisoner by now.'

'Tim is a prisoner.'

'In Germany, that's not the same thing. I try not to think about him. He's obviously not interested in me.' He had replied to her letter, but he was not in a position to say much more than that he was well, that the parcel she had sent him had arrived and the socks and toothpaste were just the job, while the cake, which he had shared with his roommates, had been a welcome addition to their rations. He said nothing of what the camp was like, nor how they were being treated, which was understandable considering the letters were censored. If she was hoping he might express affection or refer to that hurtful letter and tell her he was sorry, she was disappointed. He had simply ended, 'Take care of yourself.'

'How do you know that?'

'He would have told me so instead of sending that cold letter as if I were someone he had just met in passing. Anyway, I've got enough on my plate at work, and so have you, without worrying about the men.'

Sheila laughed. 'And the rationing and the shortage of hair grips and torch batteries . . .'

'Safety pins and lipstick.'

'I don't suppose the Yanks are short of anything,' Sheila said. 'They are going to make a difference, aren't they? To the war, I mean.'

'Of course they are. The signs are good. Jerry bit off more than he could chew with the Russians. The tide has turned there.'

'Helped by the stuff taken to Russia by the Arctic convoys. Chris died helping them.'

It was funny how they went from laughter to gloom in the space of a few seconds, Prue thought. 'I know, try not to think about it. Let's go out for a bike ride. We can stop at the Duncombe Arms on the way back.'

Sheila was involved in the Christmas entertainment at Bletchley Park, now part of the Bletchley Park Drama Group organised by Shaun Wylie, one of the very clever people who worked in Hut Eight, but who liked to relax with amateur dramatics. They were, for the most part, amateurs though there were a few peacetime professional performers among the diverse people working at Bletchley Park. Amateur or not, they were expected to put on a professional performance. What with rehearsals and the show itself on Boxing Day, she had little time to think about her visit to Longfordham Hall.

'You are getting too high and mighty for your own good,' her aunt said, when she told her where she was going. 'Hob-nobbing with the gentry won't make you one. Pride comes before a fall and you will take a tumble, you mark my words.'

'Take no notice,' Prue told her later. 'She's only jealous.'

Nevertheless, she was a bundle of nerves by the time they left Longfordham station, where an elderly man met them with a pony and trap. 'The Rolls is laid up, my lady,' he said, opening the little door at the back to hand them in. 'Beauty, here, don't need petrol.'

It was only just over a mile to Longfordham Hall and they were soon trotting along the lanes between leafless hedges. It had been raining and the potholes were full of water, but their driver steered the outfit skilfully around them. Turning at the crossroads, they encountered Ronnie cycling towards them. He dismounted and grinned. 'Watcha, Mr Tom,' he called out.

Their driver, conscious of his passengers, ignored him, so the boy turned his attention to the ladies. They were very smart ladies with their felt hats and leather gloves. And then he stared at Sheila. She stared back, even screwing round in her seat to watch him after they had passed him. 'I could swear that was Ronnie Barlow,' she said.

'So it is, miss,' Thomas said. 'He's an evacuee.'

'Is that the one who stole the vegetables, Mr Green?' Prue asked.

'Yes, m'lady.'

'Any more trouble?'

'No, m'lady.'

Sheila laughed. 'I remember you telling me about him, Prue, but I didn't realise I knew him. He lived in the next street to us. He was always in trouble. Don't tell me he's turned over a new leaf.'

'Seems like it, miss,' Thomas said, as they turned in at the lodge gates and made their way up the drive flanked by leafless trees.

The pony was brought to a halt at the door of a large mansion in warm red brick. On either side rows of long windows gleamed in the winter sunshine. Sheila looked upwards. Another row of windows matched those of the ground floor and above that smaller ones. And above that a crenulated roof with a tower at each corner and a flagpole in the middle. 'Welcome to Longfordham Hall,' Prue said.

Tom came round to open the door and hand them down and then they were standing on the gravel and he was driving away. Someone had opened the front door. Prue raced up the steps, leaving Sheila to follow. She braced herself to meet the Earl and Countess.

Prue hugged her mother and kissed her father's cheek, then drew Sheila forward and introduced her. 'So this is our songbird,' the Earl said. 'You are very welcome, Miss Phipps. Prue has told us so much about you.' He had a lovely smile and twinkling eyes and she quite forgot her terror.

'Do come in,' her ladyship said. 'Prue will show you round. Luncheon will be at one.'

Sheila looked round for her case, but it was already being borne away by the servant who had opened the door to them. Prue was following him, so she went after them.

She knew she would find it difficult to adapt to the kind of life they lived at Longfordham Hall and was terrified she would embarrass herself and Prue, who simply laughed. 'Just be yourself,' she told her when she came to Sheila's room to help her dress for dinner in the green dress she had worn the Christmas before. Prue was already dressed in a long blue silk dress that clung to her figure. 'They'll love you. My parents are not ogres, you know. I wish Gillie were here, he would soon put you at your ease.'

'Have you heard from him lately?'

'No and don't expect to, but Mama has had a card from him and he is apparently well. Turn about and let me help you with the buttons. Anyway, you won't be the only one feeling strange. Mama has invited some officers from the American base for dinner and I wouldn't mind betting they will be floundering. They don't have aristocrats in America and we seem to fascinate them, as if we had two heads or something.'

There were four of them, they discovered, when they went down to the drawing room where the Earl and Countess were entertaining them.

'Ah, Prue, come and meet our American friends,' her father said. 'Major Norton Drake, Captain Johnnie Howard, Lieutenants Vernon Greenbaum and Martin Youngman. My daughter Lady Prudence . . .'

'Oh, please, no formality, I'm Prue and this is my friend, Sheila Phipps.'

'Are you an aristocrat, too?' Johnnie asked Sheila. It sounded like 'a wrist o crat' the way he said it.

'No, I'm ordinary.'

'No, Miss Phipps, you are not or'nary, no way.'

'Of course not,' Prue said. 'Sheila is our famous songbird.'

'Songbird?' Johnnie queried, turning to Sheila. 'Famous?'

'No, she's just teasing.'

'I am not,' Prue insisted. 'Sheila is already making a name for herself. One day she will be as famous as Vera Lynn.'

The butler came to announce that dinner was served, which saved Sheila's blushes, and they paired up to go to the dining room, led by the Earl and Countess, followed by Prue with Major Drake, then Sheila and Captain Howard and the lieutenants bringing up the rear.

The Countess had been determined to impress and they were served consommé, then roast duck and for dessert, a trifle laden with fruit and cream. There was wine too.

'This is swell,' the major said. 'I didn't know you could eat so well in little old England.'

'Normally we don't,' Prue said. 'This is a special occasion. Sheila and I couldn't get here for Christmas, so we are making up for it now.'

'We are lucky,' the Countess explained. 'We can grow most of our food.' She laughed. 'Even the ducks.'

'Then we are most privileged to share it with you, ma'am,' Johnnie said.

The Countess was a good hostess and she swiftly turned the conversation to the men and what they did.

'I'm in Admin,' the major said. He was a big man, several years older than the others. He had a large moustache beginning to grey and more grey hair at his temples. 'My flying days are over. Johnnie here is a pilot, Vernon and Martin are part of his crew.'

'And how many make a crew, Captain?'

'Ten, ma'am,' Johnnie answered. 'Vernon is my co-pilot and Martin is the navigator. Then we have a radio operator, a bombardier and five gunners.'

'We hear you all taking off,' the Earl said. 'Can't fail to. I never heard such a deafening noise, shakes the house to its foundations. Sometimes I wonder if you'll clear the chimney pots.'

'I am sorry about that, sir, but I'm afraid it can't be helped.'

'I realise that. My wife counts them going out and tries to count them coming back, but I fear some don't return.'

'No. Losses are high.'

'Why do you fly in daylight? Wouldn't it be safer to fly at night?'

'Neither is safe,' Major Drake said diplomatically. 'The RAF go at night, we go during the day, it doubles the problems for Hitler.'

'Tim flew at night and he wasn't safe,' Prue said quietly.

'My daughter's young man is in the RAF,' the Countess explained. 'He was shot down over Germany and is a prisoner of war.'

'Gee, I'm sorry,' the men murmured.

'At least he is alive,' Prue said. Obviously her mother thought she had made it up with Tim, but she could hardly contradict her in front of their guests. 'Poor Sheila's boyfriend was in the navy. His ship was torpedoed and he was lost.'

Sheila had been quietly eating her dinner, not taking part in the conversation, but now all eyes turned towards her. She felt the colour flare in her face as they offered condolences. Johnnie, who was sitting opposite her, smiled in sympathy. He had auburn hair, a little like her own, grey-green eyes, and beautiful white teeth. 'Thank you,' she murmured.

'Let us talk of something more cheerful,' the Earl said. 'I hear you are going to organise a dance at the base to see the New Year in.'

'Yes, sir,' Johnnie said, taking his eyes from Sheila to answer him. 'I hope Lady Prudence and Miss Phipps will come. It is being properly organised and the young ladies will be fetched and brought home afterwards, escorted by ladies of our Red Cross. They will be perfectly safe.'

'We'd love to come,' Prue said, answering for both of them.

The transport was a canvas-covered truck with a bench seat down each side. Prue and Sheila were the last to be picked up because the

Hall was closest to the base. The Countess came out to speak to the American driver and the two American Red Cross ladies who were to act as chaperones. Apparently satisfied, she stepped back and waved them away.

The truck was full of girls and young ladies, all dressed in their finery for the occasion. They had curled their hair and put on make-up and nylon stockings given to them by the Americans. The arrival of Prue and her friend sent them into an embarrassed silence, until Prue put them at their ease by introducing Sheila and chatting to them about their families and what they had been doing. They were too overawed to ask her what she did. Five minutes later, they were driven onto the base and drew up outside a brick building.

The flap at the back of the truck was lifted and an American voice said, 'Welcome, ladies, welcome. I'm Johnnie Howard. There're others inside waiting to meet you.' He held out his hand to the first of the girls, who stepped demurely down the steps he had propped against the truck. One by one, they gained the Tarmac and entered the building.

Once inside, they were conducted to a cloakroom by the Red Cross ladies and from there to the dance hall. It was a large room but even so it was heaving with people. At one end a band was playing music for dancing. All along one side, tables groaned under the food laid out on them: ham and turkey, chicken, succulent pies, white bread rolls, lavishly buttered, sandwiches oozing fillings, cakes, trifles topped with real cream, bowls of punch, cans of Coca-Cola and at one end a barrel of beer. Many of the girls had never seen such plenty all at once, even in peacetime, and they eyed the table hungrily.

But food was not on the minds of their hosts. Every girl was soon dancing with an eager American. Prue went off to dance with Major Drake. Sheila, standing watching the gyrating couples, found her view blocked by Johnnie Howard.

'Dance?' he queried, holding out his hand. She took it and allowed herself to be led into the middle of the throng. It was a rip-roaring affair, as unlike ballroom dancing as it was possible to be. At first she tried to move demurely, but that was difficult as she found herself pulled this way and that and she let herself go, caught up in the atmosphere and the music. It was impossible to talk.

When it ended, he took her back to her place but as Prue was busy chatting on the other side of the room, he stayed with her. 'Do you live in Longfordham?' he asked her. 'Why haven't I seen you about? I would surely have remembered someone as pretty as you if I had.'

She laughed at this blatant flattery. 'I don't live in the village, Captain. I'm staying with Lady Prudence.'

'Hey, forget the captain. I'm Johnnie.'

'Then, Johnnie, no more Miss Phipps.'

'Sheila, tell me about yourself. We didn't have a chance to talk together the other evening.'

'Nothing much to tell. I was born in London, went to school, left to work in a grocer's shop and then the war came.'

'Then what?'

'My home was bombed, reduced to rubble. I lost everyone, mother, father, five brothers and sisters.'

'Gee, that's tough. I'm sorry.'

'It's all right, you don't need to apologise. There's a chance my oldest brother might have survived, but we don't know. I've been searching for him on and off ever since.' She blinked hard and smiled. 'I didn't mean to trouble you with it.'

'What do you do now? Still serving in a grocer's store?'

'No. I'm an office worker. I live with my aunt.' She realised the conversation could become tricky if he kept asking her questions and added, 'What about you? Where are you from?'

'I come from Idaho but I was born in England.'

'You mean you're English?'

'No. I was adopted when I was only a few weeks old. My pop is an American right through, Mom was English but she's American now. They met during the last war.'

'Do you know who your real parents were?'

'No, but I'm kinda curious. I might try and find out about them while I'm here.'

'Have you been to England before?'

'No, never. I promised Mom I'd look up the grandparents while I was here, but I haven't managed it yet. I'm going on my next furlough.'

'Furlough?'

'You call it leave.'

'Where do they live?'

'In Derbyshire.' He paused as a senior officer entered the room and went round tapping some of the airmen on the shoulder. They excused themselves and left.

'Where are they going?' she asked.

'To bed. They are the ones flying tomorrow. They'll be called at four-thirty, so they try and get some sleep in early. Doesn't always work though.'

'You aren't flying tomorrow then?'

'No. Say, do you want to dance again?' The music had softened and the band were playing 'Yours'. Already some couples were clasped in a tight embrace, hardly moving from the spot. He took her hand and led her onto the floor.

He wasn't like the others. He held her properly, just a little bit closer than she had been taught, but it was fine. It seemed a long time since she had been held in a man's arms; she felt warm and protected. He smelt of aftershave. She began to hum the tune and then to sing in an undertone.

'Sing for us,' he said.

'I can't.'

'Oh come on.' He stopped dancing and grabbed her hand to propel her towards the stage. 'What's it to be?'

The band was still playing the same tune. After a little hesitation, she picked up the microphone and began to sing 'Yours'. At first everyone kept on dancing, then one by one they stopped and turned towards her as the clear voice rose.

There was silence while she sang, then enthusiastic applause and demands for an encore. She followed it with 'I'll be with you in apple blossom time' and then all the popular tunes, one after another, some sweetly sentimental, others more robust like 'Chattanooga Choo Choo' and 'Ma, he's making eyes at me'. They wouldn't let her stop. And then it turned into a sing-song, with everyone joining in. An hour later, breathless but triumphant, she was rescued by Prue. 'You wowed them,' she said. 'Come and have some of this delicious food.'

Towards midnight, the eating and dancing stopped and someone turned on a wireless so they could hear the chimes of Big Ben. Silently they listened and on the twelfth stroke they turned to each other. 'Happy New Year,' they said to whoever was nearest, followed by, 'May it bring all you hope for.'

'Victory,' someone said. 'An end to war.'

'And going home.'

'Hear! Hear!'

Johnnie seized Sheila in his arms and kissed her. 'Happy New Year, Songbird,' he murmured.

Caught up in the euphoria, she kissed him back.

When the transport took the girls back, he sat beside the driver and helped her out at the door of the Hall. 'Can I see you again?' he asked.

'It depends what Prue wants to do. We're only here for a week.'

'Then we ought to make the most of it. I'll be flying some of the time, but if we're lucky we're back by evening.'

'How will I know?'

'You'll hear us come back. I'll come up to the Hall, shall I?'

'I don't know about that. I'm only a guest . . .'

'Course he can come,' Prue put in as she joined her on the gravel. 'You make what arrangements you like. Don't mind me.'

'Then I'll be seeing you,' he said and climbed back into the truck.

Sheila was woken next morning by a thunderous noise which shook the windows and did nothing to help her headache. Too much punch, too much good food, too much noise and excitement. She crept out of bed, went along to the bathroom where hot water came out of an ordinary tap, had a wash, dressed and crept downstairs. There was no one about. She could hear sounds from the back of the house and made her way towards them. They led her to the kitchen where two staff were already at work preparing breakfast.

'I'm sorry, I didn't mean to intrude. I was looking for a glass of water and an aspirin.'

'That's all right, miss, I'll get you some.' The older of the two women fetched a glass and a packet of Alka-Seltzer from a cupboard. She filled the glass and stirred the powder into the water. 'There, you drink that down. It was rare ol' night up at the base, I gather.'

'Yes, it was.' She gulped down the liquid. 'I think I'll go outside for a breath of fresh air.'

'You do that, but wrap up warm, it's freezing out. Breakfast will be about an hour.'

She found her coat, gloves and scarf in the cloakroom by the front door and let herself out of the house.

Her route took her through the gardens, its leafless shrubs adorned with frosty cobwebs, glistening in the morning sun. It had been a lovely night, the men were so friendly and polite and anxious to please. She had noticed one or two of the girls slipping out on the arm of an airman, but Johnnie had stuck close to her and made sure she enjoyed herself without being bothered by the more amorous of his colleagues. He was a real gentleman and had treated her like royalty, except for that kiss. She felt as if she had known him all her life, which was silly considering she had only just met him.

She opened a gate in a wall and found herself in another garden, where neat rows of Brussel sprouts and winter cabbage stood in otherwise bare earth. On the far side was a greenhouse and a shed. She walked towards them. She could see someone in the greenhouse and supposed it was a gardener. He came out as she approached.

'Ronnie Barlow,' she said. 'I thought it was you I saw in the lane. What are you doing in the Earl's garden?'

'I work here on Saturdays and in the school holidays.'

'Work? Ronnie Barlow working? Don't make me laugh.'

'I do too and you've no call to mock. You're no better'n me, even if you do hob-nob with the gentry. You even talk like them now.'

'I'm not hob-nobbing, Lady Prudence is my friend.'

'Does she know where you come from?'

'Course she does, but I bet the Earl doesn't know the truth about you.'

'What truth would you be meaning, Sheila Phipps?'

Sheila Phipps was a slum child just like himself and she knew the kind of life he had led before the war, with a father notorious for being in and out of prison and a mother who had the reputation of being 'easy' whenever her husband was banged up. He had learnt that very early in his young life, just as he had learnt that anything not closely guarded was fair game. He had been up before the magistrates a couple of times himself but had been let off with a caution on account of his age and the fact that he had had no one to guide him.

He had guidance now in the shape of Mr and Mrs Potts, Auntie Jean he called her, and Tom Green and Miss Green, who was Tom's daughter. They had shown him another, better way. It didn't mean he was averse to making a quick profit, but that was altogether different from taking things that didn't belong to him. He hadn't done that for ages. But mud sticks and if everyone in the village heard about his dad, they would all turn against him. He might even be sent back to his mother.

'Your pa is a jailbird and you're none too honest yourself,' she said. 'Like father, like son. I heard about you stealing things from his lordship's garden. Is that what you're doing now?'

'No, it ain't. And I ain't like Pa. That's a lie. If you say one word about Pa, I'll . . .'

'You'll what?'

He floundered, searching his memory for something to hold against her. 'I'll tell about you and Johnnie kissing. I saw you. I was watching through the window. That's what tarts do.'

About to ask him what he knew about tarts, she desisted, remembering his mother's reputation. 'There's nothing secret about that,' she said, laughing. 'Everyone was doing it and you should have been in bed.'

'You won't say anything, will you?' His cockiness left him suddenly and he was pleading. 'I ain't done nothin' bad, I swear. I like it here. I don' want to be sent home again.'

'I won't say anything. Just so long as you behave, you can keep your secret.'

She left him and made her way back to the house. Later she would see Johnnie again. Oh, she knew what they said about Yanks and the girls who went out with them, but that didn't apply to Johnnie. Anyway, he was half English.

Chapter Eleven

'Johnnie, how lovely to see you.' Martha Fletcher dragged him into the little cottage and hugged him to her ample bosom. There were tears in her eyes. 'Come on in. Make yourself at home. It's been so long and we have such a lot to talk about.'

He disentangled himself from her embrace and followed her down a narrow hall and through a door into a sitting room. It was so tiny and low-ceilinged it made him feel like an awkward giant. There was a good fire in the grate with a rocking chair beside it from which a little man with white hair rose to greet him.

'He's here, Percy,' she said. 'He's here at last.'

'So I see.' He held out his hand for Johnnie to shake. 'Welcome, my boy, welcome. Come and sit down. Martha will have some tea ready in the shake of a lamb's tail. Did you have a good journey? The trains are terrible, I know . . .'

'I didn't come by rail, I drove up,' Johnnie said. 'I wanted to take my time and see the countryside. My major let me have a jeep. I parked it outside. Is it OK there?'

'I should move it round the back if I were you or the kids will be clambering all over it. There's a farm gate. I'll show you. Let me find my boots and a coat. It's a bit nippy out there.' He looked Johnnie up and down. 'You look well wrapped up. Don't s'pose you're worried about clothing coupons.'

'No.'

The jeep was soon parked in a field behind the house where Grandfather Fletcher kept a couple of pigs and a few hens. 'Keeps us in eggs and bacon,' he said. 'Like eggs and bacon, do you?'

'Sure do.'

Once back in the house, they divested themselves of their outer garments and settled in front of the fire. Martha brought in a tea tray and a plate of cakes. 'Made fresh this morning,' she said, offering the plate to Johnnie.

He took one. 'I don't want to deprive you of your rations, Grandmother,' he said. 'I've brought some things in my bag for you.'

'Bless you,' she said.

He fetched his bag from the hall where he had dropped it and took out tins of corned beef, peaches and condensed milk, a packet of butter, a jar of jam and another of maple syrup, a box of chocolates and two oranges, all of which he put on the table.

'My goodness, manna from heaven,' she said. 'We haven't seen anything like this since the start of the war. Thank you, thank you, but you didn't have to do it, you know. We would have welcomed you without anything. Our grandson from America.'

The old man laughed. 'She'll talk about her grandson from America 'til the cows come home to anyone who'll listen.'

'You've grown into a fine young man,' she said. 'So handsome too. No wonder Freda is so proud of you. You must tell us all about yourself. Freda sent us photos of you growing up and the house and your pony, but her letters have become more and more infrequent since the war started. I am sure she writes, I expect the letters get lost.'

'I don't get to hear very often either,' he said.

'She's all right, isn't she?' the old lady asked. 'What with your father dying and you growing up so fast and going into the air force . . .'

'She is managing just fine,' he said. 'She has lots of friends, they visit with her and she visits with them.'

'At least she doesn't have to worry about the Blitz. We're in the country, but we get air raid warnings and hear the bombers flying over. Now and again a stray bomb drops nearby, but we've been lucky, not like London and Liverpool and places like that. I wouldn't like to live there.'

'Are you in bombers?' Percy asked.

'Sure am.'

'Then you're giving them what they deserve.'

'Yes.'

'After tea, we'll take a stroll to the Nag's Head, if you like,' he said. 'With a bit o' luck, they'll have some beer.'

Johnnie had been disgusted by English beer when he first arrived, but as there wasn't anything else to be had he was acquiring a taste for it. 'Fine,' he said. 'Anything you say.'

'How long can you stay?' his grandmother asked, refilling his tea cup. That was another thing he was learning to like, a good English brew.

'Two more days, if it's no trouble to you. I promised I'd meet my crew in London later in the week. They've gone to see the sights.' There had been an outcry when he told them he wasn't going to London with them and was proposing to travel round the country and go to a village called Clowne which they thought was a huge joke. When they realised he was serious, they had made him promise to join them for the last few of days of their leave. He was going to meet up with Martin and Vernon at the Grosvenor, whose ballroom had been turned into a US officers' mess. After they had been round the sights, he was going to lose them and meet with Sheila.

'Of course it's no trouble,' she said. 'Glad to have you. We've got a lot of catching up to do.'

'Lot of bomb damage in London,' his grandfather said, putting a spill to the fire to light his pipe. 'Everything sandbagged up and the art treasures taken away for safety.' He sighed. 'Still, I suppose there are still places to see. The theatres and music halls are still open, I believe. I haven't been since I retired.'

Johnnie didn't know how he was going to broach the subject of his birth mother and realised he would have to be patient and let the conversation take its course. He was quizzed about his life in America and how different it was from life in England and the words they used which had different meanings and caused confusion or hilarity. They wanted to know about his schooling and what he intended to do after the war.

'I don't know,' he said. 'I could go back to being a locomotive engineer like Pops, but I might do something different.'

'You're not married, I know,' his grandmother said. 'Your mother would have told us if you were, but have you got a girlfriend?'

'Several,' he said, laughing. 'Though I have met an English girl I kinda like. I'm going to meet her in London after I've seen the boys and she's going to show me round her place.' The mission on New Year's Day had been the last one for a week. The weather had turned nasty and half the bombers hadn't found the target and there had been collisions and crashes due to poor visibility. Flying had been stopped for the rest of the week. He had used the time to good effect, going for walks and cycle rides with Sheila. Sometimes Lady Prudence and Major Drake made up a foursome, when it was followed by a meal at Longfordham Hall. He was beginning to feel quite at home there. The week had come to an end all too soon, but he had been writing to Sheila at a Foreign Office address since then. He had no idea where she actually lived. He gathered the place and what she did was secret. It didn't bother him.

'Would you stay in England? You know if . . .'

'Don't think I would. I know I was born here, but I'm American through and through.'

'We hoped, when your father died, your mother might come back here to live,' she said, a little wistfully.

'She's like me, American as pumpkin pie.'

'That's enough, Martha,' her husband said. 'Freda won't come back and you know it.'

'Why?' Johnnie asked. Was this the moment to ask the questions that plagued him?

'Leave it, boy. Martha, how's that meal coming along?'

She rose and left the room. The old man watched her go and turned to Johnnie. 'You know you were adopted?' He kept his voice low.

'Yes, Mom and Pops told me when I was a kid, but they didn't say anything more except my real parents didn't want me.'

'And you are wondering why?'

Yes. It sounds disloyal . . .'

'It is that.'

'I don't mean to be. I couldn't have had better parents. I loved them both and I would never do anything to hurt Mom. It's why I wouldn't push her, but I'm kinda restive about it. Why didn't my real mother want me?'

'Sometimes you have to do wrong to do right,' the old man

said. 'There's nothing to be gained by raking up the past.'

'Now you have fired me up. Who did wrong? Was it you?'

'No, but we condoned what was done. For your sake, boy, only for your sake. Let sleeping dogs lie. I can hear Martha calling us to go for our tea.' He stood up. 'Not another word, d'you hear?'

'I hear.'

He followed the old man into the next room, as tiny as the first, where a table was laid for three and Martha was putting steaming dishes onto it. 'Roast chicken,' she said. 'And all the trimmings. We saved the bird until you came.' She laughed suddenly. 'It must have thought its luck was in when it escaped at Christmas time.'

They talked of many things as they ate, but did not broach the subject that was eating away at him. 'Do wrong to do right'? What had the old man meant by that? Had his adoption been illegal? Had he simply been handed over? Had he been stolen? What would the consequences of that be in English law? His grandfather had titillated his curiosity and then forbidden him to mention it again. But he couldn't let it rest. If his grandparents wouldn't tell him, where else could he go?

He waited until they were in the Nag's Head with glasses of warm beer in front of them. The British didn't seem to go in for refrigerators. 'Grandpa,' he said. 'I know you said not to mention it again, but I've just got to know. Who was my mother? I mean the woman who gave birth to me.'

The old man puffed on his pipe while Johnnie waited for an answer. 'I wish I'd never said anything now. Better to be ignorant. In any case I don't know the whole story. Your father kept it to himself.'

'You mean the man I call Pops or the one who made me?'

'Same thing.'

'I don't understand. Are you saying Pops is not only my adopted father, he is my real father?'

'That's about the size of it.'

He was shocked into silence for several seconds. This was leading up to be a real riddle. He smiled suddenly. 'When I was a kid, people often used to say I looked like him and we used to laugh about it.'

'You are like him.'

'But Mom's not my real mother?'

'Course she's real. She's had you since you were three weeks old and you couldn't have asked for better.'

'I know that, it's not in dispute. But what about before I was three weeks old?'

'You'll have to ask someone else about that.' He paused. 'Not Martha.'

'OK, who?'

'Mayhap your other grandmother.'

'Other grandmother?' This was news to him. 'Who is she and where can I find her?'

'You sure you want to know? You might be sorry.'

'OK, so I'll be sorry. You can't send me back to the war not knowing. You never know . . .' He stopped, letting the remainder of the sentence hang in the air.

'I'll have to think about it. Ask me again before you leave. Now, are you going to get the next round in, or not?'

Johnnie knew he would get no further, not then. He rose and took their glasses back to the bar to have them refilled.

Dear Ma and Pa,

I had a couple of days leave and met Johnnie in London. We went round all the sights, Buckingham Palace, Houses of

Parliament and the tower and we went to a concert at the British Museum. I took him to West Ham to show him where we lived and introduced him to Bob and June and Noel.

Noel is growing up fast and toddling now. He always comes to me to be picked up and cuddled when I go there. He is beginning to talk and can say Mummy and Daddy and several other words June has taught him. If his real parents, or some close relative, were to turn up to claim him, June would be heartbroken. It made me think of Johnnie and his search for his real parents. He's had no luck so far, but if he found them, what would his adopted mother feel like? I am not sure it is a good idea to go looking, but I haven't said so.

I am getting to know him more and more. We get on really well, there is no stiffness or embarrassing silences and we can laugh together over the differences in the language, American is not the same as English. I have been teaching him some English ways and learning some of his. He knows all about you and the kids, and about Charlie being missing. He even said he would help me try and find him when we both have longer time together, but we have no idea when that might be. Am I in love? I don't know. If he proposed and wanted me to join him in America after his tour of duty ended, would I go? Could I bear to leave you and Charlie behind? I don't know, I really don't. There were fresh flowers on your graves when I visited, but June said she hadn't put them there. She has done in the past, but not lately. I suppose it must be one of your church friends.

Prue is very worried about her brother and Tim. I do my best to cheer her up like she cheered me up when I first came here and when I heard Chris had gone down with his ship. I still find that hard to believe. I am really sorry about the way

I turned him down and read his last letter to me over and over again. I can feel his hurt as I read, and the worst of it is that I can't tell him so. Johnnie says he understands but I don't think he does really.

The weather is cold and it's a job to keep warm, but we manage somehow.

Until we meet again,
Your ever-loving daughter,
Sheila

She closed the book and put it away in her box, carefully locking it. She couldn't bear the thought of her aunt seeing it again. Ever since they had come back from Longfordham, her mockery had become worse. It would be awful if she found out about Johnnie. She put on a thicker cardigan as she went downstairs to join her aunt.

It had been cold on the destroyer as it ploughed through the broken ice of the Arctic, but that cold had been nothing compared to what Chris was feeling on shore. Lief and Gunnar, both strong, weather-beaten men, had provided him with warm clothes and several blankets and hidden him in a hut on the mountain. Every few days they brought food and drink. The language was a great barrier, he could not ask them what they intended to do with him and would not have understood their answer if he could. There was a village down by the shoreline, which, in the short summer months, was free of snow, but most of the time it was covered in a blanket of white. How many people down there knew of his existence, he did not know, but he had seen Germans patrolling on shore and their motor boats in the fjord. He understood that was why his saviours dare not have him in their homes.

He must be a great burden to them: feeding him could not be easy and his diet consisted mostly of fish and black bread. But they always appeared cheerful and talked all the while they were with him, waving their arms about, pointing higher up the mountain to the east, or down to the village and the sea. Perhaps they were telling him of their plans, explaining their intentions, but as he could not understand he had to trust them.

They were fishermen, as every man in the village was, and they had a two-masted wooden boat about fifty feet long, called the *Gabbi*. The Germans could hardly stop them fishing, it was their livelihood after all, and they were allowed diesel for their engines but they were not allowed outside a certain distance from land. It was a regulation they frequently broke if they wanted to find the fish. When the wind was in the right direction, they eked out the diesel by using the sails.

They had been outside the permitted zone when they had come across the debris from the sunken destroyer and spotted a couple of bodies on a piece of wood. One was dead but Chris was still alive, although only just. They had hauled him aboard their boat, stripped off his freezing wet garments and wrapped him in blankets. He had been unaware of was happening to him until he thawed out and understood from the gesticulations how they had rescued him. He was given hot soup which warmed his insides, all too conscious of how lucky he had been. The Arctic was no place to be cast adrift. He had tried to ask what had become of the other ships, other survivors. His answer was a shrug. He wasn't sure if that meant he was the only one or not.

They had left him lying on one of the bunks while they finished fishing, then they made for their home village. It was on the mainland, close to the northern side of a deep fjord, sheltered from the Arctic storms by a host of small islands. It was still winter and dark for most of the day. At midday there was a kind of twilight, but that was all. They had sailed in under this darkness, as sure of their way as cats on a roof, and dropped anchor.

He was too weak to walk and so they waited until night when the Germans were shut into the fug of their guardroom before carrying him ashore. He had been taken to Leif's house where he was given food and drink and put to bed. The next day, they had put him on a sled and dragged him up to the hut. It was by no means a simple operation, even in daylight; in the dark it was hazardous. The side of the fjord rose steeply from the water and they had to take a zig-zag course, often manhandling the sled. By the time they arrived at the hut, they were all exhausted. After resting and trying unsuccessfully to make him understand their intentions, they had left him with several blankets, food and drink, but no fire and no weapon. The hut had become his home.

It was lonely up there. He passed the time watching the shore and village through the binoculars they had given him. There was a row of houses and a tiny church. A rough road stopped at a small quay and continued on the other side of the fjord. Travelling from one side to the other was done in their own boats or by the ferry. He spent hours watching it coming and going. He could see that everyone boarding it had to show papers of some sort, so any idea he might leave that way was out of the question. But it was the coming and going of the ferry that enabled him to count off the days. He would watch Gunner and Lief make ready for sea and chug away from the jetty, wishing he was going with them. They were usually gone two or three days and when they came back he felt a certain lifting of his spirits, knowing they would come up and see him before they left again.

An arctic fox came padding round one night in search of food and he put scraps out for it, admiring its thick glossy coat that turned from white to grey and then a pale brown as winter gave way to summer. Several times he was awed by red and green lights that flickered across the northern sky.

There was also plenty of time to think and his thoughts turned to home, his mother and brothers and sisters. They must have been told he had perished. He imagined how they must have received the news, especially his mother who had wailed when he left and not hidden the fact that she didn't expect to see him again. Had she told Sheila? Did Sheila think he was dead too? Did she care? After all, she had not answered his letters. He had really messed things up there.

She had been a feisty little thing at school, fiercely protective of her brothers and sisters and ready to scrap with anyone in their defence, including him if it came to a confrontation between his siblings and hers. She was bright, even in those days, and would have gone on to grammar school if her parents could have afforded the uniform and the bus fares to get her there. But she was still a cut above all the other children, always clean, well-spoken and polite.

The last time he had seen her she had been smartly dressed, her auburn hair rolled up over a scarf, her face lightly made up. And she spoke like a toff. Someone, and he supposed it was the people she worked with, had brought about the change and put ideas into her head. No, he told himself severely, that wasn't fair, everyone had a right to try and better themselves. If he still wanted her, it was up to him to match it. Sitting in his snow-bound hut, he pondered the problem. He had worked in a garage before the war which was probably why he was put in the engine room of the destroyer. It had been sheer luck that he had been on deck when the torpedo struck. Luck also that he had been found when he had: he could not have lasted another five minutes. There had to be a reason for that.

When summer came, there were a few more hours of daylight and a noticeable rise in temperature. The spruce and pine trees shed their burden of snow and lower down the slopes on the side of the fjord, alpine flowers grew in the crevices. He was fit and strong again and had been given a pair of skis and was teaching himself to use them. But he had to keep a sharp look out for other people, not just the Germans, but the locals too, some of whom, afraid for their lives, might very well report seeing him. He was impatient to be on his way and wondered how far it was to the Swedish border and how hazardous the journey would be.

He tried to find out from Gunnar when he came up one day, drawing a rough map in the snow. Gunnar put his hand on his arm and shook his head vehemently. Chris drew a calendar in the snow with numbered squares. 'How long?' he asked pointing, first at the calendar and then out over the fjord to the west. 'How long?'

Gunnar shrugged and Chris gave up.

He didn't see either Lief or Gunner after that for ten days and the food they had left him was all but gone. He began to wonder if they had been lost at sea, but dismissed that idea; they were too experienced, too good at handling their small craft for that to happen. Unless they had fallen foul of a German patrol. He was beginning to panic when Lief appeared with a newcomer who greeted Chris in English.

'I am the school master from the other side of the fjord,' he told him, shaking his hand. 'Lief fetched me so that I might explain why you must wait here. I know you are anxious to leave, but it must be done with the least risk to the people of the village, you must understand that. The Germans can be brutal in their reprisals.'

'I do understand, but I have been here some time and I must be a drain on the resources of the good people of the village who have been looking after me, not to mention a risk.'

'Yes, that is one reason you must be patient. There is a big search going on and you must not be caught up in it.'

'Are they searching for me?'

'No, they know nothing of you. This is someone else. I cannot tell you more.'

'I thought about trying to get to Sweden.'

'You would never make it alone and none of the village men dare leave the village long enough to take you. Their absence would be noted.' He smiled. 'But do not despair. Plans are afoot to help you, but you must be patient until all the arrangements are in place. Whatever you do, you must not show yourself.'

Lief spoke to the schoolmaster who turned to Chris. 'Lief asked me to tell you that no one will be able to visit you for a little while and he will leave extra food for you. There is a flask of hot soup and another of coffee but when that is gone, you must drink cold water. If you see a blue curtain on Lief's washing line, you must leave the hut and hide in the forest. It will mean the Germans are searching everywhere and that might include this hut. For the sake of everyone in the village, you must not be found.'

'I understand.'

The schoolmaster, whose name he never learnt, shook his hand again and left with Lief. He realised as never before just how much the Norwegians had risked, were still risking, to help him. He went back into the hut, to wait and keep watch. At the first sign of a German on the slopes below him, he would bury all the evidence he had been there in the deepest snow, and leave. Even if he died in the attempt, he would have to make his own way to Sweden.

* * *

With the spring and the arrival of the daffodils and tulips came a feeling of optimism and people in Britain began talking about 'after the war'. The newspapers that Prue and Sheila read were full of plans for post-war reconstruction and a proposed welfare state covering health, unemployment and old age, when everyone in the country would be looked after 'from the cradle to the grave'. It was going to be paid for with a national insurance scheme to which every adult would have to contribute. Before that could happen, the war had to be won. The signs were good. The tide was turning and Churchill and Roosevelt had met in Casablanca to plot their strategy for the remainder of the war. Hitler wasn't going to make it easy.

'Dilly' Knox, one of the cleverest cryptographers at Bletchley, had died in February and that had been a real setback. He had been gifted, but highly strung and his tantrums were legendary. He had also been very protective of the girls working with him and they were miserable at his passing. His place was taken by Alan Turing, the one everyone called 'the Prof'. He was busy designing a new machine, an advance on the bombes. If anyone apart from those working on it heard about it, they did not say so. They were all bound by the Official Secrets Act and there was no risk anyone outside BP would come to hear of it.

The German army and air force codes were being broken daily and those who could benefit from the knowledge were alerted, often as soon as, and sometimes before, the German commanders themselves received their orders. Prue was proud to be part of that and, as she became used to German military phraseology and abbreviations, found her work easier. Jews were being sent to Germany and their fate was unimaginable, so too were able-bodied Frenchmen shipped off to work in German industrial plants where they would be at the mercy of Allied bombing. She worried about Gillie and wondered if Tim was as well-treated as he implied in his cryptic note, the only one she had received from him.

How could he tell Prue what it was like to be a prisoner of war? It was boring and frustrating. There were entertainments, games, lectures, all laid on by the men themselves, and there were frequent attempts to escape, almost all of which failed. Tunnels were begun and discovered before they could be put to use. Some made the attempt during an air raid, when the lights in the camp were extinguished, but the guards were wise to that and set the dogs loose in the compound to deter them. Those that did manage to get out of the compound were returned after a few days and locked in solitary confinement for a week as a punishment. Some were shot. When that happened, everyone went about with long faces until someone came up with another hare-brained scheme.

He was biding his time, observing and making mental notes, talking to the guards and building a picture of the terrain outside the camp. He was helped in this by the recaptured prisoners who were quizzed unmercifully when they were returned to the fold. His aim was to get back into the war but, more than that, he wanted to see Prue again. Receiving her letter had lifted his spirits even though she had not mentioned that last letter he had written trying to explain himself. Perhaps she had been embarrassed by it, or perhaps she had not received it. The post was notoriously unreliable. He couldn't say it all again on a flimsy piece of airmail paper, not big enough for more than a couple of meaningless sentences.

In the meantime he studiously went to his German classes and practised on the guards, who seemed to think they were winning him round to believing Germany would triumph. He did nothing to disabuse them of the idea. At night, when the camp was quiet, he lay on his bunk plotting. It was not enough to escape from the camp, he had to be able to stay out and move about without creating suspicion, to make his way to a neutral country. There was Sweden to the north, which meant finding a ship on the Baltic coast and possibly stowing away, Switzerland which was landlocked and surrounded by occupied countries where he might be stuck for the duration, or way down south to Spain or Portugal, which meant passing through France, fully occupied since a combined Allied expeditionary force had landed in North Africa and worried Hitler into thinking the south of France might be next. There was no longer a *zone libre.* The advantage of going that way was that he believed there were organised escape lines which might help him.

Setting his sights on England, home, his parents and Prue, gave him something to focus on, a goal to attain. What would he say to Prue? Would she let him explain how he felt? Could they go back to the cosy relationship they had had before that disastrous weekend in Huntingdon? He hoped so.

Everyone had been immeasurably cheered when they heard through the camp grape vine about the breeching of the German dams by RAF bombers in May.

'It must have taken a helluva lot of guts to fly that low,' Patrick said as they stood watching a cricket match on the compound which didn't have a single blade of grass on it. 'And in the dark too.' He and Patrick Duffey, as flight lieutenants, had been separated from the rest of their crew who were in the other half of the camp.

'Just shows it can be done,' Tim said. 'Accurate bombing, I mean.'

Pat laughed. 'Yes, one in the eye for the yanks and their precision bombing.'

'I'm getting out of here.'

'When?'

'I've thought of a plan.'

'Let's hear it then.'

They left the cricket match and dawdled round the perimeter of the camp. 'We change places with two of the other ranks and make our escape while we're on the road to the factory. They will dress in our clothes and take our place at roll call and we won't be missed.' Unlike the other ranks, the officers did not have to work and so were never taken outside the camp.

'How do you know we can get away from the march? The men are closely guarded. And I bet it's been tried before.'

'So what if it has? We'll get the men to create a diversion on the bridge, just long enough for us to vault over the wall and hide. Then we wait until the column has gone into the factory and make our way across country to the railway line. If we follow that, we might be able to hop on a train.'

'We will need identity cards, permits to travel, all that sort of thing. And a good cover story.'

'We can get all of that.'

'Have you put the idea to the Escape Committee?'

'Yes. They've approved. But they won't keep the men for more than one roll call and then they go back to their own quarters and pretend they've been sick and never went on the work party. It might be a day or two before Jerry puts two and two together, time enough for us to get well away.'

'But what about the men? Will they agree?'

'If it's put to them nicely and we compensate them. I'll give one of them my wristwatch, he can sell it to the goons to buy whatever he fancies. It's a pity because Prue gave it to me, but needs must. You've got something you are prepared to sacrifice, haven't you?'

'My last Red Cross parcel and my harmonica.'

Tim laughed. Patrick and his mouth organ were a bane to the men in the hut because he insisted on practising when they wanted to sleep. 'So, are you with me?'

'You bet.'

Later that afternoon, he was lying on his bunk, pretending to read but mentally rehearsing what he would say to Prue when he saw her again, when the air raid siren went. He joined the crowd in the doorway to look up at the sky. Above them they could see the dark outline of heavy bombers. 'Flying fortresses,' someone said. 'I hope they don't mistake us for a factory.'

Chapter Twelve

The fortresses, coming from bases all over East Anglia, had assembled over the Wash into the tight formations they employed to maximise safety. Johnnie had taken up his position just behind the leader's left flank. Behind him other fortresses were lining up. Around them buzzed the fighters, who would escort them as far as the German border, when they would peel off to return to their bases. While they were there, everyone felt comparatively safe. No one liked it when they were left to fly on alone, deep into enemy territory.

They had been woken as usual at four in the morning, had their breakfast and gone to the briefing, where they sat smoking and speculating about what lay behind the sheet that covered the map. Their curiosity had been satisfied when the base commander came in and pulled it aside. Schweinfurt and its ball bearing factories. A groan went up from everyone when they saw the red line, beginning at the Wash and stretching over Europe deep into Germany. This would be no milk run.

Cloud cover would be light over the target, they had been told, but a little heavier over the assembly point and they would need to be careful making up the formation. Johnnie hadn't liked the sound of that; hundreds of bombers arriving from all over East Anglia milling about to take up their correct positions was bad enough when the skies were clear, but in cloud it was asking for collisions. He said nothing of his fears to the crew, but he didn't need to, they all knew the score.

No one had said very much while they got into flying gear and went out to the fortress. It was Louis, the ball turret gunner, who spotted the name painted on the side of their fortress. 'What's that?' he queried, pointing at it.

'You can read, can't you?' Johnnie said. 'It says "Songbird".' He had asked the ground crew to paint it on in white letters. They had illustrated it too, with the picture of a colourful bird sitting on a twig.

'I didn't know you were into ornithology.'

'He isn't,' Vernon said. 'His songbird don't have feathers.'

'Oh, right. I see. Let's hope she keeps us flying.'

'Bound to,' Martin said, laughing. 'She's a bird, after all.'

He ignored their banter. Most of the fortresses had names painted on them, though they hadn't chosen one before, but he had suddenly wanted to let the world know that his songbird was special. 'Get aboard,' he told them, then walked all round the aircraft accompanied by the chief mechanic, before climbing into his own seat and doing the routine pre-flight checks.

The sun came up over the eastern horizon and lit the sky in a golden glow as the formation finished assembling and headed out east. While the fighters were there and Martin was busy with his charts, he could relax a little and his thoughts turned to Sheila.

They'd hit it off right from the start, falling into a comfortable companionship. She was easy to talk to and he found he could tell her things he wouldn't have told anyone else. He was aware of the dangers of reading too much into a chance acquaintance; many of his buddies had come unstuck when they discovered the girls were only after what they could get. It worked the other way too, when English girls had taken the easy-going generosity and flattery of the America GIs at face value, only to realise what they had thought of as love had no more substance than a puff of wind. He must be careful not to do that to Sheila. A chaste kiss was all he had allowed himself.

Besides, he still didn't know exactly who he was. After three days with the Fletcher grandparents, during which they fed him well and introduced him to almost everyone in the village, he knew no more. He had wandered round the village on his own on one occasion, exploring and thinking: this is where Mom grew up, where she went to school, people here must have known her. 'Pretty little thing, she was,' he was told by one chatty old lady standing at her house door. She had just finished whitening the step. 'We were sorry when she left, but there is nothing for a young girl round here and nothing much for the men to do except go down the mine or on the railways. No doubt she was better off in America.'

It was a coal mining area and he had seen the black-faced miners coming off their shifts. Grandpa Fletcher had been a miner before he retired and he had told him tales of what the miners had to endure underground that made flying bombers sound like child's play. 'Did you know my father?' he asked the old lady.

'When he was a young lad, but he didn't fancy the mines, so he went away and we didn't see him again until just before the wedding. Bit of a surprise that was, him being so much older than your ma and them getting married in London an' all instead of here and then clearing off to America.' She looked him up and down. 'You are like him to look at.'

'So I've been told.' Did that mean Pops wasn't American but English? This mystery, far from being solved, was becoming deeper and he didn't know what to believe.

'How is your ma? Well is she?'

'Yes, very well.'

'Good. Perhaps now you've broken the ice, she'll come home. Not until after the war, of course. Not much point in coming here now.'

'Perhaps,' he said, and left her.

The conversation had given him food for thought. He had never known where his father had been born and brought up. It was a revelation to think that his parents had known each other in childhood; the way the woman had spoken and looked at him made him think she believed Mom had given birth to him before the wedding. There had been both curiosity and disapproval in her voice. Was that the general view?

On his last day, when his bag was packed, the jeep's gasoline tank filled from the cans he had brought with him and it was almost time to go, he found his grandfather feeding the pigs in the field. 'Time to go if I'm to reach London by nightfall,' he said. 'It's been swell meeting you.'

'Yes, for us too. You must come again.'

'I will if I'm given the chance.' He paused. 'You said ask again before I left. You know about . . .'

'I was hoping you'd forget all about it. Can't you see, it won't do a ha'porth of good to go poking about?'

'I need to know. I'll keep it to myself.'

'I can't tell you. I don't know the ins and outs of it. The only people who knew the whole truth, apart from your dad, is your mother and your other grandmother and she's in a nursing home. She's ga-ga and you won't get much sense out of her, if any at all.'

On the way to London he had called in at the address he had been given. Although it had once been a substantial mansion, it reeked of urine and carbolic. The entrance hall had polished black and white tiles, the doors leading off it heavy-stained oak, the stairs wide and shallow, with a half landing halfway up. Johnnie could hear noises, shouting and singing, but could see no one. The receptionist he had spoken to had disappeared along the corridor to see if Matron was available to speak to him. He stood in the middle of the floor, cap in hand, waiting.

When the receptionist returned, he had followed her along the corridor and was ushered into an office. A plump woman in a nurse's uniform and a huge white cap rose from a desk and came towards him, hand outstretched. 'How can I help you, Captain?'

'You can see Verity, by all means,' she had said when he explained his errand. 'But I doubt you'll get much sense out of her.'

'How long has she been here?'

'Some years. She was here when I arrived in 1936.' She went to a cupboard and extracted a heavy ledger. 'Let me see, it was soon after the last war, I think.' She began turning pages. 'Ah, here it is. She was admitted in June 1921.'

He whistled. 'Twenty-two years. Who put her in here and who pays for her keep?'

'She was referred to us by her general practitioner and her husband. He set up a trust fund for her before he died.'

'Did she have a son, more than one perhaps?'

'If she did, I never saw him.'

'I think I must have the wrong lady. According to my

information she had a son who emigrated to America. That's where I come in.'

'Oh, I see. Do you still want to see her?'

'Yes. I need to be sure.'

She had conducted him along a corridor to a large room in which dozens of women sat in a circle round the edge of the room. Some were shouting, some singing, some silent and seemingly unaware of their surroundings. Feeling more like turning on his heel than staying to talk to any of them, he stood uncertainly just inside the doorway while the matron spoke to one of the white-coated attendants. 'We'll have her brought to the interview room,' she told him. 'It will be more private, but a nurse will have to stay with her. Her behaviour can be somewhat unpredictable. Follow me.'

In a trance-like state he had followed the ample back of the matron to a small room which was barely furnished with three chairs and a table. He sat down and a few moments later a nurse wheeled an emaciated woman into the room in a wheelchair. She was simply dressed in clean clothes and her white hair was cut short and combed back from her face. He stood up.

'Verity, this gentleman has come to talk to you,' the nurse told her.

He drew up a chair next to the wheelchair and sat down. 'Do you know who I am?'

'Clifford, of course.'

'I am not Clifford. My name is Johnnie. Johnnie Howard and I'm in the United States Air Force. I come from America.'

'Liar.' She spat the word. 'Liar and scoundrel. You think putting me in here will shut me up, do you? Well, it won't. I'll tell the world.' Her voice rose to a scream and she began beating her right hand on the arm of the wheelchair. The left lay useless in her lap.

It was all he could do to remain calm. 'What will you tell the world?'

'You know.' She continued to rant but although most of the words were incoherent, he did catch some of them: evil, judgment day and sins of the fathers, then something about her dinner which had displeased her and an argument she had had with someone that seemed to have no bearing on his presence. Then she suddenly ran out of steam, fell back in her chair and shut her eyes. 'I'm tired. I don't want to talk about it any more.'

He had realised the futility of going on with the interview and stood up to leave, still unsure whether she was his grandmother or not. He suddenly remembered the little teddy bear he had put in his pocket. He pulled it out and touched her shoulder. 'Do you recognise this?'

She opened her eyes wide and, seeing the toy, made a lunge to grab it and in doing so fell out of her chair. He put the toy back in his pocket and helped the nurse to haul her back. 'I think she's had enough, don't you?' the nurse said.

'Yes. I'm sorry.' He touched the old lady's wrinkled hand. 'I'm sorry, ma'am, I truly am.'

On the way out, he tapped on the matron's door. 'I appreciate your help, Matron,' he told her when he had obeyed the call to enter.

'Did you find out what you wanted to know?'

'I'm not sure. She seemed to think I was someone else. Her son, I think.'

'You think her son was your father?'

'I'd been told that, but Pop's name wasn't Clifford. Have you any other documents that might help?'

'One or two. I looked them up while you were with her. Would you like a cup of tea while you read them? I can't let you take them away, I'm afraid.'

An hour later he left, his head in a whirl of contradictions. Was she or was she not his grandmother? She had been admitted to the home after a stroke which left her partially paralysed. Her husband, who had been badly gassed in what had become known as The Great War, was already an invalid and could not look after her. He had died himself soon afterwards, but had left her well provided for. They had a son called Clifford but they had lost touch with him. He had never heard the name Clifford, so it couldn't be his father, could it? On the other hand she seemed to recognise that little teddy bear. A grainy, sepia photograph had been among the documents, of a man, a woman and a child. The woman was just recognisable as the Verity he had just left and he supposed the man, standing stiffly at her side, was her husband and the boy their son. He was about three years old and still in the dresses they put on little boys in those days until they were old enough for shorts. Could that be his father? He would have to go back to Grandpa Fletcher and make him talk. *Do wrong to do right*, those words echoed in his brain. Someone had done wrong.

'Dutch coast coming up.' Martin's voice came to him over the intercom. 'Watch out for flak.'

From then on he was too busy to think about anything but getting his fort to the target and safely home again.

There was pandemonium on the bridge. The orderly column of prisoners had inexplicably started to fight among themselves. Fists were flying and some of the men were wrestling on the floor. While the guards tried to separate them and restore order, Tim and Patrick took the opportunity to vault over the wall, scramble down the bank and under the bridge.

They hardly dare breathe as they pressed themselves against the wall and waited. After a while the noise died down and they heard the men singing 'It's a long way to Tipperary' as they formed up to continue their march to the factory. 'It worked,' Tim said. 'They've gone. Let's get out of here before we're spotted.'

Crouching and running, they crossed a field and flung themselves into a ditch. As soon as they had regained their breath, they set off again. Tim had studied the map which one of the navigators had drawn after being recaptured, but they hadn't brought it away with them. It was too useful to be given away. Once they went too near a farmhouse and set the dogs barking, which had them running for their lives, but apparently they hadn't been seen or heard and they took more care after that.

'Shall we risk trying to buy a ticket?' Patrick said, as they found the railway line just short of a station. By then they were ten miles away from the camp. They had forged identities as Hungarian workers. Neither Tim nor Pat spoke Hungarian but they were gambling that few Germans did and they could communicate in German if they had to. But were they far enough away from the camp for their disappearance to have been discovered and railway staff alerted?

'If we can get on a train we'll be further away quicker,' Patrick said when Tim voiced his doubts. 'The further away we are, the better our chances.'

'True, but this is only a quiet country station, the sort of place where everyone knows everyone else. We'll stand out like a sore thumb. Let's try and jump a goods wagon. We can buy tickets further up the line, Cologne say, where we can merge in with the crowd.'

This seemed sensible, so they hid in a shed until dusk when they emerged to run along the line to where some goods wagons were being shunted. 'Make sure they are going in the right direction,' Patrick said, following Tim along the line of wagons.

'We want to go west not east, don't forget. Ally or not, I don't want to end up in Russia.'

The line stretched away from the station in both directions, but the engine which was being hooked to the wagons was definitely facing west, if the setting sun was anything to go by. They pulled open a wagon door and hauled themselves up and quickly pulled the door shut again.

'What's that smell?' Tim asked and bumped into something hanging from the roof. 'God! It's a body. Let's get out of here.'

It was too late, the train had started to move. They sat on the floor close to the door where a crack let in a little fresh air. 'The first time we stop, I'm off out of it,' Patrick said. 'You can do what you like.'

'I'm with you, old man.' Tim laughed suddenly. 'At least it might put the guards off searching too diligently.'

'And when we get on a proper passenger train with tickets and all, everyone will steer well clear of us.'

'True. It's an ill wind.' He delved in his pocket for cigarettes and matches. The cigarettes smelt horrible too, but the smoke might keep the other odours away. And then he laughed. Striking a match had lit up their travelling companions: rows of pig carcases. 'I wonder if they are going to be used as food,' Tim said. 'I had my suspicions about the so-called pork we were served in the camp. Whenever we had it, half of us were ill.'

'I'll never eat pork again in my life.'

'Nor me.' He stubbed out his cigarette and leant against the side of the truck. 'I'm going to try and get some shut-eye. I should do the same if I were you.'

It wasn't easy to sleep. The rattle of the wagon was loud in their ears and the carcases creaked on their hooks. Besides, they were too wound up. They had left the camp some way behind, but there was still a very long way to go and hazards at every stage. Tim had rehearsed every mile of the journey in his head and tried to think of ways to counter any setbacks they might meet, but in the end it all boiled down to luck. They had to get to Belgium and find the address in Brussels he had been given by the escape committee. How they knew of it he had no idea, probably from one of the prisoners who had been recaptured. Here they might find help, always provided the address was still safe. If it wasn't they would have to improvise; he was determined he wasn't going to be taken back to that camp.

They were woken by a thunderous jolting as the train stopped and then began going backwards. 'I think we've landed up somewhere,' Tim said, pulling the door open a crack, letting in a blast of fresh air. They breathed in deeply. The movement stopped and there was silence.

It was daylight. Cautiously, Tim put his head out and looked along the track. 'They are unhooking the engine,' he said. 'Let's get out of here before they put another one on the other end and we start going back the way we came.'

'Do you know where we are?'

'No, but I'm not going to wait to find out. As soon as that worker moves out of sight, I'm jumping. You follow.'

In no time at all they were rolling down a steep embankment, at the bottom of which was a river. Tim just managed to stop himself ending up in the water and then Pat careered into him and they both had to scramble to stay dry. 'I wouldn't have minded a bath,' Pat said as they lay panting on the bank. 'But I didn't fancy going all day in wet clothes. Difficult to explain away.'

'True. Let's find somewhere to lay up until dark, then we can find out where we are.'

They walked along the river bank wondering if they ought to

be on the other side, but neither fancied a swim. They had eaten the provisions they had brought with them and were hungry and thirsty but daren't go in search of food. Tim had a bar of chocolate from his last Red Cross parcel and they shared that as they walked. 'You know, if we could find a boat, we could perhaps row down the river,' Patrick said. 'It would be quicker than walking.'

'True, but the loss might set the alarm bells ringing and rivers around these parts tend to end up in the Baltic.'

'We've been travelling most of the day at a fair old lick, so do you think we are still in Germany?'

'No idea.'

Pat laughed. 'You're the navigator.'

'True, but it's not a navigator we need right now. If the sky is clear tonight I can work out the direction to take, but it won't help over country boundaries.'

They were coming to some houses, which had gardens down to the water's edge, and there were small boats hauled up on the grass. 'I don't think it's a good idea to take one of those,' Tim said as they hesitated whether to go on. 'Someone is bound to see us trying to launch it.'

'Perhaps after dark we could. Let's hide in that boathouse.'

They crept into the wooden building from the river side and found a cabin cruiser anchored inside. They clambered aboard and found two comfortable bunks and were soon stretched out. 'We had better take it in turns to stay awake,' Tim said. 'I'll watch first.'

'We could travel a fair way on this,' Pat murmured half asleep.

While Pat slept, Tim went round the boat searching for clues as to their whereabouts. There was fresh water in a large bottle that fed the basin in the galley and a packet of stale biscuits in a cupboard, but there was no petrol in the tank. As a means of transport, the boat was useless. He was eating a biscuit and was about to screw the packet up when he noticed the wording on it. It wasn't in German, he could recognise that, but it was similar. He left the boat and walked round it. The name on its bows wasn't German either, but that probably didn't signify anything; boat owners did not have to stick to names in their own language. Were they in Holland? Belgium? Denmark? He was sure they had been travelling west when they set out: had the train changed direction while they dozed? It was imperative to find out.

He went back inside and shook Pat awake. 'I'm going to try and find out where we are. You stay here. If I don't come back in a couple of hours, get going on your own. Don't wait for me.'

'I'll come with you.'

'No. Two of us together might attract attention.'

He left the boathouse on the landward side and made his way up the garden and round the side of a substantial house, darting from bush to bush and keeping an eye out for anyone looking out of the windows. If they were in Holland, the owners might be sympathetic, even helpful, but on the other hand Holland was an occupied country and its inhabitants under the thumb of their German masters – they might be afraid to help. They might be collaborators and all too ready to betray escapees.

He reached a small residential road and made his way along it, trying to look as if he belonged there and was on his way to work. He came to a junction and found himself in a sizeable town where the roads were busier and there were German troops everywhere. There was also a lot of bomb damage but he tried not to think that he might have been one of those inflicting it. Trying not to appear too curious, he furtively watched the civilians. They were thin, ill-clad and grey-faced and scuttled past the German soldiers they met in the street. He concluded they were more likely to be an occupied people than members of the so-called master race.

He made his way into a church and picked up a hymn book. In the flyleaf it stated: St Jacobus Kirke Enschede. They were in Holland, but only just. The German border was very close. It was probably where the goods train had been uncoupled. He heard the door swing open and hurriedly went to kneel at the altar, debating his next step. Someone was walking up the aisle. He swung round to see a parson coming towards him. '*Goedendag*,' the man said.

His meaning was clear and Tim repeated the word back to him.

The man laughed and said. 'You are English.' And when Tim looked startled, added, 'Do not be afraid. Follow me.' He turned and left the church. Tim did not hesitate for long before deciding to go after him, although he was on the alert to make a run for it if he had to.

The parson was in no hurry, he walked sedately, nodding to acquaintances as he passed and even saying '*Goedendag*,' to some Germans who were standing on the pavement. Tim held his breath as he passed them too. The Dutchman had had no difficulty in identifying him as English; did that mean he stuck out like a sore thumb, even wearing the civilian clothes he had been provided with in the camp? They were made from unpicked and dyed uniforms but the tailor had made a good job of them.

Ten minutes later, he was back where he started and the parson was ushering him into the house he had been so careful to skirt around. Sitting at the kitchen table was Patrick and a young woman, drinking ersatz coffee. Tim turned to the cleric. 'You followed me from here?'

'Yes. My name is Johannes, by the way, and this is Hildegarde. You do not need to know our real names. Madame owns this house. We were talking together when we saw you creep by the kitchen window. I followed to see what you would do and Madame went down to the boathouse and rescued your compatriot. Sit down and drink some coffee. You are perfectly safe for the moment.'

Tim sat, was given a cup of scalding coffee and then began an interrogation in impeccable English. Name, date and place of birth, school and university was only the beginning. He was thoroughly grilled. What squadron was he in, where was he shot down, where was he held prisoner, how did he escape? What identification did he carry on him? All he had were the forged documents which were carefully scrutinised.

'Not bad,' Johannes said. 'They would probably get by a routine search, but not a Gestapo cross-examination.'

'I've had my turn,' Patrick said, grinning. 'They are a suspicious pair.'

'We have to be,' Madame said. 'The Nazis have been known to infiltrate their own people as escaped allied prisoners. So far, we have been able to identify them. Needless to say, they did not return to their masters.'

'I sincerely hope you are not thinking along those lines for us,' Tim said.

'No, I think you are who you say you are,' Johannes said. 'But you will stay here overnight while we check out what you have told us. If all is well, we can help you on your way.'

'Thank you,' Tim said. 'That's better than we hoped for. We were making for Brussels. We have an address to go to in Avenue Voltaire.'

'Are you sure it's safe?'

'It was two months ago.'

'A lot can happen in two months.'

'Yes, we know we have to approach with care.'

Johannes stood up. 'I will leave you with Hildegarde now. Tomorrow I will return and we will talk some more.' He shook hands with them and left.

The two men turned to each other and grinned. They had fallen on their feet and Lady Luck was with them. So far.

Hildegarde let them have a hot bath, giving them some old clothes of her late husband's to wear while she cleaned the suits they had been wearing. 'I'm beginning to feel human again,' Tim said, emerging from the bathroom with his skin pink and shiny.

'What was that dreadful smell on your clothes?' Hildegarde asked him, while Pat took his turn in the bathroom.

'Pork that had gone off. It was in the freight wagon we hitched a lift on. Sorry about that.'

'I think I have got rid of most of it.'

'Thank you. You speak very good English.'

'English is – or was – taught in most Dutch schools, Flight Lieutenant, but my husband was English. He was arrested by the Nazis when Holland was occupied. They hanged him. So you see, I have no love for the Germans. I have my revenge by helping Allied escapees. I used to use my boat until I could not obtain any more petrol for it. But you will be in good hands tomorrow.'

'We wouldn't want to put you at risk.'

'Everything we do is risky these days, but so far I am not suspected. I even help out at the German headquarters in the town and pretend to be cheerful about it. It helps because sometimes I hear about escaped prisoners they are seeking.'

'Have you heard about us?'

'Not so far. Now I will make some soup and stew some plums from the tree in the garden and after that I will show you where you are to sleep. It would be best if you stayed in your room until I call you to come down, just to be on the safe side.'

'We will do exactly as you say, madame.'

Johannes returned the next morning, coming up the garden from the river. He greeted Hildegarde, who had called the men down to a breakfast of toast and home-made preserve, washed down with more ersatz coffee. 'Come with me,' he said, refusing coffee, saying there was no time.

They said goodbye to Hildegarde and followed the parson down to the water's edge where a barge with a smoking chimney was moored. Johannes led them on board and introduced them to a big man with a blonde beard dressed in oilskin trousers and a thick pullover. 'This is Dick,' he said. 'He will take you to Belgium.'

They shook Dick's hand and then Johannes', who wished them good luck and went back on shore to watch as the barge pulled away.

Dick took them down-river as far as Antwerp. He was apparently well known to the authorities who stopped him and searched his load of firewood at various points along the way. When that happened, the fugitives were hidden in the bilge. Dick had sectioned off a compartment that was fairly dry but it was a tight squeeze for both of them at once and they lived in fear of being discovered as they listened to the sound of heavy boots on deck and German voices added to Dick's. Their saviour was in no hurry to rid himself of his visitors and sat down to drink cognac with them, before bidding them a cheery '*Dag*' as they left.

In Antwerp they were smuggled off the boat and onto a train going to Brussels. There was a scary moment when the Gestapo came along the train examining papers. Dick was unconvinced that the identity cards and work permits they had would fool men who were paid to be suspicious of everyone. He diverted the guard's attention with some triviality they could not understand but it gave the two escapees the opportunity to slip past and find a carriage which had already been searched.

In Brussels, not wanting to risk the address they had been given, Dick handed them over to his own contact. They were taken to a safe house and stayed there three weeks while new identity documents, complete with new photographs and travel passes, were obtained for them. Tim's fair hair was dyed dark brown and he was given a pair of horn-rimmed spectacles. Patrick sported untidy brown hair and an equally untidy beard, which made Tim laugh because Pat was known for his fastidiousness. It was while they were there they learnt that everyone connected to the address at Avenue Voltaire had been betrayed and several British airmen had been captured in the round-up that followed. They thanked their lucky stars for Johannes and Dick.

From Brussels they were taken to Paris by a middle-aged man called Jacques who left them with a contact on the top floor of a luxury apartment block. They were not told who owned it, but were looked after by an elegant French lady who told them her name was Anne. They didn't think it was her real name; no one in the risky business of helping escapees used their own names. Two days later, they were on their way to Lyon, accompanied by Anne.

The train was packed with German troops, foreign workers, among whom they counted themselves, women, children and old men; there were no seats to be had. They stood in the corridor not talking but feeling confident, almost blasé. Everyone they had met so far had been thoroughly efficient and knew exactly what they were doing. But even the best-laid plans could go wrong as they discovered when half a dozen Gestapo boarded the train at Orleans and went along it inspecting everyone's papers and hauling several people out onto the platform. They protested strongly and one man resisted so strenuously he was struck with the butt of the soldier's rifle and went down on his knees, his nose pouring blood. Women were shrieking, children sobbing.

'What's happening?' Tim whispered to Anne.

'They've had a tip-off that there are escaped prisoners on the train.'

'What do we do?'

'Follow me.'

He beckoned to Pat who was a little further away, and they pushed their way down the length of the train until they came to the guard's van. The guard was known to Anne. As soon as he saw the men with her, he understood the problem. He took the lid off a metal crate on wheels and beckoned to Pat to climb in. When he had put the lid back on, he pulled forward another crate and Tim squeezed himself into it. 'Will we be safe in here?' Tim asked.

'Not if you stay on the train,' the guard said. 'The Gestapo are very thorough, especially if they are sure there are fugitives on board.'

'They found out about us?'

The man shrugged. 'Who knows? I'm going to wheel the crates out onto the platform. It's up to you to get yourself out and away when the hullabaloo has died down.'

'Anne?'

'I'll stay with you as long as I can,' Anne said. 'Then I must go back to Paris.'

'Could we get on the next train?'

'Too risky. If the Boche don't find anyone on this train, they will search the next.' She pushed his head down so that the lid could be replaced and a few seconds later he felt himself being wheeled down a ramp. In the confined space of the crate, he felt battered and bruised and short of air to breathe. He could hear Anne speaking to someone, telling whoever it was that the crates would be collected by truck and they were to be taken outside to wait for it. Then he was on his way again. 'What have you got in here?' a man's voice asked. 'Stones?'

'I don't know,' she answered. 'I'm only the courier, but I know it's important for the war effort whatever it is. Best not to ask.'

They stopped. He heard the man thank Anne, presumably for a tip, and then there was silence for several minutes. Tim was feeling cramped but there was no room to move. At last the lid was removed and Anne peered in at him. 'Get out quickly,' she said, then went to let Patrick out and told him the same thing. They tumbled out but neither could stand properly until the circulation returned to their legs. They were outside the station in a yard where several vehicles were parked, most of them German military vehicles.

'Let's walk,' she said, and took each by the arm. 'Be relaxed, laugh a little. We are having fun.'

They walked down the road away from the station, pretending carefree chatter. Behind them they heard the train leaving and a little later they were passed by several of the military vehicles they had seen. One truck was full of civilians, guarded by soldiers with rifles. 'We could have been with them,' Tim said. 'If it hadn't been for Anne and that guard.'

'Too true,' Pat said. 'But what now?'

'A bus,' she said. 'We can't trust this line for the next few days, so I'm going to take you on a little detour.'

The detour meant boarding a bus which, like the train, was full to overflowing with no way of escape if it were searched. They sat, not daring to speak as they were carried mile after mile across the French countryside. They were going west, not south, which did not augur well, but Anne had been good so far, so they had to trust her. They left the bus at Auxerre where they went into a café and each had a cup of coffee and a stale bun.

'What now?' Pat asked

'I need to think,' she said. 'This is off my usual route and I'm not sure of contacts.' She rose. 'Sit still and drink another cup of coffee. I'll be back.'

After half an hour, they became worried that she had abandoned them. 'Supposing she's gone to give us up?' Pat whispered. 'Are we going to sit here and let it happen?'

'Why would she do that?'

'I don't know, do I? We can't get caught now, can we? Not after coming so far.'

'What do you suggest?'

'Make a run for it?'

'No, but we could hide somewhere and keep watch. See if she comes back and who with.'

'OK.' They rose and walked to do the door, just as Anne returned.

'Leaving me, gentlemen?' she queried, smiling.

'No, no, of course not,' Tim said. 'We didn't like the look of some of the patrons; they seemed a bit too curious for comfort.'

She laughed, obviously not believing him. 'Come with me.'

She took them to a house a few streets away and introduced them to a man called Pierre. 'This is where I leave you and Pierre takes over,' she said. 'I need to report what happened today, warn the rest of the people not to send any more men down the line for a few days. You were lucky.'

'We realise that,' Tim said. 'And we are very grateful. After the war, when the world is at peace, we might meet again. You never know.'

'You never know,' she repeated, then reached up and kissed his cheek. 'Goodbye and good luck.' She moved on to Pat and kissed him too. And then she was gone.

They turned to Pierre. He was a big man, middle-aged, already balding. He was a man of few words, perhaps not too pleased to have these two pushed onto him so unexpectedly. 'The lady belongs to a different line from me,' he said. 'We don't have contact with each other. I don't know how she came to hear of me. It is worrying.'

'Are you worried about us or her?' Tim asked.

'Both. I am not stirring from here, nor are you, until I have checked you all out.'

'Fair enough,' Tim said. 'We are in your hands.'

'If you don't want to help us, we'll be on our way,' Pat put in.

'No, don't do that. You risk your own lives and those of a great many other people if you are caught. I will not take any longer than I can help. In the meantime, please make yourselves comfortable. My wife will show you to your room, where you must stay until it is time to move you. She will bring you food and wine.'

They were conducted to a room in the attic. It was sparsely furnished with two single beds, two chairs and a table. Its daylight came from a skylight in the sloping roof. Here their hostess left them. But she took care to lock the door. 'We're stuck now,' Patrick said. 'I told you we should have made a run for it.'

Tim stretched out on one of the beds and watched his friend prowling about the room. 'Well, I am inclined to trust them. Johannes didn't let us down and neither did Dick nor Anne. They know what there are doing and we don't. I'm going to make the most of this bed and sleep. I advise you to do the same.'

Pat flung himself on the other bed and was soon snoring. Tim lay awake, going over their journey so far and what might still be to come. They had come safely more than halfway, out of Germany, across Holland and Belgium and into France. There were still hazards to be met, obstacles to be overcome, and they would need to keep their wits about them, but he was more optimistic than he had been for some time.

After three days locked in Pierre's attic and a grilling from someone whose name they never discovered, they had been judged genuine and set off hidden in the back of a dilapidated van driven by Pierre. What fuel it used Tim did not know, but the engine coughed and spluttered and would not go faster than fifteen miles an hour. It seemed a lifetime had passed by the time they entered the small town of Ville Sainte Jeanne and drew up outside a bicycle repair shop. Here they were given some soup and bread and a bottle of wine to share between them.

When that had been consumed, their host, who said his name was Paul, placed a ladder against the trapdoor in the roof and invited them to climb it. 'I am afraid I cannot offer you a more comfortable hiding place,' he said. 'But the Boche are particularly busy at the moment and causing problems. Please do not make a noise. I have to leave you, but I will be back.'

They climbed the ladder and stretched out in the confined space, where there was no room to sit upright, let alone stand. The trapdoor was firmly shut behind them.

'He's taking the ladder away,' Pat said. 'We can't get out. He could leave us here to die and nobody would be any the wiser.'

'Leaving the ladder would direct German eyes to the trapdoor, wouldn't it?' Tim said. 'Without it they probably wouldn't look upwards.'

'Could we get out over the roof?' Pat nodded towards a small skylight above their heads.

'I'm not even going to try.'

Pat continued to grumble, mainly about the heat because the loft was like an oven, but Tim ignored him and let his mind drift. His parents would be glad to see him safely home, he did not doubt that. His doubts were centred on Prue. The first thing he would do as soon as he arrived back on home soil would be to telephone her and arrange to meet. She would agree to that, wouldn't she? On second thoughts, perhaps he wouldn't telephone, he would just turn up. He spent a pleasant half hour imagining a joyful reunion, until he realised it was over eighteen months since he had seen her and in that time she could have found someone else. After all, she was lovely to look at, self-assured, titled and wealthy. She would not be short of suitors. It made his impatience all the more difficult to bear.

Chapter Thirteen

'What's the matter, Prue?' Sheila stopped singing 'Deep in the Heart of Texas' and turned to her friend. They had had their evening meal with Constance, who had gone out afterwards to a parish council meeting, leaving them to wash up. 'You look as if you've lost a guinea and found a sixpence. Are you worried about Tim and your brother?'

'Course I am. Wouldn't you be?' She stood a washed plate in the rack for Sheila to dry. 'Sorry, I didn't mean to snap.'

'That's all right. Have you had bad news?'

'I've had no news at all.'

'I'm sorry, Prue.'

'Not your fault.' She emptied the bowl into the sink and wiped it before standing it on its end on the draining board as she had seen Constance and Sheila do. Before she came to Bletchley she had never washed up in her life and even now she did not do it while Mrs Tranter was in the house. The lady would not allow her to demean herself doing something so mundane, but was quite content to sit talking to her while Sheila did it all.

'Then cheer yourself up. When the war's over, Tim will come home and it will be happy reunions all round.'

'But will it? It's been a long time and heaven knows what he's been through in the meantime. And he was the one who severed our relationship, not me.'

'He wrote to you from the camp.'

'Only because I sent him a parcel.'

'Don't be so pessimistic. At least he's alive.' Sheila paused, thinking of Chris and Charlie, then shook herself. 'Come on, let's go for a bike ride. It's too nice an evening to stay indoors.'

It wasn't only Tim Prue was worried about; she assumed he was comparatively safe in a prisoner of war camp, but some of the messages interpreted at Bletchley were about what was happening in France. It was through these messages that she learnt that the German authorities had arrested all British and American men, women and children still living in what had been the free zone and deported them to Germany, considering them a risk in the event of an Allied invasion. She read about the conditions in concentration camps and the massacre of Jews in their thousands. Meticulous at keeping records, the camp commanders announced their numbers in the same way as her father would brag about the number of pheasants they had bagged at a shoot on the estate. How could human beings do that to each other? It made her fearful for captured resistance fighters and their treatment at the hands of the Gestapo. She did not know Gillie's codename, so she had no idea where he was, what he was doing and if he were safe. The worry of that, she kept to herself. Her parents were still receiving postcards from him, but she was not at all sure they deceived her mother, though she pretended they did.

'Gillie is safe and well and we are not to worry that he can't get home for a bit,' she had told Prue the last time she was home.

'He is kept hard at work and missing us. He remembered Papa's birthday and sent him a new pipe. We have to write to the War Office to reply, like we used to do for you before we learnt the address of your lodgings.'

'It's done when people move around a lot,' Prue had told her. 'It saves having to keep telling people you've moved.'

'You haven't moved.'

'I might have done in the beginning. I'm more settled now.'

'Are you comfortable there? It doesn't sound like anything you've been used to.'

'No, of course it isn't but it's OK, and I've got Sheila for company.'

'You wouldn't have had anything to do with her before the war.'

'I know and it would have been my loss. She is a lovely person and has taught me a thing or two about courage and loyalty, and making the best of what you've got.'

'There's no news about her brother, then?'

'No. I think he must be dead. I think, in her heart of hearts, she knows it too, but she hasn't actually said so.'

'Is she still seeing that American?'

'Johnnie, yes, they meet now and again and correspond.'

'Will they make a go of it?'

'I don't know. I don't think she knows. There's plenty of time. After the war . . .'

'After the war. Everyone is saying that nowadays. When do you think that will be?'

'I have no idea.'

'I hope it will be soon. I am so tired of it all.'

'We all are, Mama. But it can't be long now.'

'And then Gillie will come home.'

'Yes.'

'Do you think he is doing anything dangerous?'

She had sighed. 'I have no idea what he's doing, Mama.' She hated telling fibs to her mother, not only about Gillie but about her own work, especially when she was sure her mother knew it and pretended to believe her. No wonder poor Mama was so tired of it all.

The last drop had brought with it rifles, ammunition, hand grenades, explosives and detonators, plus French money in the form of coins and banknotes. Gilbert had no idea how London had come by them and wondered if they were genuine or had been forged, just as his identity papers had been.

Some of the explosives had been put to good use blowing up an ammunition train standing in a siding in the marshalling yards, which had the added advantage of damaging the nearby buildings and tearing up the line. French workmen were repairing the damage, but they were taking their time about it. Equipment and materials kept mysteriously disappearing. And of course there had been German reprisals and that was hard to stomach. They had a sadistic way of doing this, arresting perfectly innocent people and shooting them, or imprisoning them as hostages against future sabotage. He tried not to think of these poor prisoners helplessly awaiting their fate. There were those who condemned the *resistants* on the grounds that they did no lasting damage and were not worth the lives that were taken as a consequence. It was a point of view with which he could sympathise.

'It has to be done,' he said on one of the few occasions when he went to the farm to speak to everyone. 'What we are doing is helping to cripple the German war machine and when the allies invade . . .'

'When is that likely to be?' Gustave demanded. 'Seems to me, they are more interested in Italy than France.'

The battle for North Africa had been won and the German army sent packing, leaving the Allies to turn their attention to Italy. They had taken Sicily and, the week before, invaded the mainland. 'I can't tell you what is in the minds of our leaders,' he said. 'But our turn will come. We must keep going.'

They went on to talk tactics and each of the men was given instructions to take to his own section, then they dispersed, leaving the farmhouse one by one. Gilbert stopped to speak to Esme. They went up to her room so that she could send her scheduled message.

'Thank you for your letters,' he said quietly when that had been done and the aerial withdrawn and put into the case with the wireless. She pulled up the corner of a rug and lifted two floorboards to reveal the hiding place for the wireless. He put it in there for her and replaced the boards and carpet.

'Was it what you wanted?'

He smiled. 'Love letters. Oh, yes. Monsieur Lebonier is a lucky man to have such a devoted sweetheart.' He had read the letters with mounting pleasure, hoping they were not entirely fictitious, but written from the heart. He was disappointed when she did not answer.

'I think the time has come for me to find a new place to work,' she said. 'I am sure the Germans are watching this farm.'

'Your cover hasn't been broken, has it?'

'I don't think so, but Anton is sometimes reckless about security and walks about with a rifle over his shoulder and a grenade in his pocket. I have spoken to him about it, but he laughs and says it's in case he comes across a lone German. There are no lone Germans, Boris, they patrol in packs, like wolves, and when they come for milk and eggs, they look about them and poke about. It makes me fearful.'

'So where do you want to go?'

'I think I should move into the town. It won't be so easy for the Germans to trace the signal in among the buildings and I might have a better chance of escaping if they come for me. We are isolated here, but there is nowhere to run to, except farm buildings and ditches. I would soon be caught.'

'Heaven forbid,' he said. 'I'll ask Paul what he suggests. I'll read the riot act to Anton too. He is putting everyone at risk, including his own mother.'

Madame had been as good as her word and carried messages backwards and forwards as she went about the business of selling her farm produce and queuing up for food. Her voluminous black skirts could hide a myriad of small items.

'So I told him.'

He stopped speaking to take her shoulders in his hands. 'Esme, you will take care, won't you?'

'Of course. And the same goes for you.'

'Don't worry, I have every intention of surviving.' He smiled. 'I should like to think you meant some of the nice things you said in your letters, and it wasn't all about deceiving the Boche.'

She laughed. 'That would be telling.'

'Damn this war, damn the Germans, damn everybody who is playing such havoc with our lives. I've got to go. I'll send word by Madame about a move, when I've found somewhere safe.'

He put his finger under her chin and raised it so that he could see her face. The strain was beginning to tell, he realised. She was far too thin and there were dark shadows under her eyes which contrasted sharply with the pale of her cheeks. 'Take care,' he said and bent to kiss her. 'From Gerard, your sweetheart,' he murmured, then clattered down the stairs, found his bicycle in the yard and pedalled away.

Before the move could be accomplished, Madame came to Paul's house with the news that Esme had been arrested. Paul had already left for work and Gilbert was there alone. 'She came into town and was stopped in a routine street search,' she told him. 'I don't know why they decided to take her in. Perhaps they didn't like the look of her identity papers or perhaps someone betrayed her. I don't know.'

Gilbert's heart sank. They had been told to prepare for such an eventuality, but the news was a shock just the same. His lovely Esme, what would the beasts do to her? 'How do you know this?' he asked.

'I was stopped in the same search, further down the road, but they weren't interested in me and let me go.'

'Why did she come to town?'

'I don't know, but she was expecting a call from London. Perhaps it was urgent and she couldn't wait for me to come back and take it for her.' She paused. 'Did you know she had been arrested before?'

'No, I didn't. When and where?'

'In 1941. She told me she had been in Fresnes prison for sabotage, but she escaped when they tried to transport her to Germany.'

He was puzzled. 'But that can't be. I met her in England.'

'She went to England on a fishing boat from Marseilles to Gibraltar. She was flown out from there. Someone in London asked her to come back. I don't give much for her chances if the Boche learn her real name.'

'My God! She never said a word of this to me. Why didn't she tell me?' He didn't know whether to be angry or full of admiration for her courage.

'We all have our secrets, Monsieur. No doubt she thought it was safer for you not to know, but she told me in case she was arrested again and you would need to know. She said if that happened, not to do anything foolish.'

He had to think quickly. 'Go home and get rid of that wireless set. Take it out of the house and make sure it can't be found. If the Boche come, stick to Arlene's cover story. Go now, please.' He watched her hurry away, then left himself to go to the bicycle shop.

'The arrest might not be anything to do with the circuit,' he told Paul. 'But we must warn everyone, shut down all letterboxes, make sure the arms and explosives are hidden well away from anyone's home and stop everyone from going anywhere near them. With luck we might avert total disaster.'

'And Arlene?' Paul queried.

'Arlene won't talk. But somehow or other we have to get her out. Is there any way you can find out where they've taken her and what they are charging her with?'

'I've got a German contact I met in *Le Coq Rouge*. He likes to talk about football. He used to be a professional player. I buy him a cognac now and again to keep him sweet. I'll see what I can find out.'

'Thank you. I'll go the rounds and make sure everyone is alerted. I'll meet you at the farm this evening.'

It took him the rest of the day to warn everyone and shut down the circuit. As far as he could tell, neither the Germans nor the *Brigade Speciale* were instituting an all-out search. It didn't mean they were safe; the Boche could simply be watching and waiting, ready to pounce on the whole group.

At nine o'clock, he set off for the farmhouse. Crossing the bridge meant showing his papers to the guards. If there had been anything wrong with Esme's, the same would probably be true of his. He decided not to risk it, but walked along the bank to a place where he knew there was a small rowing boat moored. It was illegal to have it, but its owner had pulled it up into a little boathouse and covered it with sacking. It had been used to help people from occupied to unoccupied France, but now there was no unoccupied France, it was still used to help escapees down the line.

He found the boat's owner and was soon being conveyed to the other bank. It was a quiet evening; not even the sound of aircraft droning overhead on their way to bomb Germany disturbed the rural peace, nothing but the quiet creaking of the oars and the occasional splash. The scene contrasted sharply with the scene going on in his head. His lovely Esme being interrogated and tortured, starved and humiliated, and no doubt keeping quiet to save his life and the lives of others in the circuit. He was fairly certain she would hold out for the forty-eight hours required of her, but would she break after that? How could he let her suffer? He was well aware that this situation was just what his bosses in London would deplore: one of their operatives being emotionally involved with another. He assumed they knew all about her previous adventures when they had encouraged her to return. Why hadn't he been told? Sometimes this fixation with security went too far. He had to keep a cool head. Nothing would be gained by rushing his fences.

He scrambled ashore on the other side and hurried to the farm. They were waiting for him: Madame, Jean, Anton, Gustave and Philippe, sitting round the kitchen table discussing the implications.

'The prison in Ville Sainte Jeanne is not big enough, nor secure enough, to keep her there for long,' Jean said. 'As soon as they suspect she is working for the resistance, they will send her to Paris and the Avenue Foche. We can't wait for that to happen.'

'But perhaps they don't know who she really is,' Madame Duport said. 'They might be holding her for some minor infringement of regulations. If that is the case and she keeps her head, she might not be detained for long. Trying to rescue her will only draw attention to the fact that she is important.'

'Oh, she will keep her head,' Gilbert said. 'Have no fear of that.'

Paul arrived at that point, having come over the bridge, using his *ausweiss*. He greeted everyone and shook hands all round before accepting a glass of rough red wine from Madame. 'Arlene is being held on suspicion of having a forged identity card,' he said. 'It has been taken away from her to be checked. I expect they will take it to the Gestapo headquarters in Auxerre.' He turned to Gilbert. 'Will it stand close scrutiny?'

'I don't know and I don't think we should wait to find out.'

'I'll go to the prison,' Madame said. 'Madeleine is supposed to be my cousin's daughter. I shall want to know why they are holding an innocent girl who has done no wrong. If the identity card is a forgery, they should blame the people in Algiers who issued it to her when her parents died.'

'It's too risky,' Gilbert said. 'You could be arrested yourself. Then we will have two of you to rescue.'

'Me? What have I done, except supply our occupiers with milk and cheese and eggs?' She gave a cracked laugh. 'They are forbidden to drink the local milk on the grounds it is a hazard to their health, but I take it to them every day. I shall remind them of that. They won't like it if they can't have it any more.'

Gilbert looked round at Jean and Anton. 'What do you say? Shall we let your mother try her way first?'

Jean, the elder of the two, shrugged. 'She will do as she wants, she always does, but I think we should stand by to go in if it all goes wrong.' He looked meaningfully at Gilbert. 'You, Boris, will stay out of it. This is a family affair.'

'No way.'

'You may be our leader when it comes to the *resistants*, Boris, but I say how we look after Maman.' He laughed. 'You will go and sell your insurance, Monsieur Lebonier, and leave this to us.'

Knowing they were quite capable of tying him up and locking him in the house, he did not argue but that didn't mean he was going to stand by and do nothing. 'Very well,' he said. 'But once she is free, I am sending her straight home. I'll get onto Dominic to have someone standing by.' Dominic was one of the *passeurs*, who organised an escape line as far as Lyon.

'Talking of Dominic,' Paul said. 'I've got two British airmen hidden in the loft of the bicycle shop. Pierre brought them this afternoon. He says they check out. Might be an idea for you to check them yourself, Boris, and arrange for their onward passage with Dominic.'

Gilbert groaned. He knew Dominic and his helpers were good at the job they did and had ferried numerous downed airmen and escaped prisoners of war down the length of France to safety in Spain, but he didn't want the complication of two airmen at this juncture. Esme's French was perfect and she could, if necessary, talk her way out of trouble en route, but hampered by two fliers who probably didn't understand a word of French or German, and would be liable to give themselves away, she would be in double jeopardy. He wished there were a way of contacting London but Madame Duport had thrown the radio in the duck pond. Even if they had it, he was not sure it was safe to use it.

'I'll sort it out tomorrow,' he said. 'I had better stay here tonight. The last thing I want is to be caught out after curfew.'

* * *

It was daylight next morning when the owner of the bicycle shop replaced the ladder and climbed up to lift the trapdoor. 'Good morning,' he said cheerfully to the two men who peered out at him. 'You may come down now. Do not make a noise. There are Germans everywhere.'

They clambered down the ladder into the back of the shop and then Tim had the surprise of his life, for facing him was Prue's brother, Gilbert.

He was about to greet him by name but he saw Gilbert shaking his head. He remained silent while Paul introduced them. They shook hands like strangers.

'How did you get here?' Gilbert asked.

Tim outlined their journey. 'We thought we were well on the way,' he said. 'Then the Gestapo boarded the train and we had to make a quick getaway in a couple of crates. Our courier took us on what she called a detour. We were passed from hand to hand and here we are.'

'I'm afraid we can't help you on your way just yet,' Gilbert said. 'We have a little problem of our own to tackle first. It might take a day or two.'

'You mean we've got to spend another two days in that loft?' Pat grumbled. 'It's the most uncomfortable place I've ever stayed in.'

'The trouble is,' Gilbert explained, 'for the moment, we are not sure how safe our safe houses are. We have had to stop people going to them. Until we know for certain or can find new places, I'm afraid it is back in the loft for you. Perhaps Paul can find some pillows to make it a little more comfortable. But you must keep silent. Paul has German customers coming and going all the time.'

Paul looked at his watch. 'It's time I opened the shop, Boris. You could take the gentlemen to my house . . .'

'No,' Gilbert said. 'You are Arlene's cousin, distant it is true, but the Boche probably know that. It's too risky.' He turned to Tim and Pat. 'I'm afraid I must ask you to return to the loft and stay there until I come and fetch you.'

Reluctantly they moved towards the ladder. 'When can we talk?' Tim asked Gilbert in an undertone. Seeing Gilbert and noting his quiet confidence had cheered him up and the pessimism brought on by their narrow squeak at Orleans and their uncomfortable night lifted. He began to think that perhaps, after all, they might make it back home.

'Later. Please go.'

They returned to their hiding place. 'I'm not sure I trust those Frenchies,' Pat said when they were once again stretched out in the loft. 'They don't seem to know what to do with us.'

'They're not all French.'

'How do you know that?'

'I know the one called Boris. He's in disguise, of course, and we mustn't say anything, but I reckon we're in good hands.'

'How well do you know him?'

'He's my girlfriend's brother.'

Pat whistled and Tim clapped his hand over his mouth. 'Keep quiet, you idiot, there's someone in the shop.'

That was how they spent their day, alternately talking in whispers and keeping silent, hardly daring to breathe when they heard voices below them. They knew daylight had faded when the cracks between the tiles darkened and disappeared.

Tim was dozing when Pat nudged him awake. Someone was replacing the ladder. The trapdoor was opened and Paul's head appeared outlined in the light from below. 'You can come down and stretch your legs and have something to eat and drink,' he said.

They followed him down and hobbled round the workshop until the feeling returned to their legs. Paul swept aside the tools, chains, pumps and brake shoes that littered his work bench and put a plate of cheese-filled bread rolls, a couple of apples, a bottle of wine and some glasses in their place. 'Sit down,' he said. 'Eat and drink. There's a privy out the back and a tap. You can use those before you go back up the ladder.'

'Oh, no, not back there again,' Pat said.

'I'm afraid so.'

'Have you solved the problem that G . . . Boris mentioned?' Tim asked.

'No, not yet. Now, if you please, back in the loft. I am going to shut up shop and go home. It is important not to deviate from my normal routine. I will return in the morning. Perhaps Boris will have good news.'

Reluctantly they returned to their hiding place.

Gilbert had been thoroughly taken aback to see Tim. He was hardly recognisable with his hair dyed and spectacles that made him look owlish. The disguise had made him smile, but it was not a smiling matter, not any of it. Now, besides freeing Esme and sending her safely on her way, he felt responsible for Tim and his friend.

'There will be three of them to go,' Gilbert told Dominic when he visited him in his surgery on the pretence of needing a medical examination. 'Arlene and two RAF escapees.'

'What about you?' Dominic put his stethoscope to Gilbert's chest and appeared to be listening to that.

'I stay. I am needed here.'

'And if Arlene has talked, or you can't get her out, you will be compromised and so will the whole circuit.'

'I'll cross that bridge when I come to it.'

'Very well. I can probably arrange an ambulance to take a very sick patient to Lyon. Can your two men carry a stretcher?'

Gilbert smiled. 'I think so.'

'Then I will arrange their new identities. They will need photos. Bring Arlene here to me when you have her safely in your hands.'

'Pierre can bring her in his van. I'll get the photos done.'

'Good. Let's hope she is successfully sprung. If not, it will be you on that stretcher.' He removed the stethoscope. 'By the way, you are as sound as a bell.'

Gilbert buttoned his shirt and went home to borrow Paul's camera, then he went to the bicycle shop, carrying it in his briefcase along with his insurance forms and brochures. It was late in the afternoon, Paul was busy putting a new wheel on a bicycle but there were no customers in the shop. They went through to the back room.

'Is it safe to fetch them down?' Gilbert asked, nodding towards the loft.

'I think so.' He went to the shop and locked the door, turning the sign from open to closed. Then he fetched the ladder and released the two men. They climbed down and hobbled round the small room. 'I'm stiff as a board,' Tim said. 'Have you come to send us on our way?'

'Not yet.'

'Damn and blast it, man, we've been cooped up long enough. If you aren't prepared to help us, we'll go on our own.'

'I'm afraid I can't let you do that. You know my name and who I am. If you are caught . . .' He let the sentence hang in the air.

'We'll kill you, if we have to,' Paul said quietly.

Tim gasped. 'You never would.'

'If you are patient it won't come to that,' Gilbert said, smiling at Tim's furious expression. 'I have not been idle today. Everything is being arranged. You need new disguises, new photographs and a new story.' He opened his case and took out the camera.

'Everywhere we go we have to do that all over again,' Pat said. 'Can't we just be ourselves? After all, we are in France, not Germany.'

'Not everyone in France is friendly,' Gilbert went on, positioning a chair against a plain brick wall. 'Many are pro-German and many others would betray you if they thought that would save their own skins or prevent their young men from being sent to forced labour. That will no doubt change the nearer we are to victory. For now, you do as you are told.'

'You are a hard nut.'

'I have to be. Tim, take off your jacket and sit here please.'

Tim did as he was told. Paul brought soap and water, a razor and a towel. 'Wash the colour out of your hair and get rid of that scar, it's looking the worse for wear anyway and then shave.' That done, Paul gave him a very short haircut.

'That's more like it,' Gilbert said, as Pat took his turn with a fresh bowl of water. 'Put this on.' He handed him a white linen coat. 'You are an ambulance attendant, name of Tomas Pinet. Your friend Pat will be Oscar Frank, also an ambulance man. You are going to escort a patient to Lyon in an ambulance.'

Pat had been shorn of his untidy locks and beard but he was left with a moustache which he lovingly stroked. 'When do we go?'

'As soon as the patient is ready.'

'The mysterious Arlene, I suppose.'

'Yes. Her safety will be in your hands, remember that will you?'

'I see,' Tim said. He paused while Gilbert set the camera up. 'When did you last see Prue?'

'Eighteen months ago, something like that. We had leave together. You've probably seen her more recently than I have.'

'Does she know where you are?'

'I think she might have an idea. When you get home you can tell her I'm OK. Don't say anything to my mother though. Now we will not speak of this again, it's too dangerous. Please sit on the chair and face the camera.'

Tim obeyed and was followed by Pat. Then they removed the coats and gave them to Paul who folded them and put them in a drawer. 'I will be back in due course,' he said. 'Stay in the loft.'

They sighed and gave themselves up to more waiting.

Esme was expecting a medical examination and if that happened she would be in trouble. All the childlike clothes and the hair in plaits would not disguise the fact that she was not a sixteen-year-old girl called Madeleine Tillon, but a mature woman. That would lead to more questions, more investigation and then the Boche would discover it was not the first time she had been in their hands. She prepared herself mentally to withstand the torture. So far, apart from constant questioning about her passport, all she had had to endure had been slaps and twisted arms. It was nothing to what could happen.

She wondered what Gillie and the Duport men were doing. She prayed desperately that they might devise some way of rescuing her before she was sent to Paris and the Avenue Foche, headquarters of the Gestapo. Once there, she was as good as dead and would probably welcome death as a release. She would never see Gilbert again, never tell him that the loving letters she had written to him were an indication of her true feelings. From what he had said, she thought he loved her too, but would that make him reckless?

The cell in which she was confined was an ordinary prison cell, bleak and smelly, with a lock on its heavy door, but it was in the corridor of the police station and not isolated. She could hear some of what was going on in the office where the public came and went with their problems. She spent much of her time with her ear to the keyhole. If the *Brigade Speciale* were going to hand her over to the Gestapo, she needed to know. She was immediately alert when she heard Madame Duport's voice loudly insisting they had detained her cousin's daughter for no good reason and demanding her immediate release.

The policeman on duty was one she knew, an ordinary gendarme, not a member of the *Brigade Speciale*. His name was Armand and he had a daughter of fourteen. Sometimes they had talked about her and Arlene's own childhood. Whether he was genuinely interested or whether it was intended to catch her out in a falsehood, she did not know, but she was careful to maintain her cover story and her childish innocence.

'I can't, you know I can't,' he said. 'Tomorrow she will be sent to Paris.'

'Paris, but why?'

'I don't know. If I could help you, I would, but it is not up to me.'

Esme began banging on her cell door and shouting in a childish voice, '*Tante Gabby! Tante Gabby!* Let me out!'

'Let me go to her. She is frightened.'

'No. I have my orders. No visitors.'

'I'll go home then and wait.' Madame's voice was loud, intending to be heard. 'But if she is not safely at home again by curfew, I shall take the matter further.' Esme could not hear Armand's reply, but after that there was silence.

When he came to bring her supper an hour before curfew, he

found her in tears. 'Don't cry, Madeleine,' he said, sitting on the bed beside her. 'Nothing will happen to you.'

'I'm frightened. You turned my aunt away. I thought you would let me go, but you didn't. What have I done wrong? I don't know what I've done. I thought I would be safe with my mother's cousin. Instead I've been locked up. Let me go, please. Please.'

'I daren't.' He picked up her empty bowl and left her.

An hour later, he came back and unlocked the door, then he walked away leaving it wide open. She peeped along the corridor. It was empty. The door to the office was ajar too. She walked forward and gingerly pushed it open. Jean and Paul were standing there waiting for her. They seized her arms and bundled her out of the door. No one spoke.

It was only a few minutes to curfew and there was no one about except a couple of German soldiers walking along the pavement. Jean and Paul pretended to be sharing a joke with her, but all the time guiding her along the street. As soon as they turned the corner, they sped along to the bicycle shop. Pierre's van was waiting outside. They helped her into the back of it. Paul went back to his shop and Jean climbed in beside Pierre.

'Sweetheart, are you OK?' Gilbert's voice came to her in the darkness and she felt his arms go about her as the van jolted its way over the cobbles.

'Boris! Oh, thank God.'

'Amen to that.' He hugged her to him. 'You can't go back to the farm, you know that, don't you?'

'No, I suppose I can't. Where are we going?'

'Dominic is going to take you down the line. It's home for you.'

'But you are coming too?'

'No, I can't, there's too much to do here.'

'Then I want to stay too.'

'No way. The Boche won't rest until they have you. You are a danger to the whole circuit.'

'Well, thanks very much for that.'

He laughed grimly. 'You are also a danger to my peace of mind, Esme. I want you safe, safe at home waiting for me to come back. And I will, I promise you. There is nothing in the world I want more than to be with you, because I love you, but not here, not now.'

'Oh, Gillie.' She lifted her face to be kissed, then laughed suddenly. 'You are a disgrace, Monsieur Lebonier, kissing a schoolgirl like that.'

'Schoolgirl be damned. When we are safe home again, I shall have your whole story out of you, Esmeralda Favelle.'

'What will happen to Armand?'

'He is neatly tied up and gagged in the back room of the police station and a nice wad of money has been taken to his wife.'

They drew up at Dominic's surgery and hurried inside, leaving Jean and Pierre to take the van back to Pierre's bakery. Dominic was waiting for them, and so were Tim and Pat in their white coats. Gilbert introduced them by their new names. Esme was taken to the bathroom where she washed the prison grime off and combed out her plaits, then put on the nightdress and bed jacket she had been given. By the time she had done that and returned to the men, the ambulance was at the door.

She clung fiercely to Gilbert. 'If you are in the slightest danger, you must come out,' she said. 'Promise me.'

'I promise. In any case, the war will soon be over. Until then, my sweet, look after yourself and wait for me.' He kissed her lightly, then helped her onto the stretcher and covered her with a blanket. He smiled. 'Don't forget you are supposed to be sick.'

He was reluctant to let go of her hand as Tim and Pat picked up the stretcher and followed Dominic out of the surgery.

'You'd better be off,' Dominic told him. 'Leave ma'amselle to us.'

He released her hand and stood and watched as they placed her in the ambulance, Tim and Pat climbed in and Dominic shut the doors. He rapped on the side and the vehicle drew away.

They were silent for some time. It was not easy to converse; the vehicle was old and very noisy and their driver was in somewhat of a hurry, so they did not even try. They were stopped for their papers when they came to the bridge that had once marked the boundary between the occupied and the free zone. Arlene pulled the blanket up round her face in case the guard was one who might recognise her, but he only gave her a cursory glance before waving them on.

Twice more they were asked for papers but whoever had forged them had done a good job and each time they were let through without trouble. Night turned to day and their driver stopped on a quiet stretch of road to fill the tank with petrol from a can he had brought with him; it was safer than trying to buy it. Here they all got out to stretch their legs and relieve themselves. 'Where are we?' Tim asked the driver.

'No need for you to know,' he said brusquely.

'I understand.'

'Please return to your places. We cannot linger.'

They climbed back into the ambulance. Arlene sat on the stretcher. 'I think we are about halfway to Lyon,' she told them.

'Is that all?' Pat said. 'I thought we must be nearly there.'

'No, we have some way to go yet. Do either of you want to have a sleep? You can take turns to use the stretcher, if you like. Of course, if we are stopped I shall have to be the patient again.'

Pat took advantage of the offer and was soon snoring gently. 'He's rather impatient,' Tim told her.

'So I gathered. But aren't you a bit impatient yourself?'

'Yes, I am. I have a girl waiting for me in England. At least, I hope she is waiting for me.'

'Boris's sister?'

'Yes. How did you know?'

'He told me.'

'What else did he tell you?'

'Not much. In our line of work it is best not to know.'

'Do you know even know his real name?'

'I know that is it Gilbert, but please don't tell me any more, not until we are safe.'

'Are you . . . you know what I mean.'

'Am I in love with a man whose name I do not even know? Is that what you are asking me?'

'Yes, I suppose so.'

'If this were peacetime and we were both in England, I should say, yes, I am, but as we are not, such things have to be left unsaid.'

'He loves you. I saw it in his eyes when he said goodbye to you. Is that the reason he is sending you back with us, so that you are safe?'

'No, I have become a liability. It is safer for everyone concerned that I should disappear.'

'How brave you are.'

She smiled deprecatingly. 'I do my job. I am sorry I have been taken off it, but I have to obey orders. Please don't ask me any more.'

'Very well, I won't.'

'Tell me about your girl. What's her name?'

'Prudence, though everyone calls her Prue.'

'What does she do?'

'She says she is a translator but I think there's more to it than that. She doesn't talk about it.'

'We all have to watch our tongues these days. Tell me about her.'

So he did; he told her about his doubts, about their misunderstanding and how he hoped to put it right and that filled in the time until their next stop when they woke Patrick so that she could lie down again. And thus they arrived at a small house on the outskirts of Lyon where Arlene ceased to be a patient and their driver left them.

They were made welcome at the house and given food and beds and the next day were guided to another safe house. They had to wait there another two days until a guide could be found to take them to the border. It had been relatively easy up until then and they were becoming a little too confident, especially as Arlene, whose French was perfect, was always able to come up with a tale that satisfied the curious.

At last a guide was found and they resumed their journey in an old van which took them to a village a few miles short of the Spanish border. Here they were taken in by an elderly lady to wait for a new guide to take them over the mountains. From then on they would have to go on foot.

Madame was very thin and not very tall. She only came up to Tim's chest. Her husband had been caught and killed by a German border control the year before, while taking escapees over the mountains into Spain, she told them.

'And yet you still shelter us,' Tim said.

'Of course. If I gave up, the enemy would have won and what my husband did would have been in vain.'

'You are very brave.'

She smiled. 'You are young and have your whole life before you. It is for the young I do what I do.'

'Aren't you afraid?'

'I would be a fool to say I am not, but it passes. Dying is easy.'

They were sitting round the table in the kitchen, eating a frugal meal as they talked. They felt safe, which was foolish of them because in the middle of the meal when they were laughing at something Pat had said, they heard an imperative knocking at the front door. 'Quick,' Madame said. 'Go out the back way. I will keep them talking.'

'We can't leave you,' Tim said, hesitating.

'Yes. You can. Go, before they break the door down.'

Pat, who was nearest the back door, ran out, closely followed by Arlene. They were in the backyard before they realised Tim had not followed them. Pat hesitated, ready to go back. And then they heard a shot, followed by another. Arlene pulled on his arm. 'Come on. There's no going back.'

Chapter Fourteen

Prue obeyed the summons to Mr Welchman's office, wondering what she had done wrong. It was unlike him to call her away from her work in the middle of a shift. Had she made a terrible blunder translating? Had she inadvertently breeched security?

When she tapped on the door and obeyed the call to enter, she discovered he was not alone. There was an airman and an ATS girl, both in uniform, sitting on chairs on the other side of his desk. The airman scrambled to his feet.

'Prue,' Colin Welchman said. 'This is Flight Lieutenant Duffey. He has something to tell you.'

Prue turned to face the young man. As far as she knew, she had never met him before. He was tall and dark and looking awkward. The girl was looking down at her hands. 'There is no easy way to tell you this,' the airman said. 'But I'm afraid Tim is dead.'

'Dead?' She sank onto a third chair, unable to take it in. She was surprised to find that she could speak. 'When? How?'

'In France. We were on the run. We almost made it.'

'Go on.'

He sat down again and leant forward. 'I was in the POW camp with Tim. He was determined to escape and get home. Unfinished business, he said. We got out together. I've been warned not to say anything of how we were helped for fear of reprisals . . .'

'I understand.' The work she did had given her an inkling of the terrible things that were happening in Germany and the occupied countries. It had been her constant fear, and now it had happened, not to Gillie, but to Tim.

'They were amazingly brave people,' he said, referring to those who had helped them. 'We had a bit of a scare when the train we were on was searched by the Gestapo, but our guide got us off in crates and took us on what she called a detour. Then, by an extraordinary coincidence, we met someone Tim knew.'

'Gillie?' she murmured.

'You knew?'

'I knew he was out there somewhere. How was he? Did he come back with you?'

'No, he didn't. I think he should have, but we couldn't persuade him. His wireless operator had been arrested and he and some others broke her out of jail and he insisted she came with us.'

'Was her name Esme, by any chance?'

'We knew her as Arlene.'

She turned towards the girl. 'You are Esme, aren't you?'

'Yes. How did you know?'

'Gillie told me about you. I am very pleased to meet you.'

'And I you, but I wish it could have been in happier circumstances.'

'Tell me what happened.'

It was Pat who answered her. 'We were dressed as ambulance men and Arlene was our patient. We went all the way to Lyon like that and then spent ages being passed from safe house to safe house because the French special police were searching for someone. We were having dinner in a kitchen near the Spanish border when Jerry arrived. We all got up to run. I was outside when I realised Tim had not followed but stayed to help our hostess who was an elderly lady. It was just like him to act the knight in shining armour. I hesitated and was going back when we heard a shot and then another. Arlene grabbed me. She said we couldn't do anything for them, so we ran for our lives across the back garden and over the wall. I felt really bad about leaving him like that. We were good pals, had been through thick and thin together and I couldn't help him when it came to the crunch.' His voice cracked and he stopped speaking.

There was silence in the room for some time. 'You are sure Tim died?' Prue asked.

'Yes,' Esme put in. 'It was reported in the newspaper the next day. We had to get out fast because the Boche were looking for us. That was in the paper too. I'm sure we'd been betrayed.'

'I'm glad I had Arlene with me,' Patrick put in. 'I'd have been picked up in no time without her. We made our way out of the town and up into the hills, hoping that country people might be more helpful than those in the town. Arlene seemed to know whom to approach and whom to avoid. One man guided us to a safe house and arranged for us to cross the Pyrenees into Spain, but the weather was against us and we were stuck at the foot of the mountains for weeks. Sometimes we would set out, only to be driven back by heavy snow or German patrols or guides not turning up, but we finally made it over the border three weeks ago. The last guide gave us directions to a village and left us there to find our own way.'

'Just you and Esme?'

'Yes. We were arrested as soon as we arrived and taken by bus to the next town and put in prison. We had heard tales of Spanish authorities sending escapees back over the border and we thought we'd had it. We spent a miserable couple of days, trying to think of a way to escape but then we were visited by a Spanish Air Force officer who spoke good English. He took us by car to a hotel. We could have walked out of there, but the Spanish airman assured us steps were in hand to take us to Gibraltar and we were to be patient. Next day we had a visit from an attaché at the British Embassy in Madrid, who grilled us about our escape. He seemed to know all about Arlene, which helped. We had to wait three more days before a car arrived and took us to Gibraltar. We were flown out of there last week. After I had been debriefed, I asked if I could tell you what happened.'

'What you have been told stays in this room,' Mr Welchman said.

Prue did not need the reminder. 'Does Tim's mother know?'

'Yes, she was told officially that he had died attempting to escape.'

'Tim talked about you a lot,' Patrick told Prue. 'He couldn't wait to get back to you. That's why he was so keen to escape. When we were in hiding, he said if he didn't make it back to tell you he loved you and was coming home to tell you so and not to take any notice of his silly letter. I am so sorry he couldn't tell you that himself.'

There was silence again. Tim had not finished with her after all; he regretted that letter. All that nonsense about not caring was nothing but a cover to conceal her hurt. She had almost convinced herself. Did that matter now? He wasn't coming back. Now it was too late.

She looked bleakly round at the others. They were watching her carefully, waiting for her to react, to say something, to burst out crying. But she couldn't, she was too numb to cry. It was as if someone had punched her in the chest and taken all her breath away.

'Take the rest of the day off,' Colin Welchman told her.

'Thank you, but I must get back to work,' she said. 'I was in the middle of a tricky message when you sent for me.' Her voice was a dull monotone; nothing they said had properly registered.

'Perhaps that would be best,' he said. 'We have to brace ourselves and carry on. Can you do that?'

'I think so.' She turned to Patrick. 'Thank you for telling me. It must have been awful for you.' Then to Esme. 'Can we talk some time?'

'Of course, but you know I can't tell you much?'

'Yes, I know.'

'I'll be here the rest of the day.' Esme said. 'I think I'm going to be thoroughly quizzed.'

Prue got up and stumbled from the room and out into the fresh air. Everything looked so normal, the grass, the lake rippling a bit in a strong breeze, the leafless trees and the huts with their smoking chimneys, just as they had been when she had entered the building, but they had the quality of a dream.

'Hey, Prue, what's wrong? You look as if you've seen a ghost.'

Prue shook herself to find Sheila in front of her with her satchel of post over her shoulder. 'Tim's dead,' she said. 'Tim's dead.'

'Oh, you poor thing.' Sheila dropped her satchel and put her arms round her. That small gesture of sympathy opened the floodgates and the tears ran down her face. 'He was shot trying to come back to me,' she sobbed.

'Oh.' Sheila picked up her bag. 'Come on, let's go and make ourselves a cup of tea.'

'I ought to go back to work.'

‘They won’t miss you for a few minutes. You need a cuppa.’ She took Prue’s arm and marched her to the hut where they could make some tea. There was no one there. Silently Sheila sat Prue down and made a pot of tea, poured out two cups and put one in front of her friend, then sat down herself. ‘Now tell me all about it. I’ve signed that damned official secrets thingy, so you needn’t worry I’ll blab.’

Prue gave her a wan smile and took a gulp of tea. ‘He escaped, got clean away, all the way from Germany to France and then he got caught when they were almost safe.’ She scrubbed at her eyes with a handkerchief. ‘The police arrived and he stayed to help an old lady. They were both shot dead.’

‘How do you know all this? No, don’t tell me, you read it in one of those messages you translate.’

‘No, he wasn’t alone. Two others survived and got home. They’ve just been to tell me. His friend said . . . said he wanted to come home to tell me he loved me . . .’

‘What did I tell you?’

‘I know, I should have kept in touch with him. It’s too late now and, in the long run, it doesn’t make any difference.’

‘It does to the way you remember him.’

‘Sheila, how did you cope? How did you find the strength?’

‘I don’t know. It comes from somewhere. You have to cope because there is no alternative. It’s this bloody, bloody war.’

Prue had never heard Sheila swear and it made her smile, which was no doubt what her friend had intended. She finished her tea and stood up. ‘The war won’t stop while I weep, so back to work.’

‘Can’t you go home?’

‘Mr Welchman said I could but I didn’t want to. I can’t talk to Mrs Tranter about it and I’d be alone brooding until you came in. I’m better here where there’s plenty to do to keep me busy. I’m going to meet someone later to learn a bit more. I'll see you at home later.' She left Sheila washing up the cups and saucers and went back to work.

How she got through the rest of her shift she could not afterwards say. As soon as she came off duty, she went to look for Esme and found her in the canteen sitting over a cup of Camp coffee, waiting for her. She looked up as Prue brought more coffee and sat down opposite her.

'How was the grilling?' Prue asked.

'OK. I was able to fill in a few details, but it's astonishing how much they already knew.' She paused, unwilling to elaborate. 'Are you all right? I've been sitting here thinking how awful it must be for you.'

'It was a shock I admit, but I'll survive. We have to, don't we?'

'Yes.' It was said quietly.

Prue had been told all she was going to be told about Tim's escape and his death, and in time she would come to accept it, but her brother, as far as they knew, was still alive. 'You must be worried about Gillie. Tell me about him.'

Esme smiled. 'He's extraordinary, brave, resourceful, calm. He never flaps. He got me out of that prison just in time. I was going to be sent to Gestapo headquarters in Paris and that would have been the end of me. It wasn't the first time I'd been in prison and I knew if they connected Arlene to the Esme they had held before I wouldn't have stood a chance.'

'You escaped before?'

'Yes.'

'Why did you go back?'

'I was asked if I would.'

'And that's all it took, a simple request?'

'I couldn't say no, could I?'

'Have you any family?'

'I did have once, in France, none in England that I know of. My mother was French, married to an Englishman, but they were both killed early in the war. I had no one to mourn if I disappeared.'

'But there's Gillie . . .'

'Yes, but I had already volunteered when I met him. We were on the same training course.'

'He loves you.'

'I know.' It was said with a sigh. 'I love him too.'

'I know roughly where he is,' Prue said. 'Tell me, how is he?'

'When I last saw him he was well but he's living on borrowed time. If the Gestapo find out who he really is they will make capital of it and he won't stand a chance. And I won't be there to help him.'

'What could you do if you were?'

Esme grinned. 'Not a lot. But the separation is unbearable. I've asked to be sent back.'

'Gillie wouldn't want that.'

'I know.' She smiled. 'I had no idea he was a viscount, not until we were in the plane coming home and Patrick told me. You could have knocked me back with a feather. I pray he comes back safely but the odds are stacked against it.' She paused. 'I'm sorry, you've had enough sadness for one day. Let's talk about something more cheerful.'

'Have you met my parents?'

'No.'

'I'll take you and introduce you. Gillie was a bit evasive when Mama asked him about girlfriends, but I can understand that. It would mean telling her what he was doing and he couldn't do that.' She was surprised to find she could still smile. 'I think Mama has guessed some of it in any case, though she has never said. She pretends the postcards she gets are coming from Gillie himself.'

'I wouldn't be able to tell her any different.'

'Oh, I know that. You'll come if I arrange it?'

'Yes, Gillie told me to get in touch with you when I arrived back. He said you would take me to his mother. That's why I came with Patrick today, though I would probably have been sent in any case. SOE work closely with the people here.'

'Where are you going when you leave here?'

'I can't tell you.' Esme chuckled and touched the side of her nose. 'Don't worry, I'll keep in touch.' She stood up. 'There's a car coming for me at five. I'd better go.'

Prue accompanied her to the main gate where a khaki-painted staff car waited for her. Patrick was standing beside it. He came forward as they approached. 'OK?' he asked Prue.

'Yes, thank you.'

'I'm glad I met you. Tim was right, you are special.'

She felt the tears rising again and blinked them away. 'So was he. What are you going to do now?'

'Go on leave and then back to Wyton. They have formed a new unit called Pathfinders since we were taken prisoner and I'm joining that. They go off ahead of the main force to identify the target and light it with flares so that the oncoming bombers can drop their bombs in the right place. We have more navigational aids than we had at the beginning. I'm told they are very effective.'

'Tim would have been glad to learn that. He hated indiscriminate bombing.'

'I know. We talked about it. In a way he was too much of a gentleman, too soft-hearted for war, but bombing is a fact of life and has to be done if we are to win.'

'Anything to achieve that is a good thing,' Esme said. 'If you could see what is being perpetrated by those beasts on the countries they occupy, you would not doubt it. We have to cripple the Nazi war machine before the invasion, if it is to succeed.'

Prue turned to her, surprise at the venom in her voice. But then why should she be surprised, after what Esme had been through? 'You aren't going back, are you?' she asked.

'They won't let me, or I would. I hate the thought of Gillie over there without me.'

'I am sure he is glad you are safe. I suppose he would be told?'

'Yes, I asked them to send a message.'

'Then try not to worry.'

She watched as they were driven off, then she found her bicycle and went back to Victoria Villa. After dinner she would write to her mother to tell her some of what had happened.

'Doh ray me . . .' Sheila's clear voice filled her small bedroom as she practised her scales. Bletchley Park had several talented performers besides herself and one of these was a professional singer who had offered to give Sheila singing lessons. Her voice was maturing into that of a seasoned performer and she practised regularly. One day she would make a living as a singer and with hard work and luck would become famous and rich. She needed that ambition to keep her going, to stop her sinking into the abyss of despair. To those around her she appeared to have overcome her grief over the loss of her parents and Charlie, Chris too, but it was still there, still a kind of ache that wouldn't go away. Her work and, particularly, her membership of the drama group kept her sane.

The fourth Christmas show of the war had come and gone and the New Year begun in the optimistic belief that by the time the next Christmas arrived, the war would be over. She could not even begin to think what she would do then. Bletchley Park was a hive of activity as more and more people joined. The motorcyclists came and went at all times of the day and night and in all weathers, just as she did her rounds whatever the weather. More buildings were being added and people were being moved from the cramped huts to larger buildings. Hut Twelve, which had had many uses in its time, was now the Education Hut and used for music classes and rehearsals. It was here she was given her singing lessons.

They had been taking their revues round the neighbouring village halls to entertain the local inhabitants and this extended audience had given her valuable experience. And it seemed she was being noticed. Only that morning she had had a letter from the BBC, asking her if she would take part in 'Music While You Work', a programme of popular music put out during the day to entertain factory workers doing vital but boring war work. It was a wonderful opportunity and she only hoped she could be given time off to do it.

She stopped singing when she heard the front doorbell and, believing her aunt was out of the house, went to answer it. Johnnie stood on the step. They stared at each other, both equally surprised. 'Johnnie,' she said at last. 'How did you find me?'

'I wasn't looking for you. I didn't know . . .' He stopped when he saw someone coming along the hall behind her.

'Who is it, Sheila?' Constance had evidently just come in the back door. She was still wearing her jacket and hat.

'It's . . .' Sheila paused.

'Captain Howard, ma'am,' he finished for her. 'Would you be Mrs Constance Tranter?'

'Yes, I am.'

'Then I've come to the right place. May I come in?'

Sheila stood to one side, allowing Constance a sight of the man as he stepped into the hall. Her aunt had never had much colour but now her face drained of what there was and she put her hand out to the wall to steady herself. 'Who . . . who are you? Where have you come from?'

'Captain Johnnie Howard, ma'am, from the US of A. I believe we have a connection . . .'

'Connection?' It was said in a croak, as if the lady had difficulty speaking.

Sheila had never seen her aunt so shaken, she looked as though she were about to faint. Puzzled, she looked from one to the other. Evidently Johnnie's visit had nothing to do with her. 'What's going on?' she said.

He turned to her. 'Why didn't you tell me where you lived? Is Mrs Tranter the aunt you spoke of?'

'Yes, she is, and there was no reason to tell you, was there? You knew how to contact me . . .'

'Through a secret address. What have you got to hide?'

'Nothing.'

He obviously didn't believe her. He turned from her to Constance. 'Can we go somewhere and speak in private? I've questions I'd like answered.'

She heaved a huge sigh. 'You had better come into the drawing room.'

She took off her hat and jacket, handed them to Sheila and led the way. He removed his cap and followed, leaving a puzzled Sheila to hang up her aunt's clothes on the hallstand and bring up the rear. Constance stopped in the doorway of the sitting room and ushered him in first, then followed and slammed the door in Sheila's face.

She stood looking at the door, furious that she had been excluded. It was a thick door and they were not raising their voices. What was Johnnie doing here? Whatever it was had certainly upset her aunt. She had never known Constance show emotion of any kind but what was this? Fear? Anger? She made her way to the kitchen and put the kettle on. She had a feeling they would all need a cup of tea and it would give her an opportunity to interrupt them.

Prue came in the back door as she was setting out the tray. Her friend was dealing with the loss of Tim in the only way she knew how, by keeping busy and cheerful. Sheila knew from bitter experience how hard that was, but it could be borne; it had to be borne. Prue was strong and she had a loving family to support her. Sheila envied her that. All she had was Aunt Constance.

'There's a jeep parked outside,' Prue said.

'Yes, it's Johnnie. He's talking to Aunt Constance.'

Prue laughed. 'You mean he's come to ask for your hand in marriage? How quaint!'

'It's not a bit funny and he hasn't come for that. He didn't know I lived here. He told Aunt Constance they had a connection.'

'Well, the Yanks often try and find their ancestors when they come over here. And Johnnie was born in England after all. Do you think he's related to your aunt?'

'If that's the case, I don't think he's altogether welcome. She turned as white as a sheet. I thought she was going to faint.'

'Really? You mean she recognised him?'

'How could she? He said he'd never been to England before. Unless he lied . . .'

'There's only one way to find out.' Prue walked up the hall, opened the drawing room door and pretended surprise. 'I'm sorry, Mrs Tranter, I didn't realise you had company.' And then to Johnnie. 'Hallo, Captain.'

'You know him too?' Constance said.

'Why yes, Sheila and I met him at my home. He is stationed at Longfordham. Does it matter?'

'No, not all.'

'Sheila is making tea. Shall I ask her to bring some in for you?'

'No.' Constance snapped. 'The captain is just leaving.'

'Oh, what a pity. I imagine he has driven from Longfordham. I'd hate to send him back without offering him refreshment.'

'Oh, very well.'

Prue turned back to Sheila. 'Bring it in.'

Sheila set the tray down on the table beside her aunt, who was shaking so much she rattled the cups and spilt the tea in the saucers.

'Here, let me do it,' Prue said. 'You seem to have had a shock. Not bad news, I hope. Johnnie, whatever have you done to the good lady?'

'I've done nothing. I don't think I'll stay for tea.' He rose to go.

'Are you coming back again?' Constance asked.

'No, I don't think so. I don't think I want to see any of you again. But at least I know the answers to my questions now.'

'No, you don't,' she said. 'You don't know anything. They lied . . .'

'I know that because of what you did, my father was a bigamist and his mother lost her reason. How d'you think that makes me feel?'

'Is that true?' Sheila asked.

'It is fact.'

'I don't know what to say.'

'Then don't say anything.' He picked up his cap and made for the door. 'If you want to know the truth, ask her.' He waved the cap at Constance and left them. They heard the jeep start up and roar off down the road.

Sheila and Prue looked at each other and then at Constance. She was crying. Tears were raining down her face and she was making no effort to stop them. It was such an unheard-of display of emotion that they were both taken aback.

'Come on, Mrs Tranter,' Prue said, moving to take her arm. 'Let me take you up to your room to lie down. Sheila will make some fresh tea and you can tell me all about it.'

Sheila watched in astonishment as her aunt allowed Prue to help her to her feet and guide her upstairs. All the stiffness had gone out of her. As she was led away, she kept saying, 'I loved him. I wouldn't have hurt him. I was ill.' It went on and on until the bedroom door shut on her. Sheila picked up the tea tray and took it back to the kitchen and began washing up, lost in speculation. Was Johnnie Constance's son? What had happened and why was he so angry? He'd been angry with her too. It wasn't her fault whatever it was.

Johnnie was hurting badly. And he was mad. All his life people had been lying to him. His whole life was a deception from beginning to end. Grandfather Fletcher had warned him not to go meddling, but he had taken no notice and insisted on being told the truth. He should have left the whole thing alone, put it behind him and gone back to believing the story he had been told in his childhood. Instead he had tormented himself by digging deeper. And he had dug a great hole for himself.

That woman, Constance Tranter, had given birth to him. She was the mother he had wondered about all his life, had wanted to meet, and now he wished he had stayed away. Pops was a bigamist. He and Mom had never been properly married. Mom must have known that and yet she condoned it. She had even taken on the raising of his baby. The reason, according to Grandfather Fletcher, was that his real mother was mad and had tried to smother him with a pillow and his life had only been saved when her husband had come home from work early and caught her at it.

'He couldn't leave you with her, could he?' Grandfather Fetcher had said. 'He couldn't be sure she wouldn't try again. So he picked you up and walked straight out and never went back.'

'Did he come to you?'

'No, to his parents. They lived in Derby. They were old and his father was an invalid. His mother couldn't cope with a baby who cried a lot and a son who didn't know whether to report his wife for attempted murder or just forget her. Then he met Freda again. They had been friends in their school days and she had always had a soft spot for him. Well, you know the rest.'

'He changed his name.'

'Yes, he didn't want his wife chasing them. That's why they went to America, so she couldn't find him. Or you. A new life they said, where no one knew their past.'

'You knew all about it at the time?'

'Yes.'

'That's a helluva secret to keep all these years.'

'It was done for the best. No one would have been the wiser if you hadn't come over here and asked so many questions.'

'But why did my mother try to smother me?'

The old man had shrugged. 'Who knows, Clifford didn't wait to find out.'

'I want to find out.'

'Boy, haven't you had enough?'

'I can't leave it at that. Where can I find her?'

'I don't know. It's too long ago.'

'OK, so where did my father live before he brought me to Derbyshire?'

'Down south somewhere. Freda might know but I don't think it's right to pester her. She's worried enough about you being in those bombers and flying over Germany. You will have to ask his mother.'

He should have known it would do no good to go back to that sanatorium; Verity had been no more lucid than she had been before. His next destination had been Somerset House to look up his own birth. He had it in black and white: Jonathan Tranter, born on the sixth of June 1918 in Bletchley, father Clifford Tranter, engineer, mother, Constance Robins. How his father had managed to obtain a birth certificate for him in the name of Jonathan Howard, which was evidently a forgery, he had no idea. Armed with the proper one he had high-tailed it straight to Bletchley and consulted the pre-war voting register. He wanted it confirmed by the only person who really knew for sure that Jonathan Howard and Jonathan Tranter were one and the same. He no longer had any doubt.

He was suddenly brought out of his reverie by the hooting of a car horn and realised he had strayed to the wrong side of the road. He pulled himself back to the left just in time to avoid a collision. He stopped in a lay-by and switched off the engine. He had better take a minute to pull himself together.

Faced with evidence, Mrs Tranter – he could not think of her as Mother – had blustered that he didn't understand, that she had never intended to harm him. He just wouldn't stop crying and she had been worn out with it and unable to cope and she was alone in the house all day with a screaming baby. She had only used the pillow to stop him crying. Clifford had come in, taken one look at her, picked up the baby and left. She hadn't seen him since. Do wrong to do right, was that what Pops had done? Did all the years of bringing him up, being the best father a man could have, count for nothing? Wasn't it good that he had been his real father and not an adopted one?

And there was Sheila. His plans to ask her to marry him before he went home at the end of his tour of duty had all crumbled to dust. How much had she known? Had she been lying to him too? She had sure been surprised to see him. Had that been guilt or innocence? Confronting Constance Tranter had not been the end of it. He started the engine, put the jeep in gear and turned back the way he had come.

Sheila finished washing up and took a fresh pot of tea up to her aunt's room where Prue took the tray from her.

'I don't want that child in here.' Her aunt's voice, coming from the bed, had been still a little watery but stronger. 'Send her away.'

'Tell you later,' Prue whispered.

Annoyed at being excluded, Sheila went back to the kitchen and began preparing the vegetables for the evening meal. She had barely started when she heard the doorbell. Sighing, she went to answer it.

'Oh, it's you again.'

'Yes. I want to talk to you. Where is she?'

'My aunt? Prue helped her to bed. She is very upset. We all are.'

'Can I come in?'

Without speaking, she opened the door wider to admit him. He followed her to the kitchen. Pretending indifference, she picked up the kitchen knife and returned to her task at the sink.

'Put that down,' he said. 'I can't talk to your back.'

She did as he asked and turned to face him. 'I thought you didn't want to see any of us again.'

'I was mad.'

'You had no right to be mad at me. I had nothing to do with whatever it is that's bugging you.'

'I know. I was wrong to shout at you. I'm all mixed up.'

'Is Aunt Constance your mother?'

'Yes, and I wish I'd never tried to find her. Except it saved me making a terrible mistake.'

'Oh.'

'Marrying you.'

'I don't remember you asking me,' she snapped. 'And I certainly don't remember saying I would.'

'Sorry. What I meant was that we would have been breaking the law. You're my cousin. It's incest. At least it is where I come from.'

'So, is that all?' She was doing her best to take it lightly but inside there was a hollow feeling that, once again, love had slipped through her fingers.

'No, it's not all. There's a helluva lot more. D'you want to hear it or not?'

She drew out a chair from the table and sat down, indicating that he should take the one opposite. 'Go on then, tell me.'

After a hesitant start, he told her everything. By the end of it he was holding both her hands across the table and she was trying not to cry.

'I can see why you are angry,' she said. 'But have you tried to understand?'

'Understand what?'

'Well, I don't know much about it, but my ma had seven children. I was the eldest, so I know a bit about having babies. It's a very emotional experience and I remember Ma saying that sometimes it all got on top of her, that she felt depressed when she really should have been happy, that she felt tied down with all the feeding and nappy changing and always being so tired. No one seemed to understand how she felt. Pa did try. He used to look after the little ones sometimes to let her go out on her own and treat herself to a new hat or something. It didn't mean she didn't love us. And she got better very quickly. Aunt Constance was older when she had you and it might have been worse for her, but taking her baby away from her was cruel, really cruel.'

'Oh, so you are blaming Pops.'

'No, I've no right to do that, and anyway he kept you and made sure you had a good life, so who am I to criticise? Perhaps he should have told you, perhaps not. I don't know. All I'm saying is, don't be angry.'

He smiled at her. 'You really are a wise old owl, aren't you?'

'Not so much of the old.'

'No, you're still my songbird. Am I forgiven?'

'Nothing to forgive. Do you know, when I first met you, I thought you reminded me of someone and now I know why. There's a family likeness, the same colour hair, yours is a bit lighter perhaps and the shape of your face is very like Ma's. Charlie's is like that too. I can imagine him growing up to be just like you.'

'Everyone says I look like Pops.'

'So you may, but the people who said that had never met Ma. You two would have got on well, I think.'

'Sometimes it slips my mind that you've had your troubles too. I'm real sorry.'

'Don't keep apologising.'

Prue came into the kitchen carrying the tea tray. 'Am I interrupting anything?'

'No,' Sheila said. 'Johnnie came back to try and explain how he felt . . .'

'Pretty awful, I expect.'

'Sheila put me straight,' he said.

Prue laughed. 'She would. She does that to me.'

'Did my aunt tell you anything?' Sheila asked.

'Quite a lot, actually. It goes some way to explaining why she is the way she is. All those years, regretting what she had done, pretending her husband had been called up and died of gas poisoning and telling her friends the baby had died too. The only way she could cope was to be hard. She fell out with your mother over it.'

'So that's why they never stayed in touch. I wonder if Ma knew what had happened to Johnnie?'

'Does Mrs Tranter know I'm back?' Johnnie asked.

'We heard the jeep draw up and then voices and she asked me who had come, so yes, she does,' Prue told him.

'Will she talk to me again?'

'Perhaps, but not today.'

'My leave ends tonight. I've got to go back.'

'Next time, then,' Prue said. 'You could try writing, preparing the way.'

'OK. I'll do that.' He stood up to leave.

Sheila followed him to the front door. 'We'll still be friends?' she queried.

'Would you like that, knowing . . .' He stopped.

'Of course. You are my cousin. I thought I didn't have any family left except Aunt Constance and now I have. I don't want to lose you.'

'Kissing cousins.' He laughed and dropped a kiss on her forehead. 'I'll write. Shall I write here or to that London address? Why is your address so secret?'

'It's not the address that's secret, but where I work. And you mustn't ask about that.'

'OK, I won't.' He put his cap on, dropped another kiss on her cheek and climbed into the jeep.

She watched him go and turned back indoors. Her aunt had

come downstairs and was busy in the kitchen cooking dinner. Sheila went to join her.

'Aunt, I'm sorry.'

'What are you sorry for?'

'I'm sorry that you have been so unhappy all these years. I didn't know . . .'

'It's my punishment.'

'Is that what you thought, that you were being punished?'

'I was, wasn't I?'

'But you were unwell. Mum used to feel like that sometimes after giving birth; she told me about it one day when she almost lost her temper with Annie. I am sure she would have understood if you had talked to her. It might have helped.'

'I was never very close to your mother, Sheila. She was lucky, she had a good husband and lots of children. Clifford wasn't like that. All he was interested in was getting on in business, climbing the ladder.' She banged a saucepan of potatoes on the stove and lit the gas under it.

'But he loved his son?'

'He doted on him.'

A pattern was beginning to emerge and Sheila could easily imagine what life had been like in Victoria Villa at that time. A woman unable to cope with motherhood, a woman jealous of her own son, a woman lacking love, a desperately unhappy woman. She was beginning to feel quite sorry for her. 'Did you ever try to trace Johnnie?'

'His name is Jonathan. Oh, I knew where he was, at least in the beginning. I wrote to Clifford but had no reply. Then I heard his father had died and his mother had had a stroke and he had gone away. After that, nothing.'

'Until today?'

'Until today.'

'How do you feel now?'

'How should I feel?' The potatoes were boiling over. She lifted the lid and turned down the gas.

'Glad your son has come back to you perhaps.'

'Has he? He didn't seem like the prodigal son to me.'

'Give him time.'

'Hm, we'll see. Are you planning to marry him?'

'No, Aunt, I am not. He is my cousin, part of my – our – family, but we are going to keep in touch. I think he would like to keep in touch with you too.'

'He's got another mother.'

'Two is better than one, don't you think?'

For the first time ever, Sheila heard Constance laugh. 'My, you've got an old head on young shoulders, miss.'

'Perhaps that's because I had a mother who talked to me and a host of brothers and sisters to help look after. And war makes people grow up fast, don't you think?'

'Probably. Now will you go and lay the table before these potatoes turn to mush.' She bent to take a pie out of the oven as she spoke. 'And then call Lady Prudence.'

Sheila went to do as she was told, smiling to herself. Her aunt was human after all, but she hadn't unbent all the way. She was still correcting her over names, still holding out a little, but it was a start. As for Johnnie, she was surprised to find she was not unhappy about losing him as a potential husband; she felt far more comfortable with him as a cousin. He went a little way to make up for the loss of Charlie.

Chapter Fifteen

It was fiddly and boring work. It wasn't as if they ever saw the finished aircraft. He wasn't even sure where the bits he was making went. All he knew was that he churned them out by the thousand and was paid well for doing so. Of course accuracy was important, but he had been doing it long enough now to do it in his sleep.

He had been too young to enlist at the beginning of the war but he could go now if he wanted, that is if he managed to pass the medical. The only reason he didn't was Bella, who worked the cutting machine next to his and with whom he lived. Both orphans of the Blitz, they had learnt to get by. Instead of relying on charitable handouts and foster homes, they had camped out in bombed-out houses, scavenged and earned a few pence running errands, buying and selling second-hand stuff, collecting discarded bottles and returning them to the makers for a penny a time. There had been a crowd of them doing the same thing, too big a crowd as it happened. They had been rounded up and the younger ones sent to children's homes.

Too old for a children's home and with no evidence that they had been doing anything illegal, he and Bella, whose real name was Isabella Malloney, had been found digs and a job, here at the factory in Croydon. The jobs were a godsend but they hadn't liked being in different digs and had soon found a couple of rooms of their own. He supposed one day they would get married, but there was plenty of time. After the war perhaps.

He looked at the clock. Two minutes to go for their dinner break. If they scuttled off on the dot of eleven, they might find themselves at the head of the queue in the canteen and have a decent half hour to eat it. He looked over at Bella and put his thumb up. She grinned and set aside the sheet of metal she was about to work on and pretended to be studying the blueprint to use the time before the hooter went. As soon as they heard it there was a mad scramble by everyone to get to the canteen and be the first in the queue.

With twenty minutes of their break still left, they found a table and sat down to enjoy liver and bacon, mashed potatoes and cabbage. Having a good meal at work saved them having to cook when they went home; they were usually too tired anyway. Away from the noise of the machinery they could enjoy 'Music While You Work' in peace. Sometimes, if they ate on the second shift, they listened to 'Workers' Playtime', which was broadcast from different factories.

'This ain't half bad,' he said. 'Not as good as my mother used to make, though.'

'Do you still miss her?'

'Course I do. All of them.'

He stopped suddenly to listen. The clear voice of someone singing 'When You Wish Upon a Star' came over the airwaves. It mesmerised him. 'My mother used to sing that,' he said. 'If I didn't know better, I would think that was her.'

'It can't be though, can it?' she said.

'Not unless you believe in ghosts. Who do you think it is?'

'Well, it's not Gracie Fields, that's for sure, nor Vera Lynn or Anne Shelton. I know their voices.'

But he wasn't listening to her; he could hear his mother singing as she dusted. '*When you wish upon a star your dreams come true.*' He blinked back unaccustomed tears.

The song ended. 'Thank you, Sheila,' the announcer said. Then to the listeners. 'A delightful song sung by a delightful singer. That was Sheila Phipps. I am sure we shall be hearing a lot more of her in future.'

His jaw dropped open. 'Sheila!' He reached across and grabbed Bella's sleeve. 'She's alive! She's alive!'

'It could be someone with the same name.'

'Not with a voice like that. Oh, Bella, I've got to find her.'

The hooter went for them to return to their work benches. He could hardly contain his excitement, but as the last three hours of their early shift wore on, his euphoria evaporated. How had she escaped the bomb? Where had she been all this time? Why had he never seen her about? How could he find her? He hadn't visited Ma and Pa's graves lately. Perhaps it was time he did. At least one question he had been asking himself over the years had been answered. There was no grave for Sheila because she had not died.

There was a policeman with Lady Winterton and Ronnie was immediately on the alert. He hadn't nicked anything for ages, but he supposed he was doing wrong using the bunker. Could they prove he had? Auntie Jean was looking as if she were going to cry and that bothered him. In his experience, grown-up people did not cry.

'Ronald,' the Countess said gently. She was wearing her WVS

uniform, which was another sign something was up. 'You are needed at home. Your mother is in hospital and asking for you.'

'In hospital? What's wrong with her? Was it a bomb?'

'No, not a bomb. She has been hurt. I don't know any details. I am going to take you to her.'

'I can go on my own.'

'I'm sure you can, but I think it is best that I come with you.'

'What's he here for?' He nodded towards the policeman. Policemen were not good news.

'Constable Finch received the news by telephone and fetched me. I am here in my capacity as billeting officer for evacuees.'

'He won't be coming to London with us?'

'No, he is needed here.'

'I will be coming back, won't I?'

The Countess looked from the constable to Mrs Potts. 'I don't know. We shall have to see.'

This sounded like very bad news. There was nothing for it but to shrug his shoulders and accompany the Countess to London.

His mother was hardly recognisable; her face was a mass of bruises and she had her arm in plaster. 'So you got here,' she said, ignoring the Countess, who stood just behind him.

'Who did this to you?' He could recognise a beating when he saw it. He'd had plenty of those himself when his pa was at home.

'That no good father of yours.'

'But I thought he was in . . .' He stopped, remembering the lady behind him.

'He's out, came home unexpected he did.'

'Oh.' He was beginning to understand. 'Where is he now?'

'I don't know. He stormed out again. The police are looking

for him. He'll probably come after you. I didn't tell him where you were, honest I didn't, but I don't suppose it will take him long to find out.'

'What do you want me to do?'

'There's some money in a box under the floorboards in the corner of my bedroom. I don't want him to find it. I've been saving up to get away. Bring it to me. And I'll have my make-up bag while you're about it. It's on my dressing table.'

'Then what?'

'Go back where you came from before you get taken into care.'

He turned to look at the Countess who had not said a word but he could see by the expression on her face she had understood. 'I'll take you,' she said.

If he could have rid himself of his escort, he might have done, but he realised it would be an unwise thing to do, especially if he wanted to avoid being picked up by the welfare or the police. And if he should encounter his father, he would be safer if he had an adult with him. There was the added advantage that the Countess went everywhere in a taxi and that was an unheard-of treat. And safer.

The house was a shambles. Pa had obviously turned everything upside down looking for money. It was also very dirty; unwashed crockery and saucepans in the sink, an unmade bed, the overpowering smell of stale perfume mixed with the odour from an overflowing ash tray. It all made him ashamed. Shame was something he had never felt before. Goodness knew what the Countess thought of it. But the box with the money was still there. He retrieved it and picked up the make-up bag. 'Let's go before he comes back,' he said.

They went out to the cab, which had been kept waiting. 'Shall we buy some flowers to take to your mother?' the Countess suggested as they were driven back to the hospital.

'If you like.' He was glad she wasn't going to quiz him about his mother and father.

They stopped at a florist's shop. It had been damaged by bombs but was still in business. There were no exotic blooms and it was too late in the year for summer flowers, but there were some bronze chrysanthemums, and her ladyship bought those. It was as they were turning to leave, Ronnie recognised another customer looking round the sparse display.

'Whatchya, Charlie,' he said.

The young man looked at him in surprise. 'Oh, it's you, Ronnie Barlow.' He looked from the boy to the lady who was evidently with him. She was not the sort Ronnie would normally associate with, probably an authority figure of some kind.

'This here's Charlie Phipps,' Ronnie told her. 'He's Sheila's brother.'

'Really?' she said. 'But I thought . . .' She turned to Charlie. 'Can you spare me a few minutes, young man?'

'Do you know my sister?' he asked eagerly. 'Do you know where she is?'

'I think I might. Shall we go and find somewhere to talk?'

Ronnie hadn't known Sheila thought her brother was dead or he could have told her he wasn't. He had seen him once before when he came home, but didn't think anything of it. He listened to the conversation between the Countess and Charlie as they sat on a park bench, but his own problems loomed large. Where was his father? Would he really come for him, make him go back to a life of crime? He didn't want that. He wanted to stay with Mr and Mrs Potts. But if he couldn't, what then?

'He's alive? Charlie's alive?' It was almost too good to be true and extraordinary that the person to be telling her this was Prue. It was just after breakfast, which she and Prue were having in the canteen. Prue had been reading a long letter from her mother which she hadn't had time to read before leaving for work. Sheila, who had been on night duty, would be going home to Victoria Villa after breakfast.

'So Mama says. She met him in London and they had a long talk. He's living with his girlfriend in a flat in Croydon and working in an aircraft factory.'

'He's well? Why hasn't he been in touch with me in all these years?'

'He thought you were dead, just as you thought he was. He realised you were alive when he heard you singing on 'Music While You Work' and he was buying flowers to take to your parents' graves when he met Mama and Ronald Barlow.'

'Ronnie?'

Prue laughed. 'That's another story.'

'I must go to him! Do you think I've got time to get to London and back before my shift tonight?'

'Sheila, you've been up all night. You need to sleep. And he will be at work. Mama has sent his address for you to write to him, then you can arrange a proper meeting. Here, you read it.' She handed the letter over.

Sheila scanned it quickly and then again more slowly. 'Oh, Prue, I hardly dare believe it. After all this time. I must go home and write to him at once.' She offered the letter back.

'You keep it. I have to go to work.' She stood up and gathered up their trays and crockery to take back to the counter. 'I'll see you later.'

Sheila cycled home as fast as her pedalling feet would take her, propped her bicycle against the wall and went in by the back door. Constance was having her breakfast in the kitchen. She had softened considerably since Johnnie's sudden arrival and his subsequent correspondence. 'Aunt, guess what? Charlie's been found.'

'That's what you thought before.'

'I know, but this time it's real. Prue's mother has met him and talked to him. He thought I had died with the others, but then he heard me singing on the radio.' She was bubbling with excitement. 'He lives in Croydon.'

'What's he been doing all this time?'

'I don't know until I meet him. I've got an address to write to. I'm going up to do it now.'

She hurried up to her room and sat on the bed to read the Countess's letter again. The Countess had explained why she was in London with Ronnie and how they had met Charlie and recounted the conversation she had had with him on the way back to Longfordham. 'He has always been unforthcoming about his past,' she had written. 'I think he was ashamed of it, but knowing I had met his mother and seen the conditions in which he had lived, he opened up. He told me all about his appalling childhood. His father is a notorious thief and his mother is a woman of easy virtue and they expected him to steal for them. He was beaten if he didn't. Being evacuated was the saving of him. He wants to lead an honest life, but there is little chance of it if he goes back to them. We could get the welfare people onto it, but that would mean putting him into a home for delinquents. I doubt that would set him on the right path. When I took him home, I spoke to Mrs Potts. She has grown very fond of him in spite of his cheeky ways and appalling manners and would like to keep him. He will soon be old enough to leave school and go to work and he likes Thomas Green, so your Papa has decided to offer him a job in the gardens if his parents agree. I don't see why they shouldn't. His mother doesn't seem to care and his father is on the run. We shall have to wait and see.'

Sheila could have told the Countess all of that, but had kept quiet because Ronnie had asked her to, and everyone ought to be given a chance. Perhaps it was just as well, considering she might not have heard about Charlie if it hadn't been for him.

She folded the two closely packed sheets and set them aside to write a long, rambling letter to Charlie, all about living with their aunt and her search for him. 'Just when I had almost given up hope, I received the wonderful news that you are alive and have been looking for me too,' she wrote. She ended, 'Can I come and see you? I've got Saturday off this week. Will you be at home then? Or would you rather come here? I can't wait to get a letter from you and to see you again. There is so much to talk about. Your loving sister, Sheila.'

She sealed it in an envelope, addressed it and put a stamp on it, then went out to post it. Saturday was only four days away but it seemed like an eternity.

'Bella, what are you doing?' Charlie asked. On her instructions, he had been to the grocer's with their ration books and bought a tiny joint of brisket, a couple of sausages, some potatoes, a cabbage and a ready-made apple pie. He put the shopping bag on the kitchen table and stood watching her. She was on her hands and knees scrubbing the kitchen lino.

'We can't have your sister seeing us in all this muck,' she said without even stopping the circular movement of the scrubbing brush. 'It goes without saying she's used to much better than this.'

He squatted down beside her. 'Bella, it's my sister you are talking about, born and raised in the East End, she's the same as us, no better, no worse, and if she tries to come here all high and mighty, I'll soon put her back in her place. Now pack that in and put that meat in the oven or we'll have nothing to give her and that would be worse.'

'All right.' She got up off her knees and handed him the brush. 'You finish it while I cook.'

The flat, which had once been the upper floor of a semi-detached house, consisted of a kitchen and a bedroom with a shared bathroom. Because they were both working long hours, housework and cooking had been a low priority. They could eat their main meal in the canteen at work, and neither bothered much about a little dust. He didn't think his sister would worry unduly about it either. But she might frown at their unmarried state. It was the first time it had crossed his mind that they were living in sin. He didn't think of it as a sin.

'Bella,' he said, when he had finished the floor and the brisket was giving off an appetising smell in the oven. 'Sit down. I want to talk to you.'

They sat on either side of the table. He reached out and took her hands in his. 'We had better say we are engaged and soon going to marry . . .'

'Charlie Phipps, now who's worried about what she will think?'

'What do you say?'

'I say no. You haven't seen your sister in years and you are going to start off with a lie.'

'It needn't be a lie.'

'And is that supposed to please me?'

'Doesn't it?'

'No, it does not. When I agree to marry someone, it will be because he loves me and I love him and he has asked me properly and bought me an engagement ring, not because he is afraid of what his sister will think.'

'I can't afford a ring.'

'I know that, silly.'

He sighed and stood up. 'OK, point taken.'

'Where are you going?'

'Out.'

'But you can't. She'll be here any minute.'

'I won't be long.' And he was gone.

'Are you Bella?' The girl who opened the door to Sheila was thin, her face had little colour except for the lipstick which was scarlet. Her hair was pale and wispy, but her blue eyes were bright and intelligent.

'Yes. You must be Sheila. Come in.' She led the way upstairs. 'I'm afraid Charlie's gone out. He'll be back soon.'

'Oh.' Sheila had walked up the road in a fever of anticipation, wondering how they would greet each other, imagining what he might look like, what he might say, only to be met with this deflating disappointment. 'You *were* expecting me?'

'Oh, yes. Do sit down.' She indicated a chair. 'I was just finishing off the dinner.'

'It smells delicious.' She watched Bella put a saucepan of potatoes on the gas. 'Tell me about Charlie.'

'What do you want to know?'

'Everything. How did you meet? Did he really believe I was dead?'

'Yes.' Bella took a seat opposite her and explained how she had pulled Charlie from the ruins and looked after him while he recovered. 'He was devastated when I told him you were dead.'

'You told him?'

'Yes. He was in hospital and fretting, so I went to find out. I was told you had died in that school. You know, the one where all those people got killed. It was why you didn't have a grave. When he heard you singing, it was like a lamp had been turned on inside him. He got that excited, I thought he'd burst into flames. And then he met that lady.'

'The Countess of Winterton. That's when I heard he was alive. I was excited too. Why did he go out, knowing I was coming?'

Bella laughed. 'I think he's gone to try and buy an engagement ring. He didn't think you would approve of us living in sin, so he said we ought to be engaged at least. He thought you had moved up in the world, knowing titled ladies and singing on the wireless an' all.'

'He's my brother, Bella, nothing changes that, nothing at all.'

The door burst open and Charlie stood there, breathing heavily. The gangling youth she had last seen was a handsome young man, rather too thin, but tall and straight, taller than she was she discovered when she scrambled to her feet to go to him. He opened his arms and she walked into them. He held her tight. 'Sheila, I'm so sorry, so sorry I wasn't here.'

'You're here now and that's all that matters.' She stepped back to appraise him, and laughed. 'Did you get it?'

'Get what?'

'The engagement ring.'

He looked across at Bella. 'You told her.'

'Why not? You weren't here. I had to tell her why.'

'I like your Bella,' Sheila said. 'And I like honesty. There's so little of it nowadays.'

'I like her too,' he said, looking at Bella. 'Very much.'

'Well, did you get the ring?' Sheila asked.

'Yes, but according to Bella I have to ask her properly and I'll do that later. Let's sit down, we've so much catching up to do.'

Bella dished up the meal. The plates were odd and so was the cutlery, but Sheila didn't even notice as they talked while they ate. When the raid started, Pa had sent him home to look after his Mum and help her with the rest of the kids. He had started out on his bike but things got a bit hot in more ways than one.

'A bomb went straight through the roof of a house, just as I was cycling past and the blast knocked me off me bike and I blacked out,' he said. 'When I came to, I was buried under a pile of rubble. I couldn't move. The bomb had started a fire, I could hear it crackling. I thought the fire brigade were bound to find me, but no one came.'

'Oh, Charlie, I wish I'd known.'

'I was there for ages. There was a beam just above my head and it was propped against a pile of bricks at one end. It was the only thing stopping the whole house from coming down on top of me. I was half afraid to try and move but I had to do something. The problem was how to get out from under that beam without dislodging everything.' He paused, remembering how he had managed to free one hand and tried to turn on his side in order to burrow his way out. He had heard falling masonry and the tiny space he occupied had been filled with brick dust. He dare not cough, dare not try that move again. Apart from the risk of bringing the remains of the house down on him, his chest hurt so much that breathing was painful.

'I got my hand round half a brick and wriggled it. It suddenly disappeared, fell down somewhere. I waited for everything to come down on me, but when it didn't I tried another one and then another. I made a hole big enough to get my head out, but by then I was done for. I thought I was going to die.'

'I found him,' Bella put in. 'I saw the top of his head and one hand and I fetched my brother and two of his friends and they dragged him out. We thought at first he was dead. His eyes were shut and his face was covered in scratches and bruises, but then he moaned, so they put him onto a door and carried him to hospital. His ribs had been crushed and his legs broken and the fingers of his left hand, the one he had used to do all the digging, were shredded and bleeding. He was in a coma for three weeks.'

'When I came round,' he went on. 'I told Bella my name and where I lived. I knew Ma would be worried about me. She promised to go and tell her where I was.'

She came back the next day with the terrible news that his whole family had perished, every single one of them. 'Your ma and the kids all died when the house got a direct hit,' she had told him, holding tight onto his good hand. 'They couldn't have known much about it. Your pa died down by the docks and your big sister died in the South Hallsville school the next day when that got hit. There were hundreds taking shelter there and they weren't able to identify them all.'

The news had laid him low for days and hindered his recovery. 'If it hadn't been for Bella, I don't think I would have got better, I'd have simply laid there and let myself die,' he said. 'But she came to the hospital every day to cheer me up. I was there three months. As soon as I could, I went home, but there was nothing left of it. I just stood there looking at that hole in the ground. It was filled with water and I imagine Mum and everyone lying there. It was horrible.'

'I know,' Sheila said. 'It was the same for me.'

'I had to convince myself they weren't there, so I went to see the graves.'

'You put flowers there, didn't you?' Sheila said. 'I wondered who it was.'

'We could have met there,' he said. 'I wonder why we didn't.'

'It was not meant to happen then, I suppose. I got sent to

Bletchley and Aunt Constance. It must have been while you were still in hospital.'

'I thought about joining the army,' he said. 'But I couldn't leave Bella.'

'They wouldn't have you,' Bella said. 'You're too knocked about.'

'I'm as fit as a flea now. But enough of me. What about you, Sheila. How did you meet a countess and how did you come to be singing on the wireless?'

Those questions were easy to answer. The only thing Sheila had to avoid was explaining about Bletchley Park. She told them she worked as a messenger in the post room of a factory doing war work and thankfully they did not ask for details. She talked about their aunt and Prue and how she met Johnnie who had turned out to be their cousin. 'Perhaps you'll meet him one day,' she said. 'You must come to Bletchley and meet our aunt too.'

'What happened to Chris Jarrett?' he asked. 'I thought you and he . . .'

'He was killed in action. In the navy. On the Arctic convoys.'

'I'm sorry. You've had a worse deal of it than I have, haven't you? But we've got good memories, haven't we?'

They went on to recall things about Ma and Pa and the younger children, some of which made them laugh, some made them sad and the time flew by. Later in the afternoon, she and Charlie took the tube to West Ham and visited the graves to leave fresh flowers. 'It's quite a trek from Croydon or I'd come more often,' he said.

'For me too, but June Bennett keeps it tidy for me. It's strange you didn't meet her either. She knew where I was.'

'I had to come in the evening, after work and there was never anyone about. We won't lose touch again, will we?'

'No, definitely not. You will invite me to the wedding won't you?'

'If Bella will have me, you will be guest of honour.'

'Of course she'll have you. There isn't any doubt of that.'

'I wish you could have someone . . .'

'I'm all right, Charlie, more than all right. I've got a career to look forward to and good friends. And now I've got you and Bella. What more could I ask for?' Except Ma and Pa and the little ones, she added silently.

She left him at the underground station; she was going to Euston to get the Bletchley train, he was going back to Croydon to propose properly to Bella. In spite of the war, life was good.

Aunt Constance was alone, listening to the wireless while she knitted a khaki sock intended for Johnnie, when Sheila came in. She put her head round the drawing room door. 'I'm back.'

'How did it go?'

'Wonderful. He's grown into a strapping handsome man and he's going to be married. We'll be invited. Where's Prue?'

'I think she has gone out with Hugh. Would you like some supper? I've had mine.'

'I'll make myself a sandwich. Would you like me to make cocoa? Then I'll tell you all about Charlie.'

'Yes, that would be nice.'

Much later, she went up to her room, washed and made ready for bed, then sat down in her pyjamas with the eiderdown about her to write her journal.

Dear Ma and Pa,

Charlie is alive! I am so excited I feel like jumping up and down and yelling it to the whole world. He isn't the fifteen-year-old I knew, and I am not seventeen any more, but he is just the same, half mischievous, half serious. He is living with his girlfriend in Croydon and they are going to be married. He has been visiting your resting place, as I have, and we never met. Isn't that strange? I am sad to think that you will not have watched us growing up. But perhaps you have. Who knows?

Aunt Constance seems happy that Charlie is alive and has told me to invite him to come and stay for a holiday. It will have to be after he is married because she would never approve of the situation as it is. Prue has gone out with Hugh. I am glad for her. Tim's death hit her very hard, but Hugh has been a wonderful support. Maybe something will come of it, maybe not. It's too soon to say. I shall have to wait for her to come back to tell her all about seeing Charlie. I am happier now than at any time since you left me.

Your ever-loving daughter,

Sheila

She closed the book, put it away in her box and snuggled down in the warmth of the bed. 'Thank you, God,' she murmured as she closed her eyes.

Hugh was not the brash young man Prue had first encountered in the chemist's shop. That had been a front to cover his insecurity. His need for strong spectacles and his bookishness meant he had been badly bullied at his public school. 'It was the wrong place for me,' he told Prue. 'Everyone was mad keen on sport. If you could play rugger, cricket or tennis you were OK, otherwise your life was made hell. When we had paper chases I used to hide in the woods and read. Of course I was punished for it.' The subject had come up because they were watching an enthusiastic game of rounders on the grass in front of the lake. 'It wasn't so much the staff as the other boys.'

'I've heard Gillie talk about that sort of thing.'

'He wasn't bullied?'

'Heavens, no! He was good at all sports. He's good at everything really.'

'Bully for him.'

'We can't all be the same, Hugh, and you have your uses.'

'Hut Eight.'

'Yes, that's important, but I wasn't thinking of that. I meant the way you've put up with me. It can't have been easy, me always going on about Gillie and Tim and weeping all over you. You've got a lot of patience.'

'It's been a privilege and a pleasure.'

They clapped as the batsman whacked the ball into the lake and set off at a run. 'Hey, he can't keep running,' someone shouted. 'Fetch another ball.'

'The lake must be full of balls,' Prue said. 'Perhaps they'll drain it after the war. I wonder what else they'll find. Do you think this place will still be here then?'

'I shouldn't think so. I expect it will be dismantled and all its secrets buried in people's memories.'

'But one day we will all die. Surely something will live on.'

'The bombes perhaps, and that Colossus that Turing is building. I can see that having some use in peacetime.'

'Do you think the war will be over soon?'

'No telling, is there? But you know as well as anyone how it's going.'

'Invasion, somewhere in France and then Germany will collapse and Gillie will come home. If he manages to live that long.'

'Hey, don't be so pessimistic.'

'Sorry.' She took his arm as they strolled away, leaving the players arguing. 'When it's all over and Gillie comes home, I am going to throw the biggest party ever.'

'And will I be invited?'

'Of course. How can you doubt it? You have been my prop these last few weeks. I don't know what I would have done without you.'

'I would like it always to be like that,' he murmured.

She deliberately chose to misunderstand him. 'I have to learn to stand on my own two feet sooner or later.'

'You are making a pretty good fist of it now.'

'Let's go to the pictures,' she said, not quite sure she wanted to delve too deeply into her feelings for him or his for her. But she didn't want to lose him. 'Sheila has gone off to meet her brother. She thought he had died when her parents were killed but he's alive and well.'

'Are you hoping . . .' He left the end of the question unfinished, but she knew what he meant.

'No. Tim is dead. Esme is sure of it.'

They went to the Studio and saw Ingrid Bergman in *For Whom the Bell Tolls*, a dramatic story of the Spanish Civil War, which in many people's eyes was a foretaste on the war they were fighting against Hitler.

It was late when he took her home. 'They'll be in bed,' she said, referring to Constance and Sheila. 'I won't ask you in.'

He dropped a kiss on her cheek and left her. The cloud which had been hanging over her for weeks had lifted and she felt alive again. She had Hugh and Sheila to thank for that. Sheila because she understood better than anyone and Hugh because she knew he loved her.

Sheila had gone to bed but she didn't wake her. There was time enough to hear about her meeting with Charlie tomorrow. There was always a tomorrow.

Chapter Sixteen

Christmas 1943

Plans for Christmas at Longfordham Hall started when Prue wrote to say she would be able to come home for the holiday and, with her parents' consent, intended to bring Sheila with her. For once, Sheila was not going to be in the Bletchley Park Christmas show.

'Let's ask Hugh,' Chloe said to Marcus when she read the letter. He was reading the newspaper while eating his breakfast and hardly paying attention. The Allied leaders, Churchill, Roosevelt and Stalin, had met in Teheran for a conference. The three leaders, so it was reported, had agreed plans for the total destruction of the German forces and nothing less than unconditional surrender would do. It looked as though the long-heralded Second Front was imminent, though none except those planning it knew where or when it would take place.

He did not doubt there would be more fighting, more loss of life, more injuries and partings, before the war was won, but there was no doubt in anyone's mind that it would end in victory for the Allies. After that there would be all the rebuilding, not only of tangible structures like houses, factories and roads, but of people's lives. Some would never be rebuilt, not as they were. He even doubted that Longfordham Hall would survive as it had done for centuries. The upkeep was getting beyond him. He said nothing of this to his wife, though he did not think she was foolish enough to believe everything would go back to being what it was before the war.

'Why not?' he murmured. 'Invite whomever you like.'

'Then let's have a proper house party.' Hosting parties had always been her forte and one she had missed since the start of the war.

'Shouldn't you wait until hostilities are over?'

'No. Nanny Bright told me I should soon hear some very good news. Worth celebrating, she said.'

'You shouldn't take any notice of her funny sayings, Chloe. She likes to pretend she can see into the future, but you know she can't. No one can.'

She sighed. 'I know, but Prue is coming home for Christmas and that's good news, isn't it? And she seems to have got over Tim, even though they had split up before he was shot down and nothing might have come of it. Besides, a party will brighten everyone up.'

'Very well. Go ahead if that's what you want.'

She set to work at once, making a guest list that could not have been more different from the lists she had prepared pre-war. Instead of just their upper-class friends, she mixed everyone up. Besides Hugh, there was Esme, Sheila, Sheila's brother and his new wife, Mrs Constance Tranter, Major Norton, Captain Johnnie Howard and his crew from the aerodrome, though thankfully they would not need to be provided with beds. Marcus laughed when he saw it. 'What on earth are you going to do with that lot?'

'I am going to do nothing but feed them and give them beds.'

'But will they mix?'

'Marcus, if I have learnt one thing from this war, it is that people are people; high and low they have the same hopes and dreams and fears as everyone else. We don't live in an ivory castle. Hugh is not exactly the man we would have chosen for our daughter, nor, come to that, would we think of Esme as a viscountess. But it's going to happen. We must adapt.'

That made him laugh. He had only a day or two before been wondering how she would cope with a post-war world when a title did not automatically command respect. He might have known she would think it out for herself. 'Has Prue told you she's going to marry Hugh?'

'Not exactly, but I can see the way the wind is blowing. Give them time.'

'And Sheila and her brother?'

'They deserve a treat. They have both been through the mill, and Prue is right, Sheila is a very special person.'

'But Mrs Tranter? Chloe, isn't that going a bit far?'

She laughed. 'I've heard Prue and Sheila talking about her and I'm curious. Besides, she's Johnnie's mother.'

'On your own head be it. I hope you can feed them all.'

'Major Norton will help with the food, I'm sure, but we can't do it without staff. I'll ask some of the villagers if they will help out with the catering and looking after the bedrooms. Mr and Mrs Potts and Mrs Burrows will come, I know. I'd ask Mrs Stevens but I'm not sure she has forgiven you for Bill, yet. On the other hand, she might take it as a slight if she wasn't asked.'

'Be your diplomatic self, my dear. It would be nice to be forgiven.'

'Then I'll speak to her.'

'It seems I am not needed.'

'Oh, yes you are. Don't think you can get away with disappearing off to your Home Guard. You will need to organise the drinks and the cutting down of a Christmas tree and perhaps a bit of shooting on Boxing Day. The men will enjoy that.'

'Very well. I'll ask Burrows about the game. He'll have a few pheasants fattening somewhere.'

She stood up and went over to where he sat and bent to put her arms about him from behind. 'You are a good sport,' she said, rubbing her cheek against his. 'I love you as much as I ever did, more if that is possible.'

He grinned with pleasure. 'And I you, my dear.'

She was in her element and by Christmas Eve everything was ready for the arrival of their guests. The food had been prepared, the beds made and towels and plenty of hot water made available. The reception rooms and the dining room had been decorated with holly and mistletoe and paper chains and the six-foot tree in the hall was ablaze with candles and trinkets. The Americans were used to coming and going and even though they had already provided much of the fare, they arrived with yet more. As far as they were concerned, the thick fog was fortuitous because they could not fly, but it might delay people coming from further afield.

Tom Green met Prue, Hugh, Sheila and Constance off the train with the pony and trap in the afternoon before it came down really heavily. He turned round almost immediately and went back for Esme.

Sheila had learnt a lot about deportment and poise, along with stagecraft over the years and she was no longer the gawky girl whom Prue had befriended. She could hold her own. It was Constance's turn to feel overwhelmed and she was as nervous as a kitten but as soon as she saw Johnnie and he came over to give her a hug, she relaxed and was soon talking to his crew. Prue made a point of making Esme welcome and that left Sheila to look out for her brother. Tom made his last trip to the station and brought Charlie and Bella. Sheila hugged them both and pulled them into the room. They stood a little to one side looking uncomfortable and answering questions in monosyllables until Johnnie came over to them. 'You must be my cousin, Charlie,' he said, holding out his hand. 'I'm Johnnie. I'm right glad to make your acquaintance.'

Charlie shook his hand. 'This is Bella, my wife.'

'Cousin-in-law, Bella, I'm glad to meet you too. Come and talk to the guys.'

Sheila watched them cross the room. Charlie was in a grey suit, white shirt and a pink bow tie and Bella in a skirt and jumper. 'Does she know we are expected to dress for dinner?' Prue whispered to her.

'I doubt it.'

'When you go up to change, bring her to my room. We'll find something for her.'

Prue, in her usual diplomatic way, prevailed upon Bella to accept a long blue skirt printed with summer flowers, and a white lace blouse. It was not the height of fashion and not couture made, but simple enough for people to think she had brought it with her. Prue, in cerise silk, and Sheila, in a dove-grey crêpe dress that had cost her fifteen clothing coupons and the same number of guineas, treated the transformation as a fun thing, doing Bella's hair for her and helping her to make up her face and the end result was a very pretty girl, who had Charlie grinning from ear to ear when he saw her.

They were having sherry in the drawing room prior to dinner when there was a commotion in the hall but before Marcus could go to investigate it, the door was flung open and Gilbert stood looking round at them all. Esme shrieked his name and ran to him, arriving just ahead of the Countess and Prue. 'What a welcome,' he said, holding her in his arms. 'Is the party for me?'

'It is now,' Prue said.

The servants were sent to fetch more cutlery and napery to make a new place setting, and everyone began talking at once. 'Hold hard,' he said, as Esme gave way to his mother and then Prue. 'Let me get inside the door.'

Still holding Esme's hand, he went round everyone, being introduced and shaking them by the hand. His mother was tearful but smiling. His father shook his hand and, deciding that was inadequate, pulled him into a hug. 'Good to have you home, Son.'

'The best Christmas present of all,' his mother added. 'Nanny Bright was right. It is more than good news, it's the best ever.'

'When did you get back?' Prue asked him, as everyone sat down.

'Three days ago. I wasn't let out until I'd been debriefed, so I couldn't let anyone know.'

'You said you wouldn't come home until it was over,' Esme murmured. Everyone was talking at once and only Prue, sitting on his other side, heard her.

'I had to. The Duports were all arrested and shot.'

She gasped. 'Oh, no. Not all of them?'

He nodded. ''Fraid so.'

'Who betrayed them?'

'I don't know, a double-dealing spy, Anton's foolishness or Madame's insistence on sticking to your cover story, all three perhaps. Everyone else scattered and I was ordered home. They sent an aircraft in to fetch me. It was touch and go.'

'Oh, Gillie, we brought it on those brave people. I don't think I can forgive myself.'

'They knew what they were doing, Esme. Please don't speak of it to anyone else.' He looked across at his sister and knew she had heard. 'Prue, that goes for you too. What happened and how we escaped has to be kept under wraps because there are people still out there, brave, resourceful people and careless talk could endanger them. I don't need to tell you that, do I?'

'Of course you don't. I know that.'

'More than we do, I'll bet.'

'What makes you say that?'

'You've been working at Bletchley Park almost from the beginning and you've never explained what you do, even when I told you I was going to France. That place is like a fort, no one can get in, so it stands to reason it's something hush-hush. The fact that Esme met you there when she was going through debriefing confirmed it as far as I am concerned.'

'And put two and two together and made five. If you must know, I translate reports from German newspapers. Anyone with a smattering of German could do it.' She had kept quiet about what she did for three years, keeping secrets was second nature to her now.

'OK, I believe you. Is that what you told Mama?'

'Yes, but she has met Esme so I expect she has put two and two together. If she has, she has kept very quiet about it.'

'What are you three whispering about?' Chloe demanded.

'Nothing, Mama,' Prue said. 'We were just wondering what's in the parcels under the tree.'

'That's a secret. You'll have to wait until tomorrow and find out.'

Her mother was another of the hundreds, no thousands, of people who had a secret to keep. It made Prue smile.

Ronnie crept out from the bunker and closed the trapdoor, pulling a pile of dead leaves over it. His goods were all safely stowed away. Bicycle parts, tools, candy, tins of Coca-Cola, packets of biscuits, and cigarettes given to him by Johnnie and his pals. There was even a half bottle of whisky and money in a lockable cash tin which he was saving to run away. He didn't want to go, but he had to, no one would want to have anything to do with him now his secret was out. He was the lowest of the low. He really should not have told Lady Winterton all that gibberish about his parents. She would make sure he was put into care.

He'd had a bit of that when he was little, but his mother had persuaded the authorities she had turned over a new leaf and he had been allowed to go back to her and his father. Half the time he never went to school and the attendance officer was always calling, knocking on the door at all times of the day. If he and his mother were alone in the house they hid and did not answer. If his father was there, he would go to the door and subject the poor man to a torrent of abuse, which sent him scurrying away and resulting in a beating for him. It was a relief when the old man was sent to prison after being caught red-handed cracking the safe in a factory after beating the caretaker insensible. He went back to school and then the war came and that was his salvation, or it would have been if his father hadn't escaped from prison and attacked his mother. He was afraid he would come looking for him, which was another reason for disappearing. He had no feelings for either of his parents, but he did have feelings for Auntie Jean and Uncle Cyril and the people up at the big house. It was a pity he was going to have to let them down.

He wasn't quite ready to go. He had a bicycle half restored that was destined for one of the American airmen and he needed the money from that. And he wanted to have one last Christmas with the Potts before he disappeared from their lives for ever. They were up at the big house helping with a party and he had been left to get his own supper and take himself off to bed. Instead he had put on his coat and scarf and taken a torch to go to the bunker and retrieve the Christmas presents he had bought for them. There was a pipe rack he had made for Uncle Cyril, Johnnie had helped him make that, and a pair of red felt slippers for Auntie Jean. They weren't new, new ones needed clothing coupons and she had charge of his, but they were as good as. He tucked them under his arm and emerged onto the driveway, but before he could set off home, someone came up behind him and gripped his arm so tightly, he yelled.

'Shut up, you little runt.' The voice was that of his father.

He twisted round to face him. By the feeble light of the torch he saw a man with a rough beard and long, matted hair, but it was undoubtedly the man he feared most in all the world. 'What do you want?'

'Food, drink and money, and then we're both off out of here.'

'You can go without me. I'm stoppin' where I am.'

'You'll do as you're told. I reckon there's plenty to be had up at that big house and they're all enjoyin' theirselves, so while they're at it, you'll go and get what I want. There's a nice handy jeep on the drive, that'll do to get us away.'

'I'm not doin' your dirty work for you no more, so clear off.'

His answer was a sharp blow to his face which sent him reeling backwards. He dropped his presents and the torch to put his hand to his stinging cheek. 'There'll be more of the same if you don't get a move on.' His arm was pushed up behind his back, making him squeal.

Ronnie thought quickly. 'I can get what you want without going up to the big house. It'd be safer too.'

Gerald Barlow picked up the torch. 'Go on.'

'I'll show you.'

There was nothing for it but to make the sacrifice. He led him to the bunker, brushed off the leaves and opened the trapdoor.

'What's down there?' his father demanded, shining the torch down the hole, revealing the makeshift ladder.

'It's where I hide my loot. There's a lot down there.'

Ronnie had hoped his father's greed would make him rush down the ladder ahead of him, but the man was wilier than that. He made Ronnie go first.

Once down, he shone the torch at the shelves put up to take Home Guard equipment. 'It's all there,' Ronnie said. 'Help yourself.'

Cyril found the whisky and made a start on it, swigging from the bottle as he poked about, fetching out things he thought would be useful or saleable. 'I need a box.'

'There's one at the back there.' The torch beam was directed to the back of the bunker where the men had started on the tunnel but which was now filled with loose earth and stones. Ronnie had always been careful not to disturb it.

Reg went to investigate. 'I can't see no box.'

'It's right at the back. Maybe it's under some of that dirt. It keeps falling.'

While the man bent to poke about in the rubble, the boy turned and scrambled up the ladder. His father heard him and swung round. 'Hey, where are you off to? I need you to help . . .'

Ronnie was out. He pulled up the ladder and slammed the trapdoor back in place. It wouldn't hold his father for long, but the lack of a ladder might deter him for a little while. He looked round and saw the boulder. He could hear his father shouting and swearing as he manoeuvred it into place. It nearly pulled his arms out of their sockets, but he managed it at last and stood panting for breath. What now? He couldn't just leave him there, could he? In any case, he might get out, then his own life wouldn't be worth living. And if he couldn't get out, he would die, and that would be murder, wouldn't it?

He wandered out onto the driveway. The fog was thicker than ever, but he knew that to his left lay the railway, the Potts' empty house and his bed, to his right Longfordham Hall and a crowd of people. Most of the people he knew, many of them had befriended him. He could hear his father shouting. If Pa died in that hole, his ghost would haunt the wood.

He began to walk up the drive. He was overtaken by a man in a sailor's cap and greatcoat. 'Is this the way to Longfordham Hall?' he asked.

'Yes. It's up there.' He pointed.

'Is that where you're going?'

'Yes.'

'Mind if I tag along?'

'If you like.' What else could he say?

He went round to the kitchen where Mrs Potts was working in the kitchen. 'Ronnie, what are you doing here? Why aren't you in bed? And who is this?'

'Christopher Jarrett,' the sailor said. 'I've come to see Sheila Phipps. She is here, isn't she?'

Ronnie stared at him. 'I know you now. You lived in West Ham. You're supposed to be dead.'

'Well, I'm not.' He turned to Mrs Potts. 'Is Sheila here?'

'I'll go and tell her you're here.'

'But, Auntie Jean,' Ronnie said. 'I've got something important to tell you.'

'It'll have to wait.' She disappeared through a door at the back of the kitchen. Ronnie turned to Chris. 'What happened to you?'

'It's a very long story.'

There was the sound of running feet and Sheila burst into the kitchen. She stopped at the sight of the sailor. He was thin and gaunt, standing there twirling his hat in his hands, but it was definitely Chris. She made no move to go to him, simply stood and stared as if he were an apparition.

'Sheila,' he said. 'Don't you know me?'

'Don't be daft. Of course I do. I'm flabbergasted.'

There were people crowding behind her, people dressed like toffs. They *were* toffs and so was Sheila in that lovely long dress with its cowl neck and narrow waist, and high-heeled shoes. Her auburn hair was elegantly waved with a sparkling comb holding it in place. All this he noticed as he stood, unspeaking, before her. This wasn't the girl he had left behind. His mother was right and he should never have come. 'She's got above herself,' she had said. 'She looks down at the likes of us since she got in with those toffs and singing on the stage an' all.'

He turned and blundered back out into the freezing fog.

Sheila ran after him. 'Chris, come back. Where are you going?'

'Home. I wish I'd never come. I wish . . .' He shook off her hand.

'Why?' She grabbed his arm again and forced him to stop and face her. 'Why come, if you are going to turn round and leave before even talking to me?'

'You've changed.'

'We all have. It's been a long time. Come back inside, Chris, it's freezing out here. My arms are all goosebumps. You will be made welcome, I promise you.'

She started to pull him back towards the house, but he resisted. 'I'm out of place in that lot.'

'Oh, Chris, you idiot.' She grabbed his face in both hands and kissed him. 'I cried buckets when I was told you were dead, and when I read the letter you left me and the ring. See, I'm wearing it.' She held up her right hand in front of his face. 'Please come inside where it's warm and tell us what happened to you.'

Reluctantly he allowed himself to be led back to the kitchen.

The guests had gone back to the drawing room. Ronnie was dancing from foot to foot, trying to get Mrs Potts to listen to him, but she was more interested in gossiping with the others in the kitchen about this strange turn of events. 'That girl will catch her death of cold out there in that flimsy dress,' she was saying.

Mrs Stevens laughed. 'No doubt he'll keep her warm. Who is he anyway? One of Miss Phipps' admirers?'

'I don't know. Ronnie, stop pulling on my arm. I've got to pour this soup into the tureen. You'll make me spill it.'

'But, Auntie Jean, it's very important.'

'Go home to bed, it can wait until the morning. If you aren't asleep by the time I come home, Father Christmas won't come.'

He laughed. 'Don't be daft, there's no such thing.'

'Oh, so you don't want any Christmas presents then?' She picked up the tureen, just as Sheila and Chris came back inside. They followed her to the dining room where everyone was waiting to begin their meal. Ronnie crept along behind them.

They all turned as Chris came in, incongruous in his navy greatcoat which was damp with fog. The butler hurried forward to take it from him. Mrs Potts set the tureen down on the sideboard, but serving it had to wait while Sheila went round introducing Chris to everyone. He exclaimed in surprise when he came to Charlie. 'You turned up after all. Sheila was always sure you would.'

'You too,' Charlie said.

'I gotta tell you,' Ronnie shouted at the top of his voice.

There was sudden silence and everyone turned towards him. Now he had their attention. 'In the woods,' he said. 'There's a man in the bunker. He's escaped . . .' Jean seized his arm to drag him away.

'You're are a very naughty boy, coming up here . . .'

'Let him be, Mrs Potts,' his lordship said quietly. Then to Ronnie, 'A man, you said?'

'Yes. Come quick. He might get out.'

'Ronnie,' Jean warned. No one took any notice of her.

Marcus stood up. 'Mrs Potts, please take the soup back to the kitchen and ask Cook to hold dinner back for a few minutes while I investigate.'

'Not on your own.' Fear made Ronnie bold. 'He's violent.'

'I'll come too.' Gilbert put down his napkin and stood up. He was followed by Hugh and Johnnie. They stopped in the gunroom to pick up shotguns, all cleaned and ready for the Boxing Day shoot. Jean Potts went back to the kitchen to tell Edith Stevens and the rest of the staff, who were not pleased that the dinner they had so lovingly prepared was going to spoil.

'I reckon it's my old man's ghost,' Edith said. 'He can't rest.'

'Don't be daft,' Cook said, emptying the soup back into the saucepan and giving the tureen to the scullery maid to wash up.

Those left behind in the dining room looked at each other. 'What an evening of excitement,' her ladyship said. 'I have never experienced anything like it. And we still haven't heard your story, Mr Jarrett. Please, do sit down.'

Sheila sat down and pulled him down into the seat vacated by Gillie.

He had not wanted his reunion with Sheila to be so public. It reminded him of that faltering proposal made in front of the man at Bletchley Park, and he was equally tongue-tied. He didn't know how to begin. He had been warned on pain of being locked up for the duration not to say a word of how he had been rescued.

'Where have you been all this time?' Sheila asked. 'Couldn't you let us know where you were? Your mother said you had gone to the bottom of the ocean.'

'I very nearly did. My ship was sunk and I found myself in the sea. I remember thinking that if I didn't get out of the water double quick I'd freeze to death and looking round for a piece of flotsam to get onto. The next thing I remember is being in a bunk on a small boat and men all round me. They had stripped off my clothes and were heaping me with blankets to try and get me warm. They talked but I couldn't understand a word they said. They took me to Norway and hid me from the Germans. I was ill for a long time. There was no way I could let anyone know I was alive.'

'How did you get away?' Sheila asked.

'I was helped. I'm not at liberty to say any more.'

Gunnar and Lief had found him hiding in the forest when the Germans finally gave up searching. He had tried to find his way out to Sweden but he kept coming back to his own ski tracks and knew he had been going round in circles. He had been cold, wet, hungry and exhausted. They took him back to the hut and gave him hot soup and boiled cod. He could tell by their broad grins that they had good news for him. He was guided down to the village and stowed away on their boat without having any idea where they were taking him. There was still a German guard post down by the jetty and they had to beware of that, but he was dressed as they were in thick trousers, an oiled wool pullover, thick socks, and a jaunty cap. They passed unnoticed and the boat was soon chugging its way out into the lead and from there to the open sea.

They had taken him to a place called Traena where they drew alongside another vessel at the jetty. He transferred from one to the other and said goodbye to Gunnar and Lief, with much laughter and back-slapping.

The boat on which he found himself was larger than the *Gabbi* and had a crew of five and a dozen passengers. Some of these were Norwegian refugees, fleeing the Germans, but two were British, though they spoke Norwegian. It was from them he learnt that the boat and its crew had made several trips from the Shetland Islands to places on the Norwegian coast, taking supplies to the Norwegian Resistance and bringing out refugees and agents. It was mostly done in the winter when the nights were long and they could go under cover of darkness. There had been delays in assembling everyone for the trip and he had only been included when Lief had spoken on his behalf and vouched for his integrity.

A day out from land they had encountered vicious storms and the engine failed them. They set sails while the engine was being repaired, but these were soon in tatters and the boat had been at the mercy of the storm. Two days they had drifted, tossed about like flotsam and he had begun to wonder if he had been saved from the destroyer only to perish within a day or two of safety. He had offered to help with the repairs and together they had at last got the engine going again and arrived at Lunna in the Shetland Islands a week overdue.

That wasn't the end of it. He was subjected to an intense debriefing and refused permission to contact his family until it was over, and then he had been sworn to secrecy about the fishing boats which went back and forth across the North Sea and were referred to by those in the know as The Shetland Bus.

'We understand,' Esme said. 'We won't ask any more questions, will we?' She looked round at the company.

'No,' Prue said. 'You are here now and it is going to be the best Christmas ever.' She looked at Sheila. 'You are quiet, my friend.'

'I'm overwhelmed.'

'So you must be. You could do with a few minutes' privacy. Take Chris into the breakfast room. I'll come and call you when the men return and dinner is served.'

Sheila took Chris's hand and led him away.

* * *

'Chris, this is like a miracle,' Sheila said, turning to face him with her hand in his. 'I can't take it in. Are you real or am I imagining things?'

'I'm real all right. Here, feel.' He put her hand against his swiftly beating heart. 'Believe it now?'

'Yes.' He pulled her to him and kissed her long and hard. He was no longer the fumbling boy she remembered, but a grown man and it was evident in the way he went about it.

'Oh, Chris, I am so pleased you are back safe and sound.'

'Really?'

'I'm sorry I treated you so badly, I really am. I was sorry almost at once and wrote to you several times but you didn't answer. But then I heard you had gone down with your ship. I felt so guilty. But here you are.' She laughed. 'Prue said, "If it is meant to be, he'll be back." And she was right, wasn't she? But how did you know where to find me?'

He laughed. 'As soon as I had been kitted out again and was free to go on leave, I went home. I was there two days, wondering whether to try and see you, when I found your letters. Ma hadn't sent them on. I might not have got them anyway, but it still made me angry. She said it was for my own good. She said she had given you my last letter because it was my dying wish and dying wishes had always to be complied with. When I read what you had written, I went to Bletchley. There was no one at Victoria Villa, but a neighbour said you had gone away for the holiday. I could only think of one place where you'd go, so I went straight back to town and called on Mrs Bennett. She knew where you were.'

'So you came.'

'I knew it was foolish but I couldn't stay away. I had to know how you felt about me. It's been a long time and you've changed.'

'Have I?'

He tried to explain the thoughts that had gone through his mind in the hut on the mountain. 'You've always been the girl for me and always will be, whatever you say, but I realise we both need time to get to know each other again and with this rotten war it's not going to be easy. I'll give it a go, if you will.'

'Of course I will.' She smiled up at him. 'But you will have to take me as the woman I have become, not the girl-child I was.'

'That's OK by me. I've done some growing up too.'

They heard sounds of the men returning and went out into the hall where Marcus was leading the way back into the dining room. They followed.

'Well?' the Countess asked.

Marcus laughed. 'You'll never believe it. That boy continues to surprise me. He had the presence of mind to lure the man into the bunker and imprison him there.'

'Was he an escaped prisoner?'

'Not a prisoner of war, which I had wrongly assumed, but his own father.'

'Oh, yes,' Chloe said. 'I remember being told he was on the run. He battered his wife and she was afraid he would get to Ronald. I told you about it.'

'Yes, but what we didn't know was that he had attacked a prison warder to escape and the warder had subsequently died. He is also wanted for murder.'

'Good heavens,' Prue said. 'But how did Ronnie know about the bunker?'

'He has known about it right from the beginning. He opened it up and has been using it for a hideaway. He had all sorts of stuff down, there, including half a bottle of whisky and some biscuits. When we opened it up, the man was dead drunk, singing at the top of his voice, and there were biscuit crumbs all over the place.'

'Don't tell me Ronnie stole them.'

'No, I don't think he did,' Johnnie said. 'I gave them to him. He wanted the whisky to give as a Christmas present. I gave him cigarettes and biscuits too.'

'And money?'

'For a bicycle. He sold several to the guys on the base.' He laughed. 'I reckon he was a fair trader, one way and another.'

'What will happen to him?' Sheila asked.

'He's not in trouble,' Marcus said. 'I've sent him home with Mrs Potts. We will talk about his future after Christmas. He wasn't at all sorry to see his father led away.' He looked round. 'Shall we get on with our dinner?'

They went into the dining room. Prue looked round at everyone. It was a strange collection of people, but they all, in their own way, contributed to each other's happiness. And for the first time for years, her mother looked more like her old self; there was more colour in her cheeks and more sparkle in her eyes. Everyone was smiling, even Constance. As for Sheila, she had come a very long way in the three years she had known her. Her parents would be very proud of her. 'Something to write home about?' Prue whispered to her.

'Yes. I'll do it later.'

Dear Ma and Pa,

I don't know where to begin. Chris is alive and well, but not allowed to talk about how he escaped. He has changed, we both have, but we have decided to take it slowly and get to know each again. I am looking forward to that. Prue's brother, Gilbert, is back from France and he can't talk about what he was doing there either. He and Esme are going to be married. She is another with secrets to keep.

Ronnie Barlow's secret is out. His father came after him and has been arrested for murder and I think Ronnie will stay with Mrs Potts permanently. As for me, I have been offered a small part in a musical to be put on at the Victoria in the spring. It will star Lupino Lane so is bound to be a success. It will mean leaving BP. I shall miss everyone but I will still be based at Victoria Villa, so I will still see Prue. Of course I shall have to keep the secret of BP, probably for ever, but I think Chris understands now he has his own secret which I will never pry into. Aunt Constance is a different person now Johnnie has found her and forgiven her and she has been able to forgive herself. We are getting along just fine.

These letters have been my lifeline, a way of coping with my loss, which I still feel bad about, but I think I can manage without them now, though you will always be in my thoughts.

Your ever-loving daughter,

Sheila